June Francis was brought up in the port of Liverpool, UK. Although she started her novel writing career by writing medieval romances, it seemed natural to also write family sagas set in her home city due to its fascinating historical background, especially as she has several mariners in her family tree and her mother was in service. She has written twenty sagas set in Merseyside, as well as in the beautiful city of Chester and Lancashire countryside.

Visit June Francis's website at: www.junefrancis.com

Also by June Francis:

JUNE FRANCIS
Mersey Girl

EBURY
PRESS

1 3 5 7 9 10 8 6 4 2

Ebury Press, an imprint of Ebury Publishing
20 Vauxhall Bridge Road,
London SW1V 2SA

Penguin
Random House
UK

Ebury Press is part of the Penguin Random House group of companies whose
addresses can be found at global.penguinrandomhouse.com

First published in the UK as *Going Home to Liverpool* in 1995 by Judy
Piatkus Publishers Ltd
This edition published in 2017

www.penguin.co.uk

A CIP catalogue record for this book is available from the British Library

ISBN 9781785039300

Typeset in India by Thomson Digital Pvt Ltd, Noida, Delhi
Printed and bound in Great Britain by Clays Ltd, St Ives PLC

Penguin Random House is committed to a sustainable future
for our business, our readers and our planet. This book is made
from Forest Stewardship Council® certified paper.

MIX
Paper from
responsible sources
FSC
www.fsc.org   FSC® C018179

Acknowledgements

My thanks go to Mary Mitchell, my Polish friend George, and Sister Borromeo of the Ursuline Convent in Brentwood, as well as my husband John, for their willingness to help me with my research.

I have tried to make the factual parts of the story as correct as I can – forgive me any mistakes. Having stressed that, I wish to emphasise that my characters are purely fictional.

Dedicated to my niece Linda Proud and
my agent Judith Murdoch –
for making my trips south always a pleasure

And Ruth said, 'Entreat me not to leave thee, or to return from following after thee; for whither thou goest, I will go; and where thou lodgest, I will lodge; thy people shall be my people, and thy God my God' — Holy Bible

Chapter One

Elizabeth Knight's feet made hardly any sound as she crossed the polished wooden parquet floor, past the statue of the Madonna of the Sea, to Mother Clare's room. Mother Ursula, the head, must be busy elsewhere. Her heart was beating fast. It was very seldom she was summoned into Mother Clare's presence and she wished Mother Bernard who had come to fetch her, had given her some idea as to why. She hoped her father was not going to stop her riding lessons. Last time she had been summoned had been almost three years ago, early in spring 1944, when her mother had been killed somewhere between their London home and Radio House where she had worked. It had seemed ironic that Elizabeth's father had been stationed on the Kentish coast at the time, trying to prevent the doodlebugs from getting through. He had been devastated by his wife's loss, much more so than Elizabeth who had spent most of her childhood and the war years as a boarder here in Essex.

She knocked and was told to enter. Mother Clare was seated behind a desk, in front of which stood a woman who was a stranger to Elizabeth. She wore a belted russet coat and a headscarf which had slipped back to reveal shoulder-length wavy copper hair. Without any preamble the elderly nun who had come from London's Forest Gate at the turn of the century to start the school, said, 'Elizabeth, this woman tells me she is your stepmother.'

'Stepmother?' Shock waves rippled through her. 'I don't understand.'

The woman's smile faded. 'Jimmy did say he would write and tell you.' The accent was not southern and she sounded both embarrassed and annoyed. 'I'm sorry I've come as a shock, but if it's any comfort he rather sprang you on me as well.'

'When?' demanded Elizabeth.

'When what? When were we married or when did he tell me about you?'

'Both, I suppose.' She could hear the anger in her own voice.

'We were married two weeks ago – and if I'd known about you then you'd have been at the wedding.'

Visions of a bride in white, of her father in a lounge suit, of bridesmaids, of smiling guests throwing confetti, filled Elizabeth's mind. 'I can't believe Daddy would do this to me,' she whispered. 'How could he leave me out?'

'I wish I knew, love.' There was sympathy in the woman's tawny eyes. 'But it was only a small affair. Nothing to get yourself worked up about. As it is when he told me about you, and that you'd a half term holiday due, I thought it only right you should come home despite the awful weather.'

Elizabeth stared at her, clenching her jaw and trying to assimilate the words. 'Why isn't he here? Why has he sent you?'

The woman didn't hesitate. 'He hasn't been too well the last few days.'

'Not well!' A sharp laugh escaped her. 'He was well enough to marry you. He probably couldn't face me with the news. He was just the same with Mummy if he was in the wrong.'

'Control yourself, Elizabeth,' said the elderly nun in a quiet voice. 'I see Mrs Knight's point in wanting to take you home and get to know you. I think it would be sensible if you packed your suitcase and went with her.'

'But, Mother Clare . . .' she turned a pleading face to the nun . . . 'I don't know her. How do we know she's telling the truth? Daddy worshipped Mummy. He wouldn't have married this – this *woman!*' She grasped at the idea and felt better. 'Yes, she's lying. It's a trick. She's out to kidnap me!'

The visitor looked amused as she took a packet of Woodbines from her pocket. 'Do me a favour, kid. Tell me what I'd get out of kidnapping you? Your dad's got no money. It's crippling him to pay the fees and all the extras at this place. It's very nice but . . .' She shrugged.

Mother Clare tapped a fountain pen on her desk. 'I think we will terminate this conversation.' Her tone was cool. 'Elizabeth, you really must control your imagination. What you said to your stepmother was impolite.'

'Don't mind me, Sister,' said the woman laconically. 'I've got five younger brothers and sisters. I know what kids are like.' She tapped the cigarette packet on the back of her hand.

'Please don't interrupt,' said the nun. 'And do not smoke in here.'

The woman raised her eyebrows but remained silent. Nor did she light a cigarette.

The nun gazed levelly at Elizabeth, whose heart sank. 'I will make a telephone call to your father. In the meantime both of you may go for a walk in the cloisters. I will send for you when I'm ready.'

Elizabeth noted again that raising of the eyebrows from the woman who called herself her stepmother but she murmured acquiescence and they left the room together.

'I won't go with you,' said Elizabeth as soon as the door was closed behind them.

'I think you will,' said the woman, placing a cigarette between her lips. 'That old nun'll make you as soon as she verifies the facts.' She took a book of matches from her pocket and lit up.

'You're not supposed to smoke out here either!' Elizabeth gazed at her with horrified fascination.

'No?' She exhaled and smiled. 'I bet there's lots of things you're not supposed to do. Are you a good girl, Lizzie? Jimmy said you were but then dads don't know everything about their daughters, do they? I know my dad thinks the sun shines out of me but I've done things he'd have pink fits over. As it is, he and the whole family were disappointed that I didn't go up home to marry but Jimmy wanted it quick and quiet. We were married in a register office and there were no guests.'

'You were married in a register office!' exclaimed Elizabeth. 'Then you're not really married.' And she smiled complacently.

'Oh yes, we are,' murmured the woman. 'Neither your dad nor me is Catholic so you can forget that.' She glanced about her as they left one corridor and walked up another. 'God, it's like a maze in here. How do you ever find your way about?'

'Easy.' Elizabeth's tone was scornful, although she remembered feeling the same about the school on her arrival a year into the war. Her mother had been an old girl and the Mother Superior had accepted Elizabeth as a boarder when others were being sent home because her mother was doing important war work and her father was in the army. Despite Elizabeth's tender years she remembered how exciting yet frightening it had been, hurrying through corridors to a basement cloakroom when a raid was on. The town was on a flight path for London and so had not completely escaped the blitz. The townsfolk had also taken shelter in the cellars beneath the convent hall, as had exhausted fire crews who were fighting the fires in East London and needed a rest.

They came to a long sunlit corridor where canaries trilled in hanging cages and plants in pots bravely put forth a few flowers. Elizabeth stopped. 'This is the cloisters,' she muttered.

'Not like I imagined,' said the woman, looking with interest at the birds. 'There are nice cloisters in Chester. All old stone and grass.'

'Chester?'

'Up north. I come from Liverpool.'

'Liverpool?'

The woman's tawny eyes scrutinised Elizabeth's smooth rosy-skinned face. 'You must have heard of it? It was the door to the country's larder during the war, and in the old days Liverpool merchants grew rich on the slave trade.' She stubbed out her cigarette in the soil of a potted hyacinth. 'Funny ol' mixture some of them were. One made money out of the suffering then used some of it to build the Bluecoat School for poor children.'

'What's that got to do with me?' said Elizabeth impatiently. 'I want to know how, if you lived all the way up there, you met Daddy?'

The woman did not speak for a moment then she said quietly, 'Even up north people leave home. As it is I met Jimmy for the first time during the war. At a training camp in Pembrokeshire when I was in the ATS.'

'But Mummy was alive then!'

'Yep.' The woman dug her hands in her pockets and smiled wryly. 'He was forever talking about her. I've never known a man so struck with his wife after so many years of marriage.'

There was a silence and Elizabeth considered that 'forever talking'. Her father could not have been in love with this woman then. She thought of her mother, who had been Daddy's senior by eight years, and looking back remembered how he always deferred to her and how she had always seemed the strong one in the marriage. This woman looked strong too. Was that why . . . ? She took a deep breath, needing an answer to another question. 'But how did you meet again? It's years since Daddy was in Pembrokeshire.'

The woman raised her eyebrows. 'I came to London. Your dad was different to the other men who were generally only after one – but never mind that – and I never forgot him. He had a bit of culture about him and was interested in the theatre like me. He said that if ever I got to London I was to look him and his wife up.'

'So you did?'

'I was desperate, kid. I was trying to make it on the stage but not having much luck. I had a job of sorts, trying to make ends meet, but life was tough. I was lonely and in need of a friendly face.'

'I see.'

'Do you?'

'Daddy's very good-looking and nice.' 'Too nice' she'd heard her mother say once, but how could anyone be too nice?

'Yes. He was nice to me and I fell for him heavily this time. No wife on the scene and he seemed really glad to see me.' There was a silence which stretched.

Elizabeth felt like saying: 'But I was on the scene,' though that hadn't strictly been true. After her mother's death, Daddy had wrapped himself up in his grief, excluding his daughter.

'I hope that old nun's not going to be long,' murmured the woman.

Elizabeth glanced at her and the woman smiled but Elizabeth did not return the smile. How could Daddy marry this northerner without telling her! The woman's smile faded and she turned away to gaze into a bird cage and whistle at its yellow inmate.

'Did you make Daddy marry you?' challenged Elizabeth, putting her arms behind her back.

The woman gave her a long cool glance. 'How would I do that, love?'

She reddened. 'Mummy could make Daddy do things.'

The woman raised her eyebrows and the corners of her mouth lifted but she made no comment.

Elizabeth was irritated and a teeny bit scared. So might the wolf have smiled when he wanted to gobble up Red Riding Hood. 'I won't go with you,' she repeated.

The woman sighed. 'I'm getting fed up of this. I want to get back before dark so don't give me any arguments. Think of your dad. He hasn't been well and needs company right now. I was hoping you'd cheer him up but if you're going to have a face like a wet Whit weekend, I could be wrong.'

Her words startled Elizabeth. 'Is Daddy really ill?'

The woman hesitated. 'There's no need for you to start worrying.'

Elizabeth thought, He can't be that ill then. 'Why didn't he want me at the wedding?' she said aloud. 'Does he really want me now? I won't come if he doesn't really want me.'

A puzzled frown drew the woman's pencilled eyebrows together. 'Don't you want to see him?'

'Of course I do. But it won't be the same, will it, if you're going to be there!' In her imagination she conjured up a picture of her father's eager-to-please features as they had looked before her mother had died. Elizabeth always remembered him like that. She felt a pain round her heart, considering how her mother's death had changed him. It was as if when she had died part of him had died too and Elizabeth had felt almost doubly bereaved. But before she could say any more to this woman her father had turned to instead of her, Mother Bernard appeared.

They went with her to be told by Mother Clare that she had been unable to get through to Mr Knight. 'Perhaps last night's snow brought the lines down?'

'So what decision have you come to, Sister?' asked the woman, looking her fully in the face. 'I do hope it's still the same as mine. Elizabeth really should see Jimmy.' There was a touch of steel in her voice.

The nun continued to gaze at her for several seconds, then she repeated her order to Elizabeth to pack her things. So there was nothing for her but to do as she was told.

Whilst she was emptying out the wardrobe in her cubicle, several girls entered the dormitory, crowding round her and asking questions which she did not want to answer. She was mortified every time she thought about the wedding she had not known anything about, and her pride was such that instead of telling them the truth she said the marriage was about to take place and she was going home to be bridesmaid. It was an anxious and rebellious Elizabeth who met the woman claiming to be her stepmother in the entrance hall.

'Ready?' she said, opening the outside door.

Anger welled up inside Elizabeth as she thought how this woman had caused her to lie to her friends. She brushed past, only to halt on the step. 'Where's the taxi?'

The woman's eyebrows rose in that disconcerting fashion. 'I've no money for taxis. Get walking, kid.'

Fury overwhelmed her and she said through her teeth, 'But I've got my suitcase! It's a long walk and the pavements are icy.'

'You'll survive,' said the woman with a cheerfulness Elizabeth thought veered on the masochistic. 'Console yourself with the thought that it'll be easier going down than up, and that if you slip I'll give you a hand up. Now move or you'll have it dark.'

I don't care, said Elizabeth inwardly. Nevertheless she moved. Strangely there was something in the woman's voice which reminded her of the mother she had scarcely known, although this woman was much younger. Twenty years younger probably. The thought shocked her and she tried not to question her father's motive for marrying a woman young enough to be his daughter.

Her temper was not improved as she slipped and slithered down Queen's Road, between large houses with gardens which in summer were a treat to the eyes. Even before they reached the railway station, her suitcase felt as if it was dragging her arm out of its socket and by the time she seated herself on the train to Liverpool Street station she was definitely in no mood to respond to any kind of overture from the woman she still considered an interloper.

It was dusk when they reached Camden Town after travelling across London by tube. Lights were flickering on in windows and curtains were being drawn. Elizabeth was cold as well as weary, apprehensive and irritated. What would Daddy expect from her? That he had not told her about his marriage signalled that he did not expect her to welcome it. And she didn't! As they splashed through dirty slush she could taste London's gritty air in her throat and against her teeth, and imagined the sweep of untrodden snow on lawns and fields as viewed that morning from her dormitory window. She could almost smell the clean sweet country air. Why had Daddy had to marry this woman? He could have moved out of London when he'd been demobbed and found a little cottage and then there would have been no need for her to board. Duty was the school motto, and she could have looked after him like a daughter should in such circumstances.

'You'll be glad to get home,' said the woman, pausing to take a turn with the suitcase.

Elizabeth made no reply. The house in London had never felt like home, perhaps because she had left it when she was six years old and never lived there for any long period of time since. With its high ceilings and the gas lamps that had existed then, she had often been frightened of shadows, imagining ghostly presences because the house was so old.

As they turned into the street where her father lived it suddenly felt darker despite the street lamps. It was as if candles had been snuffed out behind all the front windows. 'Damn!' muttered the woman, quickening her pace. 'Power cut. I hope Jimmy has some candles handy.'

They came to the house and the woman dropped the suitcase and fumbled in her handbag. Elizabeth waited as she put the key in the latch and pushed open the door. The woman's hand went to the light switch then she withdrew it. 'Almost forgot,' she murmured, and walked into the lobby in the darkness. Then she stopped abruptly causing Elizabeth to collide with her. 'Can you smell it?'

The girl sniffed, forgetting her antipathy for the moment. 'Gas.' She sensed the woman frowning and suddenly a prickle of apprehension scraped down her spine. What if something had happened to her father? Instinctively she drew closer to the woman as hesitantly they sniffed their way towards the kitchen.

The woman opened the door and the smell of gas overwhelmed them. They drew back hastily as it caught them by the throat. 'God!' gasped the woman. 'You get up by the front door and open it wide.'

'What about Daddy?' croaked Elizabeth. 'Do you think he's in there?' By now her eyes were accustomed to the darkness and she could faintly make out the woman's face. She watched her drag a scarf from her head and, bundling it up, cover her nose and mouth before plunging into the room.

Elizabeth hesitated then rushed up the lobby and flung open the front door. She took a deep breath of the London air she had scorned earlier before heading back up the lobby with a handkerchief pressed over her own mouth and nose.

The woman was bending over a huddled shape on the floor in front of the cooker. Without turning her head she said huskily, 'There's no gas coming from here now, mightn't have been for a while, but open that window.'

Elizabeth did as she was told, conscious of the blood pulsing sluggishly through her veins. The lock on the sash window refused to budge and she broke a fingernail. Losing patience and almost breath she took off a shoe and smashed one of the panes. She inhaled gratefully before making her way across the floor.

The woman was slumped across her father's body. She lifted her head. 'Sorry, kid.' Her voice was slurred. 'But I think he's been dead for some time.'

Elizabeth thought: But he can't be dead. I've come to see him. I want to know why he needed this woman more than me! She's mistaken! Fresh air's what he needs.

Frantically she shoved the interloper away from her father's body and noticed that the oven door was open. She slipped her hands beneath his armpits and heaved him away from the cooker, dragging him across the cold tiled floor and out to the front door. Then she looked into his face and was filled with a worse dread as her fingers sought for a pulse but could find none. Her mind struggled with the truth as tears welled up inside her. Then she became aware of the cold air chilling the back of her neck and remembered the woman who had tried to save him. Slowly she stood and went back up the lobby, aware that the smell of gas had dispersed a little.

The woman was still huddled on the floor and the fear which churned Elizabeth's stomach intensified. Please, please, don't *you* be dead, she thought, and shook her roughly. 'Wake up!' she yelled. 'Wake up!'

The woman's head lolled like a rag doll's on her shoulders but her eyelids lifted a little. 'Wh-what are . . . you . . . doing?' Her voice was a whisper.

'Holy Mary, thank God you're not dead,' gasped Elizabeth, relief mixing with her fear so potently that she felt dizzy.

The woman forced back her eyelids and pushed herself up from the floor into a sitting position. She looked about her slowly before her eyes returned to Elizabeth's face. 'Where's Jimmy?'

Elizabeth eased her throat but even so her voice came out like a frog's mating croak. 'I dragged him to the front door. I think he's dead, like you said. What are we going to do?'

There was a short silence and she wondered if the woman had taken in what she had said. Then the woman held out both hands and muttered, 'Help me up, love. Me legs don't feel like they quite belong to me.'

Elizabeth gripped her fingers and hoisted her to her feet. For a moment she thought the woman was going to collapse but she steadied herself and, leaning on Elizabeth's shoulder, walked slowly into the lobby. They went over to where her father lay, and as she looked down at him the tears came into Elizabeth's eyes and she wanted to howl.

'Stop that now,' said the woman, her own voice sounding raw. 'Save your crying 'til later. We've got to get him inside and decide what we're going to do.'

Elizabeth's sobs shuddered to a halt and she wiped her eyes with the back of a hand and stared at her. 'What are we going to do?'

'Deal with Jimmy as I said – hope the fire's still in, make a cup of tea. And wait until the lights come on before we call the police.'

'The police! Why should we call them?' Her voice was stark. 'We need a priest.' It was what the nuns would have

advocated. 'Although it's too late for Daddy.' She felt the
tears start again.

'Don't start crying.' The woman sounded weary as she
put an arm round her. 'The police always have to be called
when something like this happens. It was an accident. Get
that firmly into your head.'

'Of course it was an accident,' said Elizabeth, wiping
her eyes and leaning against the woman's shoulder. 'What
else could it be?'

'Exactly. The gas ran out. He put a couple of coppers
in the meter and forgot to switch the oven off. Now let's
get you inside then I'll see to him. You've had a terrible
shock.'

Elizabeth did not argue but leaned against her as they
carefully felt their way into the living room.

The oven, thought Elizabeth. 'Why should Daddy have
the oven on?' she said aloud, shivering as she lowered
herself on to the sofa in front of a fire that was only a
heap of cinders.

The woman did not answer but sat with her head in
her hands for a moment before rising and going into the
lobby. Elizabeth hesitated, then decided it was not fair to
leave it to her and followed her out. Without a word she
helped her drag her father further up the lobby so they
could close the door and shut out the cold. 'What now?'
she asked, her teeth chattering.

'We'll put him in the parlour, have a drink – I think
I'm in need of something stronger than tea. There's some
sherry we bought when we got married. I know you're
too young but it'll put a bit of heart into us. Oh, and we'll

get a sheet and couple of blankets off the beds and wrap them round us. By the time we've done that I hope to God the gas'll have all gone, the lights'll have come on and we can have a fire and a cuppa.' A sigh escaped her. 'Now, lift.'

Elizabeth lifted, trying to block out all thoughts that would distract her from doing what she had to.

After the woman had covered her father with the sheet, the pair of them sat in the living room on the sofa with a blanket apiece, sipping sherry in the dark. There was a sense of unreality about the situation. Perhaps it was unreal? thought Elizabeth. A dream? But the woman was here and she couldn't have imagined her. Besides, surely one couldn't taste and feel in a dream? Dear sweet Jesus! she was getting all muddled. She cleared her throat. 'The oven? Daddy couldn't cook.'

'He might have put it on to warm the kitchen.'

Elizabeth had not thought of that and was relieved.

The woman continued, 'We didn't have much coal, what with the rationing and him not having found a job since leaving the army. That was another thing I didn't know about until we were married. I was a bit of a dafty. I believed everything he told me.' Her voice was filled with self-mockery. 'He's been living on your mam's money but it's all gone now. He didn't have any himself. He told me she married him for his charm and good looks when he came to work on the family farm, but he loved her all right. He could have married better if it had just been for money. He didn't pay last week's rent by the way. I did with me last wages. That's why I thought you should come home. You're his daughter and he should have told you the way things were instead of pretending.' She paused. 'How old are you? Thirteen? Fourteen?'

'Fourteen a month ago.' Elizabeth's voice was low and uneven. She was conscious of a hollowness inside her, a mixture of hunger and loss. Her head felt light and the woman's words seemed to echo inside her brain. Was it true what this woman was saying? She had never known how her parents had met. As for what she had said about money, it sounded as if things couldn't be worse.

'And a young fourteen, I bet,' murmured the woman. 'He talked of your staying on at school, thought it was important that you got a good education so you could support yourself. I wonder – is that where I came in? He must have been mad . . .' Her tone was thoughtful.

'What do you mean?' Elizabeth stirred herself to respond.

The woman did not answer but uncurled herself and got to her feet. 'I'm going to put a penny in the meter and chance making a cuppa.'

Elizabeth rose hurriedly and followed her from the room, still clutching the blanket around her shoulders. She did not want to be alone. 'There might be some gas still around.'

'We'll open the back door wide. I suppose we could try getting a fire going but it would mean traipsing down the cellar in the dark.'

Elizabeth considered. 'What about Mrs Slater next-door? She'd give us a cup of tea.'

'I'd rather not bother the neighbours about this, kid. She might come poking her nose in and we don't want that.'

'We could stay in her house.'

'And what about your dad? She'll ask questions. I want to deal with this in my way. God willing, it'll work out best in the long run.'

Elizabeth said no more but was relieved when the woman changed her mind about lighting the gas ring on the cooker because the smell of gas still hung in the air. She went down into the cellar and Elizabeth felt a faint stirring of admiration. It was eerie enough where she was, without plunging into a place she remembered as cobwebby and spooky.

It took some time to get a fire going and a kettle to boil but there was a hypnotic quality about waiting for both and her thoughts were partially distracted from the body in the parlour. Once the woman went and clicked on the light switch but there was still no power. It was not until they were warming their hands round cups of tea that the bulb overhead flooded light into the room.

Immediately the woman went over to the mantelshelf but Elizabeth could not see what she was doing because she had her back towards her and her body blocked Elizabeth's view. After a few seconds she left the room. When she returned she dropped a crumpled ball of paper on to the fire and stood watching it burn. Then she went into the lobby, lifted the telephone receiver and dialled.

'Your name is Mrs Phyllis Mary Knight?' The policeman checked his notes.

The woman gazed gravely at him. 'We were married only two weeks ago.' Her voice was unsteady and she dabbed at her eyes with a dainty embroidered handkerchief.

Elizabeth sat quietly in a corner watching them, hoping to be ignored.

'You knew your husband was ill?'

'Not until an hour ago when his doctor told me. He seemed very well.'

Her answer took Elizabeth by surprise and she thought, You're a liar, Phyllis Mary Knight.

'You found no note?'

'Note?' Somehow the woman managed to infuse overwhelming astonishment into the single word as her eyes slowly filled with tears. 'You can't be suggesting –'

'Please don't cry, Mrs Knight,' said the policeman hastily. 'In cases like these we always have to ask. Perhaps we could just run over your statement again? And then, if we could talk to your stepdaughter . . .'

'D'you have to?' There was a tremor in her voice. 'This has all been a terrible shock to her. She hadn't seen her daddy since Christmas.'

'We'll be gentle with her.'

Phyllis sighed. 'Can't I stay with her? I mean, she's so young.'

I'm not that young, thought Elizabeth indignantly. And you're not so old yourself!

'Of course, madam.' The policeman began to read through his notes.

Elizabeth listened keenly and realised there were a couple of things the woman had wrong. Elizabeth had not been by her side when she had found Jimmy's body near the cooker, and neither had they carried him outside together. But why should Phyllis lie?

It was not until the policeman started to question Elizabeth that his earlier mention of a note flashed into her mind. She remembered the paper that Phyllis had thrown on to the fire, the open oven door, and how the woman had tried to save Daddy's life. Putting these facts together, she reckoned she knew why Phyllis was lying to the police, so she followed suit.

The policeman seemed satisfied with her answers and put his notebook away. 'There'll have to be an inquest, Mrs Knight,' he said. 'You just speak up like you have to me and I can't see you having any problems.'

'Thank you, officer.' Phyllis smiled her gratitude. 'Let me see you out.'

Elizabeth watched them leave the room. Picking up a blanket from a chair, she wrapped it tightly about her and curled up on the sofa. Her father's body had been taken away and she was still trying to come to terms with that.

Phyllis reappeared and went to stand by the fireplace. She gazed down at Elizabeth with a faint smile on her heart-shaped face. 'Jimmy said you weren't soft.'

'What did the note say?' Elizabeth's voice was stiff with the effort of controlling her emotions.

There was a moment's hesitation. 'It said he had cancer. There was going to be a lot of pain and he didn't want you to see him suffering.'

'Me? But I hardly ever saw him, and I wanted to! I feel like I hardly knew him. It wasn't me he killed himself for.' She covered her face with her hands. 'Holy Mary, Mother of God, I don't want to believe he killed himself! He'll never be allowed into Heaven.'

'Don't believe it then. Carry on pretending it was an accident,' the woman said lightly. 'As for me, I've got to accept, from what he said about going to your mother in the note, that he certainly didn't marry me for love but because he knew *you* were going to need someone. God only knows why he picked me.' Her hands were unsteady as she lit a cigarette.

'I have an aunt.' Elizabeth's voice was tight and she plucked the edge of the blanket. 'Not that I've ever seen her. She was Mummy's sister. They fell out when Mummy got married.'

'Have you any idea where she lives?'

Elizabeth shook her head, realising afresh how little she knew about her parents' lives before she was born. The full significance of her father's death suddenly hit her. 'You said he had no money? No money at all.'

'That's right. Hopefully there'll be some insurance but I can't see there being enough over after the funeral to keep you in knickers, never mind that convent school in the country.'

Elizabeth stared wide-eyed and her spirits plummeted even further. 'Then what's going to happen to me?' she stammered. 'Will I live here w-with you?'

'No.' Her stepmother inhaled and then blew out a cloud of smoke. 'I wouldn't stay in this house now for a gold clock. I came to London hoping to see my name up in lights.' For an instant her expression showed deep disappointment, then she shrugged. 'Another dream down the swanny. I'm skint and I'd like to see my family.'

'You mean . . .?'

'I'm going home to Liverpool.'

'But what about me?' repeated Elizabeth, feeling utterly lost. 'You're my – you're my – stepmother!' She managed to make the word sound like an accusation.

Phyllis stared at her and slowly smiled. 'So I am. In that case, I suppose you'd best come with me. But I warn you now, I don't like moaners. So if you have any complaints, keep your mouth shut. Now let's get to bed. I've a feeling the next few days are going to be rough.'

Elizabeth did not argue. She had a strong conviction this was an understatement but saw no other option open to her at that moment but to stay close to this woman who was her stepmother and now her father's widow.

Chapter Two

Elizabeth was still sticking close to her stepmother as they came out of a side exit of Lime Street station in Liverpool. She narrowly missed being knocked over by a porter with a trolley because she was gazing about her and not liking what she saw. Grime-encrusted snow was heaped like molehills along the edge of the pavement and the light from the street lamps shone on cleared but wet cobbled streets. The buildings looked drab and the fact that her stepmother was humming a tune beneath her breath caused Elizabeth to wonder what there was to be so cheerful about.

She kept quiet, conscious of her dependency on the woman who had told her she didn't like moaners. Not that Elizabeth didn't have plenty to moan about. The journey had been terrible. The train had been stuck in snowdrifts just north of Rugby and they'd had to wait hours before the army, with German prisoners-of-war, had come to dig them out. All this on top of a fortnight during which there had been moments when she had sunk into a mire of despondency from which she felt unable to lift herself. Her stepmother had alternately cosseted and chivvied her, and during the inquest and funeral had held her hand tightly as if she really was her mother and shared the grief Elizabeth was feeling. Yet she had told the girl to call her Phyl, saying it was impossible for either of them to feel comfortable with the term 'Mother'.

The coroner had pronounced a verdict of accidental death although he had touched on the possibility of suicide. Why hadn't James Knight switched off the gas as soon as he had become aware of its strong smell? According to the deceased's doctor, he had known he had a disease which was life-destroying. Suicide could have been on his mind. But in the absence of a note the coroner considered it wrong to bring in such a verdict which could only intensify the suffering of his wife and daughter. The verdict had been such a relief that neither of them referred to the piece of paper Phyl had burnt. Afterwards there had been the funeral to get through but Elizabeth did not want to think about that now.

'Are you OK, Lizzie?' Phyl's concerned tawny eyes scanned her pale face. 'You're not going to faint on me?'

'I'm fine,' she said brightly. 'It-it's different to Essex.' It still hurt when she thought of all that she had left behind.

Phyl smiled. 'We do have country round about here, and we have the Mersey and beaches and seaside resorts with all the fun of the fair. You'll see it won't be as bad as you think.' She waved a hand towards the back of a building. 'That's the Empire theatre. It's where I won a talent competition, singing and dancing. It does have a more distinguished frontage, just as good as any theatre in London. And wait 'til you see St George's Hall. It's all pillars and marble and Victorian grandeur. But not today.

We haven't got time, and besides we'll have to walk home and it's a couple of miles.'

Elizabeth tried to conceal her dismay. 'You should have said you had no money left. I wouldn't have asked for tea and a bun.'

'It doesn't matter now. It'll be good to stretch our legs. Although, like you, I'd prefer to be without the suitcases.'

Two miles! thought Elizabeth. It would have been nothing to her without the suitcase and in the countryside – but two miles on icy pavements! Even so she fell into step beside her stepmother and tried not to make comparisons as they came to a road with dimly lit shops. After all, shops were shops wherever you went, only the names were different. Here the snow had turned to slush but had started to freeze again so that it was crunchy underfoot.

'This is London Road,' said Phyl. 'Every Easter, Whit and Christmas we used to come here to buy material for dresses at TJ's. That was before Billy and the tiddlers arrived. There were me two sisters and Mam and me. Mam loved pink. She's a great believer in pink for a girl, blue for a boy. I got real sick of it. I remember yelling at her one day that it was sickly and sweet, just like coconut ice. My sister Lois, who can be a right smarm, said I should count my blessings. Mam agreed and Lois got a sweet while I was smacked.'

'Perhaps you should have kept quiet?'

Phyl pulled a face. 'That's me, though. I say what I think. Even so, you can tell you've never been driven mad by brothers and sisters.'

'That's not *my* fault. But girls at school were enough to make me tear my hair out at times,' said Elizabeth, changing her suitcase to her other hand.

'Jealousy and bitchiness, I suppose,' murmured Phyl. 'It's different with boys. They like to be top dog and expect you to wait on them, whatever their age. Although I reckon our boys being a bit like that is down to Mam having four daughters.' She was silent a moment. 'You're going to find it quite different.'

Elizabeth did not doubt it. She looked forward to meeting Phyl's family with a mixture of curiosity and dread. Brentwood Boys' School was only five minutes away from the Ursuline convent school but it might as well have been on the moon. The male sex was a mystery to Elizabeth. Her only contacts of any importance had been her father, and Father Doyle who had taken care of the convent school's spiritual needs. Both he and Mother Clare had written expressing their sympathy over her father's death and regret that she'd had to leave. They wished her success and happiness in her new life and said she would remain in their prayers. Those prayers were a comforting thought; like having an umbrella in case it rained. At that moment she felt a snowflake, feather-light, land on her nose, which brought her back to the present.

'I reckon we could be in for it,' said Phyl, taking hold of her sleeve. 'We'll cross here. This is Monument Place. See that statue of a man on a horse? He's George III. Money was raised by public subscription to put it up. He went mad, didn't he?'

'So they say.' Elizabeth turned up her collar as more snowflakes drifted down.

'I wish I still had my army boots and thick socks. These old shoes let in,' said Phyl, lengthening her stride.

Elizabeth said nothing. Her lace ups were six months old and comfortable, and her black mackintosh was new. Phyl wore the black astrakhan coat and black fur hat she had bought for the funeral. As they forged on their suitcases felt heavier with each step. By the time they had trudged the length of a road called Moss Street, those first few snowflakes had turned into a blizzard which slowed them down and froze them to the marrow. The noise of the traffic was muted and even the sound of the wheels of a handcart crossing into Shaw Street would have been deadened if they had not squeaked.

From beneath the brim of her school hat, Elizabeth glanced in its direction, having noticed that Phyl's expression had brightened as she looked at the man pushing the cart. The collar of his ragged jacket was turned up and the cloth cap he wore was pulled forward so that Elizabeth could not see his face properly, but it was obvious that Phyl had recognised him.

'Alex Payne, as I live and breathe!' she cried. 'Give us a lend of a bit of your handcart.' She did not wait for a response but heaved her suitcase on to the cart among bric-a-brac, jam jars and rags. She reached for Elizabeth's too but she hung on to it. She did not know this man but he was a totter and she didn't trust the breed.

He was staring back at Phyl in obvious amazement, blinking snowflakes from his dark eyelashes. His weather-beaten face was flushed with the cold and he looked grim. When he spoke, his voice was harsh. 'What are you doing here, slumming it? I thought you were living it up in the posh south?'

Elizabeth watched Phyl's smile fade and wanted to hit him. What did he mean, *posh south?* Hadn't he ever heard of the poverty in London and the hovels of some farmworkers?

'Hardly, Alex,' said Phyl. 'I'm on me uppers. I've a hole as big as the mouth of the Mersey tunnel in my shoe and not a bean to my name.'

His expression changed to one of puzzlement. 'But I heard you'd wed. I thought things were going well for you?'

'I wed all right but now I'm a widow. What brought you back here? I thought you'd run away for good.'

'Me and the sea didn't suit.' He breathed deeply as he heaved on the handles of the cart. 'And when I got back you'd gone to do your bit for King and country. It wasn't long before I followed suit.'

Phyl wrinkled her nose. 'But why come back here after being demobbed? What about Canada, lumberjacks, and mounties who always get their man?'

'Don't keep reminding me of what I said when I was a kid,' Alex said roughly. 'Things change, Phyl.' He glanced at Elizabeth who stared back at him, coldly enough to freeze a snowball in the tropics. 'Who's the girl?'

'This is Lizzie, my stepdaughter. And don't make any wisecracks about wicked stepmothers.' Phyl smiled up at him and gripped one of the cart handles. 'Remember the shows we used to put on in your dad's yard when Nan worked there? Cinderella and all that.'

'You put on,' he rasped. 'I was just one of your lackeys.'

'But you enjoyed them.'

He grinned and Elizabeth was taken aback. There was something heart-twistingly attractive about him when he smiled. Margaretta McDonald would have called him a heart throb. She had been a day girl whose mother worked at the Selo film factory in Brentwood, an avid picturegoer who took Margaretta regularly to the Electric Palace in the High Street. Tyrone Power was her favourite film star. Margaretta had smuggled a photograph of him into school and several of the girls had drooled over him. Elizabeth stared at Alex Payne intently. Had he once been Phyl's heart throb?

'I got a whacking from Pa for letting you use the stock,' he said, seemingly unaware of Elizabeth's intense stare. 'Some were good quality clothes from those houses round the park.'

'I never thought you'd come back and work for your father again,' said Phyl, shaking her head. 'How is he? And where's your horse?' She looked around her as if expecting to see the animal.

Elizabeth's ears pricked up at the word 'horse'. It had been really upsetting for her having to give up riding lessons.

'He's thrown a shoe. As for Dad, he's dead. Suddenly keeled over two days after I got back from Palestine.' His expression was bleak once more, as if the blizzard had got in behind his eyes.

'So you've taken over? You surprise me. You said you'd never work in the business again.'

'Things don't always work out the way you want them to,' he said bitterly. 'So stop harping on the past, Phyl.' He heaved on the cart, pulling it out of her grasp as he turned at the end of some gardens into Eastbourne Street.

His words and actions took Elizabeth, as well as Phyl, by surprise but it was only Phyl who slipped and landed flat on her back. 'Alex, wait!' she cried. 'I didn't mean – and I haven't asked –' But he didn't stop. Instead he carried on at a cracking pace, putting more and more distance between them.

Elizabeth gazed after him. He had a horse! The heart throb had a horse! She hoped he and Phyl hadn't fallen out for good. Then she remembered he had her step-mother's suitcase and started after him.

Phyl called her back. 'Don't bother. I must have touched him on the raw.'

Elizabeth hesitated. 'But he's got your suitcase.'

'He'll drop it off at our house and likely tell them we're on our way. Which I'm not sure whether I'm glad about or not,' she said. 'Sometimes surprise is best.'

'What do you mean?' Elizabeth helped her up.

Phyl grimaced and rubbed her backside. 'Never mind. Let's get walking. Just follow the tracks.'

They did just that with Phyl giving a running commentary, pointing out the local Orange Lodge meeting hall. Elizabeth did not like asking what the Orange stood for. She was more interested in the Dolls' Hospital in Whitefield Road. 'Our Lois broke me doll's muggin head one Christmas,' said Phyl. 'It was brand new. I'm sure she did it on purpose 'cos hers wasn't as good. It took me ages to forgive her.'

Elizabeth thought, Lois sounds like a girl I knew at school, and tried not to be apprehensive. She peered through the whirling snowflakes which were somehow hypnotic. She was weary and felt herself drifting. What was she doing here? The buildings and landscape were so unfamiliar that she could have been in the Antarctic. She thought of Scott and of the man who had walked out into the snow to die.

'Not far now,' said Phyl, and there was pleasure in her voice. 'See, there's the chandler's where I used to get block salt and candles for Mam.'

Elizabeth blinked and stared but could see no cause to celebrate. It was just another shop on a corner, except it was opposite a school. 'Prince Rupert's School,' Phyl informed her. 'He was a cousin of Charles II, so naturally on the side of the cavaliers during the Civil War. Liverpool had a castle in those days down by the river and it was besieged.'

'Has the castle gone now?' She tried to show interest, but her feet were freezing. She slithered over a grating outside a pub, sending snow down into the cellar.

'Yep. Well before my time and Nan's. But there's still a Castle Street.' They cut across the bombed site where a water tank left over from the war seemed to hunch against the storm. Next came a wide entry lit by a gas lamp on a yard wall. They turned right and Phyl stopped. 'We're here,' she said, and released a heartfelt breath.

Elizabeth wiped her face with a sodden glove and stared at the sooty red brick wall of the tall house with its flat sash windows and brown front door minus a knocker. Above was a fanlight with some kind of plaque in it. Phyl's suitcase stood on the snowy pavement in front of a freshly snowed upon step. Elizabeth did not know why she had imagined it differently but she had hoped for at least a small front garden with a tree. There was not even an enclosed forecourt, only the pavement. She had an overwhelming desire to burst into tears because suddenly she felt homesick and far from home.

'I hope someone's in or at least a fire's lit,' said Phyl, stepping back to gaze up at the roof. Elizabeth stepped back also and saw a trickle of smoke fighting massed snowflakes. 'Thank God,' muttered Phyl, and fumbled inside the letter box. 'Damn, my hands are too cold to grip the key on the string!' She banged on the door with her fist and continued until there came the sound of footsteps hurrying up the lobby and a voice telling them to hold their horses.

The door opened and a middle-aged woman stood silhouetted against the light coming from an inner room. She had greying brown hair and a pear-shaped face, was plump and wore a flowered pinnie.

'Good heavens, it's our Phyl!' she gasped. 'What on earth are you doing here, girl?'

'Oh, Mam!' cried Phyl, and threw herself at the woman, much to Elizabeth's astonishment. Phyl had not lost control once in the last two weeks.

'Now what's this? What's this?' The woman patted her back as she stared curiously over her shoulder at Elizabeth.

There was a lump the size of a hen's egg in Elizabeth's throat at the sight of such emotion and she couldn't have spoken to save her life. Not once could she remember being hugged by her mother.

Phyl wailed, 'Jimmy's dead! Not that he ever loved me. I thought he did but he didn't, and I never got to be on the London stage, and everything's been bloody awful!'

'Oh dear,' sighed her mother. 'I knew you'd rushed into it. My eldest daughter's wedding and none of us at it. Still, there's no need to swear, luv. We'll have none of that in this house. Come on in. A cup of tea'll soon calm you down.' She ushered her up the lobby.

Still feeling giddy with that surge of emotion, Elizabeth winced as she picked up the suitcases and followed the two women inside, past a door on the left and a darkened stairway into a room that lay straight ahead.

'Where's Dad?' sniffed Phyl, pulling away from her mother and wiping her eyes. 'I thought he'd be here.'

'He is! And a right nuisance he's being at the moment, but that's men for you,' said her mother. 'Although I probably shouldn't be saying that with your man dead. How did it happen?'

Phyl shot a glance at Elizabeth who said swiftly, 'An accident.' She did not want even Phyl's parents to know what her father had done. 'Daddy fell downstairs.'

'Daddy?'

Phyl looked at her mother, 'Mam, this is Lizzie. She's Jimmy's daughter. I know,' she added hastily. 'You never knew he had a daughter. Neither did I. She's been away at boarding school since just after Christmas. Even when

we were coast watching in Kent Jimmy never mentioned –'
She stopped abruptly.

'You poor little thing,' said Phyl's mother, eyeing
Elizabeth sympathetically. 'Although you're not so little.'

'I'm fourteen.' She held out a hand, not wanting to
think about how she hadn't been important enough for
him to tell Phyl about her. It hurt. 'How do you do, Mrs –'

'Eccles,' prompted Phyl. 'Maisie Eccles.'

'Nice to meet you, luv,' said Phyl's mother. 'You'd
best call me Aunt Maisie. We already have a Nan Eccles
here. Now sit yourself down.'

Elizabeth did as she was told, perching awkwardly on
the edge of a dining chair. She glanced about her. Somehow
it felt more strange being indoors and for a moment she
fought panic. She gazed at the fire struggling for its life
in the blackleaded grate and at the loaded clothes rack
hung from the ceiling. There was a strange odour in the
air which mingled with the smell of damp washing. She
thought of the laundry housed in an old stable block back
at the convent school, imagined the croquet lawn and the
old mulberry bush.

'Where's Dad?' said Phyl. 'You haven't told me yet.'
Her mother sighed. 'Can't you smell it?'

Involuntarily Elizabeth glanced at Phyl, who was looking at her. Both of them were united in dark memory of
the evening her father had died.

'I – can smell something,' said Phyl slowly.

'It's shellac. He's had it since before the war from that
place in Rumford Street. You'd think it was going to be
the twelfth of July tomorrow and he was true Orange,

when all the time the truth is he's making the plaques for money.'

'He enjoys it, Mam. He's artistic, is Dad.'

Elizabeth wondered what they were talking about but did not like to ask. She watched Phyl's mother – she could not think of her as Aunt yet – go to the closed door at the other end of the room and pull it open. Immediately the faint resinous smell grew stronger. 'Sam, we've got visitors!' she said. 'Come out of there and stop sulking.'

'I'm not sulking, woman.' The man had his back to them and did not turn. Elizabeth could just about make out that he was heavy-shouldered and had thick whiteish hair. 'And watch your tongue,' he added. 'I'm not yer slave.'

Phyl shot across the room to place her arms around his waist and press her face against his back.

'Who's that?' said the man.

'Guess who?' Phyl's voice was melted treacle warm as she stepped back.

He turned slowly on his heel and his hand reached out to switch off the gas ring, his broad face softening. 'About time too, lass,' he said. 'Yer not looking so good. What yer need is a pan of scouse to put some flesh on them bones.'

Once more Elizabeth was aware of a tightness in her throat but this time there was a pain in the region of her heart as well.

'I dreamed of scouse.' Phyl linked an arm through her father's. 'It had real meat in it.' She smiled. 'I never could swallow jellied eels. Just like I couldn't cockles from Moreton.'

'You must have smelt the scouse from London then,' said her mother. 'Not that there's much left and I was saving it for our Billy's lunch tomorrer. Still, you'd best have it if you're fancying.'

'I'm not fancying like that, Mam,' said Phyl quickly. 'Not in a thousand years.' She glanced at Elizabeth. 'We're just starving, aren't we, kid?'

She nodded, aware of Sam's eyes on her. 'Who's she?' Phyl told him.

'The poor kid looks frozen,' he said. 'Get over to the fire, lass, and thaw out.' He went to the fireplace, opening up the fire's heart with a poker before throwing on all the coal in the bucket that had stood next to the hearth.

Elizabeth saw Phyl's mother's mouth open but her husband threw her a glance and she remained silent. Elizabeth guessed he'd used up the evening's coal allowance and the thought that he was prepared to do that for them both warmed her as much as the flickering fire.

Phyl's mother picked up the metal teapot from the hob. 'Tea, I think,' she murmured and went into the scullery. Her husband followed with the empty bucket.

'Well, you heard me dad,' said Phyl, smiling at her. 'Come on, kid.' She seized Elizabeth's arms and propelled her ramrod-straight body to a chair in front of the fire. 'Sit down and thaw out.'

'He's kind,' said Elizabeth in a low voice. 'He didn't shout at you for bringing me here.'

'He doesn't know we're stopping yet,' Phyl teased her as she eased the damp coat from her shoulders. 'Even when he does he's not going to tell us to git. I'm family and you're with me. It's going to be a bit crowded but we'll squeeze in somewhere.' She glanced about her. 'I wonder where everyone is? I suppose the tiddlers could be in bed, but the others . . .' Her voice trailed off as the door to the lobby opened.

A black cat shot into the room. Its fur was sodden and sticking to its shivering body. It headed for the fireplace ahead of an elderly woman whose cheeks were chubby and rosy. The headscarf she wore was tartan and it, like the front of the long old fashioned coat she wore, was covered in melting snow. She followed the cat over to the fire, nudging it out of the way with her booted foot before holding out purplish-looking hands to the blaze.

Elizabeth stared at her in fascinated disbelief, reminded of all the witches she had read about in fairy stories when she'd been home occasionally on holiday. Then the cat sprang on to her lap and she yelped as its claws dug in.

The woman glanced her way and cackled. 'Stranger in the camp and that mog knows it. You'd better watch your Ps and Qs or you'll be furrit, girl.'

'Hello, Nan,' said Phyl, flashing a reassuring smile in Elizabeth's direction. 'How are you doing?'

The old woman grinned, showing teeth that looked like her own. 'I'm frightening folk. I likes doing that and it's better than thems laughing at me. So don't yous laugh.' She poked a finger in Elizabeth's direction.

'I'm not laughing, and I'm not frightened of you,' she said stoutly, determined to mean it.

'Of course yous are. I frightens meself at times. When the sky's clear and the moon's high an' the big black bats fly.' The old woman stilled and for a moment her face wore a blank expression which strangely did make the blood freeze in Elizabeth's veins. Then she shook her head and when she spoke again her tone was completely different. 'Something smells good, but who's burning it?'

'It's not the dinner, Nan,' said Phyl. 'Dad's started work early on his King Billy plaques.'

'King Billy in the fanlight and the girls in pretty frocks – that's how I knows this is the right house.' The old woman grinned and plonked herself down in the rocking chair the other side of the fireplace and stared at Elizabeth. 'Who's the girl? She's not my Jean.'

'This is Lizzie. She's my stepdaughter and has never set foot in Liverpool before,' explained Phyl. 'You can help me show her around, Nan.'

An uncertain expression flitted across the old woman's face. 'Don't know about that. Liverpool's changed – places have gone. Completely disappeared.'

Before any more could be said, Phyl's mother bustled in carrying two plates. Her steps faltered and she said firmly, 'You're not having seconds, Nan, so don't be looking for any. And why aren't you in your own room?'

The old woman beamed up at her. 'I've been looking for my Jean. It's cold outside and me fire's gone out.'

'I'll make you a cup of tea,' retorted Phyl's mother, placing several plates on the table. 'And you can have a sugar buttie. Now keep that cat away from the table or I'll give it what for. Come and get it, Phyl, and you, Lizzie. Get a move on before it gets cold.' She vanished into the scullery once more.

Elizabeth did as she was told, accepting that from now on she would be called Lizzie in this house. Phyl, Maisie, Sam, Billy. They were all no-nonsense names. She picked up a spoon and gingerly prodded the liquid sludge which looked more like potato soup than anything, but she'd eaten worse and besides she was famished.

'I'll have it if yous don't want it.' The grandmother had come to sit beside her.

'I want it,' said Elizabeth, putting a protective hand around her plate. Even so as she ate she was aware that the woman was watching every spoonful going to her mouth. Elizabeth was determined not to be put off. She needed food, to be strong, to grow, to work, make money and return south where she belonged.

The last spoonful gone, she wiped round the plate with a hunk of bread. 'Enjoyed that?' Phyl smiled across at her. Elizabeth nodded as she leaned back, no longer hungry for food, only for the familiar.

The door to the lobby opened and a youth entered. He stopped abruptly and looked at the pair of them before going over to the fire and peeling off a single damp glove and placing it on the fireguard.

'Say hello, Billy,' said Phyl.

Her brother looked at her. 'Hello, Billy' he repeated in mock obedience. 'Who's she? And wharra you doin' here?'

'She's the cat's mother,' put in the grandmother, nodding sagely.

'She's Lizzie,' said Phyl, a smile in her voice. 'She's my stepdaughter and I'm widowed and I'm here because I missed your happy little face so much.'

'I didn't know yer had a stepdaughter.' Billy strolled over to the table. 'Yer didn't get famous then?'

'Oh, aye, I was on at Drury Lane every night.' Phyl sighed. 'You could express your condolences, little brother. We've been through a terrible time.'

'Sorry.' He flicked a glance at Elizabeth. 'Sorry to you, too, but I didn't know yer dad, did I? We weren't invited to the wedding.'

'Neither was I,' she said stiffly.

Billy glanced at Phyl. 'That doesn't seem fair if she lived down there.'

'No,' said Phyl shortly.

He glanced down at their plates. 'Is that me tomorrer's dinner you've just ate?'

Before they could answer his father entered the room. 'Say no more, lad. Yer sister and the lass were starving. They've come all the way through the snow.'

'Are they stopping?'

'Of course we're stopping,' said Phyl, glancing at her mother. 'Did you expect us to sleep outside? We'll squeeze in somewhere until I can get meself a job and better accommodation.'

'What d'you mean, better?' said her mother, raising her eyebrows in a manner that was familiar to Elizabeth. 'There's nothing wrong with my house.'

'Did I say there was?' countered Phyl. 'It's just that I know it's going to be a squash.'

'It'll be that all right,' said her mother. 'I don't know where I'm going to put you.'

'There's the attic,' said Sam, rasping a fingernail across his chin. 'I know it's full of junk but it can be got rid of. Might fetch a bob or two which you could have, our Phyl.'

She nodded. 'I could ask Alex. I see he's back.'

'We'll think about that.' Her father's voice was terse.

Elizabeth wondered what he had against the heart throb.

Before Phyl could answer that remark, Billy drawled, 'Have you been up to the attic lately, Dad? It's like an icebox and there's a slate missing from the roof. You're not going to be able to fix it in this weather.'

'Don't worry, Dad. It can wait,' said Phyl. 'We'll doss down somewhere.'

'Yous can sleep in my bed,' said her grandmother. She grinned at Elizabeth. 'I's have me own speck safe from them black bats.'

Elizabeth wanted to ask where was that and what were these black bats but her mouth had gone dry because the old woman's talk did frighten her a little.

Phyl patted her grandmother's hand. 'Thanks for the offer, Nan. We'll take you up on that.'

Elizabeth wanted to say, No, no, no! She's mad. You can't trust witches not to do something to you in your sleep. But before her imagination could run away with her, the door opened again and two girls entered, older than herself but younger than Phyl. One was silvery pale, slim and pretty, the other brown-haired and plump.

'Well, look who's here!' said the silver one, her cool eyes sweeping over her eldest sister. 'It's our Phyl, looking like the Black Widow. We never expected her back, did we, Dot? We thought she'd migrated south like a swallow, but for good.'

'We did, Lo,' said Dot, nodding vigorously. 'But it's nice to see her back.' She smiled at Phyl. 'Have you brought your husband?'

'She's a widow, you daft nit,' said Billy. 'But don't compare her with the black one in the yard. She has a tongue like a knife – when she bothers to answer you. The girl's the stepdaughter, by the way.'

'Stepdaughter! Good God!' exclaimed Lois, her gaze touching on Elizabeth before fixing on her sister. 'You've landed yourself, haven't you, Phyl? What's happened to your ambitions to be a star?'

'Oh shut up,' said Phyl, scowling. 'Don't remind me. Things don't always work out the way you expect.'

Elizabeth thought, that was what the heart throb said.

'Poor you.' Dot sighed. Her button mouth had 'ooohed' in sympathy at the mention of Phyl's being a widow and she'd nodded several times during Billy's comments. Now she went over to her eldest sister and put an arm round her, pressing her cheek against hers. 'I won't upset you by asking anything. How did it happen?'

'You have asked her something,' said Lois, toying with a fingernail. 'And she doesn't look upset to me. On the contrary, she looks better than I've seen her for a long time.'

'Do you expect me to cry all over you?' said Phyl sweetly.

'That'll be the day,' said Lois. 'Since when did you ever come to me for sympathy? How long are you stopping?'

'As long as it takes to find a job and another place.'

'And how long will that be?'

'Give me a chance.' Phyl's voice was calm but her tawny eyes smouldered.

Her father moved away from the table and placed an arm around her. 'Now don't you two start. Phyl can stay here as long as she needs to. This hasn't stopped being her home just because she went away.'

'I only asked a question,' said Lois in a sulky voice. 'She's my sister, isn't she? I like to take an interest.'

At that moment her mother came in from the scullery and immediately Lois's expression changed. 'Dad's been biting my head off, Mam. Our Phyl isn't home five minutes and he's taking her side. I only wanted to know how long she was stopping. It was a fair question, wasn't it?' she said in pleading tones.

'Of course it was, luv.' Her mother's face softened.

'If I'm expected to share our teensy-weensy room it stands to reason I need to know how long she's stopping.' She gave a Cheshire Cat smile to Phyl. 'Not that you couldn't sleep with the kids. I'm sure they've more room than me and our Dot.'

'I wouldn't share a room with you again for all the tea in China,' said Phyl, returning her smile. 'Tonight we're sleeping with Nan. When the weather improves, Lizzie and me'll clear out the attic.'

'The attic!' Lois's face fell. 'Why haven't I ever been offered the attic? Our Dot snores.'

'No I don't,' said her sister indignantly. 'You're making that up.'

'Girls, girls!' said her mother, holding up her hands. 'I don't know what our visitor will think.'

'Lizzie's not a visitor,' said Phyl seriously. She glanced at Elizabeth and stretched out a hand. 'She's part of this family now, God help her. I did tell her how nice you all were. Now you're making me out a liar.'

Dot smiled at Elizabeth. 'We are nice. Honestly.'

'Speak for yerself,' muttered Billy. His father frowned at him and immediately he pinned a smile on his face. 'Lizzie, we are, we are!'

His father shook his head in a long suffering manner. 'I'm going to bed. I've got work in the morning. Don't forget to lock up, one of yer.'

Phyl said, 'I think me and Lizzie'll go to bed, too. We're exhausted. Coming, Nan?'

'Yus, girl.' She eased herself up. 'Where's me mog? If the black bats come I want to make sure he's safe.'

'Right, Nan,' said Phyl. 'Lizzie, get your suitcase.'

Elizabeth picked it up and followed her with mixed feelings. Part of her was glad to be out of reach of Lois's waspish tongue, the other part was worrying about the old woman. As she trailed in Phyl's and her grandmother's wake, she heard the old woman say, 'I knew a Lizzie once. She married the King. Good lad he is. Knows his duty. Just like the one who lights me fire in the morning and never charges me a penny.'

Elizabeth had an overwhelming desire to make a loud noise, to laugh or yell. She wanted to go home but there was no place now she could call *her* home.

She entered the parlour. The light from the hissing flames which leaked from a torn gas mantle sent shadows fluttering round the room. It was eerie. She could make out the shape of a double bed against a wall, a couple of easy chairs, a cloth-covered table, a sideboard and several small tables. She was surprised it all fitted in.

'There should be room enough for my Jean when she comes home again,' said the grandmother, patting the plump eiderdown before pulling back the covers. 'See thems there? Them's good sheets and pillowcases I embroidered 'specially for her.'

'They're lovely, Nan,' said Phyl. 'You were always a dab hand with a needle.'

'Yus. I make nice things,' said her grandmother, shuffling away from them across the room. 'Nighty night, God bless yous.' She disappeared under the table.

Elizabeth rubbed her eyes. She knew she was tired. Perhaps she was seeing things. 'Did she really go under that table, Phyl?' she whispered.

Phyl yawned. 'Yes. She thinks the war's still on. That's her speck where she hides from the black bats.'

'These black bats . . .' said Elizabeth hesitantly. 'They're not real?'

'Her name for the German bombers.' Phyl lowered her voice. 'My Auntie Jean was killed in the blitz and Nan went a bit queer afterwards. She'd had a cousin Jean, as well, who died in the war.'

Elizabeth considered 'queer' another of Phyl's understatements but perhaps they wouldn't be bewitched in their beds after all. But Mary, Mother of God, what a house and what a family! And she hadn't met them all yet! She did not know what to make of the boy, Billy. She didn't like Lois. The mother and Dot seemed OK. The father too. She experienced an ache inside her thinking of him because all fathers made her think of her own now. He had let her down. He had killed himself without even saying goodbye, and she knew for certain he hadn't told Phyl that she existed years before when they had first met, and he had talked forever about her mother. She had always known her mother was the most important person in his life but never to such an extent that he would not give a thought to abandoning his only daughter. Perhaps her mother's sister had been right all those years ago when she had disapproved of the marriage? Elizabeth wished she knew where her aunt lived. She was real family and surely lived in the south. Despite Phyl saying she was part of her family now, Elizabeth did not feel it. Nor were they tied to her by blood. They were virtually strangers. Her heart ached for the familiar sights and sounds and people of her southern upbringing.

Impulsively she said, 'Phyl, do you think there's any hope of my finding my aunt one day?'

Phyl glanced up from her open suitcase. 'What have you got to go on? Very little. She was your mother's sister, that's all. You're better accepting things as they are, luv. I know this isn't what you're used to but I'm afraid no stinking rich relative is going to come and rescue you from this wicked stepmother.' She smiled. 'You're stuck with me for now.'

'I didn't say you were wicked!' Elizabeth was mortified.

'No, of course you didn't. Sorry. I'm just waiting for our Lois to make that kind of crack, though.'

'You're nicer than her,' said Elizabeth, again impulsively. 'She reminds me of the Snow Queen in the story, all silver and ice and coldness. You're like autumn, warm and golden and lovely.'

Phyl flushed. 'Good God! I never thought you could say such nice things! Perhaps everything'll work out OK after all. I'll look after you, don't you worry, Lizzie luv. As for our Lois, don't let her get to you. She was just born with a boulder-sized chip on her shoulder.'

There was silence as they undressed. Then Phyl turned out the gas and said as she slid into bed next to Elizabeth:

'I wonder who this Black Widow is our Lo and Billy spoke about?'

'There's lots of widows since the war so Mother Bernard said,' murmured Elizabeth, hesitating to put her feet further down between the cold sheets.

'True.' Phyl lightly slapped her knees.

Slowly Elizabeth straightened her legs so her feet reached the colder recesses of the bed. Phyl's arm slipped round her and she snuggled up to her. It was not the first time they had shared a bed. The night her father had died Phyl had asked did she want to sleep in her own room or with her? Elizabeth had preferred the stranger Phyl had been then, to being alone that terrible night. Now her stepmother was no longer a stranger, but Liverpool and her family were going to take some getting used to. How was Elizabeth going to cope with it all? Before she could start worrying, the exertions of the day took their toll and she fell asleep.

Chapter Three

It was the sound of a door opening that woke Elizabeth. She lifted her head from the pillow and glanced in the direction of the window where a shaft of sunlight had managed to find a gap between the curtains. Her spirits lifted and she shot out of bed despite the cold and padded across the lino to pull aside a curtain. She scratched at the frosty flowers on the glass and looked up the street where the sun sparkled on snow-trimmed privet hedges. She could see children sliding on the icy road and hear their voices. She was reminded of a glittering Christmas card. All that was needed was a church, a choir, and a red-breasted robin. Instead there was a bread van immediately opposite, a huddle of sparrows squabbling for crumbs in the gutter, and footprints going and coming in the direction of this house. 'Hither, page, come stand by me,' she murmured.

The bed creaked. 'What did you say?' Phyl was leaning on an elbow and staring at her from bleary eyes.

'I was thinking of "Good King Wenceslas". There's footprints in the snow going from here.'

'They'll be our Billy's. He does a paper round.' Phyl reached for the clothes she had worn yesterday. 'Get yourself dressed before you catch your death.'

Elizabeth moved away from the window at the same moment that Nan Eccles appeared from beneath the table. The old woman sat up, her booted feet stretched out in front of her. A blanket hung from the table like a screen behind her and another covered her shoulders. She still wore a headscarf but had taken off her coat to reveal that she had on a thick man's cardigan beneath. The black mog crept out from under the blanket screen and stretched before going over to the door and miaowing.

Elizabeth was aware of a giggle rising inside her but before it could escape, Phyl said, 'Hello, Nan. Want a hand up?'

A seraphic expression lit the old woman's face. 'Hello, Jeangirl. I was wondering where yous were.'

Phyl and Elizabeth exchanged glances and Phyl groaned.

There was a knock on the door. 'That'll be me lad,' said Nan Eccles. 'Come in, boy,' she called.

Elizabeth shot across the room and scrambled beneath the bedcovers as Billy entered. He was carrying wood chips, newspaper and a loaf.

Phyl sat on a spindle-backed chair and said, 'I can light it if you like. I know you've got school.'

'It's OK.' He shook his red-brown hair in his grand-mother's direction. 'What do you think of her? Since there's been power cuts and shortages she's been worse than ever. I've told her the war's over but it hasn't sunk in.'

'I wouldn't be worrying,' said Phyl. 'She'd not be doing anyone any harm and she's probably warmer sleeping in her clothes under the table than you are upstairs.'

'But she'll smell sleeping in her clothes . . .' Elizabeth's voice trailed off at the look on their faces.

'Sure she does,' said Billy, staring at her from unfriendly eyes. 'She hasn't taken her clothes off in days. But if you want to drag in the tin bath from the yard, fill it from kettles on the fire and dunk her in it, you're welcome. Of course, you'll have to go and queue up for more coal, but where's the money coming from if you're lucky enough to get any?'

'That's enough,' said Phyl. 'Lizzie wasn't thinking.'

'Obviously! Or she'd have kept her mouth shut.'

'That's enough, I said.' Phyl frowned and cuffed him across the head. 'It's going to be hard enough for her up here as it is.'

'It's not going to be a picnic for us either if she's got finicky ways,' Billy muttered, dodging his sister's hand as it came up again. He dropped on his knees in front of the fireplace.

'I wouldn't call getting washed "finicky",' said Elizabeth defiantly. 'Cleanliness is next to godliness. The nuns taught us that.'

'Nuns! Blood—' He cut off the word in time and glanced at his sister. 'Is she a blinkin' Catholic?'

'No she's not,' said Phyl, sounding just as defiant as Elizabeth. 'She boarded at a convent school, that's all. She's C of E.'

'Boarding school?' Billy's expression was incredulous. 'She sounds like one of those characters out of our Mary's comic. The Heroine of the Lower Third or something. I can't believe it! What's she doing here?'

'Oh, shut up, you! Where's your manners?' Phyl was half laughing. 'You should be making her feel welcome. How would you have liked to have been sent away from home? Have a bit of sympathy.'

Elizabeth could keep silent no longer. 'What's wrong with boarding school?' she demanded. 'We had a swimming pool and a roller skating rink. There were plays and concerts to get involved in – and I took riding lessons.'

'Holy hell!' Billy was staring at her with fascination. 'She *is* a character out of a book.'

'No, I'm not!' She was enraged.

'I bet you're spoilt. Daddy had plenty of dough, did he?'

'That's enough.' Phyl's smile had vanished.

'Mummy had it, actually,' said Elizabeth, scowling at him.

'Actually,' mimicked Billy, speaking as if he had plums in his mouth.

'Enough!' This time Phyl's palm caught him a stinging smack across his cheek.

Elizabeth experienced a lovely sensation of pleasure. She hoped it hurt. Boys were horrible.

'Now get on with lighting that fire,' ordered Phyl firmly. 'We want to get dressed. We've things to do. And not a word from you either, Lizzie.'

Elizabeth would have loved to have said more but she remembered how the nuns had tried to teach her to behave with a sense of decorum and good manners so just stared with disdain at Billy, noting his square chin as he raked out the ashes, and considering how she would like to slap his face as Phyl had done. She had never realised she had such a thirst for revenge inside her. Still the nuns were forever saying all human beings were sinners and needed to repent.

'We'll have some toast when the fire's going nicely,' piped up Nan Eccles, startling her. 'There's mutton dripping and I've money if yous need it, Jeangirl.'

'Thanks, Nan,' said Phyl. 'But I'm not taking money from you if you're short.'

'What's mine is yours, girl.' The old woman scurried between the furniture like a busy little crab, to take a small bowl from the sideboard cupboard. 'Tasty it is.' She smacked her lips and put the bowl on the table before delving into a drawer and bringing out a thick blue paper cylinder to place beside the bowl. 'The gasman gave me this. I've been saving it for a rainy day. Yous can have it.'

Phyl's expression was uncertain. 'Are you sure, Nan?'

'Yous my Jean, aren't yous?' she said belligerently.

Her granddaughter smiled and hugged her. 'I'll be anyone you want me to be.'

The fire was burning reasonably vigorously now so Billy moved out of the way. 'I'll have to get.' He jerked a head in Elizabeth's direction. 'What are you going to do about her then? I take it she won't be going to no convent boarding school here.' He grinned. 'I could drop a note to the headmistress at ours if you want?'

Elizabeth's head shot up. 'I'm not going to a mixed school.'

Phyl wrinkled her nose. 'I don't know what to do.'

'You're going to have to do something,' said Billy. 'You'll have the man from the school board round otherwise.'

'Perhaps she could go to yours for now?'

Elizabeth gave a theatrical sign to draw their attention. 'I don't see why I can't go to a convent school. Aren't there any in Liverpool?'

'Of course there are,' said Phyl, raising her eyebrows in that speaking fashion. 'Liverpool's snowing in Irish Catholics.'

'Why's that?' said Elizabeth, without thinking.

'Because of Ireland, dummy,' said Billy impatiently. 'It's just across the Irish Sea and Liverpool's first port of call for most of its inhabitants.' He moved over to the table and cut the crust from the loaf he had brought.

'Well, that's OK then. Mother Borromeo is Irish, from Kerry, and she's clever. I'll go to a convent school here.'

Billy shook his head in disbelief. 'Haven't you told her anything, our Phyl? Hasn't she heard of the Orange and Green?' He glanced at his grandmother. 'Any connie onnie, Nan?' he said, before giving Elizabeth his attention once more. 'Listen, Lizzie girl, Mam's family is as Orange as marmalade, so it goes without saying most of us are too. We're for King and country. The other lot are for the Pope and the old Emerald Isle. Ta, Nan!' He took the tin of condensed milk from her.

'I'm not as orange as marmalade,' said Phyl. 'And neither is Dad and Nan.'

Elizabeth sighed heavily again. 'This is real educational but it's not getting me any closer to a school. I'm not orange so I might as well be green.'

'You can't be,' said Phyl, shaking her head. 'Not in this house. Mam wouldn't allow it and you have to keep on her right side.'

'Then what am I going to do?' said Elizabeth, dismayed.

Phyl was silent a moment. 'I'll do something. But you might have to go to Billy's school for a bit.'

Elizabeth's heart felt as if it had dropped into her stomach. Billy caught her eye. 'Don't look so worried, kid,' he surprised her by saying. 'The girls are kept separate from the boys. We have the top floors, they have the bottom. There's separate playgrounds, too, so you don't have to get worked up about that either. Just take a few plums out of your mouth and you'll survive.'

'I'm not going to change the way I talk,' she said, tossing back her long dark hair.

'Suit yourself. But our Phyl managed it. She took elocution lessons so she could talk the gear on stage.' He shot his sister a quick smile.

'I'll write a note for you to take,' said Phyl. 'Wait a mo'.'

She scribbled hurriedly on a piece of paper and handed it to him and kissed his cheek. 'You can go now.'

He wiped off the kiss, said tarrah, bit into his buttie and left the room.

Elizabeth slid out of bed. 'I'm not going to change the way I speak,' she said firmly.

'No, love,' said Phyl, pulling up her knickers under her nightie.

Elizabeth dressed swiftly in a blue wool frock. '*He* and the rest of them don't talk like your nan.'

'No. She grew up round Netherfield Road, a real scouser.' Phyl had dressed and was now slicing bread. 'Nan moved into this house when she married Grandad.

His mother was dead but his father was alive and I believe
he was a right old tyrant, but Nan could handle him. She
hasn't always been the way she is now.' She handed
Elizabeth a toasting fork and a slice of bread.

'I wasn't criticising.'

'Of course you weren't.' Phyl patted her head. 'Don't
be worrying about the way you talk. You'll be a five-day
wonder. You'll get skitted, but take it in the right spirit
and you'll survive.'

Elizabeth was quiet. She had survived being different
before but no longer wanted just to survive. She wanted
to have fun. She felt miserable as she held the toasting
fork and her mind wandered to just a few weeks ago. Her
life had changed so quickly.

'Toast's burning,' said Nan Eccles, nudging her arm.

Elizabeth could have wept but blew out the flames
instead and tossed the blackened bread on the hearth.

Immediately Nan Eccles picked it up and brushed ash
from it. 'Yous'll have to eat this, girl.' Her tone was severe.
'Can't have any waste.' This time Elizabeth could not
contain herself and a tear rolled down her cheek. 'Now,
girl, don't take it like that.' The old woman patted her
shoulder and concerned grey eyes stared into hers. 'I'll
eat it. The black'll be good for me ol' teeth. Yous do
another.'

Elizabeth sniffed and rubbed her eyes with the back
of her hand. 'I didn't mean to burn it.'

'I knows that. Here.' She fumbled in a pocket and
produced a penny. Taking the girl's hand, she pressed it
on her palm. 'Get yerself some sweeties.'

Elizabeth gazed at the penny and was grateful for the thought behind it. 'Can you afford it? And do we have the points?'

'Yous don't throw a gift back in a person's face, girl,' growled Nan Eccles, like an angry Yorkshire terrier. 'Now hurry up with that toast so us can get the kettle on.'

The toast spread with dripping and sprinkled with salt was tasty and met with Elizabeth's approval. She was hungry and anything would have tasted good. Everything still felt strange but she was more relaxed as she watched Nan Eccles crunch the blackened bread. 'Did she mean it about it being good for her teeth?' she whispered to Phyl.

'Of course she did. Sometimes she uses soot.' Phyl smiled. 'Feel better now?'

'Yes. What are we going to do after breakfast?'

'Have a look at the attic and then I'll go and see about finding a job. Not that I wouldn't just like to stay here in the warm, but Nan won't be able to keep the fire going all day, not the way coal rationing is. I thought everything would improve with the mines being nationalised and miners' wages going up.'

Elizabeth gazed about the room and understood what Phyl meant about not moving. It looked different. Shafts of sunlight gilded the solid furniture. Good quality stuff by the look of it. The big sideboard shone as if it had been recently polished. The old woman might not look after herself as well as she should but the sheets had been clean. Elizabeth only hoped the lavatory was.

It was upstairs on the first floor in a tiny room which Phyl informed her had once been part of the bedroom next to it. Sam was a plasterer by trade and could turn his hand to lots of things but he could not do anything about the weather and Elizabeth had to pour water from a pail down the lavatory pan because a pipe was frozen.

As she came down the dark stairway she found the bottom stair occupied. Two heads turned and she found herself being scrutinised by a boy and a girl, both of whom looked several years younger than herself.

'You're a girl,' said the boy in a gloomy voice, getting to his feet. He was already dressed for outdoors in a brown tweed coat and fawn balaclava. 'I had hopes there'd been a mistake. Might as well git to school now I've seen yer.' Without another word he walked towards the front door and slammed it behind him.

'Dad'd have him for doing that. He says it ruins the hinges,' said the girl, uncurling gracefully and flicking back the two long sandy plaits that hung beneath her pixie hood. 'I'd best be going, too. I'm Mary by the way.' She held out a hand. 'Don't mind our Trev. He's the baby of the family and only has the cat to boss. I'm pleased to meet you.'

'I'm pleased to meet you, too,' said Elizabeth, considering Mary's manners made up for her brother's rudeness.

'You'll soon get used to us. See you tonight.' She waved a hand as she went down the lobby. The door opened and closed gently.

Phyl came out of the parlour. 'You've met the tiddlers then?'

'Mary's nice, but your younger brother was hoping I was a boy,' she said ruefully.

'I told you, he hates there being so many females in the house. Poor lad.' Phyl's tone was cheerful. 'Ready to go up the apples and pears? We won't disturb Mam. She likes to have a quiet cuppa and a quick tidy after the family have gone. She's a cleaner at Prince Rupert's School, though not until after four o'clock, but queuing for food takes up a lot of her time.' She started upstairs. 'I don't know whether you felt it last night but there were lumps in that flock mattress of Nan's. She's probably had it since the Boer War.' Elizabeth had not noticed and said she'd been beautifully comfortable. Phyl looked surprised but made no comment.

They came to the attic, which felt as Billy had said like an icebox. The wallpaper was peeling off in places and snow had drifted in through the hole in the roof and frozen on top of an old treadle sewing machine. There were cardboard boxes with oddments in, an old pram, a couple of broken chairs and several plaster plaques resting against a wall.

Phyl patted the sewing machine. 'Nan's.' Then she tucked her hands under her armpits. 'Hell, it is cold! I think we'll have to wait until the thaw comes before moving up here.'

'We'll have to get rid of the junk.'

'We'll pop into Alex's yard. I'm sure I can persuade him to do it.'

'Your dad didn't sound enthusiastic about him,' murmured Elizabeth.

'Hmmm! I wonder why? He didn't use to mind him when he was a lad.' Her expression was thoughtful as she moved over to the window and gazed out. Elizabeth followed her over and saw that it looked out over a large yard with a minute iced-over pond shimmering in the sun. There was an area of frozen bushes, a wooden hutch type building and a patch of smooth snow.

Phyl turned away. 'Are you coming, Lizzie? You might as well start getting to know the area. Besides the fresh air'll do you good.'

Elizabeth thought there was enough fresh air in the attic but she agreed and followed her downstairs.

ALEXANDER PAYNE, SCRAP METALS, SALVAGE MERCHANT, WOOLLEN AND COTTON RAGS AND BAGGINGS was blazoned on large double gates. Elizabeth followed Phyl through a small doorway set in one of the gates leading into a cobbled yard. A handcart rested against the side of a building and there was an open shed with scrap metal piled high beneath its roof. Through a doorway she could make out the shapes of neatly bundled rags, and there was another building next to that one which looked as if it might be stabling. On the other side of the yard was a building which housed an office and above it what looked like living quarters because green curtains hung at the windows.

'I remember,' said Phyl, gazing about her with pleasure on her lively face, 'when Nan worked here and used to wash some of the secondhand clothes in a large tub and string them across the yard. When they were dry and ironed she would take them to a stall in Paddy's Market down Scottie Road where some of the best customers were Indian seamen straight off the ships.'

'Is the river far away?'

Phyl wrinkled her nose. 'Perhaps half a mile from Lime Street. I'm no good at working out distances. I've walked it from here and it takes about an hour and a bit in comfy shoes.'

There was the sound of breaking glass. It caused them to start and Phyl raced across the yard in the direction of the noise. Elizabeth followed her.

Before they reached the shed a young woman emerged, dressed in a black skirt, a black jumper and a black head-scarf. Her small face seemed to be made up of angles and sharp points. She looked far from pleased to see them and stopped short, wrapping her arms about her. 'What d'you want? If you're looking for him, he's out.' Her voice was flat and unwelcoming.

'I take it you're referring to Alex?' said Phyl, politely.

'You're a friend of his, are you?' There was a hint of derision in the words. 'Well, as I say, he's out.' She turned her back on them and walked in the direction of the office.

Phyl glanced at Elizabeth who was beginning to recognise a certain stubborn expression on her stepmother's face and guessed she wasn't about to leave. They headed towards the office. 'Excuse me,' said Phyl, pushing open the door, 'may I ask who you are?'

'You may,' said the woman, seating herself in the chair behind a large oak desk. 'But it doesn't mean I'm going to tell you.'

'I take it you work here?'

The woman picked up a pencil and tapped it on the desk. 'Persistent, aren't you?' Her eyes were resentful. 'What does it look like to you?'

'I haven't seen you doing any work yet. You could be trespassing.'

'Don't be daft! You can tell you haven't been round here for a while. I live here! Ask people. They'll tell you about me.'

Phyl stared. 'You're lying!' She rested her outspread hands on the desk. 'You can't live here, unless – surely you and Alex aren't married?' She sounded dumbfounded.

A humourless little smile played round the woman's mouth. 'Definitely not! Now if there's nothing else, you can leave or it'll be you getting done for trespassing.' There was an edge to her voice.

Phyl didn't move. 'Where's Alex?'

The woman got to her feet in one swift impatient movement. 'Who the hell do you think you are to keep asking me questions? He's out, I tell you! Gone into town to see a woman about a clock he thinks is an antique. Probably isn't. He's one for making mistakes! Leave your name and I'll tell him you called.'

Phyl straightened. 'It doesn't matter. I'll call back. Thanks for your help.' She walked out of the office and Elizabeth traipsed after her.

'Do you think she's the Black Widow Billy mentioned?'

'That's just what I was thinking.' Phyl's brows knitted together. 'But who the hell is she? And what does she mean, she lives there? I can't believe that Alex and she could . . .' She caught herself up and looked at Elizabeth with a smile that was obviously forced. She wondered what Phyl had been about to say. It definitely wasn't what she did say. 'Let's go home and have a cuppa tea. I've gone completely off the idea of looking for a job right now.'

Elizabeth did not argue. She felt like a cuppa and a warm by the fire herself.

Maisie was just on her way out when they reached the house. 'I didn't expect you two back so early,' she said, frowning. 'Don't go stoking the fire. The little coal we've got has to last. I can't stop or the queue at the fish shop'll be a mile long.' She made to go up the street but Phyl caught hold of her sleeve.

'Hang on, Mam. I haven't given you our ration books. Besides, I want to ask you something.'

'Hurry up then,' said her mother, looking impatient. 'Or we won't even be having fishcakes for tea.'

'There's a girl in Alex's yard dressed in black. She said she lives there. D'you know anything about her?'

Maisie sighed. 'I knew you couldn't keep your nose out.'

'Well?' demanded her daughter.

'I've only heard tittle-tattle.' She swung her oiled cloth shopping bag. 'Nobody knows anything for sure. They're all making guesses about her being the lad's fancy piece. She has a baby but no one so far has found out its sex or whether it's his or not. She isn't one for giving out information. No one's seen the baby. Only heard it crying, poor little thing.'

Phyl's hand slipped from her sleeve and she said slowly, 'Mam, you can't believe that Alex –'

'She lives in those rooms over the office and speaks to him something terrible. That's what I've heard. It makes you wonder.' Maisie glanced at Elizabeth and lowered her voice but the girl still heard her say, 'We all know the sort of thing some people got up to during the war regardless of whether they were married or not.'

Phyl shrugged impatiently. 'If it's a baby it couldn't have been the war.'

Her mother pursed her lips. 'You asked me so I've told you. You're best avoiding him. Now I'm off. We can sort out ration books later.' She bustled away, catching up with a woman who'd just come out of her house a few doors away and walking on up the street with her.

Phyl stared after her and after several silent moments had passed Elizabeth said, 'What are you going to do?'

'I need to think so we'll have that cup of tea and then I'm going back to the yard.'

'But your mother said –'

Phyl's expression fixed into determined lines and she squeezed Elizabeth's arm. 'You don't always do what mothers say, kid. Not when you get older anyway.'

'Can I go with you?' Elizabeth's curiosity was thoroughly aroused, and besides, if the heart throb returned to the yard so might his horse.

Phyl smiled suddenly. 'I suppose you can tag along. Now let's get that cup of tea. I'm freezing.'

'You back again?' The Black Widow gazed at Phyl from unfriendly eyes as she stood behind the desk, her palms pressed against its edge.

'Obviously,' said Phyl. 'Is Alex back?'

'No.'

'We'll wait then.' She parked her bottom on the desk which was littered with papers.

'You shouldn't do that,' protested the woman. 'He'll be furious. That desk is his pride and joy.'

'My weight won't do it any harm,' said Phyl. 'And somehow I don't think you're going to offer us a chair.'

The woman glared at her before walking out of the office and through the door to the rear.

Phyl grinned conspiratorially at Elizabeth. 'That's routed her. I wouldn't be behaving like this if she'd been a bit more friendly.' She slid off the desk and sat on the chair behind it.

'It's a lovely old desk,' said Elizabeth, sitting where Phyl had sat and swinging her legs. She stroked the dark wood. 'He must know something about furniture.'

'Learnt it from his dear ol' dad,' said Phyl, as she began to tidy the papers on the desk. 'Old man Payne used to empty houses before the war. Nan got some of the furniture in the parlour from him. He had a secondhand shop.' She began to sing softly as she continued to tidy the desk. Then suddenly she fell silent. Elizabeth too had heard the hooves clattering on the cobbles. She slid off the desk and hurried over to the door and outside with Phyl.

They saw the horse and cart but there was no one sitting on the seat at the front. They were just in time, though, to see the back of someone vanishing inside the outhouse which the Black Widow had vacated earlier. Phyl hurried in that direction but Elizabeth sauntered over to the black shaggy horse standing between the shafts. She presumed it was the heart throb who had given him a nose bag.

'Hello, beauty,' she said softly, halting a couple of feet away. The horse looked at her before carrying on munching.

The heart throb's voice sounded across the yard. 'I'll kill her!'

Elizabeth turned to see him reappear in the doorway of the outhouse. 'What's wrong?' her stepmother's voice was not loud but it carried.

'She's smashed two crateloads of jam jars, that's what!'

Phyl seized hold of his arm but barely managed to impede his speedy progress towards the office. 'Why should she do that?' Her voice was puzzled.

'Because she's bloody vindictive, that's why! I don't know why I put up with it.' He stopped abruptly and stared down at Phyl, then towards Elizabeth, then back to Phyl. 'I didn't think you'd be here this quick. Curiosity get the better of you?'

'That's not nice, Alex.' She sounded hurt.

'It's true, though.' His expression was grim.

'Of course it's true. We played a lot together in the old days. We were mates. Naturally I'm interested in what you're up to.'

'You could have chosen your words better.' Some of the anger had gone out of his voice. He shot a glance at Elizabeth. 'Why isn't she at school?'

'Have a heart,' protested Phyl. 'She's only just come.'

Elizabeth decided to seize her opportunity. 'I like your horse. I'll groom him for you if you have no one else to do it. I do have some experience.'

He stared at her and a lop-sided smile created a crease in his left cheek. 'Do you want paying?'

'I'd do it for love.' She glanced at Phyl, whose eyebrows rose.

'Don't act hasty,' murmured her stepmother. 'If you're going to work for Alex, he should pay you. Think on, I'm not going to be able to give you pocket money. I haven't got a job yet, and even when I do get one money'll be tight.'

Alex looked at Phyl. 'Depending on which way you look at it, this could be your lucky day. There's a job going in the shop in Wavertree Road. The girl left unexpectedly yesterday. Her sweetheart's home from Egypt and she's getting married. It's yours if you want it.'

Without hesitating Phyl said, 'I'll take it. Although you do realise I know nothing about antiques.'

'I don't deal in antiques,' said Alex, his eyes narrowing. 'Did Doreen give you that idea?'

'If she's the woman in black, then yes she did,' said Phyl, smiling. 'Something about a clock. Was it worth anything?'

He shrugged. 'It could be. Anyhow the shop deals in anything I can get my hands on that I can sell. I've got to go there now so I'll take you with me if you like? You can meet Harry. He's the old bloke who works in the back room fixing things for me.'

'OK if Lizzie comes?'

He glanced at Elizabeth. 'She's only skinny. I think we'll manage to squeeze her in. She can sit in the middle so she doesn't fall off. And there's a blanket in the back. Put it over your legs.'

'I won't fall off,' said Elizabeth, beaming at him. 'Thank you very much, Mr –' She had forgotten his surname.

'Payne,' he supplied succinctly, removing the nosebag. He patted the horse and told them to hop up.

He sprang up on the other side of Elizabeth, shoving her up so that she was squashed between him and Phyl. He unlooped the reins and almost hit Elizabeth in the eye with his elbow. She had never been so intimately close to a man, not even her father, and found the experience unnerving. He smelt of horse and soap and something indefinably male; not BO though, like some priests. He made a clicking noise with his tongue and teeth. The horse moved, circled round, and headed towards the open gate.

'Remember Richie Harding throwing stones at us when we were pushing the handcart along here years ago?' said Phyl, speaking across Elizabeth, her arm resting along the iron rail at the back of the seat.

'I got a belting for bloodying his nose,' said Alex. 'His mam complained to the ol' man and he took her word for it that I'd started it.'

'That was unfair! Why didn't you tell me?'

'What would have been the use? He wouldn't have believed you either. He blamed you for half the trouble I got into. You were older than me after all.'

'Eighteen months!' protested Phyl. 'You're all of twenty-three now. Time you caught up.'

'I feel older,' he murmured, glancing at her. 'Whereas you look younger.'

'Flatterer! If you think that's going to get you out of explaining who that Doreen is, you've another thing coming.'

'I'm your boss now, remember? Have a bit of respect.' His expression was mild but there was a hint of firmness in his voice.

He glanced down at Elizabeth who was watching his handling of the reins. 'Have you ever driven a horse and cart?'

She lifted her eyes to his and realised they were deep blue. He winked and she blushed. 'I've only ridden. I'd be worried about the horse getting away from me. You handle him very well.'

'Thanks.' There was a smile in his voice.

'Do you two mind?' said Phyl, tapping Elizabeth's shoulder. 'Horses ain't what I want to talk about. Alex, you're not really going to pull rank, are you? I only ask about the Black Widow because I'm worried about your reputation, lovey. Dad all but froze when I mentioned asking you to empty our attic.'

'Then I'd better not empty your attic,' he said softly. 'I believe in steering away from angry fathers.'

She frowned. 'Alex, you can't mean that? You're just the person to do it. We'll have to pick our moment, that's all. Anyway there's no rush. I don't want it doing until the weather gets better.' He stayed silent. 'Please, Alex,' she said in wheedling tones.

'We'll see. Anything interesting up there?'

'Bits and bobs. Nan's old sewing machine.'

'There's a pram and wall plaques,' put in Elizabeth.

'Perhaps I'll come,' he said, causing the horse to slow to a walk as they approached the main road. He glanced at Phyl. 'Your dad still making them plaques, then?'

'It's extra money. And in our house there's always a need for that.'

'I used to enjoy watching your dad work. He reminded me of a stone mason, only your dad's material is softer.' He hesitated. 'If you could get him interested then we'd probably be able to sell some through the shop.'

'I'd have to prove to him that you're someone to be trusted,' said Phyl, and leaned across Elizabeth. 'Take that expression off your face, Alex. Who is she and why is she living in your house?'

He flicked the reins and the horse broke into a trot, past a church on an island in the middle of the road and then the register office and the Hippodrome on the other side. 'I knew as soon as I saw you yesterday you wouldn't give me any peace.' His tone was exasperated. 'I don't really want to talk about it but I suppose you'll think the worst if I don't.'

'I wouldn't think the worst,' said Phyl swiftly, adding, 'It's not your baby, is it?'

'Such faith in me,' he said dryly. 'I suppose you won't shut up until you know everything.'

She smiled and reached across to press his knee.

Elizabeth was now thoroughly distracted from watching Alex's hands as they controlled the horse and her eyes went to his face. He looked far from gratified. 'The baby is the son of an army mate of mine who was killed in Jerusalem. It was an accident but Doreen, his widow,

has to have someone to blame so she blames me.' His
tone was ragged. 'The pair of us were on guard duty, you
see. When it came to being relieved, our relief started
messing about. We were the enemy and they were going
to shoot us. All pretend. The only thing was that Dougie
had left the safety catch off the machine gun and they
did shoot us.'

'Hell!' breathed Phyl.

'How awful,' said Elizabeth, her imagination painting
a picture for her.

'It was hellish.' His smile was taut. 'Doreen won't
accept that Dougie made the mistake. She says the army
only has my word for it and she doesn't consider a rag
and bone man's word good enough.'

'Then why on earth do you put up with her?' cried
Phyl. 'Yer daft!'

'A stupid promise to Dougie that if anything happened
to him . . . she has no family.'

Phyl groaned. 'How many times have I heard that
before?'

'What d'you mean?' asked Elizabeth. 'Where have you
heard it before?'

Her stepmother glanced at her and said crossly, 'You
shouldn't be listening to this, big ears.'

'I can't help listening.' Her voice was indignant. 'I'm
a piggy in the middle.'

Alex grinned. 'Hear that, Phyl. No more questions.'

'Oh, come off it, Alex,' she said. 'You can't stop there.
If this woman hates you so much, why does she stay?'

His smile faded. 'Three guesses.'

'To get as much money out of you as she can?'

He laughed. 'The ol' man didn't leave a fortune. But you're right in one way.'

Elizabeth had been thinking of stories she'd read.

'Revenge,' she said with relish. 'She wants to make your life miserable.'

'Right!' said Alex. 'But there's a third thing.' He hesitated. 'She isn't a natural mother and I happen to be good with Syd.'

'You!' exclaimed Phyl, before adding hurriedly, 'Of course, Nan taught you how to look after your baby sister when your mam died.' She sighed. 'That was tragic.'

'Don't remind me.' His dark brows drew together. 'You know, Phyl, you could help Doreen . . .'

She said lightly, 'Don't ask. I have five younger sisters and brothers. It's put me off babies for life.'

'But you know how to handle them. You could give her advice. She might listen to you. You're young! You're a widow!'

'Me and her have already met,' murmured Phyl, taking out a cigarette. 'I don't think she'll listen to me.'

He sighed. 'What the hell did you say to her?'

'Nothing!'

Elizabeth grinned. Alex glanced at her. 'What did she say?'

'I'm not telling,' she said firmly. 'Perhaps Mrs Eccles could help Doreen?'

'Mrs Eccles has enough to do,' said Phyl.

'Doreen wouldn't ask,' said Alex. 'She hates the people roundsabout. Says they're all talking about her.'

'That's because they are,' said Phyl. 'And can you
blame them when she's so unfriendly and living on your
premises?'

Alex made no reply and they lapsed into silence. None
of them spoke until he stopped the horse and cart outside
a shop not far from the Maypole dairy in Wavertree Road.

Elizabeth liked the shop. It was interesting because it
was crammed with different things. She liked Harry
Blaithwaite, too. He was tall but stooped, and had a bald-
ing head and lined face; his eyes were kind. When he
shook her hand, his grip was warm. 'So yer from down
south?' he said. 'I wus in Lundon when I was a ship's
carpenter with the Harrison line. You might perhaps
know it?'

She had to deny that. 'I didn't go down to the docks
much but I like being by water.'

He looked gratified. 'You'll have to go down the
Pierhead, girl. It's a fine sight seeing all the ships on the
river.' He put a hand on her shoulder. 'But right now
you've to come with me in the back while Mr Payne
explains a few things to Mrs Knight.'

Elizabeth went with him, barely managing to squeeze
her way between a huge sideboard and a table piled high
with jugs and bowls. There was also an old bicycle, minus
gear chain and brakes, on which she narrowly avoided
snagging her black lisle stockings. In the back room there
was shelving with tins of paint and pots of glue, and on
the floor in different stages of repair were pieces of furniture. Harry beckoned her over to a workbench where
there were a couple of boxes. She liked old things and

touched the lid of one of them with reverence. Its lid was inlaid with different coloured woods and inside there were thimbles, a cross stitch needlecase, several cotton reels and hooks and buttons.

'Many a woman'll find a use for those there buttons,' said Harry. 'You can put them on a tray for me if yer like.'

Elizabeth scooped up a handful of mother of pearl buttons, letting them pour through her fingers like shale, and remembered a trip to Southend-on-Sea. For a moment she felt overwhelmingly homesick, then Harry nudged her arm.

His eyes were twinkling as he offered her a pair of metal cylinders which were attached to the other box. She took hold of them and swifter than she had time to ask what they were for, he turned a small handle on the box. She felt a mild tingling which grew into a burning sensation as he turned the handle faster and faster. He stopped and she dropped the handles hurriedly, her palms stinging. 'What is it?'

'It's the Victorians' remedy for nervous complaints.' He grinned. 'Perhaps the boss should borrow it for that Mrs Bradshaw who works at the yard? Right gob she has on her most of the time.'

'She's lost her husband,' said Elizabeth.

'Aye! But so have thousands of others. Yer stepmam's a widda but she's brought a smile to the boss's face. Old friends, he said, and yer can tell he likes her.'

Elizabeth thought about that. How much did the two old friends like each other? They had argued, but what did that mean? Perhaps one day they might marry? She was uncertain how she felt about that. Would their feelings for each other exclude her? She did not like that thought. 'Phyl was broken-hearted when my father died,' she lied. 'It's just that she doesn't believe in wearing her heart on her sleeve.' She had read that phrase in a book somewhere.

'She looks like a woman who'd put a brave face on things.' He patted Elizabeth's shoulder. 'But some women aren't meant to be alone, girl.' He looked down at her worried face and smiled. 'I'm an ol' romantic. Yer mustn't mind me. Now how about yer putting the kettle on to make us all a nice cup of tea?'

He showed her the sink and the tiny gas ring in the corner and where the tea caddy was. As he worked he told her about his wife who had the rheumatics real bad and about his daughter who was a good girl and helped her mam as best she could with a family of her own to look after. She listened with half an ear, wishing Phyl and Mr Payne would stop taking so long to talk in the shop. She did not know if she was glad or not when her step-mother came through on her own.

Phyl smiled at her. 'He's gone. But he suggested I stay here a while and get the hang of things. Is that OK with you, Harry?'

'Of course, missus. I take it the girl's stopping too?'

Phyl leaned against the workbench and smiled as she took a cup from Elizabeth. 'You don't mind staying, do you, love?'

'Of course not.' She grinned her relief. 'I think I'll enjoy it.'

'Good. You can help me out by polishing the furniture.'

By five o'clock they had sold a dozen buttons, a pink vase which Elizabeth considered hideous but Phyl praised to high heaven to a customer, several cups and saucers, a battered kettle and a couple of hardly used tea towels. There had been a number of browsers whom Elizabeth had been ordered to keep her eyes on whilst putting a shine on an Edwardian mahogany sideboard with elephantine feet that took up most of a wall.

Phyl decided to call it a day and Elizabeth didn't know whether she was glad or sorry. Her feet ached but part of her had no wish to go back to the Eccles household, to listen to Lois's sharp tongue and to face the younger brother's resentment.

As they walked up Wavertree Road, Phyl said thoughtfully, 'I think I might enjoy working in the shop. Although it can never match up to being on stage.'

'Perhaps you might go back to it one day?' said Elizabeth, gazing into a Sayer's bakery window at several empty cakestands and thinking how hungry she was.

'Chance would be a fine thing,' said Phyl wryly, slipping a hand through her arm. 'Sometimes reality has to be faced, kid, and dreams have to go out of the window. Life often lands you with choices but it can also come up with compensations.'

'In what way?'

She smiled. 'Too soon to say. But I'm not complaining about anything.'

Elizabeth looked at her and thought, What she's saying is she's not complaining about having to put up with me. Despite not wanting to come north she realised her good

fortune in having Phyl to shoulder the responsibility of
taking care of her. The last thing she wanted was to be
considered a nuisance and she vowed that she would do
her best to be of help. They walked on in companionable
silence and came to Durning Road where they caught a
tram.

It was only when Elizabeth followed Phyl indoors at
the Eccleses' and heard Billy saying, 'I gave that note in,
our Phyl, and the headmistress wishes to see you both on
Monday,' that she remembered school and was filled with
a stomach-churning dread.

Chapter Four

'Now you're going to be fine,' said Phyl, dragging on her coat.

'Will you be seeing Mr Payne?' asked Elizabeth, who would rather have been going to the shop than to school. They had gone to see the headmistress yesterday and Elizabeth had hoped for a stay of grace, believing there would be a need for a school uniform, but it seemed there was not. So they had decided she might as well wear the Ursuline brown pleated pinafore dress and cream cotton blouse from her old school and that was what she was dressed in now. She felt a cheat.

'Hopefully,' said Phyl, fishing a glove out of her coat pocket. 'But if he doesn't call in at the shop I'll go to the yard on the way home. After all he did say he wanted me to befriend dear little Doreen.'

'I'd like to be there to see her face when you turn up again.' Elizabeth made her voice sound cheerful although her stomach was churning and she cuddled the cat close, finding the act comforting.

Phyl grimaced. 'Do you like babies, Lizzie?'

'I don't know.' The question surprised her. 'I've never been round them much. A friend at school had a baby sister. She was kept in a pram all the time I was there.'

'That's no introduction to baby care,' said Phyl. 'You need to hold them to see if it does anything to you – and the way you're holding that cat you could be a natural.' She turned to Billy who had just got in from his newspaper round and was leaning against the doorjamb, looking fed up. 'You'll take care of Lizzie now, me lad?'

'Yeah, yeah!'

'Good.' Phyl kissed his cheek, her grandmother's then Lizzie's before hurrying out. They heard her shouting a tarrah to the whole household before the front door slammed.

Nan Eccles rose to her feet, a determined expression on her wrinkled face. 'Yous heard her. Time to get yer skates on and get to school.'

'Give us a chance, Nan,' said Billy, reaching for the connie onnie tin. 'There's plenty of time.'

'Kids always say that.' She looked accusingly at Elizabeth. 'Come on, girl. Yous have to move yerself.'

She did not feel like moving. She felt rebellious and so stayed where she was. The old woman slapped her lightly on the leg. 'Yous haven't got cloth ears, have yer, girl?'

'No, of course not!' She withdrew her legs hurriedly and tucked them beneath her on the chair.

'I'd move if I was you,' said Billy, a gleam in his brown eyes as he spread connie onnie on bread. 'She'll whack yer harder if you don't, even if it's only with her hand.'

Elizabeth's nerves jumped but she made no sign of her apprehension. She had never been hit before. 'She'd better not,' she said firmly.

'She won't if you do as you're told,' said Billy in a reasonable voice. 'You've got to go so why look for trouble? I don't want you making me late, so move.'

'You don't have to wait for me. I'm not stupid! I know where the school is.' Elizabeth's words came out jerkily. 'I can find my way there without you.'

'You can do that tomorrow but I told Phyl I'd look after you today, so I'm doing it.' He frowned. 'Now move! You've got five minutes.'

She would have liked to defy him but there was something in his expression that made her think if she didn't move he might drag her out of the chair. Wasn't she glad now she'd never had a brother? To have put up with being bossed around by someone like him all her growing life would have been unbearable. She uncurled herself, and still nursing the cat, stalked out of the room, closing the door behind her.

Billy grinned and sat in the chair she had vacated.

'Yous told her, boy,' said his grandmother, resting a hand on the back of the chair.

'Yeah, Nan.' He stretched out his legs towards the fire.

'But don't be thinking yous is staying there,' she said, prodding him in the back. 'Yous can move too or I'll have yer!'

Elizabeth would have dragged her feet even more than she did but the lavatory was cold, and besides it would be a relief getting out of the house. Even so when Billy shouted upstairs for her she did not rush herself but strolled down.

She was out of sight round the bend when she heard Phyl's mother say, 'Do you have to yell like that, me

laddo? You'll have the neighbours complaining. Although
it is time she moved herself. I don't know what it was
like where she came from but she's going to have to start
considering other people more.'

Elizabeth stopped, angry that Phyl's mother should
consider her selfish.

'She's a girl,' she heard Trev say. 'All girls are pests.'

'Shut up,' said Mary. 'You're only small fry.'

'I am not!'

There came the sound of a scuffle and then a yelp.
Elizabeth hurried downstairs, only to be brought to a halt
by Trev stretched out on the bottom stair. Phyl's mother
was standing in the kitchen doorway, holding a scarlet-
faced Mary by one of her plaits. 'Let me get at him, Mam.
He kicked me,' she yelled.

'He hardly touched you,' said Billy. 'Don't be a cry
baby.'

'Shut up the lot of you,' said his mother. 'And Trevor,
get up and let Lizzie past.'

The boy sat up but as Elizabeth went to step round
him he lay out again and she fell on top of him. 'You
stupid –' she began but got no further. Billy dragged her
off Trev and put her on her feet.

'Stop messing about and let's be going,' he said. 'If
yer hadn't been doing everything at a snail's pace none
of this would have happened.'

The injustice of the remark left her speechless and she
was fuming as she followed him outside. It was another
sunny day and the air felt as if the weather forecast's promise
of a thaw ahead might come true. She thought longingly

of her school in the south, of its gardens and the surround-
ing countryside as spring unfurled. She felt like crying.

'What's the matter with you?' said Billy, looking down
at her. 'Cat got your tongue?'

'Leave me alone,' she muttered.

'If that's what makes you happy.' He said no more and
when another boy joined them he began to talk about Billy
Liddle and Jimmy Balmer. She knew the two men played
for Liverpool football team because Billy and his dad had
been discussing them on Saturday evening. According to
Billy they were the greatest football heroes of all time.

They came to the park which Phyl had taken her through
yesterday and Elizabeth felt a moment of exhilaration.
She dawdled so that the two boys gradually drew ahead.
She was alone and here was some real green space with
trees, swings and a maypole. With a little imagination she
could be somewhere else. For a moment she was happy,
then unexpectedly her father's death intruded on
her thoughts and she felt a familiar panic. She hurried
after the two boys, wondering if Phyl ever felt like this
when she thought of that huddled figure in front of the
cooker. Could she mention it to her? How would she feel
talking about it? Had Phyl really loved Daddy? Since
seeing her with Mr Payne Elizabeth did not know what
to believe. Perhaps it would be best to forget it? So she
set aside her uncertainties and buried her fears deep.

Billy was waiting, leaning against one of the blackened
sandstone gate posts at the other end of the park. 'If you
don't move yourself,' he said impatiently, 'the gates'll be
shut and we'll be for it. Now shift!'

She shifted but did not hurry enough to keep up with him. She did not want to go to this school where she would not know anyone. This time he did not bother waiting for her and perversely she felt annoyed about that. Wasn't he supposed to be looking after her? When she saw a crowd of children, squabbling and talking, she slowed down even more. By the time she neared the school there was no sign of Billy and there were few other children around, only a group of lads throwing snowballs at each other.

Elizabeth made to skirt around them but had only gone a few yards when a snowball hit her in the back, then another and another. Melting snow trickled down her neck, dampening the collar of her blouse. Misery and frustration erupted into anger and she whirled round. Scooping up a handful of snow, she threw it in the boys' direction. One of them let out a cheer and there was a positive flurry of snowballs going back and forth with the boys getting closer and closer until a couple of them grabbed her, threw her to the ground and rolled her in the snow. She screamed and hit out at them but they just laughed until a shout caused them to leave her and run.

Shivering and furious with them, and herself for allowing herself to be provoked, Elizabeth stumbled to her feet and along the street. It could not have been a less impressive start, she thought, but it got worse. The gates to the girls' entrance were locked and the yard was empty.

She slumped against the railings. Phyl was going to be furious with her. What could she do? You didn't want to go in there, anyway, said a little voice in her head.

What are you worrying about? Get away from here. You'd have caught your death sitting in damp clothes anyway.

Moving away from the gates, she thrust her cold hands in her pockets and felt the outline of the penny Nan Eccles had given her the other day. Remembering there was a road round the corner with plenty of shops which Phyl had shown her, she headed in that direction, part running, part skipping, to keep warm. She found the bakery and bought a halfpenny bun.

'Shouldn't yer be in school, luv?' asked the girl who served her.

Elizabeth's heart missed a beat and she retorted swiftly, 'I'm not from round here. I'm – I'm on holiday. My aunt's sick and Mother and I have come up to look after her.'

The girl smiled. 'Well, I must admit you don't sound like one of us.'

No, thought Elizabeth, because I'm not and I don't want to be after today! I want to go home. But she had no home. She didn't belong anywhere or to anyone. She was a waif and stray.

She left the shop and walked in the opposite direction to the school, aware of an unexpected sense of freedom. She took her time, gazing in those shop windows not obscured by queues of housewives, and eventually came to a crossroads. On the opposite corner was the Eastern District Post Office. To her right was Low Hill, which she remembered from having travelled it in the horse and cart with Mr Payne and Phyl. Ahead the way sloped steeply downwards. In the distance the buildings and snowcapped roofs seemed to be floating in a smoky haze. There was something attractive about the scene.

The longer she stood there the more tearful she felt, and she realised it was because it reminded her of when her mother had walked her to the top of Primrose Hill to see part of London spread out like a relief map, with Regent's Park and St Paul's easily recognisable. Her mother had told her how the trees had been chopped down on top of the hill to make room for a gun emplacement because war was coming and that was why she was going to school in the country.

The memory faded and homesickness and a sense of loss swamped her. Her mother was gone and she knew so little about her. She'd like to have known more but it was too late. Then that voice in her head spoke. But your mother had a sister. Perhaps there is someone in the south who knows where she lives? Maybe at the convent school? After all *she* was an old girl. Why hadn't Elizabeth thought of that before? If only I had some money, she thought desperately, I'd go and look for my aunt. She imagined her relation's delight when she turned up on her doorstep. She'd be old, of course, and glad of Elizabeth's offer to look after her in payment for a roof over her head and her keep.

She began to walk down the hill. The happy thought of someone of her own family in the south kept her going until she reached Monument Place with the statue of George III on its plinth opposite T. J. Hughes' departmental store. Then reality stepped in. She was hungry again. She had eaten little at breakfast, having been too apprehensive about school.

She was confident she could find her way back to the Eccles household, but what if Phyl's mam was in? She would start asking questions and Elizabeth felt sick at the thought of what she might say if told the truth. But what was the alternative? She couldn't wander round this strange city all day. She would just have to hope the mam would be out and the fire still in so she could have a slice of toast. The thought of hot toast clinched it.

The house was empty when Elizabeth let herself in with the key on the string behind the door. But it didn't appear to be her day otherwise. She kicked at the dead cinders in the fireplace and despaired. 'You miserable house,' she cried aloud. 'I hate you!' It did not matter that it had been just as cold in the south, that the convent school and Victorian terrace in London had never been what most would call real homes. They had been familiar and nothing was up here in the north. She was cold, lonely, hungry and anxious, and wanted nothing more than to see familiar sights and faces. Still, there was nothing she could do about it and so there was no use in moaning.

She swallowed her tears and hung up her mackintosh, taking off her sodden brown lisle stockings. She found the black ones Phyl had bought her for the funeral and put them on, adjusting the elastic garters carefully. She changed her blouse and pinafore for the plaid frock which had been after-school wear at the convent school. Then she cut a slice of bread. She looked in the sideboard cupboard for something to put on it. There was no jam or butter that she could see, only the tin of condensed milk which she found too sweet. She poked further into the cupboard and discovered a small rectangular-shaped tin right at the back which made a noise. She took off the lid and inside there was money.

Elizabeth could scarcely believe it. The coins were mostly copper but it was real money. Surely there was enough here to get her home? The thought brought on a twinge of conscience. No, she couldn't take it. It wasn't hers. She put the tin back. You could borrow it, said that little voice in her head. Leave a note, an IOU. 'No, I couldn't' The words echoed around the room.

You wouldn't have to take it all, whispered the voice.

'No, I wouldn't, would I?' she said. 'Even so, what would Phyl say?' She imagined her stepmother's face when she discovered Elizabeth hadn't been to school and her saying 'I hate moaners'. Elizabeth would have liked to moan to someone at that moment.

She took a couple of handfuls of copper and carried it over to the table. It looked a lot of money. She wrote a note in pencil, saying that she would pay the money back when she could, that she was going to the convent school and hopefully they would know where her aunt lived. She even confessed about school and told Phyl not to worry about her. Then she placed the slip of paper with the tin on the table before cramming her nightie into her suitcase, which she had not unpacked completely yet, along with her damp clothes.

She glanced at herself in a mirror as she donned her mackintosh and thought, I look just like a kid even if my chest is sprouting. They might ask questions . . .

She considered carefully before taking from the top of the chest of drawers Phyl's face powder, rouge and lipstick. Elizabeth applied them liberally. There was a small, almost empty bottle of Evening in Paris and she removed the teeny rubber stopper and dabbed perfume behind her ears and on her wrists. She was enjoying herself now and was quite pleased with the scent although it didn't smell as expensive as the one her mother had kept on her dressing table. Tears dampened Elizabeth's eyelashes. She dabbed them away carefully. Then she looked down at the heavy lace-up shoes and knew they would not do. Her gaze swept the room and she saw Phyl's only pair of high heels in a corner. Did she dare? They would give her height and make her look even more grown up.

She dared.

The man in the ticket office watched Elizabeth push more coins through the hole in the glass with a long suffering expression.

'Emptied yer piggy bank, have yer, luv?'

'Yes.' She blushed as she watched him start to count and crossed her fingers but even before he spoke she knew there was not enough.

'Yer two bob short. You'd best go home and cum back.'

'But I haven't got any more money.' She felt herself go hot and cold. 'Couldn't you let me have a ticket for less?' she pleaded. 'I'll bring the money in next time I come. The trouble is my aunt's sick and I'm all the family she's got. She needs me.'

'Sorry, luv. No can do.'

'But you must let me,' she stammered.

'I don't know what yer running away from, luv, but I'd go home if I were you.' His tone was kind but implacable. 'Now, could you take yer money back and move away from me winder?'

With her colour even higher, and wishing she had emptied the whole tin back at the house, Elizabeth fumbled for the coins, dropping some and having to bend and pick them up, wobbling and going over on the high heels as she did so. A man wearing a bowler hat and a raincoat tutted away behind her, saying that it shouldn't be allowed and they should clear the streets. She did not know what he was talking about but left feeling all kinds of fool.

She took a rest outside the railway station, leaning against a wall and dreading the journey back to the house. Walking in high heels was more difficult than she had realised, especially on slippery pavements. She should have kept up with Billy and none of this would have happened. Hopefully, though, she would have time to put the money back and rip up the note. The large clock up high on the station wall had said two-thirty. Getting places had taken her longer than she'd realised.

Where did she get a tram? Elizabeth glanced across the road at the huge impressive blackened building with lots of pillars and a plateau with statues of people on horses and a couple of lions. Lions! But Lime Street wasn't a bit like Trafalgar Square. Again she felt homesick.

A tram drew up, blocking the view, and she would have gone to ask the conductor what number to get for

Everton but at that moment a man wearing a sailor's uniform stopped in front of her. 'Hello, doll. You doing anything?' he said.

Was he addressing her? 'I beg your pardon?' said Elizabeth in that posh voice Billy had criticised.

'Would you like a drink?' His eyes ran swiftly over the shape of her in the belted mackintosh and then down to her shapely calves in the black stockings. 'Whaddya say?'

A hot drink sounded lovely. 'That would be nice. But why should you buy me a drink?' Her tone was puzzled.

'Why?' He stopped chewing and grinned. 'Come on, doll. I like playing games as much as the next man but you know why.'

'No, I don't.' She stared at him, suddenly feeling uncomfortable.

'Lizzie, you daft idiot!' Billy's voice took her completely by surprise as he seized her arm and pulled her away.

'Beat it, kid,' snarled the sailor, and took a grip on Elizabeth's other arm.

She looked at Billy who ignored her and glared at the sailor. 'This is my sister, mate, so beat it. Me big brothers aren't far behind and they'll knock your block off if they find you with your hands on her.'

'Who'd you think you're kiddin', kid?' The sailor clenched his free hand. 'This one's mine so get lost.'

'I'm not yours!' cried Elizabeth in a shocked voice. She thought, he's big! And Phyl's not going to like it one little bit if Billy gets hurt because of me! 'Oh, Mary,

Mother of God,' she cried, clutching Billy's jacket. 'Don't let them hit me! I didn't mean to run away from school!'

The sailor dropped her arm as if treated by Harry's Victorian remedy for nerves, and disappeared inside the railway station.

Elizabeth thought Billy would be pleased at the result of her words but he shook her hard and muttered, 'I could kill you, putting me to all this trouble.'

'I'm sorry! I'm sorry!' she gasped.

He released her abruptly. 'Ah, well! You're not as thick as I thought. You have got some nous.'

'What do you mean?' She had been quite pleased with herself a minute ago.

'With all that muck on your face and standing here, don't you realise what you look like?'

She touched her mouth. 'I wanted to look older.'

'Well, you do, but that's not a good thing, hanging around here. Although looking at you close up, you can tell you're only a kid playing at being grown up. He obviously likes them like that, though.'

She scowled, irritated by what she considered a terrible insult. 'I'm not a kid. And he only wanted to take me for a drink of coffee and I was cold. I didn't like him, though. Not once he threatened you.'

'I should blinkin' hope not!' He rubbed his chin. 'I suppose you couldn't be expected to know. Even so, don't do it again.'

'What?'

He sighed. 'Forget it. Who am I to take away yer innocence? You have a word with our Phyl about the birds and the bees. They don't seem to have given yer much of an education down in that convent. Anyhow, don't say a word of this to Mam or our Phyl. It's bad enough your not going to school and pinching Nan's money. You're a thief, do you realise that?'

She reddened. 'I'm not a thief! I'd have paid it back.'

'How?'

Elizabeth had no answer to that but she had a question of her own to ask. 'How did you find out where I'd gone so quickly?'

'Your class teacher sent a monitor to ask me what had happened to you. I had to lie! I told them you'd gone down with the 'flu.'

She was surprised and touched that he should lie for her. 'You lied to that sailor, too.'

'He doesn't matter. Teachers do. I went home at lunch-time like I normally do but you weren't there. I saw your note. At first I thought, Who cares? Good riddance. So I went back to school – it was footie practice in the park. Then I got to thinking, our Phyl's not going to like it. She'll blame me. So I told me mate to tell Sir I'd been kicked in the shins and I was bleeding and had to go home.'

Her amazement grew. 'You told all those lies for me! Won't you get into trouble?'

He shrugged. 'If I do, I'll make sure you don't get off scot-free. Anyhow what are you doing hanging around out here with that muck on your face? Wouldn't they let you on the train?'

'I didn't have enough money.' Unexpectedly her eyes filled with tears.

He groaned. 'Don't turn on the taps. Let's go and have a cup of tea in the Kardomah.'

'What?' The suggestion stemmed the tears.

'We won't touch Nan's money,' he said hastily, jingling the coins in his pocket. 'I earn me own. Yer'll have to wipe that lipstick off, mind, and behave yourself.'

She wiped her mouth with the back of her hand. 'Will that do?'

'I suppose so.' He started to walk. 'Perhaps we can go to the Tatler as well.'

She could not believe what was happening. Why should he do this for her? 'What's the Tatler?'

'It's a news theatre and they show cartoons as well. That'll cheer you up. But we'll have to be home in time for me paper round and before our Phyl gets in.'

She agreed and wobbled in his tracks, going over on a heel which hurt and caused her to yelp. He glanced back at her and shook his head, then with obvious reluctance held out an arm. She seized it as a drowning man would grab a lifebelt and with her hanging on to him, they walked in the direction of Church Street.

The cartoons were funny. What wasn't were the pictures of a bombing in Jerusalem and she remembered that the new state of Israel was struggling to be established in the Holy Land. Palestine, she thought. Wasn't that where Mr Payne had been with the army? She mentioned it to Billy when they came out of the pictures.

'He was wounded,' he said. 'Some kind of accident. His mate was killed.'

'I know. He told Phyl. The Black Widow blames him for it, but he didn't do it.'

Billy looked at her uncomprehendingly.

'The Black Widow is the mate's widow and the baby is his. Mr Payne promised him he would look after her because she has no family,' explained Elizabeth.

'So they're not carrying on?' he said softly. 'Our Phyl should tell Dad all this. I've always thought ol' Paynie was OK. Me Nan still goes round the yard sometimes and she never gets chased when he's there.' He chuckled. 'Did our Phyl tell yer how Nan used to boil up bones for his ol' man to sell to the glue factory? They made smashin' soup. She used to give me clackers as well. They made a great noise.' He looked at her. 'Does it worry you, our Phyl taking an interest in Paynie?'

'Why should it?' Elizabeth said as casually as she could. 'They're just old friends. And besides, Phyl's only just widowed.'

'That's true. I suppose she must have been in love with yer dad?'

'Isn't that why people marry?'

He stared at her as if trying to make up his mind about something and when he spoke she felt certain it wasn't what he had meant to say. 'We'll have to tell our Phyl the truth about yer not going to school. She'll have to write yer a sicknote . . . and another thing, don't be worrying about any other lads picking on yer. Just say yer related to me.'

She smiled. 'You're my step-uncle.'

He groaned. 'Don't tell them that! Just give me name
and they'll know they'll be furrit.'

'Yes, Billy.' She felt like Rebecca out of Sir Walter
Scott's *Ivanhoe,* unexpectedly having found a champion
to fight her cause. Still he was not going to be able to
prevent Phyl from being cross with her, but that was
something she would just have to face up to.

'It'd better not happen again,' said Phyl severely, wriggling
her stockinged toes as she held them out to the fire.

'No,' said Elizabeth, perching on the edge of a chair in
Nan Eccles's room. 'I'm sorry. Billy said you could write
a note saying I've had the 'flu and everything'll be OK.'

Phyl sighed heavily. 'I can't say you've had the 'flu.
You wouldn't be going back to school tomorrow if that
was true.'

'You can say you thought it was the 'flu but it was
only the common cold instead.'

'More lies,' said Phyl dryly. 'I hope it's not going to
become a habit with you, Lizzie.'

Elizabeth felt her cheeks reddening. Her conscience
bothered her terribly because she hadn't told Phyl anything
about trying to run away, but she only murmured, 'Of
course it's not. But if we told the truth it might only
complicate matters.'

'Right! You say nothing of this to anyone at all. You
don't know what it's like in this house. You can hardly
do a thing without everybody wanting to know the ins
and outs of it, and I don't want our Lois saying I've taken
on too much by bringing you up here.'

'They can pull my toe nails out with pincers and I still won't squeal,' said Elizabeth solemnly.

Phyl's lips twitched. 'I don't think there'll be any need for that. You sound like you've been reading the boys' comics.'

'I found a couple under a sofa cushion. I'm hoping they'll give me an understanding of the male mind.'

'They all like to consider themselves heroes,' said Phyl, rubbing her cold toes. 'Most aren't.'

'What about Mr Payne? He was wounded in Palestine. Isn't he some kind of hero?'

Phyl's eyes widened. 'I'd forgotten about him being shot. I wonder where the bullets hit him?' She smiled. 'I must ask him to show me his scars.'

'Did you go to the yard on the way home to see him and the Black Widow?'

'I didn't. I was tired and cold so I couldn't be bothered making the effort to be friendly. Besides, I want her out of there. Alex is too soft-hearted for his own good. People'll still think the worst even when I tell them the truth.'

Elizabeth wasn't exactly sure why they should think the worst of him when he was doing a kindness but she said nothing and leaned on the table with her chin in her hand. 'Perhaps being even more friendly with Mr Payne is the best way to get rid of her?' She was thinking she wouldn't mind going round to the yard with Phyl and asking about grooming his horse.

Phyl sat back and put her feet on the brass fender. 'I have thought of it but I didn't think you would.' She sounded amused.

'It makes sense. She doesn't seem to like you so she'll want to leave.' Elizabeth's brows puckered. 'The only trouble is, how will Mr Payne feel if he's soft-hearted and she hasn't anywhere to go?'

'I'm hoping he won't be *that* soft-hearted.' Phyl got up and went out of the room, leaving Elizabeth wondering again what her stepmother felt about Mr Payne. Could she love him and have fallen out of love with Daddy because he had let them both down? How many men could someone love? Was it possible to love several at the same time? It was a completely new thought to her because she had grown up with her parents' example of being everything to each other before her.

She stared into the fire. Then Nan Eccles's voice from the other side of the window penetrated her thoughts. 'Cum on, mog. Time we wus indoors. If them black bats cum I wants to be ready for 'em.'

Elizabeth grinned but rose swiftly and put the kettle on the fire. She would show this family she was not selfish. She put all thoughts of Phyl and Alex Payne and love out of her mind. There were more worrying things to face than that. There was school for a start. But it did not hold the awful dread it had that morning because of Billy's promise to be her champion.

Chapter Five

'How did it go?'

Elizabeth swung round at the touch on her shoulder and was relieved when she saw it was Billy, although she felt suddenly shy. He was with a couple of other youths just yards from the girls' school gate. 'OK,' she said gruffly.

'Is that it? OK!' He grinned.

She reddened. 'All right then. The lessons were too easy and they don't do Latin. When I asked why not, the teacher said it was a dead language and no good to anyone. Later some girls called me a snob, a tuppenny ha'penny toff and fancy pants, but I've survived.'

'Shouldn't have mentioned the Latin. Yer'll get yer leg pulled. Priests spout Latin, not ordinary people.' He shook his head as if he couldn't comprehend her. 'See you back home.' He gave a casual wave and went on ahead with his mates.

Elizabeth wished he had offered to walk with her. She had not told him about the girl who had deliberately trodden on her foot, and she was feeling lonely and lost again.

Somebody bumped her from behind and she turned quickly.

'Sorry,' said another girl. 'It was my fault. I was rushing. I have to get home and get the tea on for me pa.'

'It's OK.' Elizabeth smiled, wanting to be friends.

'I'd – I'd stop and talk,' gabbled the girl whom she recognised from sitting behind her in class, 'only –' Her voice trailed off and she glanced over her shoulder.

'Only what?' said Elizabeth.

'Yer talk lovely,' said the girl in a rush. 'I could listen to yer for ages.'

'Could you?' Elizabeth was taken completely by surprise but the remark perked her up. 'Most of the others don't think like you.'

'Yer're talking about Thelma,' said the other girl gloomily. 'She's the class bully. She told me not to speak to yer and she'll pick on me if she finds out I have.'

'Why should you be scared of her?'

The girl did not look like a victim. She was well developed and had nice features. She could have been pretty if her face had not been covered by a mass of freckles. She wore a huge pink bow in her thick dark brown hair cut just below her ears and her clothes were clean if a little short and well worn.

'She has a gang,' said the girl. 'They're real tough. They'll give me a Chinese burn or summit – and probably you as well.'

'I'm not scared of them,' said Elizabeth with untested courage.

'Yer not?' The girl's face lit up and she fell into step beside her as they walked in the direction of Shiel Road. 'I'm Brenda, by the way. Perhaps we could be friends?

Tell me, how d'yer know Billy Eccles? I couldn't help noticing yer talking to him.'

'His sister's my stepmother so we're sort of related.'

'Lucky you,' sighed Brenda. 'He's the cock of the school. No wonder yer not frightened of Thelma and her gang.'

'What's the cock of the school?' asked Elizabeth, her expression puzzled.

Brenda stopped and stared at her, smiling. 'Yer don't know that?'

'No.' She felt stupid.

'He's the best fighter going, of course! Yer should be proud of him. I wish I had a bruvver like him at home. Then perhaps –' She broke off abruptly, apprehension written clearly on her face.

Elizabeth glanced over her shoulder, almost expecting to see Thelma but there was no one there. 'What is it?'

'I've – I've got to rush,' said Brenda, backing away. 'Pa gets real angry if I haven't got his tea ready. I'll see yer in the morning.' She turned and raced along the street, leaving Elizabeth to make her own way home alone.

'Well, how did it go?' Phyl's reflection smiled at Elizabeth's in the mirror over the sideboard in the parlour as she dragged a brush through her tangled hair. 'Was it as bad as you thought it would be?'

'It was OK.' For a moment Thelma's name had hovered on her lips but she spoke of Brenda instead.

'Sounds like she's got no mother,' murmured Phyl, pursing her mouth and applying lipstick.

'She's definitely got no brothers and she sounded scared of her dad.' Brenda's fear bothered her. 'At least Daddy never frightened me except for that one time,' she said hesitantly.

'We can both be thankful for that,' said Phyl, placing the lipstick on the sideboard. She glanced at Nan Eccles who was fastening a bonnet on the cat, and whispered, 'It's not easy to forget, is it, love?'

Elizabeth felt that peculiar panic. 'It happens unexpectedly. Suddenly he's there in my mind.'

'Me too.' Phyl squeezed her shoulder and scrutinised her features. 'D'you want to stay in or would you like to come to the scrapyard with me?'

'Come with you,' said Elizabeth positively, and scrambled from the chair and went to fetch her mackintosh.

When they reached the yard the gates were locked and so was the little door set in it. Phyl banged on it and called Alex's name but nobody came. 'Damn!' she said, huddling inside her coat. 'He can't be able to hear.'

'Perhaps he's not in?' Elizabeth felt just as disappointed.

'Where would he be on a night like this?' muttered Phyl. 'No, he's probably got the wireless on. Perhaps I could climb the gate?'

'You're joking!'

Phyl smiled at her. 'Don't be stuffy. You can lend me your back and then I'll be able to get a grip higher up. Aren't I glad you're a nice tall girl.'

Elizabeth felt pleased by the remark, although she muttered, 'I wish I wasn't now. You might fall.'

'Stop moaning and bend over.'

Elizabeth groaned but did as she was told, wincing as first Phyl's knee dug into her back and then the heel of her shoe. She rose slowly and so did Phyl. 'I've got a grip now so you can relax.'

But relaxing was the last thing Elizabeth could do as she watched her stepmother pull herself up and over the gate. There was a yelp and then silence.

I knew it! she thought, and shouted Phyl's name several times. There was no response and she was aware of the thudding of her heart. She hoped Phyl was not dead but since her father's death was inclined to look on the dark side of things.

Climbing was not Elizabeth's forte but she had been reasonably good at the high jump. She took a run at the gate, managed to get a grip, but before she could climb higher a voice said, 'What the hell d'you think you're doing?' Startled, she lost her hold and slid down the gate.

Two hands seized her by the waist and turned her round. She struggled, then realised it was Alex Payne. He looked angry as well as surprised and she did not blame him. 'What are *you* playing at?'

She felt breathless. 'I wasn't doing anything wrong. It's Phyl. She thought you were inside and couldn't hear. So she climbed the gates and must have fallen because she doesn't answer me.'

He frowned and released her. 'The idiot!' he muttered, delving into his overcoat pocket and bringing out a set of keys. He inserted one inside the lock of the small door and within seconds they were both inside the yard.

Phyl was sprawled on the cobbles. They knelt one on each side of her. 'She's breathing,' said Elizabeth, her voice high with relief.

Alex ran his hands lightly over Phyl's limbs. She groaned, her eyelids fluttered, opened, and she blinked up at them. 'You fool!' said Alex. 'Your ankle, is it?'

'Yes, dammit,' she whispered.

'What about your head?'

'A bit. I don't think I've cracked it open. I heard Lizzie calling but I just didn't have the breath to answer her.'

'Right! Let's get you up,' said Alex cheerfully. 'Lizzie you take the keys.' He dropped them in the pocket of her mac. 'You'll have to open the office door. It's the Yale key. I don't know what the hell Doreen's thinking about, not coming out.'

Elizabeth hurried over to the office and was just inserting the right key in the lock when she became aware of a baby crying. So Doreen was in, she thought. Had she recognised Phyl's voice and so ignored it? She found the light switch and clicked it on. Then she held the door open so Alex could carry Phyl inside.

He set her down on a chair and glanced at Elizabeth. 'Go up, love, and see how Syd is.'

'Syd!' she exclaimed, taken aback.

'He's the baby,' he said. 'Doreen's baby.'

That did not help her. 'Isn't she there? Won't she look after him?'

'I think she must have gone out. It's not the first time she's left him and locked the gates behind her.' His face was tight with annoyance.

Elizabeth shot a look in Phyl's direction but found no help there. Her face was grazed down one side and she looked dazed. Elizabeth did not like saying she did not know anything about babies to this man who presumed she did. She remembered how Doreen had gone through the door to the rear of the office so did the same with a feeling of trepidation.

She found a passageway with several doors opening off it and to the right a flight of stairs. She went up them and found the door at the top unlocked. The light had been left on and she immediately saw the baby standing in a cot at the far side of the room. He gazed at her and stopped crying with a heartrending hiccup. His bottom lip continued to quiver and he drooled. Perhaps he was teething, she thought, remembering something that the friend with the baby sister had said. She crossed what was obviously a bedsitting room because there was a single bed and a sink and cooker in it, and wondered how to deal with the baby. He was larger than she had imagined.

'Hello, Syd,' she said hesitantly. 'I'm Lizzie.'

He relinquished his hold on the bars, held out a hand, made some kind of noise in his throat and began to wobble. She managed to grab him before he fell and hoisted him out of the cot. He was wet. 'Yeuk!' she exclaimed, holding him out at arm's length and remembering a bit more what she had been told about babies. Disgusting nappies! But this baby did not smell too disgusting. 'Now how do I do this?' she said aloud. 'And what do I do with you while I find a clean nappy?'

'He's not going to answer you,' said a voice from over by the door. It sounded amused.

Elizabeth could feel the heat rushing to her face as she turned towards Mr Payne. The baby swung in her arms as she did so, and chuckled. 'Did Phyl tell you I've never changed a nappy before?' she said lamely.

He nodded, picking up a towel from the back of a chair and coming over to her. 'It's easy once you know how.'

She felt slightly embarrassed, not knowing how to respond to that remark. 'H-how is Phyl?' she muttered.

'Resting in my part of the house. It's only a sprain. Fetch me a nappy and a nightgown from the clothes horse, there's a good girl.'

'You're going to change him?' She could hear the relief in her voice.

'Don't go round telling everyone,' he said gravely. 'All the women'll think me only half a man instead of the philanderer they believe me.'

Elizabeth was not sure what a philanderer was so she just smiled and did as she was told before kneeling on the floor where he had placed the baby on the towel and was in the process of removing its wet nappy. He smiled at her. 'You haven't finished. Light the gas fire and warm a wet flannel, there's a luv. Then fetch me the jar of zinc and castor oil by the sink.'

She did as ordered and then dropped beside him and the kicking baby who was now dressed only in his vest. 'He looks sore,' she said, feeling slightly embarrassed at this, her first sight of the male sexual organ.

'Nappy rash.' His tone was short as he took the flannel from her.

'Poor little thing,' she murmured as Syd whimpered. 'Did Phyl say it was Nan Eccles who taught you how to look after babies?'

'That's right. Unscrew the jar for me, luv. My mam died and left us with a baby. I was eight at the time.'

'You had no aunties?'

'Only one aunt and we didn't trust her. Anyhow me and the ol' man wanted to keep my sister. She was a beauty.'

'Where is she now?'

'Dead. Diphtheria. She was six years old.' His voice sounded suddenly raw as if the memory still had the power to hurt him.

Elizabeth looked down at his hand as he smeared the cream round the baby's little whatsits. 'It must have broken your hearts,' she said diffidently.

He was silent and she watched him fold the clean nappy and fasten it about Syd with a safety pin at each hip.

'D'you think you can remember how to do this?' he said, glancing at her. 'You could be of help to Doreen, I reckon she's feeling trapped and that's why she's such a nark.'

'A nark?'

'Moaner, misery, complainer.' He grimaced. 'I reckon she's not much older than you, you know.'

'I'm fourteen.'

'Fourteen. Almost a young lady.' He smiled at her. 'Doreen's twenty. I know she looks older but grief can do that to a person.' He paused in the act of putting on Syd's nightgown. 'D'you think you'd like to help her?'

Elizabeth hesitated. 'She mightn't want me. And what about your horse?'

'My horse?' He grinned and held Syd out to her. 'Here, take him. Get used to the feel of him. I'm sure Doreen won't chase you. I'll fetch you a cup of tea – and maybe I'll give you a trial where Blackie's concerned.'

Blackie! He couldn't have been called anything else with his colouring. She smiled as Syd wobbled in her inexperienced hold and moved an arm up his back to steady him.

Alex took a bottle from out of the cot and there was a gleam in his eyes as he stared at her. 'I think you'll cope. You'll have to change the bottom sheet. I'll see you get paid.'

Paid for what? Elizabeth thought as he left. She gazed down at the baby and Syd gazed up at her from big blue eyes as he sucked his thumb. 'I'm stupid,' she said severely. 'I should have said I couldn't do it.'

He smiled, showing a couple of teeth, and she found herself responding as she went in search of a dry sheet.

Elizabeth was just in the process of extricating Syd from beneath the table, having decided the safest place for him was on the floor whilst she changed the sheet, when Alex came back.

He placed a cup of tea on the table and a piece of shop-bought cake. From his trouser pocket he withdrew the feeding bottle half-filled with tea. As soon as Syd saw it he bounced in Elizabeth's arms and held out a hand.

'He'll probably be asleep in five minutes,' said Alex, relinquishing his hold on the bottle. 'Put him on his side in the cot and then you can relax. There's some magazines on the shelf in the corner. As soon as Doreen comes in I'll walk you and Phyl home.'

'Thanks.' Elizabeth sat on a chair with Syd on her knee. 'You said something about getting paid?' she said boldly.

'Impatient, aren't we?' There was a faint smile in his eyes as he took a coin from his pocket, placing it on the saucer next to her teacup. 'By the way, if you're that interested in horses you should call in at the blacksmith's – William Morgan Osborne's, no less. A bit of a mouthful. His yard's somewhere between the shop on the corner and Wong's Chinese laundry in Boundary Lane which you crossed on your way here.' Without another word he walked out of the room, perhaps not realising the pleasure this information had given her.

It was an hour before she heard footsteps in the yard and the sound of voices below. A few minutes later Doreen entered the room, her thin face set. She kicked off her shoes and sat on a chair, glowering at Elizabeth. 'Why should you want to babysit for me?' she demanded.

For a second Elizabeth considered saying that she didn't and couldn't wait to get out of here, but she changed her mind. 'For money,' she said. 'I want to save up so I can go back south one day. He's paid me for this evening so you don't have to give me anything.' She stood.

'I wasn't going to! He owes me. Sit down again. Is that where you come from? Down south.'

Elizabeth remained standing. 'I said so, didn't I?'

Doreen jerked her head. 'She's not from the south. What is she to him?'

Her manner irritated Elizabeth even more than it had the other day. 'Why don't you ask Mr Payne?' she said forcefully. 'Now if you don't mind I'll have to go. I have school in the morning.'

'Hoity toity, aren't we?' Doreen got to her feet, her mouth set in a straight line. 'He's a murderer, you know. You can tell her that from me. Then perhaps she won't think him so nice!'

A murderer? Elizabeth almost repeated, but bit back the words and walked downstairs. Phyl asked if she was ready to go and she nodded wordlessly. Alex helped Phyl outside.

The air felt slightly warmer but Elizabeth was barely conscious of it. Surely it couldn't be true that Alex Payne really was a murderer? If it was, how could Doreen possibly feel safe under his roof? She must be referring to her husband's death and her belief that Alex Payne had been responsible. Of course Alex could have lied to her and Phyl. Elizabeth considered that. Then the remembrance of his gentle hands soothing cream on to Syd's chapped skin came back to her and she dismissed the thought.

'What did the Black Widow have to say to you?' asked Phyl later as she gingerly stretched her legs under the bedclothes. 'Alex said something about your babysitting for her. Does she want you to?'

'She didn't say if she did or didn't.' Elizabeth slid into bed beside her. 'She did say Alex was a murderer?'

'Alex!' Phyl stared at her. 'She's daft. But you called him Alex.'

Elizabeth reddened. 'Sorry. It's just that you call him Alex and it slipped out.'

Phyl sighed and snuggled down in bed. 'He's a softie,' she said in a muffled voice. 'He'll make life easier for her. You should have refused. While she stays there people'll continue to talk.'

'Mr Payne made it difficult for me to refuse.' She kept it to herself about Blackie. 'He says she's only twenty. Perhaps . . .' A thought suddenly occurred to her.

'Perhaps what?'

'Nothing.' It was a daft idea that Alex Payne and the Black Widow could once have been in love and that he could have killed her husband after all. A *crime passionel?* She had heard it said that love could turn to hate.

'Don't go telling anyone we went there tonight,' murmured Phyl. 'Dad would kick up a rumpus.'

'Have you told them about your job?' whispered Elizabeth, suddenly remembering that Nan Eccles was asleep under the table.

'Of course. And they both disapprove.' Phyl yawned. 'Now get to sleep and let's hope the snow's all gone in the morning so I can get to work with this ankle, without breaking my neck.'

Elizabeth and Phyl were wakened as dawn lit the sky.

'The flood's come,' said Nan Eccles, bending over them. 'Me ducks'll be pleased.'

'Go back to sleep, Nan,' groaned Phyl. 'You're getting worse.' She pulled the bedcovers over her head.

'Nos I'm not. Me feets are wet.'

Phyl made no answer but Elizabeth, who was lying on her side on the edge of the bed, forced her eyelids open and looked down to see water seeping under the door. She blinked, then shot up against her pillow and shook Phyl. 'She's right! There's water everywhere!'

Phyl sat up and looked bleary-eyed about her. 'Bloody hell! You're right! Action stations!' She forced her eyes wider and slid out of bed, winced, then limped towards the door. Nan Eccles and Elizabeth, who felt a peculiar exhilaration, pit-patted after her. Phyl took the stairs carefully while Nan Eccles beckoned Elizabeth into the kitchen. There was a huge bubble on the ceiling which water was seeping through but it had already found another place to come through and was running down the wall in a corner.

'Yous help us to put the rug outside on the line,' ordered the old woman.

Elizabeth did not argue and once out in the yard became aware of the drip-drip of melting snow everywhere.

'Yous carry in the bucket,' said Nan Eccles. 'Yous'll be needing it. I'm going to see me ducks.' Elizabeth would have liked to see them, too, but guessed she'd be more useful indoors.

Phyl's mother was in the kitchen, dressed but in her bare feet. 'What a b—mess!' she said. 'Light the gas under the kettle, Lizzie. We'll have to have a cup of tea. It's not worth doing anything 'til Sam's turned the water off in the street. Now where's those girls?'

'We're here, Mam,' said Phyl, entering the room. 'Our Lo's not moving, though. Typical.'

'Water's off, Mam,' shouted Trev, appearing in the doorway in pyjamas and wellies.

'Good lad! Go and shout our Lois with that big loud voice.' She threw a cloth in Elizabeth's direction. 'Don't stand there staring, girl. Get working! And that goes for you three, too,' she added, addressing her daughters.

Elizabeth did not argue, wanting to prove to Phyl's mother that she could be of use. She got down on her knees, noticing that her cloth consisted of a ragged pair of sage green drawers, and began soaking up the water. The flannelette did it beautifully.

Lois arrived on the scene when most of the water had been mopped up; as did Nan Eccles carrying a struggling white duck. 'Thems'll be happy now,' she declared, beaming at everyone. 'Ice going and soon thems'll be laying again.'

'Trust her to be concerned only about her stupid ducks,' muttered Lois, standing in front of the fire which Billy had just lit and blocking out its heat for everyone else.

'That's enough of that,' said Sam, planting himself down in his chair and wiping his hands on a towel. 'Yer'll show respect to your grandmother. I didn't see you rushing to help.'

'I was tired. I'd been working hard all day. I don't see why I should be picked on,' said Lois sniffily. 'Our Phyl wasn't showing much respect for your feelings last night. I saw her walking home arm in arm with Alex Payne.'

There was silence and everyone looked at Phyl.

'It's not true, is it?' said Sam in a tone that made it obvious to everyone that he didn't want it to be so.

'It's no use her denying it,' said Lois. 'I saw them.'

'If you saw them, then you saw me,' said Elizabeth impulsively. Phyl was looking pale after doing so much with her sore ankle and Elizabeth considered Lois a sneak. 'He was helping her because she'd slipped on the ice and hurt her ankle.'

Lois shot her a poisonous look.

'Hurt your ankle?' said Sam, his mood obviously softening. 'And you've just mopped all this water up. You should have rested, lass.'

'How could I, Dad? When Lollopy Loo over there stayed in bed,' said Phyl, her eyes glinting. 'Having said that, I am over twenty-one and have been away from home. Don't you think I'm old and wise enough to pick my own friends, Dad?'

'That's as maybe,' said Sam, looking harassed. 'But while you're under my roof you'll respect my wishes where Alex Payne's concerned. I know what you've said about that girl that's staying there, but it's still not right.'

'But I've been in the house now, Dad. He lives downstairs and she's up in a bedsit,' said Phyl forcefully. 'You ask Lizzie.'

'You took a young girl into that house of sin?' said her mother, sounding vexed.

'She's always been sneaky,' said Lois, folding her arms across her breasts and smirking.

Phyl's expression stiffened. 'Nobody's asking for any more of your comments,' she snapped, 'so shut up.'

Elizabeth took a deep breath. 'It's not a house of sin and they aren't living in sin. So leave Phyl alone.'

'Did I hear right?' said Maisie.

Elizabeth quailed as the whole family stared at her.

'What do you know about living in sin?' asked Dot, wide-eyed.

'The girls used to talk a lot about sin in the convent school,' she stammered. 'Especially sins of the flesh. But I always imagined people needed to love each other to risk hell and damnation. Doreen and Mr Payne don't.'

'Convent!' Lois tittered. 'What is it you've brought into the house, Phyl?'

'Oh, be quiet,' said her elder sister scornfully. 'You already know about that. But there you have it, family! They're not living in sin.'

Her mother looked scandalised. 'I think this has gone far enough. Have you all forgotten our Mary and Trev are here? Now not another word out of any of you.'

'Can't I even ask if we're having porridge?' said Trev indignantly.

'Don't be stupid,' drawled Billy, reaching for the bread and connie onnie tin and winking at Elizabeth.

'Sins of the flesh,' murmured Mary, who was standing next to her. 'Don't the words have a lovely feel? I wish I knew what they meant. You obviously do, Lizzie. Perhaps you can explain them to me?'

'I think it's something to do with having babies and not being married,' she muttered, and hurried out of the room and into the parlour to get ready for school before anyone could say any more. She found herself trembling and wished herself anywhere but where she was. It was so hard living with a family and for a while back there even Phyl had seemed a stranger again.

The door opened and it was her stepmother.

'Thanks for the defence,' she said, smiling. 'I appreciated it. But do you really know what living in sin means?' Elizabeth hesitated, then repeated what she had said to Mary. 'Near enough,' said Phyl with a wry smile. She looked as if she would have said more but shrugged and offered to plait Lizzie's hair.

'Will Mr Payne still empty out the attic after what your dad said?' asked Elizabeth, gazing at the still damp floor.

Phyl tapped the side of her nose. 'I think the less said about that the better. But you know, Lizzie, I'm a very determined person.' She tied the single plait with a yellow ribbon. 'Now shall we brave the lions' den together and see if Mam's making enough porridge for us? Then it's school and work, and let's hope we both have a good day to make up for its lousy start.'

'I thought I told you,' said Thelma, pushing Brenda in the chest and against a wall in the school yard. Several of Thelma's gang clustered around Elizabeth and the other girl, concealing them from any watching eyes.

'If you only thought it then perhaps you didn't tell her,' said Elizabeth, feeling she had to defend the other girl, even as she strove to keep the tremor out of her own voice.

'Don't be smart with me.' Thelma turned from Brenda and gripped Elizabeth's wrist with both hands, twisting them in opposite ways and dragging the skin painfully.

Thelma watched Elizabeth's face but she made no sound. 'Now keep that mouth shut!' Thelma released her. 'It's me that's talking to old smelly pants here.'

Elizabeth knew it would be wiser to keep silent but her wrist was hurting and she felt angry about that. Who did this girl think she was? 'She doesn't smell,' she muttered. 'If there's a stench round her it's coming from you. You've got the manners of a pig.'

Fury then pleasure lit Thelma's eyes. 'It takes one to know one,' she said, and ground her heel into Elizabeth's foot. 'I can see we're going to have fun wiv you,' she said softly.

Elizabeth gritted her teeth and rode the pain. It was several seconds before she was able to say, 'I wouldn't be so sure if I was you. Billy Eccles is related to me and I don't think he's going to be pleased when I tell him about this.'

There was a murmur from a couple of the girls and Thelma looked taken aback. Then she recovered herself and said, 'Who cares? He can't help yer in here, and outside I've got two brothers bigger than him.'

'But I'd luv a date with him,' cried one of the girls. 'Maybe yer should leave her alone, Thel?'

'And maybe you should shut yer mouth,' said Thelma, casting her a darkling glance.

'Miss is coming,' hissed a short blonde girl.

Thelma dug a finger into Elizabeth's abdomen. 'One word out of you and yer'll get worse.'

Elizabeth did not need the warning. She knew of old that teachers could not always be there when one needed them and bullies had subtler ways of hitting back than purely physical means, but at least for now Thelma had gone.

Brenda linked her arm through Elizabeth's and walked her away hurriedly. Her face was flooded with pleasure and she pressed her cheek against Elizabeth's shoulder. 'I've never had a friend like you. I'm really grateful.'

'It's you that befriended me,' said Elizabeth, feeling slightly uncomfortable and wishing she could free her arm without hurting Brenda's feeling.

Fortunately at that moment the bell rang for lessons and thankfully she detached herself and hurried into line, wishing Phyl would hurry up and do something to get her out of this school. On the way home, to try and compensate, she did a detour and went home up Boundary Lane and found the gate to the smithie open. She slipped inside and to her delight discovered the blacksmith shoeing a horse. He glanced up at her but remained silent as he nailed the shoe into place. When he finished he asked her what she wanted. 'I just came to watch,' she said, flushing. 'I like horses, you see.'

'You'll be the girl from London? Well, I don't mind you coming in as long as you don't make a nuisance of yerself by nattering or getting in me way.'

That was enough for Elizabeth and during the following week when Thelma continued to make a nuisance of herself she often dropped in at the blacksmith's and calmed herself down watching him work. Sometimes she was not the only child there and he talked to them about how the way the number of motor vehicles was growing and threatening the livelihood of men like him in the city, although at the moment there were still enough working horses around to keep them busy.

Elizabeth considered telling Billy about Thelma but the girl had partially convinced her that there was little he could do. She toyed with the idea of telling Phyl but did not want to appear a moaner. Especially when Phyl told her that she was going to get Alex to empty the attic the following Saturday evening.

'What about your dad?'

'In case you haven't noticed,' she said in a teasing voice, 'Mam and Dad always go to the pictures on Saturday nights. Our Lois should definitely be out because she's got a new boyfriend. You should see the cut of him!' She pulled a comical face. 'Cowboy boots and a stetson, no less. Our Dot says he has relations in the Wild West.'

Elizabeth could not resist a smile at the picture conjured up because since coming to Liverpool she had already seen several cowboy films. 'Does he sing?'

Phyl grinned. 'You mean like Gene Autry or Roy Rogers? I must ask. Perhaps he neighs like Trigger!'

'What about the rest? Will they tell about Al—Mr Payne coming?'

'Don't worry about them.' Phyl narrowed her eyes as she powdered her nose. 'As for Dad, I'll tell him once it's done. Now how about a trip to the flicks? Gene Kelly's on and I just love his dancing.'

Elizabeth did not need asking twice. She was fast becoming a dedicated picturegoer.

*

'What's Paynie doing here?' asked Billy of Elizabeth as he came out of the kitchen into the lobby where she was standing at the bottom of the stairs.

'He's come to empty the attic.'

Billy whistled. 'Dad'll have a fit.'

'Phyl's hoping it'll be done before he gets back,' she whispered. 'Perhaps we should offer to give them a hand?' She was thinking that Alex Payne still had not set a date for that trial with Blackie.

'We should keep an eye on them anyway.' He winked at her. 'Dad wouldn't like them being up there on their own.'

Elizabeth made no reply but began to climb the stairs. Billy passed her, taking two steps at a time.

'No snogging, you two,' she heard him say as he reached the top of the stairs.

'If we want to snog, we'll snog,' said Phyl. 'Anyway, what are you doing here?'

'I came to offer a hand.'

Elizabeth entered the room to see Phyl and Alex standing close to each other over by the window. Her stepmother had her arm around his waist and his dark hair was ruffled. The sight did not please her and she wanted to push them apart.

'Are the two of you offering to help?' asked Alex.

'Why else would I be here?' said Elizabeth, trying not to sound irritated.

He stared at her, a quizzical expression in his eyes. 'Right you are then. Get cracking. You can carry those plaques down. Billy, can you manage a couple of chairs?'

'I'm not an eight-stone weakling,' said Billy scornfully, and placing one chair upside down on the other, walked out.

Elizabeth followed with several plaques.

Billy hissed over his shoulder, 'I don't get our Phyl. Once she was all for going on the stage. Now your dad's hardly cold in his grave and she's snuggling up to Paynie! I think she's become over-sexed. Mam blames everything on the war. Maybe she's right.'

'What do you mean over-sexed? And what's the war got to do with it?' said Elizabeth.

He stopped on the stairs and looked up at her. 'I thought you knew something when you said all that the other week about sins of the flesh, but you still don't, do yer?'

'About what?'

He sighed. 'I told yer. Have a word with our Phyl about the birds and the bees.' And frustratingly he carried on downstairs without another word.

Several trips later, and after giving Blackie a carrot, Billy said he'd had enough. 'I'm getting out of here,' he said, dusting his hands. 'The pair of them have done nowt except talk up there and tell us what to do. I'm sick and tired of it. That pram was the last straw.'

Elizabeth agreed, brushing a hand across her damp forehead. She was disappointed in the two upstairs because she had hoped Alex Payne might have mentioned Blackie and babysitting. She had no money worth mentioning and it would be extremely useful to earn some. 'I think I'll come with you,' she said.

He paused in the act of donning a jacket. 'You haven't been asked.'

'Please, please, let me come?' she begged, putting her hands together and bowing in front of him. She was becoming accustomed to Billy and believed that in some ways boys were not so different from girls. She quite liked him. Trev, though, still treated her like she was poison.

He grinned. 'Such nice manners. I don't know if I should let you, frankly. Our Phyl wouldn't approve.'

'The mood I'm in, I don't care,' said Elizabeth.

'You're getting gutsy. OK! As long as you don't start moaning that you wanna come back here after five minutes.'

'I never moan,' she said, and buttoning her cardigan she followed him outside.

There was a slight breeze but it was not cold and spring was to be seen in the swelling buds and tiny leaves on trees along the park side of Rocky Lane. Leaving the lane they climbed on to the embankment and followed the railway line until Billy stopped. Elizabeth looked about her, wondering why he had chosen to come here. 'This is called the Black Hills,' he said, taking a piece of metal from a pocket. 'Don't ask me why.' He began to dig.

'What are you doing?' She dropped on her knees in the grass.

'Looking for bullets.'

'Bullets?' she echoed, thinking she must have misheard him.

He lifted his head. 'An ammunition train went up roundsabout here and shells and all sorts of stuff buried themselves in the soil.'

'Holy Mary!' Elizabeth crossed herself and shot to her feet, staring nervously but with a peculiar thrill of excitement at the ground all around her.

Billy flashed her a severe glance. 'You'll have to get out of that habit. Or Mam'll have something else to complain about where you're concerned. I don't think she's got over you and sins of the flesh yet.'

'It's not that easy when you've been brought up on it.'

'OK. Now sit down and stop looking like you think you're going to be blown up any minute. I've been here dozens of times and I'm still alive.'

She sat down again. 'A bomb made a mess of part of the top floor of Trinity block at school during the war and it'd only been built in '39.'

Without looking up he said, 'Anyone killed?'

'No.' She felt melancholy, remembering her years in the care of the nuns when she had not worried about money and what being over-sexed meant.

His head lifted. 'I thought the convent was in the country where it was nice and safe?' There was a hint of scorn in his voice.

She bridled. 'In a country town – but there was a Marconi radio telegraph place nearby with several masts. I suppose Jerry wanted to destroy that. And if Jerry'd invaded he would have got to us first!'

He grinned. 'OK, OK. Keep yer hair on. I'm not looking for an argument.'

They were silent for a while and then she said, 'What'll you do with the bullets?'

'When I hear a train coming I go and put several on the rail and there's a nice little explosion.'

She could not believe him. 'Surely that's dangerous?'

'That's the whole point!' His eyes gleamed. 'But if you're going to sound like Mam or one of me sisters and get all scared, you can scat. I have enough of that at home. If you're staying, don't hover over me.'

Elizabeth sat further away from him, suitably chastened. She gazed about her, letting the peace get to her.

'Train coming,' said Billy, startling her into wakefulness.

She watched as he slid down the embankment. A few seconds later he was bounding up the slope towards her. 'Go, Lizzie,' he yelled. 'Go!' He bundled her over the brow as the goods train rattled along, and they lay in the grass, his arm flung protectively across her. The sound of the train almost swallowed up the muffled explosion but he grinned conspiratorially at her. 'You're not bad-looking,' he said, and kissed her. 'D'you want to have a go when the next train comes?'

It was her first kiss and she wondered whether it was this or his question that caused her heart to appear to flip over. She hesitated, wondering if he would kiss her again and then perhaps she would know.

'Well?' he demanded. 'Are you a scaredy cat or what?'

She sighed inwardly and decided she might as well keep up the honour of the south.

'Good!' he said. 'I thought you had guts!'

Afterwards, when the deed was done, Elizabeth wondered what he would have told Phyl if she'd slipped and those guts he admired had been spilt all over the railway line. It was a crazy thing to have done but it had certainly been more exciting than emptying out the attic.

Elizabeth expected a ticking off for leaving the job half done but it wasn't quite like that. 'What do you think you were doing just waltzing off the way you did without a word?' said Phyl. 'Alex was going to give you both money for icecreams.'

'Couldn't he still?' Elizabeth said hopefully.

Phyl grinned and handed over a sixpence. 'Be prepared for fireworks when Dad comes in.'

'Do you have to tell him?'

'If I don't,' said Phyl soberly, 'one of the neighbours is sure to ask Mam what the horse and cart were doing outside our house.'

Sam was coldly angry. 'I sometimes wonder what happened to the daughter who joined the ATS. You've changed. In the old days you wouldn't have deliberately deceived me.'

Phyl tilted her chin and squared her shoulders. 'I haven't deceived you. I told you I was going to ask him to empty the attic and that's what I did.'

He said almost grudgingly, 'Aye, you did. But I didn't think you would after what I said a short while ago.'

'Did you listen to me and Lizzie at all?' she said with a flash of anger. 'You're just not prepared to think any good of Alex. He had a hard upbringing and you should be more sympathetic.'

'I try to believe there's some good in most people,' said her father, resting both hands on the table and lowering his voice. 'But I can't believe a man of his age and a young woman can live under the same roof without something going on. People can put on an act so it appears that they don't like each other, yer know.'

Phyl opened her mouth but obviously thought better of it and without any appearance of haste walked out of the room.

Elizabeth followed her because Phyl's dad's words bothered her. 'Do you think it's true what he said? That people can put on an act about not liking each other?'

'What would be the purpose in Alex's case?' Phyl lit a cigarette, her expression moody. 'People still think the worst. Look at Dad, and he's normally a tolerant so-and-so. If only he realised how tough things are for Alex. He's got the taxman breathing down his neck because his old man left the books in a heck of a mess.' She placed her cigarette in a glass dish, took off her skirt and draped it over the end of the bed, standing in a flesh-coloured underslip which showed her hourglass shape. 'If you can call them books. The accounts are piles and piles of bits of paper with pencilled figures on them. And he never used a bank! The shop's different. We have proper cash books there.' She smiled. 'Alex's emptying a house in Priory Road on Monday and I've asked him to see what he can find in the way of second-hand bedroom furniture for us. He said I can pay him back weekly. I'm planning on painting the attic over Easter. You can help with the painting and we'll strip the walls this week.'

'I've never done anything like that,' said Elizabeth.

Phyl lay on the bed and blew out a smoke ring. 'It can't be any harder than painting scenery and I've done a little bit of that in me time.' A sigh escaped her and for several minutes she lay there staring up at the ceiling. Then she shook herself and said, 'Just think, soon we'll have a room of our own.'

Elizabeth thought about that but her relief lay not in vacating the parlour but in the realisation that there would be no school around Easter, which meant no Thelma for two whole weeks. Alleluia!

Chapter Six

Easter Sunday arrived and there were high winds. Elizabeth was aware that Phyl kept looking at the sky. Maisie and Sam were dithering over whether to cross the Mersey and visit Maisie's sister in Moreton on the Wirral with the rest of the family or to stay at home. Fortunately the winds, which brought with them the smell of the sea, kept the rain away and despite the sun not making an appearance they left the house about noon.

Phyl danced upstairs, singing 'One Fine Day' from *Madame Butterfly*. Elizabeth followed, wondering if her high spirits had anything to do with Alex.

They had nearly finished emulsioning the last wall a primrose colour when Phyl, who had frequently glanced out of the window, dropped her brush on a sheet of newspaper and ran downstairs.

Elizabeth went over to the window and saw Blackie with the cart at the opening to the entry of the next street. Clever, she thought, watching Phyl open the backyard door and greet Alex with a kiss. Elizabeth bit on her lower lip, wondering why he was here? Then she noticed Harry from the shop and saw there was furniture in the large cart and remembered what Phyl had said a week or so ago and hurried downstairs to see if she could help. On the way she picked a faded apple from the bowl on the sideboard to give to Blackie.

'I suppose it would have been wiser to wait until we'd finished with the gloss,' said Phyl, half an hour or so later. Yet even as she spoke her hand was stroking the surface of the second-hand oak dressing table.

'What yer need is some nice bright curtains at the windus,' said Harry, drawing on his pipe.

'I plan on getting yellow and white gingham,' said Phyl. 'Gingham always looks clean.'

'Clean but cheap,' said Alex with a faint smile.

'One has to cut one's cloth,' said Phyl gravely, and smiled at Elizabeth. 'When we're rich we'll get better, won't we kid?'

'Of course.' She felt excited. 'Then we'll buy gold brocade with huge tassels. We'll have a mansion, of course, and velvet footstools and a four-poster bed.'

Phyl laughed. 'I'll be thinking I'm the Queen of the May if ever I have tassels and velvet footstools.'

'Is that your dream, Lizzie?' teased Alex.

'What? The footstools and the tassels or the mansion and being Queen of the May?'

'All of them.'

She shook her head, a smile playing round her lips. 'I'd have to find myself a rich husband and they don't grow on trees.'

'Good thing too,' he said, his eyes twinkling. 'Otherwise the rest of us wouldn't stand a chance. Harry, didn't we have something for Lizzie?'

'Aye, Mr Payne. But I think we've left it in the shop.'
The old man got to his feet, placing his pipe in the breast
pocket of his jacket.

'Something for me?' stammered Elizabeth.

'It's nothing fancy. I just thought a girl your age might
like it. D'you mind going back, Harry? Then you can go
home.'

'Don't mind at all. Wife's gone to her bruther's. Perhaps
Miss Lizzie'd like to come with me?'

'That's a good idea,' said Phyl softly, glancing at Alex.
'We can finish the painting while you're away.'

'You can take Blackie,' said Alex to Elizabeth. 'Perhaps
you'd like to have a go at handling the reins and then
Harry'll take him to the yard. You can find your own way
back from there easy enough.'

'Are you sure?' breathed Elizabeth, giving him a beau-
teous smile. 'I mean Blackie might get away from me – and
what about traffic?'

His eyes held hers and seemed to infuse confidence
into her. 'He's not a young tearaway! The old boy's getting
on, almost ready for the knackers. As for traffic, he's used
to it. And besides it's Easter Sunday. The streets'll be quiet
and he could find his way to the shop blinkered.'

'Go on, Lizzie,' said Phyl, putting her hand through
Alex's arm. 'Don't look a gift horse in the mouth.'

Elizabeth did not argue any further but went out with
Harry.

It's strange how it's come back to me, she thought, as
she held the reins loosely in one hand as they went along

Hall Lane in the direction of St Mary's church. When Harry had first handed the reins to her she had almost wrapped them tightly round her hands like most novices were prone to do, which could be dangerous if the horse bolted. It was different of course to riding. There was not that sense of physical and sometimes almost spiritual oneness with the horse for a start. Most of the control was done with the fingers and occasionally the voice. Yet there was a need for some mental affinity between horse and handler. In a situation where control was needed Blackie would soon detect any nervousness or fear she might feel. For now, though, she felt good sitting high above the street behind the horse, aware of the occasional glance from passers-by. For the moment it did not matter that her surroundings were city streets instead of the green fields and woods of her own countryside because she was content.

The 'something' turned out to be a small high-heeled dancing shoe with a full bottle of Evening in Paris in it.

'Yer mightn't want the scent,' said Harry. 'But Mr Payne thought you might like to put your bits and pieces inside the shoe.'

'Oh, I like the scent,' said Elizabeth, unscrewing the bottle and dabbing perfume behind her ears. The smell reminded her of the day Billy had rescued her from the sailor and taken her to the Tatler. She thought about him kissing her on the embankment and wondered if he would do it again. 'What's the shoe made of?' She stroked the blue shiny surface, thinking of Cinderella's slipper and a scrap dealer who was kind but far too much of a heart-throb for her peace of mind. Had he and Phyl deliberately set out to get rid of her?

'Phenolic,' said Harry. 'But if you want to know any more yer'll have to ask Mr Payne. He takes an interest in these things.'

Elizabeth glanced around the shop. 'I'd like to work here.' She took a black fan painted with red and blue flowers from the top of a table and fanned herself with it, fluttering her eyelashes.

Harry grinned. 'Yer remind me of Margaret Lockwood in one of them costume dramas.'

'I like her looks. I've seen her picture in a magazine. D'you think if I ask Phyl she'd have me help her on Saturdays?'

'She'd have to ask the boss.'

Elizabeth dropped the fan and said thoughtfully, 'He probably couldn't afford to pay me as well. Phyl said something about the taxman. Besides I think I'd still prefer looking after Blackie. Although I could do that Sundays and evenings.' She thought of Alex and Phyl back at the house on their own and wondered if they were kissing. She felt restless and reminded Harry they had to get back.

Elizabeth let herself into the house with the key on the string and closed the door quietly. She took off her shoes and tiptoed up the stairs. She knew she was behaving badly but she did so much want to see what Phyl and Alex got up to when alone. She reached the top floor and just like a peeping Tom, knelt and put an eye to the keyhole. Her heart was beating suffocatingly fast.

They had taken off their shoes and Phyl lay on top of Alex on the bare mattress on the bed beneath the window. She was rubbing against him in a way that made Elizabeth feel peculiar in the pit of her stomach. Her foot was moving sinuously against his ankle and one of his hands was stroking her back.

'Stop it, Phyl,' he murmured. 'You're not going to get round me. I can't just throw her out the way you say. There's Syd. You know the way housing is since the war. Where could they go?'

'Harden your heart,' said Phyl, kissing his ear. 'Girls like her can always find someone to take them in.'

'You don't know what you're talking about!' He sounded exasperated. 'You've never been alone with a baby with no family to turn to.'

'OK. OK! Forget I said it. But you might end up sorrier than you are now!' She kissed him hard on the mouth and his hands moved down to rest on the curve of her hips.

Elizabeth fell back on her haunches, hating herself and suffering that excluded feeling which she'd lived with most of her life. She crept downstairs and clattered up them again before opening the door and walking straight in. They had on their shoes but the top of Alex's shirt was unbuttoned. He appeared to be glad to see her so she decided to make the most of it.

'I wondered if I could work in the shop on Saturdays,' she said, standing straight, her hands clasped behind her back.

'Why?' asked Phyl calmly, lighting a cigarette.

'To make money, of course.' Elizabeth's tone was almost scornful. 'And there's Blackie as well. I could look after him.'

Alex's eyes gleamed with amusement. 'Is all this money you want to make to save up for that mansion?'

She hesitated, cross with him for allowing Phyl to lie on him the way she had. 'It's to go south, of course! It's where I belong. Well?' she demanded.

He raised an eyebrow. 'I'll think about it. Did you like your present?'

Some of the anger seeped out of her. 'Yes, thank you. Harry said you could tell me more about it? And could you tell me anymore about perfume bottles?'

'It's Art Deco and made in the thirties. But years ago women bought their perfume in plain bottles and those who were rich transferred it to fancy bottles they kept on their dressing tables. Then the makers decided –'

'I remember my mother had a fancy bottle,' she intervened, her voice cracking. 'It had sharp edges and a puffer with a pink tassel.' She drew an unsteady breath. 'I'd forgotten about it until now. Just think, it's been in my head all this time, waiting for me to remember.'

'You must miss your mother,' said Alex gently.

Elizabeth felt the tears start and, filled with embarrassment, she fled.

Once she was outside the house she carried on running until she was breathless. It did not matter where she was going, only that she put as much distance between Alex and Phyl and herself as she could. Her feet took her down into the city, between closed shops and bombed sites where grass and weeds grew and the smell of the sea was stronger. Eventually she came to the river where there were ships, ocean-going liners and fussy little ferry boats. The water was grey and choppy and there appeared to be hundreds of men, women and children milling around. It felt very different from the Thames by Westminster where she had been wont to go sometimes due to her interest in old buildings along the riverside. The air was salty and seagulls swooped and flew up again like so many pieces of whirling newspaper. Slowly, she breathed in the sea air deeply and she calmed down.

A woman wheeling a pram stopped and waved a hand to her. Elizabeth looked at her and did not recognise her for a moment, then she realised it was the Black Widow but no longer wearing black. 'Hello,' muttered Elizabeth.

'Hello, yourself,' said Doreen in a surprisingly chirpy voice. 'You look as if you've lost a shilling and found a farthing.'

Elizabeth forced a smile. 'You sound happy.'

'I've escaped, haven't I?' She held her head a little to one side. 'It wasn't easy when I didn't have the pram.' Elizabeth stared at the vehicle and recognised it as the one from the Eccleses' attic. 'I've been across the river to New Brighton,' said Doreen. 'I walked round the fair and then sat on the promenade, watching people. I could have clicked if it hadn't been for Syd.' There was surprise and satisfaction in her tone. 'Are you on your own?'

'Yes,' she said, hardly able to believe the change in the woman since last they had met. What did she mean, 'clicked'?

'Where's *she*?' asked Doreen.

'You mean my stepmother?'

'So that's who she is!'

'Yes. She's with Al—Mr Payne.'

Doreen's smile vanished and her eyes glinted. 'You never told her then?'

'Told her what?'

'About him being a murderer. You didn't believe me, did you?'

'Mr Payne doesn't act like a murderer,' said Elizabeth, flushing. 'He's kind.'

'What's that got to do with it? Even murderers are probably nice to their mothers. How many do you know?' Doreen tossed her hair back. 'There's probably hundreds walking around. So many people died in the war.'

Elizabeth began to wonder if this was how Alice in Wonderland had felt when talking to the Mad Hatter. 'Yes. But they weren't murdered, although I suppose you could say Hitler murdered them. Your husband's death was an accident and the war's over.'

'My private one isn't.' Doreen's face was set like flint. Then suddenly she smiled. 'You walking my way?' She whirled the pram around so that Elizabeth could see Syd. He gazed at her with his big blue eyes and gave her a four-toothed smile.

She had been going to say no but seeing Syd caused her to change her mind. 'I suppose I can.'

They hardly spoke on the return journey but when they came to the scrapyard Doreen asked her to come in. Elizabeth hesitated, wondering whether Phyl might be worrying about her. Then she remembered how she had lain with Alex on the bed and felt uneasy and irritated.

Once upstairs in the flat Doreen made no mention of Alex or Phyl, but instead put a record on her gramophone with lines like 'leave your worries on the doorstep'. She gave Elizabeth tea and Madeira cake, and asked her to feed Syd while she drank out of the brown bottle that had been tucked away under the pram cover. She danced around the room with Elizabeth watching her in fascinated disbelief as she fed Syd a bottle with crushed rusk in it.

After his bottle he needed changing and Elizabeth could see Doreen making no effort to do it so she had to go herself. Her first two attempts resulted in his nappy falling down but the third time she got it almost right. Doreen clapped her hands.

'You can be my babysitter. I've started to feel alive again but I've got to get out of this place more often and *he* complains if I leave Syd alone. Trevor Howard is on at the Hippodrome next week in *Green for Danger.* You can come on Saturday.'

'OK,' said Elizabeth, not sure after all Doreen's queer talk about murderers and the war whether she wanted the job or not but she liked Syd and was curious about a few things. 'Why did you come and live here if you don't like Mr Payne?'

'I had no money and my landlady didn't want a baby around. I only met Doug a few months before he was sent out to Palestine and so I stayed on in my old digs.' Doreen subsided on the rug in front of the gas fire, a faraway look in her eyes. 'I never thought he'd die. The war was over so I could hardly believe it when it happened. *He* came round and tried to make me see how he said it happened, but I saw it how it was. Afterwards I was determined to make him suffer.' Her eyes had hardened as she was speaking and Elizabeth felt as if a hedgehog was rolling down her spine.

'He's been good to you,' she said strongly. 'You should be grateful. He even got you the pram.'

Doreen's mouth set stubbornly. 'I'm not saying any more. You can go now. Just put Syd down to sleep.'

Elizabeth said no more but placed the sleepy child in his cot and with a swift goodbye left the flat. She arrived in the yard as Alex came through the gate and would not have stopped if he hadn't called her.

'What the hell are you doing here?' he demanded. 'We've been looking all over for you.'

'You shouldn't have bothered. I'm not a child. I'm perfectly capable of looking after myself,' she replied stiffly.

He rested his back against the wall, dark brows drawn together. 'You ungrateful little bitch,' he said softly.

She was shocked. 'I'm not a bitch! And you shouldn't call me one. It's not a good example of how one should speak.'

He did not apologise. 'You're selfish then. You were upset so Phyl was worried about you. She's sure something has been disturbing you lately. Has it?'

Nice of her to notice, thought Elizabeth. Perceptive.

'What's wrong, Lizzie?' said Alex quietly.

The sudden unexpected gentleness in his voice brought an unwelcome lump to her throat, but she did wonder if he really cared or whether his interest was purely down to Phyl. She could hardly tell him she was worried about his relationship with her stepmother. Instead she said, 'I'm unhappy at school. Phyl said she'd see about finding me the equivalent to the one I attended in Brentwood, and I'm worried if she doesn't do something soon I'll not get in, even for the autumn term.'

'I see.' He straightened. 'I'll speak to her about it if you like. Anything else?'

'The Saturday job in the shop? Blackie?' she enquired hopefully. 'I groomed him when we got back. You ask Harry.'

'I believe you. But I couldn't pay you much. As for the shop . . .' He shook his head. 'Maybe nearer Christmas when we get busy. Anyway, what are you doing here?'

Glad that he hadn't turned down her request completely, she told him about meeting Doreen and being hired as Syd's babysitter.

He smiled. 'You've definitely got something. There's not many people she's friendly with.'

Elizabeth thought about that. 'Perhaps she sees me as an outsider like herself?'

He nodded as if he understood. 'But the longer you're here, the more you'll fit in.'

'Perhaps,' she said. 'Perhaps not. I'd best go.'

'See you around.' He left her and went inside the office.

When Elizabeth arrived back at the house the family had all come home.

'So you're back?' said Sam, glancing up from his newspaper.

The answer to that remark seemed obvious to her and she could not understand why they were all staring at her. 'What's wrong?' She suddenly wondered if Sam had caught Alex in the house.

'Do you know how worried our Phyl's been about you? We were just about to send out a search party,' said Maisie.

'I'm sorry. I didn't think you'd all be worried.' She glanced at Phyl, wondering why Sam wasn't furious with her. 'I walked to the Pierhead and had no money so I had to walk all the way back again. I thought with us having finished the painting it would be OK.'

'You should have said where you were going,' said Phyl, shrugging. 'It's OK. Just don't do it again.'

'I'd have got me bottom smacked if I'd gone off without saying where I was going,' said Trev, glowering at Elizabeth. 'It's not fair. Girls get away with murder.'

'No, we don't,' said Mary immediately. 'I've had my bottom smacked.'

'That's enough,' said Sam. 'We've had a good day so let's not have any fighting.' He turned to Phyl. 'How did the painting go, lass?'

'Fine.' She glanced round the circle of faces. 'Nobody's to go in the attic, by the way. I don't want any smutty fingers on the paintwork so I've locked the door. When it's all ready you can see it.'

'Jolly dee,' murmured Lois, not looking up from the Mills & Boon book she had borrowed from the library in the newsagent's round the corner. 'Can we have supper now Wandering Lizzie's returned?'

No more was said by the rest of the family about Elizabeth's having gone missing but a week later when they saw the finished attic with its yellow and white gingham curtains and the bed with matching cover and the good quality secondhand furniture, Lois blurted out, 'It's not fair that Lizzie should be up here with our Phyl. It should be me.'

'How d'you work that out?' said Phyl, leaning against the windowsill.

'I'm next to eldest,' said Lois, folding her arms across her chest. 'Elders get the best in the family and if Lizzie's a real part of this family then the rules apply to her.'

'Hold on there,' said her father. 'I remember someone saying they wouldn't share their room with their eldest sister.'

Lois's smile was honeyed. 'As if I meant it, Dad. I'm willing to pay halves towards everything up here. I'm sure our Phyl could do with a bit of financial help. I mean, where did she get this furniture?'

'I bought it off someone whose elderly father had died.' Phyl's smile was just as sweet as her sister's. 'And I don't want your money. When one of us leaves it could prove difficult cutting everything right down the middle.'

'That settles that then,' said Sam, heading for the door accompanied by the youngest two in the family.

Lois pouted at her sisters and flounced out of the room.

'I wonder how the furniture got here,' said Billy, sotto voce, against Elizabeth's ear. 'No one's asking. I reckon Dad's in no mood for another argument with his favourite daughter.

'Damn,' said Dot, surprising Elizabeth. 'For a minute I thought I was going to get rid of our Lois. I reckon you'd be more peaceful to live with, Lizzie.' She winked at her before going out with her mother who had managed to hold her tongue throughout the whole episode.

'Well,' said Phyl, 'aren't you going, Billy?'

He got to his feet. 'I was just wondering whether to put in a bid meself as the elder son but –'

'Out!' said his sister, pushing him towards the door.

He grinned and left.

'Typical of this family,' said Phyl, going over to the bed and stretching out on it. 'Anything you have they all want a bite of the cherry. I wonder what Nan'll think when we don't sleep in the parlour tonight?'

Elizabeth was too concerned with her own problems to worry about Nan Eccles's feeling at the moment. 'I'm babysitting for the Black Widow tomorrow night, although she's stopped wearing black. I'll give you half the money. It must have cost you a bit for the furniture.'

'Shut up about money and save it for the new uniform you might need,' said Phyl, without opening her eyes. 'You can stop worrying about school. I've made an appointment to see the headmistress to discuss your situation and ask her advice.'

'You can tell her I'm being bullied. That might help.'

'Figures,' said Phyl, not sounding surprised. 'Anyway I'm sorry I'd forgotten. It was something Alex said that reminded me.'

'I'm glad about that.' She wondered what Alex had said but did not ask.

Phyl opened her eyes and sat up. 'Are you sure you want to babysit for that Doreen?'

'I'm sure,' said Elizabeth, and impulsively hugged Phyl. 'And if I can make money in any other way to help pay for everything then I'll bloody well do it!'

'Elizabeth!' said Phyl sounding shocked. 'Go wash your mouth out with soap! I don't know what's got into you. Our Billy's company, no doubt.'

'Sorry,' said Elizabeth meekly. 'I won't say it again.'

Knowing that Phyl was going to take steps made returning to school after the Easter holidays easier for Elizabeth. She half-expected to be summoned to the headmistress's office and asked who was bullying her but it did not happen. Yet as the days passed she became aware that the teachers on playground duty seemed to be more vigilant, although Thelma still pinched and prodded her covertly when they were lining up. Elizabeth was beginning to believe that bullying was a fact of life and how one dealt with it was preparation for the tough, grown-up world. She was more concerned about Brenda.

When Elizabeth told her she might be leaving, the girl flung her arms round her and begged her not to go. 'It's only the thought of you being here that helps me cope,' she cried.

'You coped before I came,' said Elizabeth uncomfortably, loosening her hold. They were outside the Cosy picture house not far from the park, and she was aware that people were staring.

'I was miserable. It's wicked at home. You've no idea,' said Brenda, shaking her head as if in pain.

'What d'you mean, wicked? Does your pa hit you?'

Brenda hung her head. 'Forget I said it. There's nothing you can do.'

'Haven't you got an aunt or an uncle who could help?' By now Elizabeth knew that Brenda lived alone with her father.

'I've got an aunt but she never visits.'

'Couldn't you visit her?'

Brenda shook her head. 'Can't.'

'Why?'

The girl turned on her and yelled, 'Stop asking me questions! There's nothing nobody can do, so forget it!' And she burst into tears.

Elizabeth wanted to run away but instead she sent up a prayer and put her arm around the girl. 'Stop it, Brenda,' she whispered. 'People are looking. We can still be friends outside school.'

'We can't. I'm never allowed out in the evenings,' she sobbed.

'At the weekends?'

Brenda stopped crying and gazed at her. 'You mean that?'

Elizabeth felt sorry for her because crying had made her appear ugly and pathetic and she blamed herself for it. 'Yes!' she said, although she realised Brenda was becoming as much of a worry to her as Thelma.

'We could go to the park,' Brenda said eagerly.

Elizabeth nodded. 'We could take Syd in his pram.'

'Who's Syd?'

Elizabeth told her about babysitting and that got them to where their homeward paths divided. It was a relief to be on her own and when she entered the house, which she was beginning to think of as home, she felt that Trev's and Lois's behaviour did not bother her half as much as Brenda's.

The next time Elizabeth babysat for Doreen she broached the subject of taking him to the park on Saturday afternoon. Doreen looked pleased. 'I can't pay you,' she said, 'but I'll make you some butties.'

Elizabeth had not really expected to be paid so it wasn't a disappointment. Never having had anything to do with babies before, she found herself rapidly getting fond of Syd. She found his attempts to feed himself and to talk and walk amusing as well as fascinating.

He took his first steps while she and Brenda were in the park, sitting on the grass, listening to a brass band playing. Elizabeth swung him up into the air, kissed him, and told him what a clever boy he was. He made that chuckling noise that made her want to laugh.

'You spoil him,' said Brenda sulkily, brushing crumbs from her lap with a violent movement. 'All babies learn to walk so what's so clever about it?'

'His mummy doesn't spoil him,' said Elizabeth seriously, 'and he has no daddy. So I think it's good for him that I do.' She chucked Syd under the chin.

'Did yer know babies grow in women's stomachs?'

'What?' Elizabeth laughed. 'That's a daft thing to say. How would they get there?'

'Up your front passage. A man puts his thing up there and plants a seed.' She shivered and wrapped her arms round herself. 'Anyway, it's not good for children to be spoilt.'

Elizabeth could not believe what Brenda had said. It seemd too incredible. She thought the girl was just trying to be clever because she was jealous but really she made herself appear stupid by saying such things. How could a baby get out of a woman's stomach? Her heart sank. She had believed that by keeping Brenda company more often she was helping her, but now Brenda was becoming possessive. Still, things would be different when they were no longer attending the same school and that was a thought to hold on to.

Phyl informed Elizabeth which school she was likely to attend just three weeks before the end of the summer term. 'It's a Church of England Girls' Grammar. The headmistress wrote to your old one in Brentwood and got a good report back about you.' She smiled. 'I felt quite proud. Almost as if you were my own daughter.'

The remark pleased Elizabeth. 'Thanks. Does the Head want to see me?'

'No. She feels certain you'll fit in, and so do I. Your confidence seems to be growing and I've noticed you're picking up a few of our funny little ways of talking. I'm glad about both. You'll cope with the changes.' Phyl paused. 'Talking about coping – how are you getting on with Doreen and Syd? Any sign of her moving out? Alex clams up if I mention her.'

'Syd's a love,' said Elizabeth, sitting on the bedcovers and clasping her arms about her hunched pyjama-clad knees. 'As for Doreen, I think she's happier than she used to be but she hasn't mentioned anything to me about leaving.' She realised her heart was beating fast. Was Phyl thinking that once Doreen moved out, she would set about getting Alex to marry her and move in with him?

Phyl frowned. 'You don't think Alex likes her, do you?'

Elizabeth thought about that. 'No. I think he's a softie as you said.' Although, she almost added, remembering how he had called her a selfish bitch, I believe he does have certain expectations and there are things he would not put up with.

Her remark, though, brought the conversation to an end and Elizabeth snuggled down under the covers, dwelling on the thought that soon there would be no more Thelma to worry about.

But Thelma was not to allow Elizabeth to leave without one final attack on her. It came when she and Brenda were on their way home. The two girls were surrounded by Thelma and her cronies, who twisted their arms behind their backs and dragged them into an entry. They were forced to face each other.

'Take a gud look at 'er, Snooty Boots,' said Thelma, pressing her knuckles into Elizabeth's back. 'Because I want yer to smash her face in.'

Elizabeth thought she must have misheard her.

'And you, Freckle Face,' Thelma nodded in Brenda's direction. 'I want a good punch from yer, right on her snout. She won't look so snooty wiv it broke.'

Brenda stared at Elizabeth from scared-silly eyes and Elizabeth realised Brenda believed Thelma was serious. She felt sick and prayed desperately to as many saints as she could remember to have Billy come along, but she had a feeling there was a cricket match that evening after school.

Thelma punched Elizabeth in the back, nearly knocking all the breath out of her, and sent her colliding into Brenda. Elizabeth pushed herself away and looked for an escape but Thelma's gang had formed a circle, closing them in. They began to chant, 'Fight, fight, fight!'

Elizabeth thought of the early Christian martyrs being thrown to the lions and then a second punch in the back sent her flying into Brenda again. 'Hit her,' yelled Thelma, 'or it'll be the worse for you!'

Elizabeth clutched Brenda's shoulder and whispered, 'Let's pretend to fight.' They had played pretend games before, acting out scenes from books. Brenda seized Elizabeth round the middle and aimed a punch at her head. She ducked just in time and realised it was not going to be easy to pretend. And it wasn't. Several times blows found a target and Elizabeth's blazer pocket was almost ripped completely off when Brenda attempted to swing her around by it. It had to finish, decided Elizabeth desperately, or she was going to be in a right mess. As Thelma and the others cheered and booed, she dragged Brenda down on to the ground and rolled her over and over in the dust. The girls encircling them moved back and suddenly *there* was the gap Elizabeth was hoping for. She pulled Brenda's arm and they were off.

They raced up the entry pursued by Thelma and her gang. In Boaler Street Elizabeth considered it safe enough to slow down. There were shoppers about and their pursuers fell back. Elizabeth had never been so relieved. Then she caught sight of her reflection in a shop window and felt shocked. 'I'm a mess,' she stammered. 'Aunt Maisie and Phyl will have fits if they see me looking like this.'

Brenda hesitated then said, 'Yer'd best come to our house. Pa shouldn't be in for an hour or so. It'll give yer time to wash yer face and tidy up.'

'Are you sure?' said Elizabeth. Brenda had always stressed that she wasn't allowed to have friends home. 'I don't want you getting into trouble.'

'Things can't be any worse than they are,' said Brenda in that tight little voice she used sometimes. 'Just hurry.'

They hurried.

Inside Brenda's house, Elizabeth tried not to make her thoughts obvious as she stood at the shallow brown stone sink in the tiny scullery of the two up, two down, but she had never been in such a dismal house. All the walls were painted black and even the curtains appeared to be blackout ones. There was an atmosphere about the place that gave her the creeps and she wondered how Brenda could bear to live there.

As if her friend had read her mind, she said in a voice of loathing, 'He painted it like this after Ma died – said it wouldn't show the dirt.'

'I-I suppose it's a fact.' Elizabeth dried her face on a ragged and rough towel.

'He ran out of paint when he got to my room so he didn't bother doing anythin' with it. It's still got the wallpaper on from before the war. Yer can see it if yer like?' Her voice brightened. 'I keep me sewing things up there and yer'll need to fix that pocket.'

Elizabeth would have preferred to go but thought it politer to agree to stay.

They climbed the stairs to the rear of the front room. There was a sharp curve at the top and almost immediately one stepped into a small front bedroom. A couple of strides took Brenda to the window and she drew the curtains so that only a narrow strip of sunlight shone through. Elizabeth watched her take a box from under the single bed that was covered with a couple of blankets. There was nothing in the way of bedroom furniture. Curtains hung at the alcoves either side of the narrow chimney breast and that was all.

'While yer sew the pocket, I'll replait yer hair,' said Brenda, handing over needle and thread. 'I've got a spare ribbon.'

They were silent as they worked and Elizabeth was glad that Brenda did not seem to want to talk about what Thelma and her gang had made them do. Almost she wished herself safe in the care of the nuns. She had just set the final stitch to her pocket when below in the street she heard heavy footsteps and then the sound of a key in the latch. She bit off the thread and placed her blazer down, glancing at Brenda. 'Is it your pa?' she whispered.

Brenda made no sign of having heard her.

'Are yer there, gerl?' shouted a man's voice.

Still Brenda was silent but slowly she began to rock backwards and forwards on the bed.

Elizabeth did not know what to do. 'Had we better go down?' she said in a low voice.

This time she seemed to have got through to Brenda, or maybe it was the sound of heavy boots on the stairs that roused her. She dragged Elizabeth off the bed and said hoarsely, 'Hide under here. If he sees yer here it'll be the worse for me. Whatever happens, don't make a noise.'

Brenda's fear communicated itself to her and Elizabeth scrambled beneath the bed. The door opened and she could see the bottom of a man's trousers. They appeared to be made of thick serge and looked greasy. The turn-ups rested on boots which were black and had metal toecaps.

'Why didn't yer answer me, gerl? And why isn't me tea ready?' He had a voice which in a strange way reminded Elizabeth of black mud. It filled her with a fearsome apprehension.

'I didn't expect yer so early,' said Brenda in a trembling voice. 'I'm sorry, Pa.'

'Sorry! You'll be sorry. Get yer drawers off!'

Elizabeth's nerves jangled frantically. He was going to smack Brenda's bottom! What could she do? Before she could make a move, the mattress sagged and dipped between the well-worn springs so that it rested on top of her head. She almost stopped breathing. Then the bed began to creak and the underside of the mattress between the spring squashed her hair as it moved up and down. Brenda's pa was groaning then suddenly all went still and quiet. The boots made an appearance again and he said, 'I'm going up the pub. Yer'd berra make sure me tea's ready this time, yer little slag, or it'll be the belt as well next time.'

'Yeah, Pa,' whispered Brenda.

The bedroom door opened and closed and there was the sound of his boots going downstairs. Then the front door slammed.

Elizabeth scrambled out as Brenda reached for her knickers. 'You mustn't tell,' said the girl wildly. 'You mustn't, mustn't tell! You get out of here and don't say nothing to nobody or he'll kill me.'

'What did he do to you?' Elizabeth could not believe her thoughts.

'Don't yer know? God, you're thick! Now get out!' Brenda made a shooing motion towards her. 'Out, out!'

Elizabeth ran and got as far as the door when she remembered her blazer and ran all the way back upstairs. Brenda was huddled on the bed, rocking herself in that peculiar way she had done earlier and did not appear to notice her in the room.

'Come with me,' said Elizabeth. Brenda ignored her. Elizabeth seized her arm but Brenda shook it off. Elizabeth was aware of a terrible feeling of helplessness and ran downstairs again. She wanted Phyl. She'd know what to do.

Elizabeth left the house without looking left or right and raced up the street, round the corner and along the road without drawing breath. At last she reached the entry which was a short cut to where home was. She was half-way through it when the sound of heavy footsteps caused her to look behind her and her heart seemed to stop beating.

He covered the distance in three strides and grabbed her. 'What's the rush, gerl?'

Elizabeth forced herself to look into the unshaven face with the lantern jaw and skin which appeared to have dirt embedded in it and she was so frightened she thought she would faint. 'I knew the blazer wasn't hers. Where were yer? Hiding behind the curtain?' He shook her with such force that her plait hit her in the face.

From somewhere she dredged up courage. 'Let me go, you filthy old man, or I'll have the law on you.' The words came out in a squeal.

'You'll what?' he said scornfully, and shook her again. 'Posh little cow, aren't we? Where did our Bren find yer?' There was a sneer in his voice as he pushed her into a narrower entry running off the main one and he began to fumble with her skirts. A scream started inside her but it was a struggle to get it out. Then she heard children's voices and running feet. He pushed her behind him and squashed her against the backyard wall.

'What are yer doing, mister?' asked a very young voice.

'Mindin' me own business, yer nosy little sod. Now beat it or the monster that lives up this entry'll come and get yer in the night.'

'What kind of monster –' came the boy's voice, but it was interrupted by a girl saying, 'Come on, our Charley. Yer know what mam says about strange men up entries.'

The children's running footsteps receded and Elizabeth felt as if she was going to die as Brenda's pa turned. Strangely it was then she found her voice. She yelled as he pressed her against the wall with one hand and pulled his thing out of his filthy trousers with the other. She kicked and kicked and he smacked her across the face. Then unexpectedly he let her go and went lumbering away up the entry. Elizabeth slumped against the wall. She could hear women's voices and one of them belonged to Phyl's mother. She had never felt so glad to hear it.

'Come on, Lizzie luv. It's all right now,' she said. 'I've got you safe.'

Despite her age and size Elizabeth was lifted off her feet and carried out of the entry and into the Eccleses' house where they laid her on the sofa. Dot had arrived home from work and was ordered to make hot sweet tea while Maisie wiped Elizabeth's face with a damp flannel. 'See where he's cut her lip,' she whispered to Dot. 'The dirty rotten swine! I'd have him castrated if I knew who he was. We'll have to keep a watch out now in case he comes after any of the other girls.'

Elizabeth wanted to say, But I do know who he is! but could not find her voice and her whole body felt as if it was an aching floating mass.

Dot sat her up and placed an arm about her shoulders and held a cup of tea to her lips. 'Come on, Lizzie, you're going to be OK.'

'Phyl,' she managed to whisper. 'She's-got-to-do-something.'

Mother and daughter exchanged looks. 'Yes, luv,' murmured Maisie. 'Don't you be worrying. We'll do something.'

Elizabeth did not have long to wait. Phyl walked into the kitchen five minutes later. She stopped abruptly at the sight of her stepdaughter stretched out on the sofa and her smile turned to a frown. 'What's happened?'

'The poor girl's had a shock,' said Maisie. 'Come in the scullery and I'll explain.'

'No!' cried Elizabeth, sitting up. 'It happened to me! I'm not a kid for you to tell her things behind my back.' She turned to Phyl. 'You've got to do something!' Her insides squirmed at the thought of what she had to say. She glanced at Maisie and said, 'I think I know what he was trying to do but I don't know why he wanted to give me a baby. I know who he is.' Maisie opened her mouth but before she could speak Elizabeth continued and told them what she thought had happened in Brenda's house.

'Something's got to be done right away,' said Phyl, her eyes intent as she stared at Elizabeth. 'That poor girl. D'you remember the number of the house?'

'It's five doors up from this end. Odd numbers.'

'You can't go on your own, Phyl,' said Maisie swiftly. 'You need a man and your dad's working late down on the Indian Buildings. What about the police?'

'You mean have them interrogating Lizzie and that poor girl? I know a man who might do something,' said Phyl quietly, and without another word she left the house.

Maisie and her daughter exchanged glances. 'Does she mean – ?' began Dot.

'I don't know but I guess we'll find out soon enough,' said her mother grimly.

Maisie tucked Elizabeth up in bed with a hot drink of whipped up egg, milk, nutmeg and treacle, as well as the *Radio Fun* and a couple of spam sandwiches. Elizabeth was really grateful and said so shyly. Maisie smiled at her and touched her cheek with a work-worn hand before going out.

The attic was full of evening sunlight reflecting off the primrose-painted walls and it seemed unbelievable to Elizabeth that all the horror that had taken place in the last few hours could happen on such a golden day. It was as the nuns always said there was real evil in the world. She shivered, wishing Phyl would come home and wondering if 'the man' was Alex.

Phyl did not return for hours and when she did it was dark in the attic and Elizabeth had dozed off several times, only to start awake when she heard a noise outside the door. But it was only the tiddlers whispering. She'd have enjoyed even Trev's company at that moment but Dot had called them away. Now Elizabeth stared in relief at Phyl as she sat sideways on the bed, gazing down at her, a faint smile on her face.

'Is Brenda OK?' she asked.

'Yes. Alex made it look like a burglary.'

'What d'you mean?' So *he* was Alex.

'He climbed over the backyard wall and broke into the house. He beat the living daylights out of the swine and then broke into the gas meter. He's putting the money in a collecting box for the Sunshine Home for Blind Babies so you don't have to worry about him being a real thief. Then we dialled 999.'

Lizzie could hardly believe that Alex could behave in such a way. 'The police! What about Brenda?'

'She was in bed and apparently didn't hear a thing.' Phyl began to undress. 'They've taken her father to hospital. Somehow I don't think he'll be coming out for a while. Brenda was taken in by a neighbour.'

'She has an aunt,' said Elizabeth, leaning forward eagerly. 'Someone should get in touch with her. But –' She frowned. 'How do you know what happened afterwards?'

'We hung around, of course! The neighbours all came out when the police and the ambulance arrived, ringing their bells like crazy. We just mingled and listened. Satisfied?'

'Yes,' said Elizabeth, pulling the bedcovers up to her chin. 'Yes,' she repeated. 'Was there much blood?'

'Lots. And I think his nose was broken,' said Phyl, getting into bed.

'Good,' said Elizabeth, although she would not have liked to have seen the blood. She lay there, looking up at the ceiling and feeling safe. 'I think we should write an anonymous letter to the police if Brenda ends back at that house with him.'

'Right,' said Phyl. There was a silence. Then she said, 'I don't really like bringing this up but I feel it's got to be said.' She hesitated. 'All that about having babies – how much do you really know?'

Elizabeth was silent a moment, then told her what Brenda had said that day in the park. 'I thought she was stupid but it was me that was daft.'

Phyl sighed. 'Poor Brenda. She'll probably never get over the experience. But sex isn't all bad, Lizzie love. With the right man it can be nice and comforting, believe me or not.'

'I used to think only married people had babies. I knew where I was believing that,' said Elizabeth sadly. 'But a woman can't have a baby every time that happens, can she? Or Brenda . . .'

'If a woman had a baby every time she did it then we'd all be standing on each other's heads!'

'How does the baby get out?'

'Normally the same way as it gets in. Weren't your periods ever explained to you?'

'I was told it was a sign I was growing up.' Elizabeth sighed. 'I don't think I want to grow up now.'

Phyl let out a heavy breath. 'Don't blame you. Life can be tough, kid. Now get to sleep. God bless.'

'God bless.' Elizabeth closed her eyes, mulling over what Phyl had said and the words followed her into her dreams. Alex was not such a softie after all, she thought with a great deal of satisfaction.

Chapter Seven

The next morning Phyl told Elizabeth she could have a couple of days off school to recover from her ordeal. She was glad of the opportunity to rest as her body felt sore and she had bruises on her upper arms and grazes on her knees and every now and again a shiver would make the hairs stand up on her arms due to the horror of that moment in the entry having not quite left her. She spent the time in the backyard sitting in the sun on a kitchen chair, watching Nan Eccles's ducks splashing about, whilst she read one of Lois's 'love taps' (Maisie's name for romantic novels). She could not help thinking that Phyl and Alex weren't the least bit like the couple in the book, who kept their distance most of the time and didn't kiss until the last page. Unbidden came thoughts of Brenda's pa, and unwilling curiosity as to how he must have treated his wife caused Elizabeth to think about marriage. People were so different, she thought, comparing the way her parents had behaved with Maisie's and Sam's behaviour. The latter were not given to hugging and kissing much in company or saying flowery things, yet it was obvious they felt comfortable in each other's company. Feeling at ease was a state that Elizabeth was beginning to appreciate.

When she returned for the last days of the summer term, a solitary Thelma surprised her by seeking her out and saying, 'I hear you're leaving and I see now yer mate's not coming back.'

'What d'you mean?' said Elizabeth, frowning.

'She's being sent to Colomendy for a holiday. You probably don't know it but that's a camp for kids near Loggerheads in North Wales. After that she's going to live with some aunt. It seems her ol' man of hers has been mistreating her so I heard me mam saying. It was terrible, she said.'

Elizabeth said lightly, 'I wonder what she'd say if she knew the way you'd behaved towards her?'

'Is that a threat?' said Thelma, bristling.

'No.' Elizabeth stared her straight in the eyes and told herself she would be leaving soon and there was no longer any need to be scared. 'But if you lay another finger on me again I'll squeal.' She walked away.

School ended without Thelma touching Elizabeth again but she felt dissatisfied with the way the girl had got away with her bullying ways. But Elizabeth could not see a way to balance the scales of justice so determined not to think about her.

The summer holidays seemed to stretch ahead into infinity and with them came a freedom Elizabeth had never experienced. In the past her leisure had nearly always been organised. She was encouraged to go out by Phyl's mother after she and Mary had washed steps and polished furniture. 'You make the most of this time, luv. All too soon you'll be grown up and going out to work. This time doesn't come again.'

There was only one problem: Elizabeth no longer had Brenda to go round with, Mary was a little too young and Elizabeth had not made any real friends among the girls in the street. She soon discovered, though, that Doreen was more than willing to let her fill an hour or more in taking Syd out in his pram. It was the same with many another young mother who was eager for a respite from baby and children, so Elizabeth sometimes found herself walking to the park with a troupe of other young baby-minders who gradually accepted her as one of them, and so she formed tentative friendships.

Sometimes when she returned Syd to his mother, Alex was there in the yard and he smiled at her and asked how she was doing? And if she had a minute maybe she'd like to refill Blackie's water container or take him fresh hay? On one occasion she had offered to muck out and Alex accepted her offer. Elizabeth always felt a warmth when she saw him, gratefully remembering how he had settled Brenda's pa.

There were days, though, when Billy asked her if she wanted to join him and a mixed group of boys and girls who roamed further afield. They visited his Aunt Kate in Moreton and went cockling. Elizabeth enjoyed the feel of the wet sand between her toes and the salt breeze in her hair and lungs. Billy kissed her but she was aware that she was not the only one he kissed, and though pleasant it was on a par with the pleasure she felt at the smell of the sea which seemed to permeate everything, but especially the cockles they took home and Maisie boiled in the large pan she used for scouse.

One day Elizabeth went alone with Billy, peapicking to Kirkby a few miles from Liverpool. It seemed a long way on the tram but she did not care about that. The sun was shining, and despite peapicking being backbreaking work she no longer felt a stranger up north. Then unexpectedly she saw Thelma along the line of peapickers and froze.

Immediately Billy noticed. 'What's up with you? Has your back gone?'

'It's Thelma Woods,' she whispered. 'She and her gang used to pick on Brenda and me. They made us fight once, I hate it that she got off scot-free.'

'Her family are a gang of knock-offs,' said Billy, glancing in Thelma's direction before popping a pod and eating the plump sweet peas inside. 'She's got a couple of brothers built like the side of a house. Not the kind of family to come up against.'

Elizabeth murmured, 'I wish –'

'That you could get back at her?'

She nodded slowly. 'She made Brenda's life even more miserable than it was.'

He ate several more peas before muttering, 'I'm not super brain but give us a mo'.' He spent the next half hour silently working and occasionally letting his gaze range the green woods, hazy in the distance. Eventually he said, almost dreamily, 'We'll give this another half hour then pay a visit to the arms dump.'

'Arms dump?'

'You'll see,' he said, and wouldn't say another word.

When the half hour was up they walked in the direction of the woods and eventually came to a place where there were broken down aeroplanes and tanks, and boys, boys, boys hiding in billowing willow herb, cow parsley and seeding grasses, as well as cockpit or gun turret, acting out scenes from the silver screen or as told to them by fathers or uncles home from the war.

'Stay here,' said Billy, indicating a patch of grass, and he vanished between a couple of tanks.

Elizabeth was glad to obey and stretched out on the ground wondering what Billy had in mind. Suddenly it seemed incredible that she should be so set on revenge. A year ago such a thought would not have been allowed to take such a hold on her. Forgiveness was a word much used in religious circles, like sin.

Something hit her cheek and instinctively her hand went to the spot. Another noise as something hit a tank a few feet away. A few seconds more and something else whizzed past her ear. She whirled and called, 'Come out, come out, wherever you are!'

A boy's head showed above a clump of cow parsley. 'Sorry. I wasn't aiming at you.'

'You must be a terrible shot.'

The rest of him made an appearance and she saw the catapult dangling from his left hand. 'Not so terrible,' he drawled. 'I've hit that tank several times. My sister's in there.'

'It's true,' called a muffled voice, and a second later a blonde head materialised above the circular opening and a girl climbed out.

The boy helped his sister down from the tank and Elizabeth gazed at them with interest. They were both fair and lanky in build and their features were extremely alike. 'Are you twins?' she asked.

The girl nodded. 'I'm Josie. He's Joe. Who are you?'

'Elizabeth Knight. But most people call me Lizzie now.'

'Elizabeth the King's wife. Lizzie's much more friendly,' said Joe, sitting cross-legged on the ground and breaking off a stem of grass and chewing on it. 'You're not from round here?'

From that moment on Elizabeth thought of herself as Lizzie. She wrinkled her nose. 'You can still tell? I thought I was starting to sound like a Scouser.'

They shook their heads. 'Naw!'

She grinned, liking the look of them. 'OK. I'm from the south.'

'London,' said Josie, nodding sagely.

'Yes, but it mightn't have been. Why does everyone up north presume that anyone from the south is from London? There are other places.'

'London's good enough for me,' said Joe solemnly. 'Fleet Street. I want to be a newshound.'

'He's already been in print,' whispered Josie, leaning towards Lizzie. 'The church magazine.'

He groaned. 'Don't tell her that! She'll think me a right wet!'

'Wet?' The expression was a new one to Lizzie.

'Wet behind the ears. A learner,' explained Joe, throwing away his piece of grass.

'But you *are* a learner,' said Josie. 'But coming on fair dinkum, Matt sez.'

'Fair dinkum? That's another one I haven't heard,' said Lizzie.

'It's Aussie slang,' said Joe. 'Matt was born in Australia, and's sort of related to us. He's OK, for a vicar.'

Lizzie brushed that aside. 'What d'you mean, sort of related? I live with sort of relations. I'm an orphan.'

Josie and Joe exchanged glances. 'Us too,' they said gravely. 'We live with Vera, our sister, and Ben, her husband. As well as their two kids and Ron, who's Ben's brother. They have a farm out Knowsley way,' said Josie.

'Who's Matt then? And where's Knowsley?'

They were about to explain when Billy appeared, carrying what looked like part of a bomb and grinning like a crazed monkey. He nodded in the twins' direction. Joe cast an interested glance at what Billy was carrying. 'That looks like a bit of an incendiary.'

'It's the tail. We're the hands of justice and we're going to wreak revenge,' he said solemnly, and winked at Lizzie.

Joe and Josie stared at them both with shining eyes. 'D'you need two more hands?'

'It could be risky,' said Billy. 'How are yer legs?'

'Legs?' said the twins.

'Can yer really run?'

They swore they could and to Lizzie's delight Billy agreed to allow them to be part of the team.

The next day the twins arrived at the Eccleses' home and were invited to join Billy and Lizzie at the bottom of the yard. With Joe's help Billy emptied the gunpowder out of the incendiary, watched by the two girls who had been solemnly warned by Billy not to breathe a word during this delicate process. If they did they would not be allowed to be there on the day of vengeance when the wrath of the Lord would fall on Thelma. It all sounded terribly exciting and maybe a bit dangerous, but Lizzie was not going to let that put her off. Josie agreed that to not be there would be awful.

The following day was another sweltering one when tar bubbled between the cobbles and the road where Thelma lived shimmered in the heat. Most mothers and children seemed to have deserted the front step for park, seaside or sunny backyard.

'Perfect,' whispered Billy, as he and Joe piled gunpowder against the Woodses' front door.

Hardly breathing, Lizzie and Josie watched from the bottom of the step as the boys came towards them, laying a snaking line down the cracked cement surface. Then Billy lit a match and they fled and hid behind the gateposts of the bombed house opposite as the flame hissed its way towards the Woodses' dwelling place.

The loudness of the explosion took them by surprise and Josie flung herself into Billy's arms. 'Holy Hell!' he said. 'I never thought it would go off like that!'

'It's just like the blitz,' said Joe in an awed whisper. 'It's blown the door in, as well as the windows.'

'Gosh, we'll be for it if we're caught,' said Lizzie. Yet she was filled with a glorious exhilaration as she stared at the billowing smoke.

Billy pushed Josie away. 'We'd best get out of here. This place might look deserted but somebody's bound to have heard the bang.'

Even as he spoke they could hear voices and the clattering of hooves.

'Best not run away,' said Lizzie, coming out from behind a gatepost. 'Do what anybody'd do in the circumstances.'

'Go and have a nose,' said Billy.

They crossed the street and the horse they'd heard halted a few feet away. Lizzie glanced at it and saw Alex jump down from the cart. Her heart flipped over.

'What's going on?' he said, coming to stand next to them. 'Billy, this isn't anything to do with you, is it?'

Lizzie felt quite indignant, as well as guilty. 'Why should he be up to anything?' she said, thinking that after all it was her revenge.

'Don't bite my head off, Liz,' drawled Alex. 'He's often up to something so he doesn't have to play the innocent with me.'

'It was probably an unexploded bomb in the garden left over from the war,' said Josie in a loud voice. 'Wouldn't you agree, Lizzie?'

Already a crowd was gathering from nowhere just like they'd been magicked there. 'Yes, I do,' said Lizzie, just as loudly.

Alex glanced at her. 'I wonder how?' he said softly. 'Are you suggesting it could have been the sun shining on a piece of glass that started a fire and set off the fuse?'

'Is that what happened?' said a woman, who had just crossed the road from the sweet shop over the way. 'I'll tell that to the fire chief when he arrives. I've just phoned the fire brigade.'

At that moment a couple of figures with coats over their head appeared through the billowing smoke, coughing a little. They lowered the coats as soon as they were clear of the smoke. One of them was Thelma, the other a lad from school whom Lizzie had heard had a bit of a reputation. 'Bully!' said Lizzie under her breath.

'Our door's on fire!' Thelma exclaimed, as if she could hardly credit it.

'Terrible,' said Lizzie. 'But I don't think the house'll burn down.'

'I don't know what Mam'll say.' Thelma looked worried. 'She'll want to know how I didn't notice it.'

'Exactly! How could you not notice a bomb?' said Joe.

'Canoodling, were yer?' said Billy innocently, with a slight swagger. 'You hadn't better tell yer mam that.'

Lizzie was suddenly aware that Alex was listening to them and felt her cheeks reddening. He stared at her and said tersely, 'The four of you get into the cart.'

'What for?' said Josie, but he did not reply, only pushed her across the road.

'Why should we do as he says?' hissed Joe. 'He's only the ragman.'

'Do as he says,' muttered Billy. 'If he tells our Phyl about this, my goose could be cooked.'

'He doesn't know it was us,' whispered Josie.

'Shut up!' said Billy. 'Girls don't half have big mouths.'

The two girls stared at him indignantly but accepted a leg up into the cart. Josie sat on an upturned table. 'He can't know.'

'He knows,' said Lizzie, sitting next to her. 'It amazes me but there are people who can read minds.'

'Aunt Lily,' said Josie with a sigh. 'She only has to look at me and I confess to things I haven't done.'

A snort escaped Billy who was standing against the side of the cart in the opposite corner to Joe. 'We're scuttled if you start confessing to this! Say nowt!'

'Say nowt to what, Billy?' Alex's head appeared over the side of the cart.

They looked at him. 'We've got nowt to say,' said Lizzie.

'Good. I'd hate to upset Phyl with this so you'd better be nice to me. I have a distinct impression that you'd have liked that house burnt to the ground.'

'We didn't intend it to burn at all,' said Lizzie, then put a hand over her mouth.

'I didn't hear that,' he breathed as he passed her. A couple of minutes later the cart jerked and they were on the move.

'Big mouth,' groaned Billy.

'He's not going to tell,' said Lizzie confidently, hanging on to a table leg.

'How can you be so sure?' asked Joe anxiously. 'I mean, I'm sure he knows Ron – our brother-in-law, and he might feel he has to tell on us. Ron delivers milk to him.'

'I just know! Stop worrying.' She was not going to tell them what Alex had whispered.

She held her face up to the warm breeze and closed her eyes against the sun as she heard the clanging of a fire engine in the distance. Revenge was glorious. But even more glorious was Alex Payne being the kind of man who would never let her down, unlike Daddy. She felt now that if Phyl could get the Black Widow to leave, and married Alex, she could quite happily live under his roof.

Chapter Eight

Lizzie glanced up from her homework and groaned as Trev entered the kitchen like a whirlwind. There would be no peace to get her maths done now. It was Friday evening and outside it was dark and murky and in Nan's parlour there was no fire lit and up in the attic it was freezing.

'Are we having it, Mam?' he said, back-heeling a ball under the couch.

'Having what?' said Maisie, who had only just come in. 'And don't put that ball there!'

'Duck apple, of course,' said Trev, eager tawny eyes so like Phyl's.

'I'll think about it.'

'But it's Hallowe'en,' he cried. 'When witches fly and there's magic about.'

His mother looked at him severely. 'Don't talk daft. There's no such thing as witches. And as for magic –' She paused and smiled into her son's excited face. 'All right! I'll confess to having bought apples and chestnuts.'

Trev hugged her round the waist. 'I knew you wouldn't forget.'

'Never mind the softsoap. Go wash your hands and face, you look a right scruff. You haven't been in that hole the men have been digging?'

'No, Mam, honestly.' He stared at her innocently.

She shook her head as if she did not quite believe him before turning to Lizzie, and Mary who was cutting out paper dolls from newspaper on the rug. 'Mary, you set the table. Lizzie, make a pot of tea. Any minute now the rest of them'll be in clamouring for food.' She was taking off her coat as she spoke. 'Where's Nan? I didn't see her light on.'

'The fire's out in there so she came in and went out again,' said Lizzie, remembering her arrival at this house well over a year ago. Even now it was easy to picture Nan Eccles flying through the air on a broomstick with Mog clinging on. All Hallows' Eve! The last chance for all the bad spirits to do their worst before All Saints' Day tomorrow. But Nan Eccles wasn't bad, just muddled, and she hoped she'd be in soon. Probably she was standing by the cocky watchman's little tent up the street, warming herself by his coke brazier. He was keeping his eye on the workings of the electricity board who were laying cables to all those households willing to pay for power.

'Have you ever had Duck Apple Night?' asked Mary, handing Lizzie her books before shaking out a white tablecloth over the chenille one. The family hadn't made a fuss of it last year.

'Never with a family,' said Lizzie. 'Daddy used to roast chestnuts on the fire sometimes.'

'Oh, we do that. But it's duck apple and bob apple that's fun.'

She wanted to ask what was the difference but decided she would probably find out soon enough.

'For bob apple you've got to be blindfolded and keep your hands behind your back,' said Billy, fastening a scarf so that it covered Lizzie's eyes. 'If you can catch an apple with your teeth it's yours.'

Lizzie nodded, trying to see with her mind's eye the position of the apples dangling on strings from the clothes rack, but Billy spun her round so fast that she had no idea where anything was. 'That's not fair,' she cried. He laughed.

'Blindfold me,' said Trev impatiently. 'I bet I can get one before her. Although my string's too short and she's bigger than me. Let it down a bit, Bill.'

Furtively Lizzie lifted the edge of her blindfold and pinpointed an apple. She was not going to let any ten year old beat her.

'I'm glad I'm not a kid any more,' said Lois, curling her feet beneath her on the couch. 'I remember how frustrating it was. The apple was forever hitting my nose but when I tried to get my teeth into it, it would always bob away.'

'Dad always made sure we all got one, though,' said Phyl, pricking chestnuts and placing them on the coal shovel and that on the glowing fire.

'Remember how we used to try and peel an apple in one piece?' said Dot.

'And throw it over our shoulder,' said Lois, 'praying it would form the letter of our future husband.'

'I don't think yours ever formed BB,' said Phyl, putting the shovel on the fire.

'What d'you mean, BB?' said Lois, taking a bottle of scarlet nail varnish from her handbag.

'Buffalo Bill.' Phyl grinned, and rose to her feet. She manipulated one of the dangling apples so that it touched Lizzie's cheek.

'Thanks,' murmured Lizzie, considering that despite cheating she was still finding catching an apple just as frustrating as Lois must have.

'Very funny,' said Lois. 'I never remembered any of yours forming an A. D'you think Alex is ever going to get rid of that woman?'

'There's nothing between them,' said Phyl, an edge to her voice. 'I've told you before.'

'Don't start, you two,' said Maisie, looking up from the newspaper. 'I wonder if your father's found Nan yet?'

'He shouldn't have gone out in this weather,' said Dot in a worried voice. 'It's not good for his chest.'

Phyl pushed an apple against Lizzie's mouth and held it there long enough for her to get her teeth into it. 'He might be talking to the cocky watchman. Nan was there earlier.'

'Are you sure you aren't doing all the chasing?' said Lois.

'What are you talking about?' said Phyl impatiently.

Dot sighed. 'Can't you shut them up, Mam?'

Lizzie took off her blindfold and saw Maisie stand and leave the room.

'You've upset Mam now,' said Billy.

'I'm not chasing him,' said Phyl, lighting a cigarette.

'You're always going round to his yard.'

'He can hardly come here,' said Phyl. 'Not with the way Dad feels.'

Lois waved a hand around to dry her nails. 'If he wants you he'd stand up to Dad.'

Phyl inhaled deeply and then blew smoke in her sister's face. 'That's a snide comment! How can you call yourself my sister and say such a thing?'

Lois coughed and nearly knocked the nail varnish over. She swore and Trev said, 'Mam'll have you for swearing.'

A chestnut exploded and they all jumped. In the silence that followed they heard the murmur of voices in the lobby. 'Dad and Nan,' said Dot, her relief obvious, and rushed out of the room. She reappeared a moment later. 'It's not Dad,' she whispered. 'They say talk of the devil. It's Alex Payne. He's got Nan and a toddler with him.'

Phyl and Lizzie exchanged looks and they both went out into the lobby. They heard Maisie saying, 'I'm sorry if she's been a trouble.' She sounded put out.

'She was no trouble,' drawled Alex. 'More of a help than anything.'

'Yous come in, lad,' said Nan Eccles, who was holding on to his arm. 'You shouldn't be out in this weather.'

'Yes, come in, Alex,' said Phyl, her voice warm, as she glanced at her mother. 'It looks like it's raining out there.'

Maisie said nothing but brushed past Lizzie and went back up the lobby, closing the kitchen door behind her.

Alex said lightly, 'At least she didn't tell me to git. That said, I'd best get back.'

'What's the rush?' demanded Phyl.

'No rush,' said Nan Eccles, dragging on his sleeve. 'Yous come in my room, lad, and warm yerself by me fire.'

'Sorry, Nan,' he said. 'But I'd best get Syd home.'

'Why have you brought him?' said Lizzie, holding her arms out to the child, who immediately stretched towards her. Alex relinquished him with a smile. 'He's getting to be a handful.'

'Where's Doreen?' she asked.

'Vanished. Left a note saying to look after Syd, and that was all. I could kill her!' His voice held a savage note.

'You're joking!' Phyl stared at him, wide-eyed.

'Would I joke over such a thing?' he demanded.

'But-but where's she gone?'

'How the hell should I know?' he rasped. 'I haven't even had time to think yet. Your nan turned up at the yard just after I discovered the note and Syd was hungry and your nan was shivering. As I said, I'd best get back and try and get organised.'

'Do you think Doreen'll come back?'

'I hope so! Then she can blinkin' pack her bags and leave. I've had enough of her moods.' He thrust his hands into his pockets, his face set in angry lines. 'What kind of mother is it who leaves her child?'

'Perhaps she just couldn't cope any more?' said Phyl. 'Children aren't everybody's cup of tea. Even so she's blinkin' selfish.'

'Too right she is,' Alex groaned, resting his shoulder against the lobby wall. 'I've got a busy day tomorrow.' He stared at Phyl.

'Don't look at me,' she said. 'I couldn't cope with him and the shop. He's at that age when he's into everything.'

'You could put him in the playpen.'

'Lizzie said he climbs up it.' She hesitated at the expression on his face. 'I know you're the boss, Alex, and if you're going to order me then I suppose I'll have to have him, but he could break things.'

There was a silence. Lizzie removed Syd's fingers from her mouth and said, 'I'll look after him. I've done it loads of times this summer.'

'But not for a whole day,' said Alex, gazing at her. 'And there's the office too. I couldn't get someone in there for tomorrow.'

'I could cope with that if it's only a matter of taking jam jars and messages. If it's anything else, people can come back when you're there.'

'Yous is a good girl,' said Nan Eccles, patting her arm. 'I could help yous.'

Phyl laughed. 'There you are, Alex, an offer too good to miss.' She linked a hand through his arm. 'Now why don't you come and have a cup of tea?'

He shook his head. 'Not this evening. I'll have to get Syd to bed. See you in the morning, Lizzie, about nine.' His smile was appreciative and he pulled gently on her plait before taking Syd from her. 'I won't forget this.'

She murmured something, having just managed to control an impulse to rest her cheek against his hand.

After he had gone there was a short silence. Then Phyl let out a sigh. 'I hope Doreen does come back and Alex does tell her to git. Now what was I doing?'

'You were roasting chestnuts,' said Lizzie.

'Chestnuts!' exclaimed Nan Eccles and smacked her lips before scuttling up the darkened lobby.

Lizzie was aware of a reluctance to talk to Phyl about what had just happened.

Sam arrived home twenty minutes later. They all stared at him where he stood in the kitchen doorway, rain dripping from the peak of his cap and his mac. The only noise was gas hissing from a piece of coal and a ghostly voice coming from the wireless. Not even Lois thought it a good idea to tell him that Alex Payne had brought his mother home.

'Thanks, Lizzie. You're a good kid,' said Alex, wheeling the sleeping Syd's pram towards the rear door in the office.

Suddenly she hated him calling her a kid. 'I'm nearly sixteen,' she said, sitting on the desk and swinging her shapely legs. 'In three months' time to be exact. It doesn't feel like eighteen months, since I came here.'

His eyes met hers and for a long moment neither of them spoke and she could feel her heart beating. 'Not grown up enough yet, though,' he said at last.

She felt that remark was a dismissal of her so-longed-for adult status and slid off the desk. 'I'm not a child,' she muttered.

'No.' There was another silence during which she did not look at him. He sighed. 'Lizzie, you must know Doreen pretty well now. Have you any idea what was on her mind for her to leave the way she has? I didn't mention it last night but she took some money which I can ill afford.'

That was mean of her, knowing he was still hard up, thought Lizzie, lifting her head. 'I know she still has it in for you,' she said. 'What exactly did she say in her note?'

'Just "I'm going away. Look after Syd".'

'She's still calling you a murderer now and again.'

'That doesn't surprise me. You don't take her seriously?'

'Of course not. You wouldn't do such a thing.'

'Thanks for the vote of confidence.' He smiled and she wanted to stay there talking to him but knew she had to go, and said so.

'I haven't paid you.'

'I offered to help,' she replied swiftly. 'What are you going to do with Syd if she doesn't come back?'

'That's my problem. Don't you worry.' He held the door open for her. 'Thanks, and tarrah, luv.'

'Tarrah, luv,' she echoed boldly, her spirits lifting on an enormous wave of sudden exuberance. With a wave of a hand she danced across the yard and out.

The family were having tea when Lizzie arrived, flushed and bright-eyed. They gazed at her as she entered the kitchen.

'Well?' enquired Lois. 'What news?'

Lizzie glanced at Phyl as she pulled a stool up to the table and squashed in next to her.

'You might as well tell if there is anything to tell,' said Phyl, licking her spoon. 'It isn't a secret.'

'There isn't anything worth telling.' Lizzie watched Maisie ladle stew into a bowl and place it in front of her. She murmured her thanks.

'I hope Alex Payne was suitably grateful to you for looking after that little lad,' said Maisie.

'Of course he was.'

'How much did he pay you?' asked Lois.

Lizzie dipped her spoon in the stew. 'I wouldn't take any money.'

'You what!' cried Maisie, resting a hand on the table. 'Every little helps, luv. It cost our Phyl more to keep you since you went to that college, when you could be out at work. He could easily afford it. You have to think of others and not be so daft.'

'Mam, don't!' said Phyl. 'You never brought us up to put a price on helping people.'

'This is Alex Payne we're talking about and a child that – that –' she glanced at Mary and Trev and stopped.

'You know that's not true,' said Lizzie fiercely.

'Sit down, woman,' muttered Sam. 'Let it drop.'

'No,' said Lizzie, the firmness in her voice taking her, as well as them, by surprise. 'I didn't take any money because Doreen stole from him.'

'The cow!' Phyl started to her feet.

'Sit down,' ordered Sam, looking worried. 'It all seems a right funny carry-on if you ask me. Surely he can't be going to keep the child if it isn't his?'

'He is 'til she comes back.'

'He really believes she'll be back?' said Dot, wide-eyed.

'He hopes,' said Lizzie, taking a round of bread from the plate in the middle of the table.

'And what d'you think?' said Sam. 'Seeing as how you seem to know more than our Phyl about what's going on with that woman.'

'I can't believe she'll forget about Syd's existence like some parents seem able to forget their children.' She was thinking about her own.

'You've answered the question, lass,' he said, smiling at her.

'Yes, she has,' said Phyl with satisfaction. 'And when she does come back we definitely know she won't be stopping because Alex has said so. So now you can all stop thinking the worst of him!'

Doreen returned a fortnight later on a Saturday when Lizzie was once again in charge of Syd and the office. Alex had arranged for a widow woman to be available during weekdays but today he'd had to slip out on business for an hour or so. Doreen was not alone and immediately drew Lizzie to one side. 'How's everything? How's my beautiful boy?' She managed to land a kiss on her son's hair as he played with a car on the floor. 'Was Alex good and mad?' she whispered.

'How am I supposed to answer that? Of course he was mad. You left him high and dry and he's had a right time trying to manage everything,' said Lizzie irritably.

'Keep your voice down,' murmured Doreen. 'I thought you were my friend. The gentleman is my new husband,

Walter Rowlands, and he only knows I've been working here and that a friend was looking after Syd.'

Lizzie could scarcely believe it. She stared at the upright, white-haired man who flashed her a friendly smile. 'Where did you meet him? He looks nice enough but isn't he – a bit – ?'

'Age isn't important,' said Doreen, shrugging warmly coated shoulders. 'He's a widower, is kind, and has a nice little house the other side of the river in Wallasey. He and his wife lost a child and never had another so he's quite happy to take Syd on. And would you believe he still has the cot and playpen up in his loft! The things people hang on to.'

'You must be glad of that. Saves you having to take them from here.'

'Too blinkin' right!' She smiled. 'I'm sorry for drawing you into this but I thought Walt deserved a honeymoon and that's why I left Syd.'

'You could have explained.'

'And spoilt a perfect opportunity to get right up Alex's nose?' For a moment Doreen's eyes held a familiar glint. Then it passed. 'Anyhow, I knew he'd find someone to help him. I just thought it would be your stepmother making the most of her chances to prove what a good little wife and mother she'll be.'

Lizzie was silent. It would feel like a betrayal to say Phyl didn't want children. Besides, she might change her mind. 'Do you want me to pack Syd's things?' she murmured.

'Yes. I don't want Walt getting the wrong idea. And be quick about it, kid. With a bit of luck I might never have to see "the boss" again.'

Lizzie felt angry at her for that remark. After all Alex had acted more like family than a boss to her but she controlled her feelings and went and did as asked.

It hurt saying goodbye to Syd who had managed to wrap himself round her heart but it was not until Alex returned that she realised she should have tried to keep Doreen there.

'I'm not blaming you, Lizzie, but she's got off scot-free with some of my money,' he said, his eyes stormy as he paced the office floor.

'I'm sorry!' The words burst from her. She was hurt by his anger after all she had done for him. 'I didn't think.'

'I said I'm not blaming you.'

'Good!' Her voice was fierce.

'She's probably kept a watch on the place, waiting for me to go.'

'Probably.'

'I didn't even get a chance to say goodbye to Syd,' he muttered, and walked out of the office and into his living quarters.

Elizabeth realised then that it wasn't just the money which had upset him. She went for a walk round the park, trying not to think about Alex being hurt, and about Syd, but she had so many memories of the toddler that the park was definitely the wrong place to go to forget him. Eventually the chill November wind dried the tears on her face and when she had control of herself she made her way home.

Phyl rejoiced when Lizzie told her Doreen had been and gone, taking Syd with her. She flung herself backwards on the bed and yelled, 'Yippee hi hey! God's in his heaven and all's right with my world! There's nothing to come between Alex and me now. Come Christmas he just might ask me to marry him.'

Lizzie was silent. Phyl sat up, wrapping her arms round her knees, and said forcefully, 'I know you must be thinking that it's not so long since your dad died – but let's be honest, kid, we didn't have much of a marriage. He used me, and the way he went didn't make me feel any the better about that. Now I want a man I know inside and out and who makes me feel good about myself. You do understand, don't you?'

'I think I do,' said Lizzie, unsmiling. 'What I can't understand is if you're not that keen on kids, why you brought me here?'

Phyl smiled. 'You've forgotten you literally forced me to.' She mimicked Lizzie's voice. '"You're my step-mother!" After that I could hardly leave you behind. Besides you're almost grown up.' She hesitated. 'You do like Alex, don't you, Lizzie? Because I presume you'll be living with us until you're old enough to take care of yourself. We'll be a happy little family.' Her face lit up. 'Remember the way he looked that first time you saw him pushing that old handcart?'

Lizzie nodded as she slid beneath the bedcovers. 'You really believe he'll ask you to marry you at Christmas?'

'Let's say I'm optimistic.' Phyl's eyes gleamed.

'What about your mam and dad?'

'I'm old enough to do what I want.' Phyl switched off the new electric light that Sam had put in by taking a connection from a bedroom below. She hummed a love song.

Lizzie knew she should have felt happy about the prospect of being part of a happy little family consisting of two people she admired. It had been what she wanted for the last year or so but now her emotions were all confused. She was scared. Scared of being out in the cold again – like a stray cat who finds warmth at a stranger's hearth only to be ousted just when it is starting to feel wanted. But what could she do? The only thing she could think of was not to let herself care too much for these people who had taken her into their lives. She turned over in bed and tried to harden her heart against Phyl and Alex but she knew it was much too late. They already occupied a special place and it was going to be impossible to eject them.

Chapter Nine

It would soon be Christmas but Phyl had not spoken to Lizzie since of her certainty that Alex would ask her to marry him. Would it happen, wouldn't it? she worried.

Lizzie glanced at Josie kneeling beside her at the communion rail. Her friend looked pale and Lizzie imagined the fuss if she fainted so propped her up with her own body. She felt a bit that way herself and hoped no one could hear her stomach rumbling. Going without breakfast before early communion and school was not a good idea. Yet it was good they could be there together. Lizzie had been thrilled on discovering the younger girl was already a pupil at the school which had accepted her.

The vicar approached with the chalice and she sought to occupy her thoughts with something more spiritual. She imagined Jesus passing round the wine at the last supper before being pinned to the cross with heavy nails and vowed to try not to be jealous if Alex did ask Phyl to marry him. Her stepmother deserved to be happy. She was good to Elizabeth, continuing to support her going to the grammar because it meant a chance of her having a better paid job when she left school. Alex was kind, too. He now insisted on paying her for grooming and mucking out Blackie regularly. It meant that she did not miss Billy too much now he was away such a lot. He had changed jobs recently, signing on a ship of the Elder Dempster line, which regularly crossed the north Atlantic to Canada, returning with a cargo of timber. Lizzie was happy that he seemed to be in his right element, enjoying the adventurous seafaring life.

It was over porridge in the school hall after Communion that Josie mentioned the party. 'Boxing Day at the farm – you will come, won't you?'

Lizzie lifted her gaze to her friend's lively face. 'I'll have to ask Phyl but I can't see her saying no. She'll probably be glad to have me out of the way.'

'Why's that? I thought you and she got on well together.'

'We do. But –' She paused, and leaning forward across the table, whispered, 'She's hoping Alex will ask her to marry him at Christmas now that Doreen's gone, and it'll be two years soon since Daddy died.'

Josie's eyelids flew wide so that her blue eyes formed perfect ovals. 'How does that make you feel? I mean, what do you call your stepmother's husband when he's not your father?'

'I'll call him Alex. After all, I've never called Phyl "Mummy" so I can't very well call him "Daddy". He's far too young.'

Josie looked thoughtful. 'I see what you mean. It's awkward with neither of them being related to you.'

'I don't always rate family ties,' said Lizzie moodily. 'You want to hear Phyl and Lois when they get going!

And my mother cut herself off from her own family. I wonder sometimes if it's because of something Phyl said a while ago. Still what's the use of worrying and wondering now?'

Josie sighed heavily. 'Poor you. But do you have to live with them? I mean, newly-weds generally want to be on their own. Not that our Vera and Ben have ever had much time on their own. There were always relations around. Our Vera would love to marry off Ron. He's her husband's brother if I haven't told you before.'

'Phyl sees us being one happy little family.'

'Nice of her.'

'She is nice. It's just that –' Lizzie shrugged and spooned up the residue of porridge in her bowl. 'Forget it. By the way, I won't be able to go shopping with you on Saturday. I'll be working in the shop on Saturdays regularly now with Christmas coming up.'

'But you'll come to the party?' said Josie. 'And ask Billy to come as well if he's home. And anyone else in the family. The more the merrier, our Vera always says. Perhaps Phyl?' Her eyes danced. 'She could be perfect for Ron, and if not he could serve to make Alex jealous and maybe he'll pop the question.'

Lizzie glanced at the brass alarm clock standing on an enormous plain pine chest of drawers in the shop window. Only another hour to go. The shop had been quite busy but now there was a lull and she was conscious of her calves aching from having been on her feet most of the day. She glanced at Phyl who was placing a couple more of Sam's plaster plaques in the window. They were moulded plaster bowls of flowers, freshly formed and painted only the week before. It amused her that now Doreen was out of the way Sam had allowed himself to be persuaded by his eldest daughter to use Alex's shop as an opening to sell more of his artistic creations and split the proceeds with him.

Phyl turned and looked at Lizzie as if suddenly aware of her scrutiny. She eased her back and smiled. 'I'll be glad to get home tonight.'

'It's good that it's been busy, though. Alex needs the money.'

'I thought he might have come in today.' She took a cigarette from a five pack of Woodbines and lit up. For a few minutes she puffed with obvious pleasure then said, 'D'you think I've been doing all the chasing where Alex is concerned?'

'You're asking me?' The question startled Lizzie.

'Why not you? Remember our Lo saying that to me ages ago?' I've been thinking lately that she could be right. And as you see more of Alex and me than she does, I'd appreciate your opinion. Do you think she's right?'

'Do I?' Her tongue stumbled over the words. 'I-I'm not there when you're doing the chasing.' For a second in her mind's eye she pictured them in the attic together. 'I mean, I'm not with you when you're alone with him.'

'So you think I am chasing him?' Phyl frowned.

'I didn't say that at all! I meant, if you were I'm not there to see it.' Her cheeks felt hot and she wished Phyl would drop the subject.

'They say men like being the hunters,' muttered Phyl.

'Perhaps you should play harder to get and make him jealous then?' she responded, remembering what Josie had said about Ronnie.

'With whom?' Phyl sighed.

'Josie's asked me to a party at the farm on Boxing Day. There's an uncle there who's about your age. She said you were welcome to come. He delivers milk and knows Alex slightly.'

Phyl pulled faces. 'I haven't been to a party for ages. I've almost forgotten what it feels like.'

'Then why not come?' urged Lizzie, wanting to bring the conversation to an end.

'Perhaps I will. Just give me a day or so to think about it.'

At that moment the doorbell jangled and a man entered wearing paint-spotted corduroy pants and a wind-cheater. He glanced round before his gaze settled on Phyl. 'Hi!' He approached her. 'You wouldn't have a fan, would you? Only we're putting on *Lady Windermere* and –'

'Oscar Wilde,' said Phyl, smiling at him. 'One of my favourites. You're in luck. I nearly threw it out – seemed no call for it.' She delved into a wicker basket and after rummaging around produced what he was searching for. She opened the fan with a surprisingly skilful flourish and fanned herself. 'What d'you think? Will it do?'

He grinned. 'It's just what we need. Thanks. How much?'

'Shall we say sixpence? Who are *we*, by the way?'

'We are an amateur dramatics group. We lapsed during the war but we've started up again.'

'I used to be on the stage,' said Phyl, her voice animated as she wrapped the fan in a piece of tissue paper. 'Been on the Empire, done pantomime. It's a wonder you're not doing that with Christmas coming.'

'We thought some people might be sick of pantomime.'

'Well, it is daft! All that changing of the sexes.' She took his money and handed over the fan, resting her elbows on the counter. 'I used to love the life. I even went to London but it was hard going – really tough. Then I married and was widowed, was broke . . .' She smiled ruefully.

He looked interested. 'You should come and join us. That's if you wouldn't think you'd be lowering yourself?' he added hastily. 'I mean, we're only amateurs but it's great fun.'

It was as if a torch had been switched on behind Phyl's eyes. 'I'd love to come.'

'Great! Listen, my name's Graham Leadbetter.' He fumbled in his pocket and produced a stub of pencil and a scrap of paper. He licked the pencil, leaving a purple mark on his tongue, and wrote before pushing the paper across the counter towards her. 'That's where we meet, the time and everything. Just turn up.' He hesitated. 'We mightn't be able to give you a part for a while but –'

'That's OK! It's the atmosphere that I love.'

'Great! Fine!' He pocketed the fan and headed for the door, turned and half-lifted a hand. 'I'll see you then.'

'See you,' called Phyl and waved. Then she gazed at the paper as if she had been handed something precious and reached for her handbag under the counter to place the paper inside.

'Are you really going to go?' asked Lizzie, amazed at how fast Phyl had worked.

'Of course! It'll take me out of myself. What a turn up for the book! It'll be marvellous being on the stage again.'

'He said he wouldn't be able to give you a part for a while.'

'I know he did.' Phyl smiled and gazed into space.

The shop door opened and Alex entered. Lizzie smiled a welcome but her stepmother did not appear to notice him and continued to stare into space. Alex moved a hand in front of her eyes. 'Phyl?'

She blinked and focused on his face. 'Hi, Alex. Did you want something?'

'I wanted to talk to you privately.' He glanced at Lizzie. 'Make us a cuppa, please, Liz.'

She nodded, knowing she was being got rid of as she went into the back room where Harry was clamping a chair with a newly glued leg. Her stomach was behaving in a peculiar way as if it was being kneaded like dough. Was this the moment when Alex would ask Phyl to marry him? As she made the tea and listened to Harry, her thoughts were on the shop.

She re-entered quietly, carrying the tray, half-expecting to see Phyl with a shining face and Alex embracing her. And it was true they were standing close but Phyl's words didn't sound lover-like. 'OK. If that's the way you want it.'

'It is.' He leaned down and kissed her cheek. 'Don't be cross with me, luv.'

'I'm not!' Her voice softened. 'It's real kind of you but you're a fool to yourself, though. If you sold it you'd get a good price?'

'I don't want it just to go to anyone,' he hissed, turning as Lizzie approached.

He took a cup from the tray. 'I believe you're going to this party Phyl's mentioned?'

'Yes. It should be fun.' She avoided looking at Phyl in case her astonishment showed.

'Billy going?'

'It depends if he's home.'

Alex smiled. 'Don't let him lead you astray.' He drained his cup, nodded at them both and left.

Phyl sighed. 'Would you believe he's going to be working over Christmas? It's a pity he isn't invited to the party.'

'Wouldn't that be defeating the object if you plan on making him jealous?'

'I suppose so. I just hope the idea works.'

Lizzie prayed that it would for Phyl's sake but before the party there was Christmas Day to enjoy.

On Christmas morning Lizzie could not believe it when she saw the doll's house. It was made in a mock Tudor style with shutters at its upper windows and flowers painted growing up its walls. The front door had a tiny green door knob and inside was a real staircase going up to the bedrooms. She stared up at Phyl. 'You're saying Alex gave it to me?'

'That's right, love. That was what the hush-hush talk was about in the shop the other day.' She lit the first of her Christmas present cigarettes. 'It used to belong to his sister. He was clearing out the loft and thought you might like it. He said it's not exactly the mansion you'd like but . . .'

'I love it,' said Lizzie with a mixture of desperation and delight. 'But dolls' houses are for kids! I'm nearly sixteen.'

'I'll have it if you don't want it,' said Mary, kneeling on the floor in front of the house, heedless of her new Christmas white stockings and pink dress.

'It's not for you,' said her mother, who was standing with Lois and Dot in the doorway, 'and get up off that floor.'

'He could have sold it,' said Lois, coiling her hair up on top of her head. 'It would have been snapped up with it being Christmas. He could have made a few bob.'

'I'll give it back,' said Lizzie immediately.

'You can't!' cried Mary. 'We could have such fun with it. Don't give it back. Please, please keep it.'

'Be quiet, Mary,' said her mother. 'It's up to Lizzie. Now get downstairs. I've got the Christmas dinner to start.' They left the room.

'Perhaps he's given it to her to get round our Phyl?' said Dot, who was standing at Lois's shoulder.

'There isn't any need,' said Lois, who'd been flashing a three diamonds engagement ring since just before midnight on Christmas Eve. 'Our Phyl would have him like a shot.' She glanced at her elder sister. 'Wouldn't you? But the Black Widow's been gone a couple of months now and still no sign of a ring.' She held out her left hand and gazed at the three diamonds. 'I LOVE YOU! That's what these diamonds say. Don't you wish you had one as nice?'

Lizzie glanced at Phyl and wished now that Alex *would* ask her to marry him. Surely he loved her? They always got on so well together and they had lain on the bed. 'I think diamonds are cold,' she muttered. 'If I was getting a ring I'd want colour. Something warm with fire in it.'

'Nobody was asking you,' said Lois without rancour. 'I was talking to my sister.'

'What if I told you Alex had asked me to marry him and I'd turned him down?' said Phyl with a glittering smile. 'Would you stop midering me then?'

Lois's expression froze. 'You really mean he has and you don't want him? That's like that song – after you get what you want you don't want it. Have you told Dad?'

'I haven't told anybody. It would be humiliating for Alex so don't you go and tell anyone about it either, or else.'

'Of course I won't,' said Lois.

'Swear it on the Bible,' said Phyl, picking up Lizzie's black leatherbound gold-leaved Bible which lay on the chest of drawers.

'Don't you trust me?' said Lois, giving a tiny laugh.

'No. Now do it.'

Lois swore, watched incredulously by Lizzie.

After she had gone there was a silence. Then Phyl said, 'Well, say it!'

'Say what?' said Lizzie.

'That I'm a liar. After our conversation the other day in the shop, what I've just told our Lo could hardly be true.' Her eyes glinted. 'But she got right up my nose going on the way she did.'

'I'm sorry. Perhaps I'm the problem?' said Lizzie, squatting on the floor in front of the dolls' house, fingering the door knob and thinking how good it was of Alex to give the house to her. 'Have you told him you want me to live with the pair of you?'

Phyl laughed shortly. 'How can I when he hasn't even asked me to live with him? What's wrong with the man! I've a good mind, if he does ask me, to really turn him down!' She left the room, slamming the door behind her.

Lizzie did not believe her and felt so sorry for her that she decided she had to do something desperate. If she was going to keep the dolls' house, which she dearly wanted to – after all grown men played with train sets, so what did age have to do with toys – then she should thank Alex. She decided to go and see him after Christmas dinner.

Lizzie found Alex in the office and for a moment she knew he was pleased to see her, then he lowered his eyes to the books and papers on the desk in front of him and scribbled something, before saying gruffly, 'What are you doing here? I thought you'd have something better to do on Christmas Day.'

'I've come to thank you for the dolls' house. It's lovely. Thank you very much.' She slid her bottom on to the corner of his desk and gazed down at the books spread out there. 'Should you be working on Christmas Day? It's a bit ol' Scrooge-like, don't you think? Although you haven't got his millions, have you?'

'I doubt Scrooge had millions.' He glanced up at her. 'Now you've thanked me you can go and enjoy yourself.'

She nearly went then, but knew she might never work up the courage to speak again if she did. 'It's not friendly wanting to get rid of me,' she murmured, swinging her legs. 'Just when I was going to tell you the latest news, too.'

'And what's that?' He put down his pen.

'Lois has just got engaged. She's flashing her ring right under Phyl's nose and it's made Phyl say things she shouldn't.'

He stared at her, his expression unreadable. 'What's she said?'

She took a deep breath. 'Firstly – have you ever thought of asking Phyl to marry you?'

There was silence and she could hear her heart beating and when he looked at her his expression was grim. 'I bet bloody ten to one Phyl doesn't know you're here!'

'You shouldn't swear in front of me,' she said, trying to be bold though her legs had turned to jelly.

'You'd make a saint swear,' he said vehemently. 'Don't you think you should leave it to Phyl and me to decide when and if we should get married?'

Her head shot up. 'So you have thought about it? It's just that I wondered if you were delaying asking her because of me? Perhaps you think having me to live with you would be hell?'

'Too right! Girls of your age can be a real pain in the ar— household, so I've heard.' He gazed at her legs. 'And besides, I'm not so sure marrying Phyl is the best thing for her.'

'Oh, but it is,' said Lizzie quickly. 'She's crazy about you. She told me. She'd jump at the opportunity of marrying you. As it is she lied to Lois to salvage her pride. She said you'd asked and she'd refused.'

He said a word that Lizzie had never heard in family circles, only from some boys in the park, and for a moment she thought he was going to explode. She slid off the desk quickly. 'I thought you'd better know in case Lois doesn't keep her promise,' she said hastily.

'What b— promise?' he demanded.

'Not to tell anyone, of course,' said Lizzie, heading for the door. 'But I wouldn't trust Lois with a barge pole, Bible or no. So it's best you know.'

Alex groaned and dropped his head on the desk. There was a brief silence before he got to his feet. His expression was one of restrained anger. 'I could strangle Phyl! Lois! The lot of you! Wasn't there enough talk about me when Doreen was here? Now they'll believe it was true and that Phyl turned me down because of something that wasn't going on.'

'But she hasn't turned you down,' said Lizzie swiftly. 'You haven't even asked her. Perhaps you should? She'll say yes and everything'll be OK.'

The anger faded from his face. 'Is this what you really want, Lizzie? Me and Phyl married.'

She hesitated. 'I want Phyl happy. She's done so much for me.'

There was another silence and he suddenly looked tired. 'Get out, Lizzie. And in future keep your nose out of my business.'

She knew she had gone too far. 'I'm sorry. It's only that I've taken so much from her. I want you both happy.'

'So me being happy does come into this?'

'Of course! She loves you. Everybody's happy when they're loved.'

He smiled faintly. 'It depends on who's doing the loving. Now go, Lizzie.'

Still she hesitated. 'You will buy her a lovely ring, won't you? One better than Lois's.'

His smile faded and his expression hardened. 'I'll remove you forcibly if you don't scram right now!'

She went.

Lizzie thought Alex might come round that Christmas evening but the only visitor was Lois's fiancé. They planned on marrying two years next March. It seemed a long time to wait but apparently they had to save up for the big day and to set up home. That was if they were lucky enough to find a place of their own. Lizzie hoped that Alex might call round on Boxing Day morning but he did not and the afternoon passed with no sign of him. As they dressed for the party Lizzie wondered if she had ruined Phyl's chances but it was too late now to worry.

She could hear a car tooting below in the street and as
Josie had said she would ask Ron to fetch them, it was
probably him. Dot calling their names clinched the
matter.

"'Shall I compare thee to a summer's day?'" recited Joe.
"'Thou art more lovely – '"

'Oh, shut up!' said Josie, nudging her twin where he
stood in front of the stove in the biggest of the farm's
back kitchens. 'We don't want to be listening to soppy
Shakespeare. We're not at school.'

'You've got no romance in your soul,' said Joe with a
theatrical sigh, holding the well-worn leather-bound book
against his chest.

'It's a good job,' she said indignantly. 'One of us has
to be practical! I've decided I'm going to be a nurse when
I grow up. Now this is a party and just because the grown-
ups are all talking and drinking in the best kitchen, it
doesn't mean to say we three have to listen to you spouting
on. Isn't that true, you lot?'

'Yes, Miss Bossy Boots,' said Billy, his hand reaching
for another mince pie from the plate on the scrubbed
kitchen table.

'I'd like to be in there,' said Lizzie positively. 'I'd love
to see if anything's happening.' She exchanged a meaning-
ful glance with Josie.

'I thought Phyl looked lovely,' said her friend. 'Is that
wave in her hair natural?'

'Naw,' said Billy. 'She has these big metal claw-type
curler things that she uses.'

'You shouldn't be giving a woman's beauty secrets away,' said Joe severely. 'Until marriage an aura of mystery should surround a woman.'

'Then comes the big shock on the wedding night,' said Billy, who was sailing on the evening tide tomorrow, 'when they take out their false teeth, remove the wig and wipe off the make-up.'

'Don't exaggerate,' said Lizzie, accepting another glass of lemonade from Josie. 'Besides, beauty is only skin deep.'

'Yes. It's what you're like inside that matters. Looks aren't everything.' Josie smoothed down the skirts of her new Princess-line dress and glanced at her reflection in the darkened window.

Lizzie smiled. 'I vote we go and join them. Isn't there a gramophone in there? We could put on some records and get them dancing.'

'I've noticed that grown-ups need at least a couple of drinks before they'll let themselves go,' said Joe.

'But they must be thinking of dancing,' said Billy. 'Because they've cleared a space in the middle of the floor. Let's go and show them how.'

'How?' said Josie. 'I can't dance.'

That seemed to settle the matter because Billy seized her hand and dragged her out of the room. Lizzie and Joe followed more sedately.

Lizzie did not know whether to be disappointed or not to find Phyl talking, not to the pleasant but slightly hard of hearing Ron, but to dark-haired Lily who was heavily pregnant and her priestly husband, Matt. He had salt and pepper hair, a tanned skin, and was forty if he was a day. Phyl called Lizzie over so she had no option but to go.

'Lizzie, Mr Gibson and his wife are going to a parish not far from Camden Town in the spring,' she said without any preamble. 'You know Primrose Hill, don't you? Isn't it the next stop up the line on the tube?'

'The station's Chalk Farm,' said Lizzie. 'It sounds very country but it's not. Although it's not too far from Regent's Park, and of course there's the Hill.'

A smile broke out over Lily's face. 'That's the kind of information I wanted, love. Matt had other things on his mind when he went down to talk to the churchwardens and the PCC. I want some grass where I can take Paul and the new baby when it comes.' There was a pause before she added, 'Your stepmother was saying you were good with children, Lizzie.'

'Did she?' She flashed a startled glance at Phyl who raised her eyebrows in that speaking way of hers. 'I haven't had much experience but I like young children, yes. Is there any reason why you mention it?'

'No overwhelming reason,' said Lily cheerfully. 'It's just that Matt thinks I should have a nanny when I get to London. So if you ever decide to go back to London, come and see us. He's of the opinion I'll find a big vicarage, a strange parish and another child too much at my age.'

'How old are you?' said Lizzie curiously.

Phyl nudged her in the ribs. 'You don't ask women their ages!'

'I don't mind,' said Lily, a good-humoured expression lighting her face. 'I'm thirty-six.'

'Mummy was thirty-eight when she had me and she was OK.'

The priest leaned forward. 'Your stepmother told us *she* went to London to get her name up in lights. Have you ever seen her on stage, Lizzie?'

His question surprised her. 'No.'

'Would you like to?'

She smiled. 'I haven't really thought about it.'

'Think about it now. Could Phyl's singing give pleasure to thousands?'

Lizzie's smile grew. 'She can sing but she gets told to shut up at home.'

'A prophet in his own country,' he said softly.

'You're referring to that bit in the Bible, meaning nobody's appreciated by people who've always known them. It's true.' Lizzie's voice was grave.

He grinned. 'How about her being an actress?'

Lizzie gave Phyl a quizzical look, remembering how it had been after her father had killed himself. 'I've seen her putting on an act,' she said firmly. 'She was very convincing.'

'There you are then, Phyl,' said Lily, squeezing her arm. 'If you have a talent you shouldn't waste it. You must definitely join the amateur dramatics and slay the audiences dead!'

'Perhaps I'll do just that,' said Phyl, her eyes bright. 'Maybe I'll go even further than the amateur dramatics.'

'Well, if you get to London, let us know,' said Lily, her eyes twinkling. 'I'd like to say to people, "I knew her before she was rich and famous".'

'I'd like to see the day!' said Phyl, responding to her smile before changing the subject, and asking Lizzie what was that peculiar dance Billy was doing.

It was not until they were getting into bed at what felt like the middle of the night that Phyl said, 'What did you make of that conversation with the dishy vicar and his wife?'

A droopy-eyed Lizzie replied in sleepy tones, 'Dishy? He has a gorgeous voice. I'll give you that.'

Phyl hunched up her knees and rested her chin on them. 'It was marvellous how they homed in on what really interested us both. I like the stage and you like kids.'

'You told them we did.'

'Yes. But I told them other things too.'

There was a silence and Lizzie closed her eyes.

'I'll definitely go along to that group now,' murmured Phyl.

'The amateur dramatics?' Lizzie yawned.

'Yes. Who knows where it might lead?'

Immediately Lizzie had a vision of Phyl dancing and singing her heart out on stage. She blinked and sat up abruptly. 'What about Alex?'

'What about him?'

'What if he asked you to marry him?'

Phyl stared at her through the darkness. 'He won't,' she said sadly. 'And Ronnie was a no go for me. You know who did make an impression on him, though? Our Dot! He didn't stop asking me about her every time we danced.' She slid down in the bed and rolled on to her side.

Lizzie gazed at her outline beneath the covers and hoped against hope that Alex would ask her to marry him. Yet as she drifted to sleep, a vision of her stepmother on stage went with her.

Lizzie was pleased when Alex came into the shop the next Saturday morning. He approached slowly, touching certain wares, picking up others and giving them a scrutiny. He stopped in front of the treadle sewing maching which had come in only yesterday and which Phyl was giving a dust. 'I remember my grandma had one of these,' he murmured, placing his foot on the treadle.

'I didn't know you'd had a grandma,' she said.

'She died when I was only a nipper. She lived in Low Wood Street up off Low Hill and was a dressmaker. I never knew my grandpa because he died at sea before I was born.' He caressed the smooth black and gold metal of the sewing machine. 'I used to love to escape up there with that view you get over the city as far as the Liver birds.'

'Was your gran your mother's mother?'

'Yes.' He hesitated. 'D'you remember my mother?'

'She must have been around but I've no recollection of her.'

'I thought she was lovely because she could get people laughing over the daftest things.' He picked up a brass door handle and turned it between his hands before placing it down carefully. 'Did you enjoy your party?'

'It was fine,' she said brightly. 'Wild. I met a nice bloke. Ron. You know him I believe. Delivers milk. He was interesting. What about you? Did you get all your work done?'

'I had to work, Phyl. I'm still a long way from being rich.'

She met his glance. 'That Doreen didn't help. Do you ever miss her?'

'Like I'd miss moths in the rags,' he drawled. 'I miss Syd, though. He livened the place up.' He hesitated. 'D'you ever think about having kids?'

'Not much. Being the eldest in a family the size of ours, you've no illusions about the work involved.'

'I like kids.' Alex dug his hands into his pockets. 'You know I haven't much money, Phyl,' he said carefully.

'I know that!'

'It'll be some time before I have any worth having. I need to buy a lorry to keep up with the times, and I'm thinking of going into the car scrap and parts business. That'll bring more in eventually. I can't think of getting married for a while.'

Lizzie stretched her ears, wondering if they had forgotten she was there.

'Why are you telling me all this?' said Phyl.

'I thought you might like to get engaged?'

There was a long silence during which Lizzie willed Phyl to accept. An engagement! That was perfect! There would be no rushing into marriage. She could have a job by the time they tied the knot so would not have to be dependent on them.

'I don't mind,' murmured Phyl, an odd note in her voice.

'Then you'll wear this ring?' He produced a screwed up piece of purple tissue from a pocket. 'It was Grandma's so it's a genuine antique.' He loosened the paper to reveal a large turquoise stone surrounded by tiny diamonds. 'If it's too big we can get it made smaller.'

'It's unusual,' said Phyl, and held out her hand.

Lizzie almost clapped as Alex pushed the ring with some force past Phyl's knuckle. She held her hand up to the light and watched the gems sparkle. 'It is pretty. I think your gran must have had smaller hands than me, though.' She smiled up at him. 'I'll cherish this.' She kissed him.

Lizzie lowered her eyes and a moment later heard Alex say, 'How d'you think your dad will take the news?'

'He could be expecting it after the way I've stuck up for you.' Phyl's voice was comforting. 'Although I thought you'd have been more concerned about how Lizzie will feel. Lizzie?'

'Yes,' she said, trying to sound as if her thoughts had been somewhere and she hadn't heard a thing. 'Did you want something?'

'Alex has asked me to marry him,' said Phyl, holding out her left hand. 'Isn't this ring lovely?'

'Lovely,' agreed Lizzie. 'Congratulations.' She beamed at them.

Alex's smile mocked her. 'You won't mind waiting for the wedding?'

'Of course not.' She dared to meet his eyes. 'I'll be off Phyl's hands by then.'

'Hardly,' she said. 'Alex, you don't mind her living with us, do you?'

'I think we're best waiting and seeing,' he murmured. 'I think Lizzie might have plans of her own by then. Now hadn't you better break the news to your dad and see what he has to say? You can take the rest of the day off. There's not going to be many customers so soon after Christmas.'

So they went home but Alex did not go in with them. 'I don't want to give your dad too many shocks at once,' he said, and kissed Phyl before leaving them.

To Lizzie's relief Sam did not appear put out by the news of his favourite daughter's engagement. 'At least he's got his head screwed on right. If he'd rushed you into marriage I wouldn't have liked it. I'm still not convinced it was all innocent about that woman.'

'Perhaps he likes widows,' said Lois, *sotto voce,* to Dot, who was sitting next to Lizzie on the couch. 'More experienced.' Aloud she said to Phyl, 'What made you change your mind about marrying him? Seeing my ring?'

'Of course not,' she said, looking amused. 'Alex was so persistent, I realised it must be real love.'

'Will we be having a party?' asked Mary.

'Parties cost money and we've just had Christmas,' said Phyl. 'You'll have to wait until the wedding but we're not rushing into that either.'

'What about Lizzie?' said her mother. 'What's she doing? Come on, girl, tell us what you think of our Phyl getting married? I suppose you'll be happy, living round there, seeing that horse when you want?'

They all stared at her and she felt an unaccustomed flash of annoyance. The interest the family took in what everyone living in the house did was something she sometimes had difficulty in accepting. She did not want to tell them her thoughts right now. They were her own. Besides how could she say she was still feeling amazed that Alex had done what she asked? 'I probably won't live with them,' she said eventually. 'Next year I'll be leaving school and getting a job.'

'Aye, lass, but you won't be earning enough to support yourself completely,' said Sam. 'Were you thinking of maybe staying on with us until yer a bit older?'

Lizzie had not considered it. She had become fond of most of them but there were times when she thought it would be good to get away from them. Even so he had a point. 'I suppose if you still wanted me I could stay on and pay my way for a while,' she said hesitantly.

'That would be a help,' said Maisie, smiling. 'We'll be two down by then, probably.'

'That settles it,' said Dot happily. 'Mam'll be glad of your money, Lizzie. And I don't mind sharing with you if you want to come down from that attic.'

Phyl banged her fist on the table, startling them all. 'Do you mind? I'll have you all know that it's me who's responsible for Lizzie until she's twenty-one! It's what *I* say that goes.'

'Gosh, our Phyl's pulling rank,' said Trev, looking gleeful as he leaned on the table over a jigsaw. 'You take her with you. It'll be another one less.'

'Enough,' said Sam. 'What are you thinking of, luv? It's better for newly-weds to be on their own.'

Phyl said, 'I say – let's wait and see. It's not going to happen today or tomorrow. Probably not for a year or two, and who knows? By then Alex might have that mansion, hey, Lizzie?'

'A mansion! That'll be the day,' murmured Lois, picking up the newspaper.

'It just might be,' said Phyl, and smiled at Lizzie. 'People do sometimes get exactly what they want.'

Lizzie wasn't so sure. Yet what was she worried about? As Phyl said, nothing was going to happen for ages.

Chapter Ten

It was March, 1951, and Lois's big day. Lizzie had never been involved in a wedding before and she found the ongoing bustle and edge-of-panic voices that filled the Eccles household from dawn onwards exciting. Fortunately Lois's cowboy-mad boyfriend had already done his National Service so the war that had broken out in Korea had not affected the wedding plans. There were to be three bridesmaids and a matron of honour. Dot, Mary and a sister of the bridegroom were dressed in pink, and according to Trev half an hour ago, had looked like three puffs of candyfloss. Phyl was the matron of honour, and was pacing the attic, dressed in a primrose organdie frock, rehearsing her part in the play the amateur dramatics group was putting on in a week's time. Billy had not managed to wangle leave so he was missing and the erstwhile mentioned Trev had stormed out of the house half an hour ago, insisting he wasn't going to wear no cissy bow tie.

Lizzie was clad in a waffle cotton dress in lilac with an open shirt-like collar and tiny pearl buttons which fastened in the front from the waist up. The skirt was flared and she had bought a pair of high-heeled white kid shoes and poplin gloves from the money she had managed to save from her job in an insurance office in North John Street, although she wasn't happy there and was on the look out for something else. Her long black hair was piled on top of her head with a whole card of hair grips struggling to keep it there. She had borrowed Phyl's Max Factor panstick and bought a Rimmel lipstick in bright red, and applied both with care. She felt extremely sophisticated and hoped she looked much older than her eighteen years.

She had been given the task of showing interested neighbours and wedding guests the presents displayed in Nan Eccles's parlour. After four years of living with the family, those round about accepted her as one of them although there were still times when Liverpudlian words and customs puzzled her, making her realise afresh that she was not one born and bred. For the moment, though, she felt as if she was one of them and was enjoying herself. But she did have a problem. The fuss generated by the wedding had confused Nan Eccles who was convinced that it was her wedding all the excitement was about.

Earlier Maisie had managed to persuade Nan out of her old coat and into a powder blue tweed suit, but she had stubbornly refused to wear the new court shoes bought for her, saying they hurt her bunions, so her feet were clad in her old down-at-heel boots. Once Maisie was out of the way the old lady produced from a drawer a length of lace curtaining which she draped over her head, and having found the wedding flowers in a box which had been delivered earlier and placed for safe keeping under her table, began to parade with Lois's bouquet of

carnations and gypsy grass up and down the lobby, chant-
ing, 'Here comes the bride, sixty inches wide!'

It was a struggle not to laugh but Lizzie had to try and
persuade her to give up the flowers. The old woman refused
to part with them and Lizzie did not want to tussle with
her in case the bouquet was damaged.

A bang on the knocker summoned Lizzie to the front
door and she opened it with her eyes brimming with
laughter.

'You look happy,' said Alex, removing his hands from
his pockets and smoothing down his newly washed dark
hair.

'It's Nan Eccles,' she said, trying not to stare though
he was looking devastating in a charcoal grey suit. What
was it about seeing a suit on him that gave her so much
pleasure? Lately she had found herself looking at him
often and enjoying the looking, and when he spoke to
her about the most ordinary things, she discovered herself
really listening to his voice. She liked the way it deepened if he felt strongly about something and when he
was amused she loved the thread of laughter that ran
through it.

She closed the door behind him and said unevenly,
'She thinks she's the bride. What should I do? Aunt Maisie
is getting ready upstairs and so is Uncle Sam.'

Alex slowly removed his gaze from Lizzie and looked
at the old woman. His smile deepened. 'I take it Lois
doesn't know about this?'

'No. She's still closeted with her handmaidens.'

'Pardon?' His eyes glinted with wry humour.

Lizzie blushed. 'I mean, she's still upstairs with the bridesmaids. Phyl's not there, though. She's in the attic learning her lines. D'you want me to fetch her?'

'Soon. First, what are we going to do about Nan Eccles? Lois is bound to kick up a fuss if she sees her.'

'I've tried to persuade her to give up the bouquet but she refuses.'

'Who can blame her? She's reliving her own big day.' Alex looked thoughtful. 'What about some other flowers? We could do a swop.'

'There's only a few daffs in the backyard.'

'What about a florist's? There's one on the corner of Edensor Terrace.' He opened the door. 'Come on. I'll run you there.'

She hesitated. 'Are you sure you wouldn't like me to fetch Phyl?'

'Why?' he said with a slight edge to his voice. 'If she's practising her part she'll only use me for a sounding board and I'd rather she didn't.'

She knew what he meant and hesitated no longer. Until the final curtain dropped there would be no getting any sense about anything else but the play from Phyl. Since joining the group she had swiftly progressed from painting scenery, prompting and walk-on roles to being their leading lady.

Lizzie slid into the front seat of the secondhand Austin, which was cosy in comparison with the cab of the lorry Alex had bought six months ago and which had caused them temporarily to fall out. The lorry had made Blackie redundant and the horse had seemed destined for the knacker's yard. Lizzie had called Alex heartless and he had got really angry, shouting at her in an exasperated voice that he couldn't afford to have a horse eating him out of pocket. He had a business to run! She saw his point eventually but still had not been able to bear the thought of Blackie becoming cat's meat.

'I went to see Josie at the farm last Sunday,' she murmured. 'Blackie's the perfect pet for her two nephews.'

He glanced at her sidelong. 'Proud of yourself, aren't you?'

She could not prevent a smile. 'It was you who gave him to them.'

'Your suggestion. One of your cleverer ones,' he murmured dryly, as he turned a corner.

She wondered what he meant by 'one of', but did not like asking. She looked out of the side window and saw a lorry going in the opposite direction with a boy hanging on to its rear end. 'Idiot!' she muttered, then realised the boy was Trev. 'Oh, heck!'

'What's up?'

'Oh, hell!' The lorry had stopped suddenly, causing Trev to swing into it and bang his face before losing his grip and falling to the ground. The lorry started up again and roared away.

'Turn round! It's Trev!' yelled Lizzie, clutching the seat. 'He's fallen off that lorry!'

Alex did not argue.

She felt all of a dither, worried about what Maisie would say and feel. The car came to a halt. Trev had risen to his feet and was stumbling along the pavement with his hand to his mouth. She slid out of the car and grabbed his arm. 'You fool, Trev! Your mam'll have you, doing such a daft thing! Now get into the car.'

He looked at her wordlessly and did as he was told without arguing which surprised her. She popped her head into the back of the car to have a closer look at him. 'You're bleeding!' she gasped, feeling dizzy. 'What have you done to yourself?' She flopped on to the seat next to him.

'I've thith me thonge.'

'You've what?' asked Alex, glancing over his shoulder.

'I've thith me thonge. I thanged me mouth and –' He stopped and held his head forward as a gush of blood trickled through the fingers held against his mouth.

'Oh Lord,' groaned Lizzie and put her head between her knees.

'Are you OK?' said Alex in a worried voice, fishing a clean white handkerchief out of his breast pocket and handing it to Trev.

'I'll be all right if I keep my eyes shut,' she gasped.

'I've thith me thonge,' repeated Trev, shaking her shoulder with his free hand. 'Youth hath thu tath me the hothpithal. Don leth Mam see me.'

Alex leaned over the back of the seat and told Trev to open his mouth and hold back his head. 'Than't.' He opened his mouth slightly and more blood came out.

Alex frowned. 'It's worse than I thought. He's right, he'll have to get it looked at.'

Lizzie lifted her head, only to lower it rapidly again. 'The wedding! What are we going to do?' she said weakly.

'We'll go back to the house and you can go in and tell them what's happened. I'll take Trev to hospital.'

Trev pulled on Lizzie's sleeve. 'I vant thu tha cum.'

She could not believe it. 'Me! You want me?' He nodded, looking vulnerable and younger than his twelve years.

She did not know what to do. 'Alex?'

'You'd best come. Just nip into the house and get someone to tell his mam and dad after we've gone. Say there's nothing to panic about. It's just a precaution.'

Lizzie did just that and then felt faint as soon as she got back into the car and saw the blood on Alex's handkerchief.

He shook his head. 'Are you always like this at the sight of blood?'

'I'll be OK,' she said faintly, leaning back next to Trev. 'Just go.'

Alex went in the direction of Alder Hey Children's Hospital in West Derby.

'Are you the father?' said the doctor, looking over his spectacles at Alex after Trev had been whisked away to a ward.

Alex said, 'I know the war aged people but –'

'He's too young,' said Lizzie indignantly.

'Sorry,' said the doctor, reddening. 'I meant, you look too young to be the father. He does have one, does he? We'll have to give him an anaesthetic and stitch the tongue back on. It's hanging by a thread. We do need a parent or guardian to sign.'

'Sure! We'll get one.' Alex lifted a hand and, taking hold of Lizzie's arm, walked her out.

'Lois isn't going to be pleased,' she said as they got into the car. She rested her head against the back of the seat, still feeling as if the blood had been drained from her.

Alex moved his tongue inside his cheek. 'Hard luck, Lois. How was Nan Eccles, by the way? Did you see her or Phyl?'

'I saw Dot. She was handling Nan.' She hesitated. 'Phyl was singing somewhere, I didn't like to disturb her.'

Alex started the car and neither of them spoke for a while. He looked stern and Lizzie was wondering if Phyl had told him about her appearing in the amateur gala revue for the Festival of Britain celebrations in the summer.

'Has she mentioned anything to you about getting married?' he said suddenly.

The question startled her. 'You mean Phyl?'

He glanced at her and his eyes were quizzical. 'Who else, luv?'

'You could have meant Dot. She's very friendly with Ronnie, Josie's brother-in-law.'

He smiled grimly. 'Very friendly. That says a lot. She'll probably be the next.'

She stared at him and felt a moment's helplessness. 'Alex, perhaps after August Phyl will be different?'

'You mean after the gala,' he said.

'So she has told you? That's a relief.'

'Did you think she mightn't?'

'I wasn't sure. She's so self-absorbed at the moment. She didn't even listen when I told her I hated where I'm working.'

'Why d'you hate it?'

'Insurance doesn't interest me.'

'I can't sack Mrs Dwyer,' he said firmly. 'She's no husband and has a son at school.'

'I wasn't asking you to give me a job!' She was pleased that he had thought of it, though.

He smiled faintly. 'Why don't you try a shipping office?'

She thought about it and liked the idea. She would write to Elder Dempster whom Billy worked for.

When they reached the Co-op Hall where the reception was nearing its conclusion, they were seized immediately by Trev's two worried parents and three of his sisters. 'I've hardly been able to eat a thing,' said Maisie. 'How is he? Where is he? Why did you rush off? You should have spoken to me and I'd have gone. I want to be with me son.' Her plump face was anxious.

'We know that,' said Lizzie soothingly. 'But it wasn't life or death and Lois would have hated you not being there. Did everything go all right?'

'Never mind that,' said Sam, squeezing her shoulder. 'How is he, girl?'

Alex told them and offered to run them there.

'That's good of you,' said Sam, looking gratified.

'I'll come as well,' said Phyl, slipping a hand through Alex's arm. 'Although you look like you need a drink, Alex luv.'

'I can wait.' He looked at Lizzie. 'Give that girl something. Did you know she goes faint at the sight of blood?'

'No!' Phyl raised her eyebrows.

Lizzie pulled a face, and putting her arm through Mary's walked away. She felt she could not bear it if Phyl started showing concern, and wished Billy was around to take her mind off Alex.

'He's an idiot is our Trev,' said Mary vehemently. 'He needs a hiding.'

'He wanted me with him. I couldn't believe it,' said Lizzie. 'He was scared of what your mam would say.'

'She'll be as sweet as apple pie until he's better. Then he'll cop it and probably won't be allowed out for a week.'

'I wouldn't let him out for a month!'

'Keeping him in for a month would drive her mad.' Mary smiled suddenly. 'Mam knows her limitations. Anyway, are you sure he's going to be OK?'

'I'm sure.' Lizzie looked about the hall. Dessert plates were being cleared away. She groaned. 'I'm starving. I suppose there's no food for me?'

'Of course there is. Mam made them put it aside.' Mary pulled on her arm. 'Come on, it'll be in the kitchen. I'll tell Aunt Kate that Mam said you could have a glass of sherry to settle your nerves. By the time you've drunk that and eaten your grub the band'll be here. Then the twins should be arriving for the evening do.'

The timing was almost as Mary said but Lizzie was discovering that she could not work up any excitement for the party. She kept watching the door for Alex's and Phyl's return. By the time they arrived the dance floor was crowded with fox trotting couples. Immediately Lizzie left the others and made her way across the floor to be joined by Dot, Ron and the bride.

'I knew something else would happen to spoil my day,' said Lois, not for the first time. 'D'you know the trouble I had getting my bouquet off Nan? And look at her now, dancing with Pete's grandad and making a show of herself.'

'Trev didn't do it on purpose,' said Phyl.

'Of course he did! You don't skip lorries by accident.'

'He was running away,' said Alex. 'Your dad had belted him for giving cheek.'

'He was an idiot,' said Lizzie in a mild voice. 'How far did he think he'd get with no money? I tried the same thing once.'

'When?' said Phyl, looking surprised.

'Does it matter?' said Alex. 'Trev wasn't thinking. Now can we forget him? He's OK and I'm starving.'

'I'll get you something,' said Phyl, smiling, and left him.

Lois drifted away and Dot and Ronnie joined the dancers on the floor. Alex looked at Lizzie. 'Are you OK now?'

'Fine.'

'Perhaps you'd like to dance then? We might as well do something as just stand here.'

She decided it would be rude to say no and went into his arms. She fitted comfortably, her head just beneath his chin. The band played a waltz, the dance once forbidden by the lady watchers of morals. She closed her eyes, thinking of *Vanity Fair* and Lady Richmond's ball before the Battle of Waterloo. The men were dressed in regimental colours and the ladies in ball gowns of pink, lilac and palest blue.

Alex swung her on to the floor and she let herself drift. How would she feel if Alex was really a soldier and going off to fight in one of the bloodiest and costliest battles in Europe before the First World War? She would not want to let him go. He had become important to her. She valued his company, his smile, even his common sense. He hadn't flipped when she had told him about Trev or when he discovered she went limp at the sight of blood. He was, as she'd seen when Thelma's house had nearly burnt down, utterly dependable. They waltzed on.

'Excuse me!' Phyl's voice sounded impatient.

Lizzie opened her eyes to see her stepmother standing in the middle of the floor with a plate in one hand and a glass of beer in the other. 'Sorry,' said Lizzie. She glanced up at Alex and had a feeling he too had been somewhere else besides the dance floor.

'Thanks, Elizabeth,' he said.

'Thank you,' she murmured, and removed herself from Phyl's presence as quickly as possible.

'Alex wanted me to run away with him tonight,' said Phyl, as she and Lizzie undressed for bed that night.

Lizzie froze. 'But you didn't?'

'Of course not, silly. It was so unlike him that I asked if he'd gone off his rocker. I mean, after our Trev how would Mam and Dad have felt? Besides, I told him I wanted the full works after having such a hole in the corner affair the last time.'

'So what did he say to that?'

'He said to forget it. That I was right and it'd be best to wait like we planned.'

'And when will that be?'

'Probably this time next year.' She yawned and dived beneath the covers.

'I'll be nineteen,' murmured Lizzie. 'Hopefully I'll be earning more money. Maybe I'll even go south.' It would be better to do that than stay watching Phyl be happy with Alex.

Phyl's head made a reappearance. 'South? I thought you felt at home here?'

'I do. But – forget it.' Lizzie shrugged. 'How was the ceremony?'

'For better, for worse, 'til death do them part. It was hard to concentrate knowing you and Alex were off to hospital with our Trev. What was all that he said about you fainting at the sight of blood? How inconvenient.'

'Very,' said Lizzie, not prepared to start explaining that she didn't normally faint, only went all queer. She burrowed down the bed, and when Phyl murmured that Lois's wedding day had turned out very differently to how they had expected, Lizzie said that she couldn't agree more, knowing she would dream about dancing with Alex for days to come.

Chapter Eleven

Lizzie walked past the bomb site in Ranelagh Street, pretending to be unaware of the catcalls from a couple of labourers working on the rebuilding of Lewis's departmental store. A week or so ago the site would have been full of people and the shouts of barrow boys would have vied with the noise of buskers and people on soapboxes telling everyone that either THE END IS NIGH or they must look to the future and get the present government out. Then the police had decided that the site was becoming dangerous due to the rebuilding so it had been closed to the public.

Lizzie had been for an interview at Booth and Co. and would be starting work at the King's Dock next week. She felt excited about the prospect. The office building looked out over the Mersey and she felt certain she would find it much more interesting there than at the insurance company. It was Alex she had to thank for the job because it was he who had suggested to Phyl that she try Booth's after Elder Dempster's and a couple of other companies had not had any vacancies. Apparently old man Payne had known one of the older Booths. Now she was off to do Alex a favour by spending the rest of the day in the shop whilst Phyl was in Southport.

Lizzie was walking a roundabout way to get there due to public transport being in a bit of a muddle as it was 12th July when the lodges of the Orange Order paraded. The whole family except for Billy, Nan and Sam, had left the house well before eight o'clock to march to the sound of flute, squeeze box and drum to Exchange Station to take one of the special trains to the seaside resort further up the coast towards Blackpool. In charge of all sixty lodges in this remembrance of William of Orange having beaten the forces of the deposed James II of England over two hundred and fifty years ago, was Brother W.H. Wilkes, Provincial Grand Master.

It still seemed strange to Lizzie that the Battle of the Boyne in Ireland should be remembered in this way. Her parents had never rejoiced in their Protestantism or Britishness, or been so fiercely loyal to King and country in the way the Eccles were. Even one of the Orangemen's marching songs referred to them being 'Sons of the Sea and British Boys', and Maisie had informed her last night that today a message would be sent to the King, whose health was causing anxiety, assuring him of their best wishes and loyalty. She glanced up at the overcast sky and prayed the rain would hold off for the day and quickened her pace.

She came to Abercrombie Square where paint was peeling from houses that once had been the joy of rich merchants. Then she saw something which took her mind completely off the Eccleses. A couple of buses had crashed into each other and were blocking the road ahead. Lizzie ran forward to find people milling about. Some were

obviously dazed and several were stretched out on the
ground. A couple of men drew heavily on cigarettes as
they leaned against a garden wall, looking grey-faced. The
traffic had come to a virtual standstill and glass crunched
beneath Lizzie's feet as she looked about her. Then to her
astonishment she saw Alex bending over someone and
without further thought went over to him. He glanced up,
she glanced down, saw blood on the woman's hair and
neck, felt the colour drain from her face and keeled over.

'That was a stupid thing to do,' chided Alex.

Lizzie's eyelids fluttered open as she felt a breeze on
her face and saw that he was fanning her with a newspaper.
She tried to sit up but he pushed her down again. 'Give
yourself a few minutes.'

'I'm OK now.' She brushed the newspaper aside and
realised she was lying on the long seat of his dilapidated
lorry. She avoided looking at him, realising that he must
have carried her there and wishing she had been aware of
it. Since Phyl had told her that Alex had asked her to run
away with him the night of Lois's wedding, she had been
trying to rid herself of the romantic dreams she had of
him but it had not worked. He intruded into her thoughts
every unguarded moment. She only hoped he was unaware
of how she felt, but – she squashed the thought. 'I've been
for my interview,' she said brightly.

'How did it go?'

'I got the job, thanks.' This time Lizzie managed to sit
upright and look about her. She was in Grove Street not
far from St Stephen's church and near the site of the

accident where a couple of ambulances were now parked. 'How's that woman? Was anyone killed?'

'She's OK. Just cuts. I don't think anyone's dead.'

'Good.' There was silence. 'I was on my way to the shop.'

'I'll give you a lift. It's good of you to help out.'

'I owe Phyl,' she said quietly. 'And I owe you for suggesting the job.'

'I was glad to help. I hope you'll be happy there.' His voice was flat as he started the engine.

'I'm sure I will be,' she said, and enthusiasm livened her voice as she began to tell him what she had already learnt about the company. 'Its trading history goes way back into early Victorian times. They imported skins for the leather trade, mainly from South America but also China and India as well. More recently they've started bringing in kangaroo skins from Australia. They have a leather factory down Berkshire way, making gloves and things, and a London office, and up here the company has branched out into the construction business.' She glanced at him. 'They had to find another way of making money because they lost ships and men to the U-boats during the war.'

'Like many another line sailing from Liverpool,' he murmured.

'Yes. I'm sure you're right.'

'I know I'm right.' His gaze flicked over her face. 'Although unlike Billy I never made a sailor. He enjoys the life, so I believe.'

'I'm sure he does. Although he doesn't really speak about it much.'

'You'd have other more interesting things to talk about, I suppose? Phyl says you and Billy are very fond of each other.'

She flushed. 'I like him, yes. What about Phyl?' she said, wanting to change the subject.

'What about Phyl?' His tone was non-committal.

'What about her and this revue for the Festival of Britain?' she persisted. 'Are you going to see her in it?'

'No.' His fingers tightened on the steering wheel. 'Unlike the last three things she's been in, she doesn't want me there.'

'She doesn't want the family either.' Lizzie tried to conceal her disappointment. 'She was great in the last one. I could hardly believe it was her! She really was the person she was playing. Couldn't you insist on going, Alex? After all, you are her fiancé.'

He pulled a comical face. 'Insist with Phyl? You must be joking! If I tried that at the moment I'd get a blast of artistic temperament. Haven't you had a dose?'

She grinned. 'It's not quite so bad as last year. Then we had her wandering round the house muttering to herself, like Lady Macbeth after the murder. She had pages of script and suddenly she'd pounce on one of us and demand we listen. Sometimes we had to play the other parts, and I was hopeless because I'd get the giggles.' She sighed. 'This revue's a lot of singing and dancing and sketches and would be fun to see. I think it's mean of her not wanting us there.'

'She must have her reasons,' he said tersely. 'Although she hasn't told me them. I suppose when she's good and

ready she just might.' He changed the subject and began
to talk about the preparations for the Festival in Liverpool,
and the conversation was kept on that impersonal level
until he dropped her off at the shop.

As preparations for the Festival of Britain hotted up,
the naval aircraft carrier HMS *Indomitable* arrived at
Gladstone Graving Dock, soon to be joined by the destroy-
ers *Battleaxe* and *Scorpion*. Almost overnight it felt as if
the years of austerity were over and a brave new future
for Liverpool lay ahead. The city was crammed with sailors
and Sam issued warnings to Lizzie and Mary to watch out
for themselves and not trust anything a royal navy rating
said. They took his advice with a pinch of salt and went
with the twins and Trev, who had quietened down since
he'd almost bitten his tongue off, to watch a band of the
Royal Marines beating the Retreat on St George's Plateau.

Patriotism was aflame inside Lizzie as she wandered
round the exhibition inside St George's Hall commemorat-
ing Queen Victoria's visit to the last festival in 1851. 'That
was before the American Civil War but after the Irish
potato famine when masses of the Irish, who didn't have
the price of a ticket to America, came to Liverpool, knowing they would get fed,' said Joe, who was an avid reader
and took an interest in all sorts of things. 'Liverpool was
doing well. Cotton was king and so was sail. Imagine the
alterations needed to ships once steam came in.'

'No wonder they needed more shipyards,' said Lizzie.

'And docks. Steam ships were bigger. They had to have
space to carry coal as well as cargo. Steam caused tre-
mendous changes in shipping.'

She was fascinated and felt some of that pride and love for Liverpool's mucky, overcrowded and often ugly streets despite the transformation wrought with flags and flowers of red, white and blue. She read with interest the pages of the *Liverpool Echo* which told of the numerous exhibitions, concerts and shows which were to take place during the three weeks of the Festival. They boasted artistes of the calibre of Sir Malcolm Sargent and Arthur Askey, Ann Ziegler and Webster Booth.

Despite their high repute Lizzie would have preferred to see Phyl in the amateur gala. As that was ruled out she was looking forward to the Pageant of Shipping and Firework Display which was to take place, naturally on and above the Mersey. She had been surprised when Phyl had said that she wanted Lizzie to go with her and Alex to the first of the firework displays. 'It's about time the three of us started doing things as a family,' she had said.

'I'm grown up now. You don't have to worry about me.' Lizzie had hastily put away the dolls' house in which she and Mary had been rearranging the furniture. 'I'm sure Alex would rather have you to himself.'

Phyl had pulled a face at her in the mirror. 'I doubt it. He's getting annoyed because I'm putting so much of myself into this revue but one has to rehearse and rehearse if one wants to go places in this business.'

'Then you should take this chance to be alone,' insisted Lizzie. 'Or don't you want to be alone with him?' she added hopefully.

'Of course I do!' Phyl pouted and applied lipstick. 'But it's as I say, I think it'll be easier with you there. Besides it's a chance for us to do things together. If you say no, you'll have me thinking you don't like my company any more. That I'm getting too old and decrepit for an eighteen year old.'

'Don't be daft! You make yourself sound ninety.'

'I'm twenty-eight.' Phyl's expression was unexpectedly serious. 'The war took my youth away.' She sighed, then smiled. 'You enjoy yours. Stop worrying and come with us. I'd like your company. I feel like I haven't talked to you properly for ages despite us sharing a bed.'

Lizzie almost said, And you know why! Because you're stage struck! But instead she had succumbed to the charm in Phyl's smile and agreed to go with her and Alex.

The evening of the firework display came round quicker than Lizzie could believe and she rushed home from work to be ready on time, only to be kept waiting because there was no sign of Phyl. As the minutes ticked by Lizzie felt tension rising inside her. After all the fuss her stepmother had made why wasn't she here? If she was much later they'd have trouble finding a good 'speck' and would miss the parade of the little ships.

When she heard a knock on the door she rushed out. It was not her stepmother but Alex who looked seriously attractive in dark trousers and jacket. 'Are you ready?'

'Yes. But Phyl's not home yet.'

'She's not coming. She phoned. An extra rehearsal. Some girl's dropped out – hysterics, nerves or chicken-pox – any excuse – so Phyl's doing something extra.' He sounded on the point of exploding and Lizzie could not blame him. After all Phyl had arranged this evening and now she was not here.

'We'll forget it then,' said Lizzie. 'You won't want to go without Phyl.'

'Why not?' His expression smouldered. 'I like fireworks! Don't you?'

'Yes. And ships.'

'Well then? Shall we go?'

She stared at him, thought, What the hell! and followed him out.

Coming towards them was Nan Eccles. She stopped in front of them, blocking the way to the car. 'Where's yous going, girl?'

'To the river, Nan,' she said cheerfully.

The old woman fixed her bright eyes on Alex. 'Yous ol' man's Payne's lad. Yous was always a good boy to your ol' lady. Us'll come with you.'

Lizzie shot a glance at Alex and he looked at her and she thought she knew exactly what he was thinking. 'I can't say it,' he murmured.

'No, I suppose not.' Her feelings were a peculiar mixture of disappointment and relief.

Alex crooked his right arm. 'Put your hand in, Grandma, and let's be going or we'll miss the start.' He opened the car door and helped Nan Eccles inside.

Lizzie clambered in after her. 'This is crazy,' she whispered to Alex. 'She could get agitated and all muddled up.'

'I know. I remember Lois's wedding day. Don't you?'

Lizzie was silent. She had a feeling he was not referring to Nan Eccles playing at brides. 'I hope she doesn't want to go aboard a ship.'

'Stop worrying,' he said softly. 'Sit back and relax.'

She obeyed, gazing out of the window but not really aware which direction they were taking because his presence seemed to fill the car. Lord, she had got it bad!

It was ten minutes later she realised they were not heading for the Pierhead. 'You're going the wrong way!'

'You know Liverpool better than me, do you?' The smile in his voice took the sting from the words.

'I know enough to know the Pierhead's down there!' she said, waving a hand in the direction of the river as they passed along Heyworth Street.

Nan Eccles seized her hand. 'See that building, girl? St George's church, made of cast iron. Let's get out.'

'We can't, Nan. We'll never get to the river if we stop. Besides I think he's lost.'

'No, I'm not.' Alex stopped the car. 'I was heading for Seaforth, thinking it would be less crowded there. But let her have a look at her old stamping ground for five minutes if she wants.'

'I should have stayed at work,' said Lizzie wryly. 'I was right on the spot there, Alex. I bet we end up seeing nothing.'

'You can't see nothing,' he said, helping both of them from the car which he'd parked along Everton Brow. The rain had stopped but the river was concealed by a misty haze.

'We won't see fireworks then,' said Lizzie, after thinking over what he had said.

'This is a daft conversation,' he murmured and took her hand as Nan Eccles scuttled in front of them before vanishing down an opening on their right. They hurried after to find her halfway down a steeply sloping street where a metal handrail was placed to aid the weak-kneed and faint-hearted.

They plunged after the old woman and Lizzie was conscious of a pleasure which seemed inexplicable in the light of what they were doing though she knew it was down to being with Alex. 'I wonder where she's going,' she murmured.

Nan Eccles had stopped at a house at the end of a row. The door was shut but she had seated herself on the front step and was gazing out over streets and streets of sooty terraced houses and factory chimneys. Her chest was rising and falling rapidly. 'This was our house,' she said, 'and time wus when me and our Jean cud race down that hill without it takin' a feather out of us.'

'Your Jean?' said Lizzie, seating herself next to her.

The old woman chewed on her gums and made no answer. Alex leaned against the wall of the house, his fingers still curled about Lizzie's.

'Me cousin Jean which used to live down Bostock Street off Scottie Road,' said Nan Eccles abruptly. 'Us'd go to the Rotunda and see the turns. Then she went away and didn't cum back. All gone now,' she muttered. 'Don't like being on me own.'

Lizzie caught the sheen of tears in her eyes and wanted to cry herself. She thought of her parents. Death was so final. 'You're not on your own, Nan,' she said gently. 'You've got us. We'll look after you.' She put her free hand on the old woman's shoulder.

There was a silence as they all looked in the direction of the river. Then suddenly they saw it.

'There's a rainbow,' said Nan, a note of awe in her rusty voice. 'Them's lucky. Perhaps I'll find me mog. Us was looking for him, wasn't us?'

'He's at home,' said Lizzie. 'We were going to the river to see the boats, remember?'

'Would you still like to go?' asked Alex, helping Nan Eccles to her feet.

'See the boats?' Her expression brightened. 'I's don't mind, lad.' She took the arm he offered and linking her other one through Lizzie's, the three of them climbed the steep hill together. Once in the car Alex decided it might be best to head for the Pierhead instead of Seaforth as it was nearer.

They missed the parade of ships. Which was perhaps just as well because the 'speck' they found up Water Street would have made it impossible for them to see much. They were in time to see aeroplanes from the carrier *Indomitable* screeching across the sky into the setting sun over New Brighton.

'Fantastic!' cried Lizzie.

Alex smiled down at her and she returned his smile. Why worry about Phyl? It was her choice not to be here. Lizzie determined to make the most of this time. His arm lay protectively across her shoulders for they were wedged tightly in a crowd that had continued to grow around them. She in turn had her arm about a trembling Nan Eccles who seemed to have shrunk since the first time they had met. 'Us thought them bats had gone,' she muttered.

'Time for us to go home, Jeangirl. It's getting dark.'

'It's OK, love,' said Lizzie in a comforting voice. 'The enemy bats have gone for good.'

'Are yous sure?'

'Believe us, Nan,' said Alex. 'You're safe with us.'

Safe, thought Lizzie, remembering how she had felt when she had seen her father dead. She wanted to feel safe for the rest of her life.

'Look,' Alex murmured. 'Lights on the river.' She followed his gaze to see coloured beams illuminating jets of water from two fireboats. Soon came the fireworks and a roar went up from both sides of the river as hundreds of rockets shot up in the air to burst like flaming chrysanthemums, showering down golden rain. 'Glad you came?' he said against her hair.

'There's no need to ask.' She did not look up at him, in case her love showed, but was terribly aware of the feel of his fingers against her neck and the jut of his hip firm against her side. She heard the explosions that hurled showers of red, green and gold up in the night sky, silhouetting ships at anchor, and it was as if they were happening in some strange way inside her body. Had there ever been such magic in her life before? Yet soon these moments would be history and tomorrow it would be back to reality.

It was past midnight when they arrived back at the house. 'Are you coming in?' whispered Lizzie.

'No, luv. You get the old girl in.' For a moment their eyes met and his fingers held hers, then he wound up the window.

Lizzie leaned against the front door while Nan Eccles hammered on it, and watched him drive away. What am I to do? she thought despairingly. My heart will break.

The door opened behind her and she fell backwards into the lobby. The same thing happening to Nan Eccles was only prevented by the prompt action of her eldest granddaughter.

'Was that Alex driving off?' asked Phyl.

'Yes.' Lizzie picked herself up off the floor and was swamped with guilt as she looked at her stepmother.

Nan Eccles shrugged off Phyl's hand. 'Us wants the lav. Desprite I am, girl.' Her voice was breathless as she lumbered towards the stairs.

'I knew he was annoyed,' sighed Phyl.

'I thought he'd explode.' Lizzie pretended to yawn, afraid Phyl might see something in her eyes. 'We took Nan with us,' she added to assuage that sense of guilt. 'I think she enjoyed it.'

'Good for Nan,' drawled Phyl, looking at her keenly. 'What about you?'

'Pure magic,' said Lizzie without thinking. Then she realised what she said and muttered, 'I'll have to go to the lav, too,' and fled.

The lavatory door stood ajar and she went up to it. Inside Nan Eccles lay on the floor. Lizzie's heart felt as if it had stopped beating and she went down on her knees. Her shaking hands sought for a pulse but there was none. For an instant she remembered doing the same thing with her father. A sob grew and grew inside her and she burst into tears. It was not the best ending to an evening that had been almost perfect.

Chapter Twelve

'I don't think yer should be doing this,' said Sam. 'Not when yer nan's barely in her grave.'

'I have to, Dad.' Phyl's eyes narrowed as she placed a pith helmet on her bright hair and, watching her actions in the mirror, sang a snatch of 'Mad Dogs and Englishmen'.

'It's all wrong,' said Lois, leaning back in a chair, eating a banana. 'I don't know how you have the heart. I'm really going to miss Nan.'

'Just like a sore toe,' murmured Mary, not looking up from her book. 'Hypocrite.'

Lizzie almost smiled.

Phyl turned round slowly and stared at her father. 'I have got a heart but the show must go on, Dad. I loved Nan. I'm going to miss her. But it'd be difficult for them to replace me at this late stage.'

'Sez you,' said Lois. 'I suppose you are the star?'

'We're all stars,' said Phyl flippantly, removing the helmet.

'But you more than others,' said Lois sardonically.

'Shut up, Lois,' grunted her father. 'Phyl needs all the confidence she can muster right now.'

'I wish you'd make up your mind, Sam,' said Maisie, glancing up from the matinee coat she was knitting for

Lois's expected baby. 'Do you want her on the stage or don't you? I know where I want her.'

'Where's that, Mam, as if I didn't know?' drawled Phyl, putting on her jacket.

'Married off to Alex. At least he seems to have got his head on right these days and is working hard.'

Phyl sighed heavily. 'Here we go again! I will be marrying him, Mam. Just have patience.' Without another word she went out, carrying the pith helmet, and slammed the door behind her.

'Well, that's that,' said Maisie, sighing.

'I wish I knew why she didn't want us there,' said Mary. 'I mean, we're her biggest fans.'

'Drop it,' said her mother. 'I want you and Lizzie to help me start sorting out Nan's room.'

'What about me?' asked Lois.

'It's time you were going home to your husband.' Maisie's voice was firm. 'It's nice to see you but you must feed that man of yours sometime.'

Lois pulled a face and Mary and Lizzie exchanged grins before getting up and leaving the room.

Lizzie sat in Nan Eccles's chair by the empty fireplace. 'It still feels strange knowing she'll never sit here again with Mog on her knee.' The cat was perched on the narrow window ledge behind the lace curtain, gazing out on the street as if watching for his mistress.

'Don't you start getting morbid,' said Maisie, opening a cupboard. 'She had a long life with never a day's illness and that's a heap more than most people get.'

'I wasn't being morbid,' said Lizzie. 'I was just remembering. She almost frightened the life out of me when I first came here.' She bent and picked up a shoebox which was still on the floor where Trev had left it the day of the funeral.

'That's her memory box,' said Maisie, sitting on a chair with a couple of tins on her knee. 'You might as well turf it out.'

'Can I keep it?' she said impulsively. 'I like old things.'

'Take it up to the attic then.' Maisie paused. 'I was thinking, Lizzie, would you go and see Alex about taking Nan's bed away? I want it shifting as soon as possible. It's not worth me waiting for our Phyl to do anything about it. We won't get any help from her until this concert's over.'

Lizzie hesitated. 'Couldn't Mary go?'

'I asked you,' said Maisie bluntly. 'I've another job for her.' She shook one of the tin boxes. 'Full of pennies. You two can share it when you've done your wack.'

Lizzie stared at the box and was reminded of the day she had almost run away. How different her life would have been if she'd had enough money and had found her aunt. She wouldn't be suffering like she was now. 'It's Sunday today,' she said, still seeking an excuse.

'So it is,' said Maisie dryly. 'But there's no rest for us, girl, not today. And I'm sure you'll find Alex in the yard. Give the man his due, he's a worker.'

Lizzie realised there was nothing for it but to go, but she took her time about it. She wanted to see Alex yet she didn't. He was Phyl's and she had to keep telling herself that. Yet still she dreamed of snuggling up to him, of being held tightly and kissed passionately.

Lizzie came to the yard. Several brokendown cars occupied a large area and Alex was tinkering with one of them. He was stripped to the waist and her heart seemed to swell inside her at the sight of him. She felt good. She liked his body. He didn't have a bit of flab but real muscles. Not the kind that Charles Atlas advocated but they were good enough for her.

He glanced up as she approached. 'What d'you want?' His tone was curt.

Immediately her soaring emotions fell slapbang flat. 'I don't want anything,' she said sullenly.

He wiped his hands on an oily rag. 'If you don't want anything then what are you doing here?'

'I haven't come here by choice,' she snapped. 'It's Phyl's mam. She wants Nan's bed taking away. Now if possible!'

'I'm expected to jump to it, am I?'

'That's the general idea. She's got plans for the parlour.'

'Any other stuff she wants to be rid of?' He reached for the checked shirt lying on a car roof.

'You're best asking her. But I should imagine so.'

His eyes narrowed against the sun as he looked at her, his fingers busy buttoning up his shirt. 'Is Phyl in?'

She shook her head. 'Dress rehearsal.'

'Figures.' His voice sounded taut. 'Has she said anything to you?'

Her nerves jumped. 'About what?'

'I've asked her to choose and she thinks it's horrible of me.' He opened the cab door of the lorry. 'Jump in. You might as well have a ride.'

Lizzie did not move. She was wondering if what he was saying had anything to do with the night of the fireworks. 'You mean, choose between you and the concert?'

'Not only the concert. The whole shebang. She's talking about some theatrical or casting agent being at the concert on the prowl for new talent. She's just like she was when she was a kid, full of dreams and nerves, and up and down like a yoyo.'

'I suppose he's the reason she doesn't want us there?'

'Yeah,' he said grimly. 'She wants to concentrate on impressing him and not have to worry about us hanging around afterwards.'

'I suppose it's understandable,' said Lizzie carefully, wrapping the end of her pony tail round a finger and trying to think of Phyl's feelings and not her own. 'She really enjoys it and I'm sure she's got talent.'

'I know that. That's why it's a worry.'

'She told Maisie that she was marrying you.' Lizzie did not look at him.

He stilled. 'Did she now? So I should know where I am.' His voice was quiet. 'But strangely enough I don't feel like I do. Are you getting into the cab or not?'

She slowly let go of her hair and said unhappily, 'I'm sure she loves you.'

'Are you?' He did not look at her but said roughly, 'Let's get going. It's pointless talking like this.' He helped her into the cab.

She slid along the seat. That brief contact had brought colour rushing to her cheeks and an indescribable yearning. 'Phyl's really been good to me,' she muttered.

'Don't we both know it?' he said. 'And that's the bloody trouble.' Savagely he pressed his foot down on the accelerator and the lorry shot off up the street.

They did not speak again and Lizzie determined to keep her distance in the future. Seeing him mixed her up something terrible.

A few days later, at almost midnight, Phyl walked into the kitchen. The family had all been waiting up for her.

'Well, did it go OK?' demanded Dot, pouncing on her.

'Let me get my jacket off,' she said, laughing.

'It went well,' said Maisie, folding the newspaper. 'I can tell by your face.'

Phyl flung her coat on the couch and went over and hugged her. 'Mam, you wanted to talk weddings. Now is the time to do it before I get caught up in rehearsals again. I'm going to suggest to Alex that we get married before Christmas. He always did want a quiet affair.'

'What do you mean, rehearsals?' said Lizzie, pushing Mog from her knee and standing up. She told herself the sooner Phyl married Alex the better.

'I'm pretty sure I've got a part in *Babes in the Wood* on at the Empire over Christmas.' Her eyes were shining like topazes. 'Jimmy Jewel and Ben Wallis are in it.' She straightened. 'Alex's bound to be pleased, don't you think?' There was almost a pleading note in her voice.

'Of course he will, luv,' said Sam. 'I take it yer did well?'

Phyl straightened up. 'I was great! Everyone said so. It was marvellous! I just hope Alex understands what this means to me.'

'He should be proud of you,' said Dot.

'I wouldn't guarantee it,' said Maisie, shoving the news-paper under a cushion. 'Men like a woman in the home. Now let's be having you. Get to bed everyone.'

All but Phyl made a move towards the door. She flopped on to the couch. 'Not me. I'm too full of pep. Lizzie, love, come back. Make us a cup of tea. Then I'll tell you all about tonight's performance.'

'I'll make tea but that's it,' she said firmly. 'I've got work in the morning and so have you.'

Phyl grimaced. 'I think I'll give it a miss. I'll probably feel shattered when I come down to earth. I wish you'd stay. I need someone to talk to.'

'You didn't need any of us earlier,' said Lizzie, and walked into the scullery.

'Are you criticising me?' said Phyl, struggling to her feet and following her out.

'I'm just telling the truth. You wanted none of us watch-ing you, but now I'm supposed to be all ears when all I can think of is bed.'

'Is that all it is?' Phyl leaned against the sink, a frown on her face as she watched Lizzie fill the kettle.

'No. It's your marrying Alex. I know you want me to live with the pair of you but I definitely don't. If you don't mind, I'd like to stay on here.'

'But I do mind,' said Phyl. She rat-tatted on the wooden draining board with her fingernails. 'I would have thought you'd be glad to get out of here? I had thought if I got more acting work and had to go away you'd be there to look after Alex.'

Lizzie did not know whether to laugh or cry. Was Phyl blind? 'You're not on! I'm eighteen and he wouldn't even be my real stepfather. What would people say?'

Phyl sighed, and reaching inside a pocket, took out a lone cigarette and lit it from the gas ring. 'You're so wise, Lizzie. Alex's very protective of his reputation these days and you are growing up.'

Lizzie was silent, thinking she was not as wise as Phyl seemed to think though she could not say that.

Phyl exhaled a stream of smoke. 'I suppose our Billy wouldn't like it either. I bet he's the real reason why you want to stick around here. You're nice and handy when he arrives home.'

Lizzie still could not believe how blind Phyl was and said flippantly, 'I have to find some way to be one step ahead of the competition. All the nice girls love a sailor.'

Phyl grinned. 'You and our Billy! Now there's an interesting combination. I couldn't be more pleased. Now hurry up with that tea. Then I really will let you get to bed.'

Lizzie wished she had not said what she had about Billy now but she supposed it was better that Phyl thought she fancied him, rather than suspect she had a pash on Alex. When next Billy came home perhaps it might help if she acted like it was for real?

But before he did Phyl came home in a twist one evening. 'Alex doesn't want to marry me before Christmas,' she told her mother.

'It's your own fault!' exclaimed Maisie, putting down her knitting. 'When's it to be then?'

'Next spring. He says he wants me to get the acting bug out of my system. He doesn't mind me sticking to the amateur dramatics but he's against me going professional.'

'So he thinks you'll settle down once the pantomime's over?' said Maisie. 'I hope he's right. When are you going to see sense, girl?'

Phyl frowned. 'Oh, be quiet, Mam. I know you're right in a way but I don't like being given ultimatums.'

'The man wants you in the home where you belong. Not prancing about on some stage. It was OK when you were younger but not now. The kitchen's where a wife belongs, luv.'

'Hmmph!' said Phyl, and walked out.

It was October before Billy had any leave worth mentioning and when he arrived home he looked ready to burst. 'I'm going to be on film in full technicolor!' he said, sweeping his mother off her feet and swinging her round the kitchen.

'Put me down, you daft ha'porth,' she demanded. 'And tell us what you're going on about?'

'I'm talking BLOOD, Mam.'

'Well, don't,' said Lizzie, smiling at him as she filed her fingernails. She was pleased to see him. Perhaps it wouldn't be so difficult to fall in love with him and out with Alex?

'I have to,' said Billy. 'The Blood Transfusion Service is making a movie to do with dockside accidents. I could become famous before our Phyl! Blood, blood, glorious blood!' he sang.

'Shut up,' said Mary in dampening tones as she looked up from her sewing. 'There's nothing glorious about it, but it's important to give it. What with the fighting still going on in Korea and now Egypt, I just might become a nurse the same as Josie when I leave school.'

'You do that, little sister,' said Billy, seizing her about the neck and pressing her face against his shoulder.

Mary struggled free. 'You get worse. When are you going back to sea?'

'Ta very much! I love you too.' He gave her a spanking kiss on the cheek.

She wiped it off. 'Tell that to one of your girlfriends,' she drawled.

'I only have two,' he said, putting his arm around his mother and Lizzie. 'How about the flicks tonight, Liz?'

'OK.' She kissed his cheek. 'How was your trip?'

'Canada's going crazy. They've got royalty fever with Princess Elizabeth and the Duke being over there. I reckon there's more flags there than there probably were here during the Festival.' He removed his arm and hugged Maisie. 'What's there to eat, my best, best girl?'

She dug him in the ribs but she was smiling. 'You're just a cupboard lover.'

Whatever a cupboard lover was, Lizzie was perfectly content to have Billy's company at the pictures that night. They sat on the back row but when he kissed her the only impression he left on her was the taste of Gibb's toothpaste and Wall's icecream. She also remembered that Doris Day and Gordon Macrae sang a lot. The next day they went to the farm and spent time with the twins. Josie took Billy away, saying she wanted to show him something, but Lizzie knew just how much her friend had missed him. She had forgotten Josie when she had joked with Phyl about liking him. They were away a while and in the meantime Lizzie had to put up with listening to Joe reading out his latest article which he planned on sending to the *Echo*.

When Billy went back to sea the family acted like Lizzie was going to miss him dreadfully and she did not deny it because Phyl and Alex were there when they teased her about him.

Life went on. There was a general election and the newspapers declared that housewives could have the decisive vote. Most Liverpool MPs retained their seats but the Conservative Party, led by Winston Churchill, won the election.

'Now let's see ol' Winnie improve things,' said Maisie with satisfaction. But the only improvement Lizzie noticed was that bacon rations went up by an ounce a week, which meant she received a whole slice on Sundays. She saw little of Phyl because of work and rehearsals.

The week before Christmas there were gale force winds so strong that ships could not leave the river and the rain was torrential, making Christmas shopping joyless. To top it all the newspapers announced that after Christmas, the bacon and sweet rations would be cut and coal would go up by six shillings a ton.

'One of these days,' said Maisie irritably, 'we'll get a government who'll make life easier for the housewife.'

'We need more women in Parliament,' said Phyl, stretching her feet towards the fire.

'We had them under Attlee,' said Alex, who had been invited to tea but seemed as restless as Trev who was staring out of the window at the teeming rain.

'That says something about the working classes,' said Lizzie, trying not to look Alex's way too often as she wielded scissors.

'Not all of them,' said Phyl in a teasing voice. 'Some still see a woman's place as being only in the kitchen.'

'Don't go on about politics,' interposed Trev. 'It's so boring. Like this weather.'

'At least you're dry and warm,' said his mother. 'Think of our Billy out there on the high seas.'

Alex glanced at Lizzie who was kneeling on the floor, cutting out a dress pattern. 'Are you worried about him?' he said in a low voice.

She raised her eyes to his face and realised it was hopeless her trying to pretend. 'No more than anyone else in the family,' she murmured. 'He's like a brother to me, that's all.'

'But I thought –' His eyes searched hers and his expression was strained when he moved away.

The new year brought more gale warnings and the realisation that Billy's ship was several days overdue. A picture in the *Echo* of a troubled freighter taking heavy seas on exposed decks didn't make the family feel any better, although a spokesman for Billy's company said there was no need to be anxious. Ships were often delayed at this time of year. Still they worried. Then came the news that Billy's ship had docked but that there had been an accident. He had been taken to the Royal Infirmary in

Pembroke Place. Billy had been on deck with a couple of men when some lumber had become loose in the stormy seas and had been injured.

Immediately his parents left for the hospital. When they returned it was obvious they were putting a brave face on things. 'It could have been worse,' said Maisie, her eyes glistening as she pleated a fold of her frock over and over. 'He could have been killed.'

'What's wrong with him?' said Mary, her lips trembling.

'He might never walk again,' said Sam, his throat moving convulsively. 'His spinal cord's been damaged and some nerves are affected. He's also got concussion.'

'Oh God!' whispered Dot. 'He was always a lad to be doing something.'

Trev had gone white but said fiercely, 'You sound like he's finished. Let's not be so bloomin' negative! He might be OK with time.'

His father did not comment but walked out and went into the backyard where he lit a cigarette. He stayed there a long time. Maisie went into the scullery and could be heard banging pans about.

Mary burst into tears. Lizzie placed her arm round her and hugged her. A lump the size of an apple felt as if it was stuck in her throat and she wished fervently that Phyl was there, but she was at the Empire because the show had to go on.

The house felt as if it had been plunged into mourning. It did not bear thinking about that Billy might never walk again. Even Lois when she called seemed to have lost her razor edge. What made it worse was that Billy had to be kept quiet and so only his parents were allowed to see him.

When finally Lizzie went to the hospital, her first glimpse of Billy did nothing to make her feel hopeful. He was Billy, yet he wasn't. The eyes which had so often been full of merriment appeared blank and she was suddenly reminded of Daddy after her mother had died. It caused her to reach out and take his hand firmly in her grasp as if it was essential to stop him slipping away. She wanted to reassure him that everything would be OK but she did not know if it would and could not lie so remained silent.

Without warning Billy freed his hand and said, 'Why don't you say something? The others had plenty to say. In fact they never bloody stopped!'

'What d'you want me to say?' said Lizzie, her eyes filling with tears. 'How are you? It seems a waste of time when I can tell by looking at you how empty you feel inside.'

Pain flashed across his face. 'Not the right thing to say.' There was a bitter note in his voice. 'You should be saying how much better I look than you thought I would.'

'What would be the point?'

'Say everything's going to be fine then!'

'Perhaps it will be?' She felt a moment's hope.

'No. My legs have no strength.'

'The feeling could come back.'

'And Donald Duck might swim the Atlantic,' he said harshly. 'You're not a bit of bloody help!'

'There's more than one way to get across something,' retorted Lizzie. 'Some ducks can fly. Your wings might only be clipped temporarily.'

He looked away and muttered, 'You're talking rubbish.'

'I'll shut up then. But it was you who wanted me to talk,' said Lizzie crossly. 'What do you want from me if it isn't talk?'

'Nothing! I'm going to be a cripple and there's nothing anyone can do about it.'

He looked so anguished that Lizzie felt as if her heart was being squeezed by a nutcracker. She did feel a kind of love for him. 'At least you're not flat on your back for life,' she said. 'You can move your arms and waist. It's only –'

'Don't say it,' he said fiercely. 'I know what I can't move.'

She was silent, then burst out, 'I wish I could do something to help. Couldn't you come home? Perhaps you'd feel better there.'

He raised bruised looking eyes to her. 'Perhaps. I'm sure they were planning on keeping me here longer, although there's nothing they can do. They're just waiting to see if time improves things. But you tell Mam and Dad I want out.'

She nodded, too choked to speak, and hurried away.

'I don't know why you had to interfere,' said Lois, resting her hands across her pregnant belly and glaring at Lizzie.

'They must have their reasons for wanting to keep him in longer.'

'Don't blame the lass,' said Sam. 'It's our Billy's choice, and if he wants out then out he comes.'

'That's if they can let us have a wheelchair,' said Maisie. 'Sister was talking about demands and shortages.'

'Insist,' said Phyl wearily, her copper hair loosened so that it spread over the back of the chair. 'Insist, insist, insist! It's the only way if you plan to get what you want.'

'Josie said the Red Cross can sometimes help with wheelchairs,' said Lizzie. She thought of her friend's bleak expression when she had told her about Billy. Josie had pleaded to see him but he had said he wanted to see no one but the family.

'Right,' said Mary, her face brightening. 'Where are you going to put him, though? He won't be able to manage the stairs.'

'Nan's parlour,' said her mother. 'We can bring his bed down and he'll have loads more space.'

'What about going to the lav?' asked Trev.

'He'll have to make do with a potty.'

Trev groaned and put his head in his hands.

His mother was silent, looking for comfort to Sam.

Lizzie thought that going to the lav was going to be the least of Billy's problems.

Lizzie's nineteenth birthday came and went with no celebration. King George VI had died peacefully in his sleep. It upset the family. 'He was a good man,' said Sam. 'He knew his duty and did it.' Nobody argued with him. Phyl's and Alex's wedding was postponed yet again and Lois gave birth to a baby boy.

At last Billy came home and to everyone's surprise made no complaints about his changed circumstances. They were so relieved that they all waited on him, rushing about doing whatever he demanded and bringing him little treats. Whole sweet rations were spent on chocolate and his favourite sherbet lemons and Lizzie thought if rations had been more generous he would have put on twice as much weight. She pitied him so was forever volunteering to go to the library or do anything else he wanted. He devoured almost as many books as he did sweets. One thing he did not do, though, was go outside the house, except to hospital, and neither would he allow any of his friends to call. He even refused to see Josie who with tears in her eyes demanded, 'Why, Liz? Does he really believe this could make a difference to the way I feel about him? Me and Joe want to help!' Lizzie told him what she had said but he still insisted that he did not want to see them. The twins went away tight-lipped but Josie came again and left little treats for him which Billy put in a drawer.

Winter blossomed into spring and Billy became moodier, less talkative, and when he did speak, far from gracious.

'Nobody's doing him any favours by kowtowing to his every whim,' said Alex to Lizzie and Phyl late one afternoon when they were at the scrapyard.

Immediately Phyl flared up. 'It's easy for you to say! He's not your brother.'

His face stiffened. 'I look on him almost as a younger brother. I've known him a long time and he's always had a nice way with him despite being a bit of a devil, but you're ruining him. He's a fighter by nature but how does he fight his way out of all that cushioning you've got round him?'

Lizzie realised he was right. 'He'll have to start doing more for himself,' she said. 'He has to get out and about.'

'It's you that does the most running round for him,' said Phyl irritably. 'I can understand that because you love him.'

'I don't do any more for him than anyone else,' said Lizzie emphatically. 'I just wish he would see Josie. I'm sure it would make a difference.'

'I'd never noticed he cared that much for her,' said Phyl, frowning.

'That's because you've got it fixed in your head that he fancies me.' Her tone was impatient.

'He does.'

'He doesn't. No more than he fancies any other girl.'

'I think you're wrong.' Phyl's heart-shaped face was set. 'Is it the thought of him being crippled that's changed you? I know you like kids and –'

'That's a lousy thing to say to Lizzie,' said Alex harshly.

'You should know her better, Phyl. She told me before it happened that Billy was just like a brother to her.'

Phyl looked at Lizzie. 'Why tell Alex that?'

'Because the whole family was talking about Billy round Christmas, that's why! Anyway there's nothing stopping him having children,' Lizzie said defensively. 'Those nerves weren't damaged. I heard your mam speaking of it to your Lois.'

Phyl said, 'Sorry.'

'It's OK.' Lizzie was hurt and her voice was cool. 'Anyway I would have thought you'd be occupying yourself with your own wedding plans, not worrying about anyone else's love life?'

'Your mistake, Lizzie,' said Alex, leaning against a car and watching her. 'Phyl has what she says is a tiny part in a play. You tell her, Phyl.'

She flushed. 'You don't have to make it sound as if I'm lying about this part.'

'Did I say that?' said Alex. 'Tell Lizzie what it is then.'

Phyl smiled. 'OK. It's one of these country house type of mysteries, Lizzie, and I have the part of a governess whom the son of the house fancies. He gets murdered and I get to be grilled by the local constabulary because I'm a suspect. I start rehearsals in Manchester next week and then we go on tour.'

'Isn't this all jolly exciting, Liz? Much more exciting than getting married,' said Alex sardonically.

'Alex, lovey, don't be like that,' said Phyl in a coaxing voice. 'You said you didn't mind! And I admit now to a need to get away from everything for a while.'

'Including me?'

'No!' She reddened. 'I meant the atmosphere at home. Mam and Dad are so worried about Billy and what kind of future there is for him.' She put her arms round Alex's waist and rested her head against his chest.

Lizzie watching them, felt pain and anger. Without a word she walked out of the yard. How could Phyl treat Alex the way she did and why didn't he put his foot down with her?

Lizzie came to the blacksmith's and paused outside. She always found it soothing watching the work going on inside and she needed soothing right now. She was about to go through the gateway when Phyl suddenly appeared. 'Alex wants you,' she said shortly. 'You'd best go back. I'll see you at home.'

Lizzie was so surprised she could not think of a thing to say. Phyl half-lifted a hand and walked on past the grocery store and round the corner.

Mystified, Lizzie retraced her steps to find Alex staring at the rusting skeletons of cars. 'What d'you want me for?' she called as she walked towards him.

'Billy,' he said succinctly.

She sighed. 'What about him?'

'I thought he might like to give Harry a hand in the workroom. Bill did woodwork at school, didn't he?'

'Yes, I'm sure he did,' she said slowly.

'If you can get him interested, tell him I'll pick him and his chair up and take him to the shop in the lorry on Monday.'

'Right!' she laughed, feeling as if a weight had fallen off her. Billy would be a fool not to say yes, and he was no fool. She felt like doing cartwheels round the yard at the thought of his getting out of the house and holding down a job and regaining his confidence. If that happened it would all be down to Alex.

'You really are a beautiful man,' she said softly. 'I can't understand why Phyl wants to go off and leave you.'

She stood on tiptoe and kissed his chin but before she could step back he seized hold of her shoulders and pulled her against him. His mouth came down over hers. For a moment she could not move or think. A tremor was racing through her so that it felt as if her limbs contained fizzy lemonade. Then she thought why is this happening when only a short time ago she left him and Phyl in each other's arms? She struggled in his grasp but he did not let her go, only holding her off from him, his hands spanning her waist.

'Lizzie, I love you,' he said.

'You can't!' she cried.

'Don't tell me what I can and can't do! I love you and I think you love me.'

She moistened her lips, wanting like crazy to believe him. 'But what about Phyl?'

'She didn't tell you?' He looked surprised.

'Alex wants you, that's all she said.'

He smiled then. 'And I do. You're all grown up and I can say that now.'

'Oh, Alex!' she said helplessly. 'Do you know what you're saying?'

'Yes! And I've wanted to say it for ages. I've broken off my engagement with Phyl. Although she's still hanging on to my ring.' He paused at the doubtful expression on her face. 'She doesn't want me, Lizzie. You know what she really wants, luv! Her name up there in lights! For a while she thought she couldn't do it but now her hopes are high.'

Lizzie knew that was true, but even so. 'Phyl didn't look happy,' she said quietly.

'No. She still believes herself in love with me but she isn't! She's failed at this acting game once before so she wants to keep hold of me for insurance – but it's over! I really knew it wouldn't work years ago. I pitied you then and that's why I agreed to an engagement. I wanted you to feel safe and happy.'

'I knew you cared for me a little.' Lizzie could still scarcely believe what was happening.

'A little! That's an understatement. I fought against loving you like hell because I knew what people would say. But I just don't care any more. I love you.'

Those words clinched it for her. 'I love you, too,' she said without a blush or further fuss. 'I've wanted you to kiss me for ages. I've wanted you to kiss me and go on kissing me and never to stop.'

His mouth touched hers experimentally. Then she was in his arms and returning his kiss with a youthful exuberant passion. She felt the strength of his reaction in the pull of his arms as he moulded her against his body. The action sent a surge of pleasure to every part of her. She wanted to make him happy and for the happiness to last for ever.

'You don't think I'm too old for you?' he said, when at last he stopped kissing her.

'No! My mother was eight years older than Daddy and they were in love 'til the day she died. And after,' she added thoughtfully. 'What does age matter?'

'I'm glad you feel like that.' He hugged her to him again. 'We'll get married as soon as we can. I'll buy us a house on the outskirts of town.'

'Have you the money?'

'Would I say it if I didn't? I've been saving. It won't be a mansion but –'

'I don't care.' She pressed closer against him. 'I'd live here with you. I'd live in a tent. I'd live –' He stopped her words with a kiss.

When eventually Lizzie could breathe evenly again, she said, 'Did you tell Phyl how you felt about me?'

Instantly his expression sobered. 'I couldn't. Not until I knew definitely how you felt.'

'It'll come as a shock to her,' she said, her brows creasing. 'You heard what she said about Billy and me?' She caught her breath. 'In fact, it'll come as a shock to them all.'

They gazed at each other, questions in their eyes. 'I don't want to hurt Phyl – or any of them,' she whispered, a sinking feeling in her chest.

'Neither do I. I mean, they've lost Nan Eccles in the last year and now it's Billy they're worrying about.' He frowned. 'But being hurt is part of life and they've hurt me in the past, Lizzie. You know that. Phyl's mam and dad weren't for having me in the family not so long back.'

'That only makes it worse,' she muttered, biting her lower lip. 'Lois'll say bitchy things about you too. I won't like that.'

'I don't care about her! But I do care about the rest of them.' He paused. 'But surely they all know how Phyl's put me on the back burner while she's pursued her dream? They'll understand.'

'They won't,' she said, positively.

There was silence and then Alex's hands slid down her arms to search for her fingers and grip them tightly. 'You're probably right. What do you want to do?'

It pleased her that he really was treating her like an adult by consulting her. She tried to think sensibly but it was not easy when even the touch of his fingers could set her tingling. 'We'll have to be patient. Let them get used to the idea that you and Phyl aren't going to get married. And if you really can help Billy, it'll be all the better for us.'

'Sensible girl.' He pulled her against him and she rested her head on his shoulder. 'We can still see each other and we can go out together. We'll just have to be discreet,' he murmured.

She nodded, and so it was settled.

As Lizzie entered the front room Billy looked up from the *Daily Mail Annual* which Mary had received for Christmas. 'Where've you been?' he demanded.

'Out.' She smiled.

'Where to?' His eyes narrowed. 'You look as if something's made you happy. I suppose you haven't given a thought to me stuck in here?'

'I always give you a thought,' she said quietly. 'Not that it always makes me happy. But I am happy this evening because I've decided I'm not going to allow you to make me and everybody else, as well as yourself, miserable for life!'

He looked taken aback before the habitual scowl of recent months dragged his mouth down again. 'Nobody's asking you to be miserable. You can clear off!'

'I should just do that,' murmured Lizzie. 'But this family's been good to me and I don't like to see them suffering. I've been to see Alex and he's offering you a job. D'you want to hear about it?'

He stared, obviously struggling with several different emotions at once. 'Why should he offer me a job? What can I do for him?' His tone was suspicious. 'It's because he feels sorry for me, isn't it?'

'What's wrong with people feeling sorry for people?' she said lightly. 'It shows that their heart is in the right place. You should be glad that Alex is prepared to take an interest in you – unless your brain was affected in that accident and not just your legs.'

'Very funny,' he rasped. 'But perhaps you're half right. You've no idea how not being able to walk affects the way you feel about yourself. Everything I did –' His voice trailed off and he looked stricken.

Lizzie put an arm about his shoulders. 'He's offering to get you out of this house so you can do something useful and earn yourself a wage.'

'You mean in that yard where everybody I know can come in and talk *down* to me?' he said bitterly. 'Because that's what people do to people in wheelchairs.'

'It's not in the yard. It's in the room at the back of the secondhand shop. He thought you might like to help Harry repairing furniture. You were OK at woodwork, weren't you?'

'Yes, but –' Several minutes passed and still he was silent. Then he said, 'No, I can't do it.'

She felt an overwhelming disappointment as well as anger. 'Coward!' she said scornfully. 'When I think *you* were the boy who dared to put bullets on a railway line,

I wonder where your guts have gone!' She walked out of the room. It took a lot not to look back but she was determined not to soften, hoping that by goading him in such a way he might be made to fight back.

Sam was alone in the kitchen, painting a plaster plaque.

'Where's Phyl?' asked Lizzie. It did not appear that her stepmother had said anything to him about the broken engagement. She went over to Sam and gazed down at the Viking ship with its billowing sail and line of shields along its prow. His ability to create pictures in plaster fascinated her and she remembered how he had tried briefly to get Billy to have a go, to take his mind off his troubles.

'Phyl came in and went straight out again with her mother. They've gone to see Lois and the baby.'

That surprised her. Phyl had been a trifle scornful over Lois having been 'caught so quick' as she called starting a baby when there were ways and means to delay such an event.

'Alex's offered Billy a job,' she blurted out.

'Oh, aye!' He lifted brown eyes that contained a desperate hope.

'Billy's being awkward.'

'That doesn't surprise me.' He sighed heavily as he swished the paintbrush in a partially filled jam jar of turps. 'What's the job?'

She told him, adding, 'Perhaps you can persuade him to give it a chance?'

He hesitated then shook his thatch of hair which so often appeared white because of plaster dust. 'He won't listen to me or anybody else at the moment, lass. And

I've been wondering if maybe it's right that he doesn't? We can only imagine what it's like for him. We can't know! You've given him something to think about. Now leave it to him.'

His words were a relief, convincing Lizzie that she was right to detach herself from Billy and his problem. If he wanted his life to change then he would have to be the one to make it happen.

She asked after Mary and Dot.

'Ron and the twins called. They've gone off to the pictures.'

'I presume that Billy wouldn't see the twins?'

'You presume right, lass. Now be a good girl and put the kettle on and make us a cup of tea.'

Lizzie did just that and then went up to the attic with a book but she scarcely read a word as she relived those moments in the yard and pondered her future. If Billy would take the job and Phyl made it to the top in the acting profession she would feel so much happier about everything.

When Phyl came to bed Lizzie considered pretending to be asleep but she was too on edge. She wanted to know how her stepmother was feeling and why she had gone to see Lois. She sat up in bed, hunching up her knees. 'How's the baby?'

'He's a plain little thing. Must be a throwback. He's not the least bit like our family or even Buffalo Bill. But she's besotted, which surprises me.' Phyl lit a cigarette and sat on the edge of the bed. Lizzie noted she still wore Alex's ring and her heart seemed to lurch sideways.

'What did Alex want you for?' said Phyl.

Immediately Lizzie felt a surge of guilt. 'He didn't tell you about Billy?' she said, although she knew Alex hadn't.

Phyl raised those expressive eyebrows. 'We weren't exactly on speaking terms when I left.' She blew a cloud of smoke. 'He's threatened before but I've always been able to get round him. I'd forgotten he can only be pushed so far. Suddenly, just like that,' she snapped her fingers, 'he decided that I needed a fright. He's broken off the engagement.'

Lizzie considered it wise to allow a shocked silence to occur as Phyl inhaled deeply. What she'd said fitted in with Alex's suspicion that Phyl would try and hang on to him. 'You think it's only temporary?' she murmured.

'I live in hope. I can't imagine life without Alex there somewhere in the background. Mam thinks I'm a fool. She got me all anxious. That's why I let her persuade me to go round to our Lois's. She thought that if I saw how happy she was with motherhood and all that, it would make me realise what I'm missing.'

'And did it?'

Phyl shrugged and then leaned closer to Lizzie. 'What if I don't make it, kid? I'm nearing thirty and my looks might start going soon.'

Lizzie thought, Alex is right! But she also realised Phyl was seriously worried. 'Of course you'll make it,' she said firmly. 'You've got talent.'

Phyl laughed shakily. 'Thanks. But you need more than talent in this business. You need to be in the right place at the right time. You need luck. You need to meet the right people. You need the right part. And despite what Alex said about the one I've got now, it is only small.'

'You'll be noticed, though,' said Lizzie without hesitation, thinking only that Phyl needed reassurance. 'You can do it. You've got something when you're on stage that makes people notice you.'

'You really think so?' she said, smiling, and glancing towards the mirror on the chest of drawers.

Lizzie smiled. 'I said so, didn't I? Now are you coming to bed?'

Phyl nodded, extinguished her cigarette and undressed. It was not until she was in bed that she said, 'You didn't tell me what Alex wanted you for?'

Lizzie told her about the job for Billy.

Phyl sighed. 'Of course. Dad said something. He's an old softie is Alex. Nice of him to be thinking of you and our Billy.'

'I told you there is no me and Billy,' said Lizzie, feeling like screaming out the truth.

Phyl said absently, 'So you did. But I don't know if I believe you. You're not that hard. Oh, well, Manchester here I come.' She turned over, leaving Lizzie feeling frustrated. Perhaps she should have screamed out the truth? It would help if she could get Billy and Josie together, then there would be fewer hurtful things said when the family were told about Alex and her. Lizzie had not forgotten Phyl's remarks in the yard. She remembered the way Alex had sprung to her defence and fell to dreaming about the moments when he had kissed her. She could see that it was not going to be easy keeping secret her feelings about him in the months to come and prayed for wisdom and patience.

Chapter Thirteen

'Gosh, it's hot,' said Dot, fanning herself with a rhubarb leaf.

'Tell her not to use that,' said Josie, glancing at Lizzie from her position in the hammock. Lizzie was lying on the grass in the shade, reading a Georgette Heyer romance. 'Those leaves are poisonous.'

'I'm not going to eat it,' said Dot, gazing about her. 'D'you think Ron's going to be long with those cows?'

'Animals come first when you're a farmer's wife, Dot. You're going to have to get used to that,' said Joe, biting on the end of his pencil but not looking up from his notepad.

She blushed. 'You're jumping the gun a bit. He hasn't asked me yet.'

'He will,' said Josie with a sigh, setting the hammock swinging as she attempted to sit up. 'He's had a letter from Great Aunt Dora and Great Uncle Dermot in Ireland and he said he can't make a decision until he's spoken to you.'

'I wish Billy would make a decision,' said Lizzie, closing her book and getting up. 'That job Alex's offered him would be good for him.'

'There's nothing we can do about it,' said Josie bitterly. 'I wish he wasn't so bloody proud.'

Joe tutted. 'Naughty, naughty. Ben would have you if he heard you swearing. You know how he hates it in women. Anyway, think on. If Ron and Dot get married, there'll be a wedding and the two families'll come together. Billy's not going to refuse to go to his sister's wedding now, is he?'

Josie's rosy face brightened then fell. 'I wouldn't put it past him.' She looked at Lizzie. 'Where are you going?'

'I've got a date.'

'Who with?' asked Dot, her face alive with interest as she leaned up on an elbow.

Lizzie tapped her nose. 'That's my business.' She softened the words with a smile, and looked at Josie. 'Don't give up hope, luv. Sometimes people get what they want. Thanks for the lunch.'

Joe pulled a face. 'D'you have to go so soon? I was going to read my latest poem to you.'

'Yes!' She blew him a kiss and left them beneath the leafy branches of the apple trees, thinking what an ideal place it would be to canoodle and dream dreams. She walked up the lane where wild dog roses grew, or Alexandra roses as Josie liked to call them because they were the emblem of Rose Day when funds were collected for the Alexandra nurses.

She caught the bus, thinking of Alex whom she was meeting in town. As yet no one had guessed what was going on. Phyl was up in Bolton and they knew little of how she was faring. She wasn't one for writing letters although she had phoned Alex since she had left. He had said she had only spoken of the play and Lizzie had wondered briefly if he was telling her all the truth. Jealousy, guilt, sexual desire, suppressing her excitement when she was meeting him . . . they did not always mix well and sometimes she felt quite sick from the depth of her emotions. She thrust Phyl from her thoughts and set her mind to anticipating her meeting with her lover.

'This is madness,' teased Alex, taking Lizzie's hand as they entered the Odeon. 'Everyone else is outside enjoying the sun and we're going to the pictures!'

'I've been in the sun,' she retorted, smiling up at him. 'It'll be cool inside and we can canoodle. D'you know the temperature is eighty-one degrees in London? Josie's relations phoned the farm and told them. Britain's having a heatwave and that's official.'

'Let's hope it's like this next June for the Coronation.' He paid at the box office and they went inside. The stalls were three-quarters empty and *Tom and Jerry* was showing. 'How is Josie? And Billy? Any change in his mood?' whispered Alex, as they sat down near the back.

'He's moody and quiet for him. No complaints today. Perhaps he'll come round yet. As for Josie . . .' She shrugged. 'I think we all need patience at the moment.'

'I remember Josie the day you set fire to that house. Billy nearly bit her head off because of something she said.'

Lizzie smiled. 'It was about confessing things. She said something about somebody only having to look at her and she confessed to things she hadn't done.' Lizzie hesitated. 'Did you ever tell Phyl about that day?'

'No. Did you?'

'You must know I didn't. I remember thinking then that you were someone I could trust and that I'd be perfectly happy living under your roof with you and Phyl.' A sigh escaped her. 'It would never have worked.'

He pulled her against him. 'It would have been a disaster.' He kissed her and she forgot all about Phyl and everyone else as the purely physical need which they were forever struggling against took over.

Alex wanted to see her to the bottom of her street but Lizzie told him to leave her at the Mission Hall. Phyl was on her mind again. She always was when Lizzie was saying goodbye to Alex and heading for the house. It was then that her fear of discovery was at its height because they were nearer to home and she wondered how long she could keep her secret.

Another month passed and the Olympics in Helsinki gripped everyone's attention and still none of the family appeared to have guessed what was going on between Lizzie and Alex because they were anticipating news from Dot and Ron.

It was a warm evening in July when Lizzie went to meet Alex on the landing stage at the Pierhead.

'Hi!' she said, slipping her hand into his as she came alongside him.

'You're late,' he murmured, without glancing up at the clock on the Liver building, and kissed the top of her nose. They were taking an evening ferry to New Brighton.

'I bring news,' she said solemnly. 'Ron's asked Sam for Dot's hand and they're getting married. In only two

months' time, would you believe! They're going on honeymoon in Ireland. His Aunt Dora and Uncle Dermot have
a farm out there which they're planning on leaving to him
because they're getting on and have no kids.' She smiled
up at him. 'Isn't that good news? Billy can hardly refuse
to go to his sister's wedding so he and Josie will see each
other at last.'

'It's great news.' His eyes scanned her face which bore
traces of sunburn from their outing to Southport a couple
of days ago. 'How does Dot feel about living in Ireland?'

'That's why they're going there – to see how she feels.
Although I suspect she knows she has little choice. She
says it'd be daft of Ron to turn down the chance of having
his own place. She's going to miss the family, of course,
but it's not as if it were Australia where his youngest sister
lives. She's got two kids and lives on this huge sheep
station in the Outback.'

He squeezed her hand. 'And all I can offer you is a
house on the edge of Liverpool!'

'And a scrapyard,' she teased, returning the pressure of
his fingers as they crossed the gangway onto the ferry boat.

He smiled as she had intended, and pulling on his hand
she dragged him up the stairs to the upper deck. It was a
lovely evening, although a little clammy, and thunder had
been forecast for later. At that moment, though, the sun
was catching the surface of the water in a wide swathe
and turning it reddish-gold. A couple of crewmen cast off
and the screws turned, foaming the water. The screeching
of seagulls sounded overhead as the boat headed towards
the point where the Mersey estuary met the Irish Sea.

'I had a phone call from Phyl,' said Alex, putting his arm around Lizzie as they watched Liverpool's dockland slide by.

Immediately she felt that guilt which thinking of Phyl brought on. 'What did she say?'

'She's in Sheffield. The play's going well. Good audiences. There's talk of the tour being extended but it's definitely going back to Manchester next week. She asked would I like to go and see her?'

Lizzie stiffened. 'What did you say?'

'What do you think I said?'

'No. But maybe you should have said, "Perhaps one day, and I'll bring Lizzie. We've got something to tell you."'

He frowned. 'And how d'you think she'd have taken that?'

She leaned back against his arm and said moodily, 'I don't know. It's just that it's hard to be patient and I have this urge to say to hell with everything and just –'

'I know.' He nuzzled the side of her neck. 'It's not easy for me either.'

She knew it wasn't. That was why they went places where there were people when really all they wanted was to be alone. She gazed over the water which still looked reddish-gold in places and noticed a buoy marking a wreck. A man at Booth's had told her a number of ships had gone down in the Mersey during the war. It was hard to imagine at that moment with the river so peaceful. She said dreamily, 'Wouldn't you love to go for a swim right now?'

'Not in the Mersey, thanks.' He hugged her against him. 'I've swum in the Red Sea and that spoilt me for British waters.'

They were silent a moment as she thought about their lives before they met. 'There was a Madonna of the Sea in the convent school,' she murmured. 'It was odd, really.'

'Why?'

'No sea at Brentwood.'

Alex smiled. 'I had some good times in Palestine but I'm only now appreciating them. For years I blocked them out of my mind.'

'Because of your friend Dougie?'

He nodded.

'And now the Black Widow's married to someone else.'

'Yep. All that grief and hatred, and then to marry again so quickly! It infuriated me at the time.'

'But Dougie lives on in Syd. She can never forget him.'

'No. You're right. Still –'

'Change the subject,' she said, smiling. 'Tell me about Jerusalem. Did it feel holy?'

An amused smile lit his face. 'I wouldn't know. I don't know what it feels like to be holy. When there's a chance of being hit by a sniper's bullet it's the last thing on your mind. Although I admit to feeling awe-struck when I saw the setting sun gleaming on the Dome of the Rock.'

'I'd love to go to the Holy Land,' she said, drawing an invisible dome on the ship's rail with the tip of a finger. 'To walk where Jesus walked. I'd like to go to Egypt as well and see the pyramids and the sphinx.'

'No chance of that for a while. I reckon there's going to be trouble over Suez. You know there's already been fighting in that area?'

She sighed. 'I remember believing that when the war was over there'd be no more fighting.'

'There'll always be fighting somewhere,' said Alex. 'They've started in Kenya now.' He frowned. 'We're getting too serious. Let's change the subject. We're nearly there.'

They were soon making their way along the pier. In Lizzie's opinion New Brighton pier could not compete with the pleasures of the pier at Southend-on-Sea which was the longest in Europe, but the resort itself did have better sand and its horizons were wider because the open sea lapped its shore. It also had history because here at the mouth of the Mersey was Fort Perch Rock Battery, which Billy had told her had been camouflaged as a tea garden, complete with painted lawns and paths, during the war.

Alex had something different to say about it. 'It was built after the Napoleonic Wars on that outcrop of sandstone.' His eyes narrowed as he looked at it. 'It was known as Black Rock and the fort was intended to protect Liverpool which in those days was growing and growing. It was from that rock – so my grandma told me her da told her – wreckers used to lure ships to their doom.'

'It sounds like something out of an historical novel,' said Lizzie, her eyes smiling into his.

'It's true!' He grinned. 'You're forgetting life was even rougher and tougher for the working classes in those days and there were rich pickings to be had from sailing craft. A ship bringing gold from the Australian fields went down off the coast of Anglesey, although that was due to a storm, so it's not surprising there were wreckers and smugglers around here.' He pointed with one hand. 'See them cliffs? There's caves there. They say they lead to secret passages that link up to a pub known as Mother Redcap's at Egremont. She was notorious. The pub's still there but it's a bit of a wreck itself now. It's reputed to have been built in the sixteenth century.'

'Fascinating,' she said, squeezing his arm, having enjoyed the history lesson. 'Now how about a long cool drink? I don't know about you but the air feels even clammier to me now.'

He did not argue and after he'd had a Guinness and she a shandy, they wandered round the busy fairground and had a ride on the Big Wheel which gave them a bird's eye view of the sands and the sea. Then it was a walk along the promenade in companionable silence. She was happy just to be in his company, to feel the muscles in his arm beneath her fingers. It struck her that even in a crowd she had a sense of being one with him.

It was when they were on the return ferry that they heard the first roll of thunder and the night sky over the Liver birds turned a dirty shade of navy blue. Lightning crackled in the air and the rain sheeted down. Lizzie's sandals were filled with water and her dress was soaked by the time they reached Alex's car. She shivered all the way to the yard and it was still raining when they arrived there.

'You can't go home like that,' he said succinctly as he helped her out. 'Come inside and dry off.'

She did as he suggested and when they entered the kitchen gratefully accepted the offer of a towel. Her long black hair was like rat's tails about her face and she began to rub it dry whilst at the same time glancing about her. It was strange to think she had not been in this room since Phyl fell off the gate and hurt her ankle. Now she had time to notice the bookshelves in an alcove to one side of the fireplace and the gramophone in the other. Alex lit the fire that was already set and left her huddling close to it, willing it to burn up quickly.

When he returned he had changed into dry pants and a sloppy joe and carried a shirt and trousers. 'I know they'll be too long but you can roll the sleeves and bottoms up while you dry your dress by the fire. I'll go and put the kettle on.' He dropped her clothes on the tiger skin rug in front of the fire and went into the back kitchen.

She glanced at the half-open door and smiled as, with difficulty, she unbuttoned the sodden pink and white striped dress to the waist and slipped it off. She also removed her damp bra and underslip, glad that she'd left off her roll-on and stockings because it had been so warm earlier. She donned the shirt, the tail of which covered her bottom, and dragged on the trousers. They were much too big and she had to keep a grip on them if they were not to fall down.

Alex entered the room, carrying a tray, and there was a gleam in his eyes as he placed it on the table. 'They look better on you than me,' he said, and coming over to her he pulled her close and kissed her.

Instinctively her arms went up round his neck and the pants fell down. 'Alex!' she muttered against his mouth.

'Lizzie, I love you,' he breathed passionately against her lips. His hands ran over her hips, caressing her bare thighs as he kissed her with such force that her head went right back.

Oh Lord, she thought as his arms went round her and he lowered her onto the floor, where inconveniently or conveniently, whichever way one looked at it, her head rested against that of the poor defunct tiger. She cleared her throat. 'Alex?'

'What, sweetheart?' he said against her throat.

'Who kissed this tiger?'

He lifted his head and looked at her. 'Kissed?'

She giggled. 'I mean killed.'

He was smiling. 'What a question to ask at a time like this! I don't know. Grandpa who was washed overboard brought it home. Now shush and kiss me.'

They kissed deeply, exuberantly and at length before he removed her knickers. She was unsure whether she was shocked or not. 'Alex? What are you doing?'

'What do you think?' He pressed his lips against her stomach and inwardly she trembled, feeling as if all at once things were moving fast towards a different stage in their relationship.

'Alex, what are you doing?' she repeated.

'What does it feel like I'm doing?' He stroked her inner thigh and she shivered with pleasure but was still doubtful of the wisdom of what was taking place. She pulled his head up and they kissed as if starved.

He took off his sloppy joe without haste and undid the shirt she wore, making her somehow more aware of her body. He rubbed against her and she was conscious of an aching restraint which became too much to bear. She watched him take off his pants and the size of his whatsit came as something of a shock. She thought about making babies and remembered Syd. 'I want you, Lizzie,' whispered Alex against her mouth. 'I'll be gentle. Do you mind?'

To be wanted was what she had wanted all her life so how could she say no? She put her arms around his neck and pulled him down, giving herself to him. He wasn't as gentle as she thought he would be, but she accepted that passion and gentleness had trouble rubbing along with each other.

Afterwards they drank tea and toasted bread by the fire while her dress steamed on the clothes horse. She thought for a while and said, 'We've committed a mortal sin.'

Alex said seriously, 'Do you want me to say sorry? I wouldn't be being honest if I did because the last half hour has been the best in my life, but it won't happen again until we're married.' She was touched and stopped worrying about mortal sin, taking his hand and holding it tightly. She thought of what Phyl had said about having babies, and about Billy, and how she would need Phyl's permission to marry Alex. A shadow darkened her eyes. Would Phyl give it?

It was past eleven o'clock by the time Lizzie arrived home but there was still a light on in the parlour. She was about to let herself in quietly by the key on the string when the door opened and Sam stood there. 'What time d'you think this is to be coming in? Where've you been?'

Her heart sank and she thought quickly. 'I'm sorry. I had to take shelter from the rain at my friend's.' It wasn't really a lie. Alex was her friend as well as her lover. 'I didn't mean to be this late. I really am sorry.'

Sam's homely face relaxed. 'It's OK, lass. These things happen. You get up to bed now and be quiet about it.'

She was about to do just what he said when Billy called out, 'Dad, I want to talk to Lizzie a minute. Let her come in here.'

She looked at Sam and he nodded and went past her up the lobby.

Lizzie opened the parlour door and went inside. Billy was lying on top of the bedclothes with Mog beside him. He frowned. 'You're dry. I thought you'd be wet.'

'I took shelter in Alex's on the way home from the pictures,' she said without thinking. 'We got talking.'

'About me, I suppose,' he grunted, his hand stroking the cat.

She was suddenly cross with him, and herself for being honest. 'You flatter yourself! It's over two months since Alex offered you that job and yet you're still moping around in here. All the beautiful weather we've had and still you've stayed put! You're stubborn and stupid, and poor Josie's miserable. She wants to help and so does Joe. He might always be spouting poetry and stuff but he's big and strong with helping out on the farm, and –' Her voice trailed off.

Billy looked down at his legs and said slowly, 'You called me a coward a while back. You were right. I know it's corny but I looked death in the face out there on the Atlantic. I've had to fight thoughts of death before I could face up to life.' He lifted his gaze. 'You tell Alex to drop by if you see him again. That's if he's still willing to take me on?'

Lizzie blinked. She could hardly believe he had just said that in the old voice. She nodded and kissed his cheek, unable to find words to express how she felt, and then she tiptoed up to bed, feeling quite dizzy with emotion after the evening she'd had.

The next morning was like someone's birthday just because Billy had said he wanted someone to push him to the library and had told his mam he was going to have a go at that job Alex had offered.

'I think I'll go to church,' said Maisie, a slight quiver in her voice as she took off her turban-style headscarf and reached for the hat she kept in the sideboard cupboard. She smiled tremulously at her elder son. 'I'm going to get down on my knees and thank God for the change in you, me lad.'

'Don't get too excited, Mam,' he drawled. 'I'm not going to take up me bed and walk.'

'No, son.' Her voice was even shakier than before. 'But miracles can happen.'

'Good God, church on a Wednesday,' said Trev, hoisting the haversack with his school books in over his shoulder. 'Are you sure it'll be open, Mam?'

'Of course it will.' She smiled at him. 'Now you get off to that Tec School or you'll be late. And you, too, Mary.

You haven't finished school yet.' She turned to Lizzie who was cramming a packet of sandwiches into her bag and eyed her carefully. 'Will you let Alex know, luv, about what our Billy says? And tell him to drop our Phyl a line in Sheffield and let her know too. I'm not much good at writing. If this doesn't bring her home for a visit, nothing will. It's time she had a go at getting back with Alex. All this gadding about from town to town at her age is a mistake if you ask me. But if she comes home now I'm sure he'd have her back like a shot. She'll need to put her skates on mind. He's a good-looking man and some find a reputation even more attractive. I did hear tell he's been seen with someone else. You wouldn't have heard anything about that, would you, Lizzie?' She looked slightly anxious.

'If I'd heard I would have told you,' said Lizzie as casually as she could despite her racing heart. She was annoyed at Maisie's assumption that Phyl only had to return and Alex would be panting for her. She thought of telling the truth but realised that on her way out to work was hardly the right time. Besides it was something that Phyl had to know first.

As she walked to the bus stop she thought of what Maisie had said. She pictured Phyl's expression when last they had spoken about Alex and remembered her stepmother saying she could not imagine life without him. She pushed the memory away, feeling suddenly vulnerable and young. She needed Alex and was glad that instead of waiting until tomorrow to see him she had a legitimate excuse to call at the yard this evening instead.

*

'You're thrilled,' said Alex, turning round from the sink where he was washing his hands.

'Of course I'm thrilled.' Lizzie leaned against a small oil-cloth topped table. 'It's such a relief to know that he's going to be sensible. You haven't changed your mind, have you? You will still give him the job?'

'If he wants it, he can have it.' He upturned the enamel bowl and reached for a towel. 'It won't be long before Harry retires. He can teach Billy all he knows before he goes.' His gaze rested on her face. 'Is that the only reason you came round to see me?'

She flicked away a fly. 'It's no use trying to hide things from you, is it?'

'So there is something you're trying to hide?' he said lightly. 'It's not that Billy's an attractive, courageous young devil, and you fancy him instead of me? That last night put you off?'

She stared at him, utterly taken aback. 'That is a joke?'

'Not a very funny one by the look on your face,' he said ruefully. 'Sorry.'

'I should think so.' She flushed. 'It's almost as bad as Phyl's accusing me of not wanting him because he couldn't walk.'

'I've said I'm sorry.'

'Yes. I'm sorry too.' She placed a hand through his arm. 'Alex, you don't still fancy Phyl, do you?'

He stared down at her. 'It's your turn now, is it? Why are you asking?'

'Because I want to know, of course.'

'You shouldn't need to ask,' he said. 'We made love last night, didn't we? Do you think I'd want to make love to you like that if I still fancied Phyl?'

She rested her head against his arm. 'I hope not. But I'm inexperienced. Did you ever make love to her in that way?'

He sighed and lifted her head by her hair. 'I'm not liking this conversation, Lizzie.'

She looked up into his face and had second thoughts. 'Neither am I. Kiss me, Alex.'

'No. Tell me what this is all about?'

'It's nothing.'

He continued to stare at her. Then he kissed her so hard that her lips tingled when he stopped. 'I'm taking you home,' he muttered, relaxing his hold on her hair.

'Why?' She touched her lips tentatively. She had rather enjoyed the hint of caveman tactics, although she had a feeling she would not have liked too much of them.

'You want me to see Billy, don't you?'

'Yes, but –' She sighed. 'Couldn't you kiss me some more?'

Suddenly his face creased into a smile. 'You're blatant. But no, I won't kiss you some more. Who knows where it might lead? Go and get in the car while I get my jacket.'

'Meanie boots,' she murmured, having picked up the phrase from Trev.

When they arrived outside the house Billy was sitting in his chair on the pavement, a book on his knee, watching

a game of rounders in progress and shouting encourage-
ment to his brother. Maisie hovered in the background
with Lois's baby balanced on her hip while Lois herself
was gossiping with one of the neighbours. As they got
out of the car Lizzie was aware that they were the focus
of several pairs of eyes.

Billy took the book from his lap and held it out to
Alex. 'I've been reading this.'

Alex showed no surprise as he took it from Billy and
Lizzie did her best to appear nonchalant as she peered
over his arm and read *Renovating Old Furniture*. 'Any
good?' asked Alex.

'I'm no expert,' replied Billy, his face reddening. 'But
I can do most joints he talks about in there and I can
french polish.'

Alex handed the book back to him. 'I'll give you a
trial. Pick you up at eight tomorrow morning. Be ready.'

'OK,' said Billy, smiling.

Lizzie could not believe it had been settled as simply
as that. She stared at Alex who nodded in Maisie's and
then Lois's direction before turning to her. 'See you tomorrow.' He leaned towards Lizzie and kissed her before
getting back into the car and driving off.

With her cheeks burning Lizzie placed an arm round
Billy's shoulders and hugged him. 'That was quick work.
I'm real made up for you.'

'He's not the only quick worker round here, is he?' intervened Lois, poking her face between them. Her blue eyes
were glacial. 'No wonder Alex broke it off with our Phyl.
You two have been carrying on! How disloyal can you get?'

'It's not true!' Lizzie straightened up swiftly.

'Isn't it? Our Phyl's always wanted Alex Payne and you took him from her.'

'It's not true,' insisted Lizzie. 'If she'd really wanted him she'd have put him first instead of acting her socks off in some play.'

'She left because she found out about the pair of you. It was all she had left,' said Lois dramatically.

'No! No!' It was all Lizzie could think of to say. The accusation made her feel worse than she had thought she would.

Maisie stepped forward and thrust the baby at Lois. 'Take your son and get inside,' she said fiercely. 'This is hardly the place to wash our dirty linen.' She pushed her daughter in the direction of the front door.

Lois marched up the lobby as Maisie turned to Lizzie. 'You get indoors too.'

Lizzie met her gaze squarely. 'I was going to go.' She followed in Lois's wake, her heart thumping in her chest, wishing that Alex had not kissed and left her the way he had. Dirty! That was how they would regard she and Alex making love, but it hadn't felt like that at all.

Lois took up a stance in front of the fireplace, ignoring her father and Mary who were both reading. She glared at Lizzie. 'You bitch!'

'That's enough of that,' said her mother, entering the room.

'We should never have taken her in, Mam,' said Lois her expression ugly. 'I knew Phyl had made a mistake. Someone else's child! She should have known better.'

'What's all the shouting about?' said Sam, lowering the newspaper. He was getting slightly deaf and lately was ignoring the disputes between his womenfolk.

'Nothing for you to worry about,' said Maisie swiftly. 'Our Billy needs you. Go and get our Trev to help you bring him in.'

Sam glanced at the faces of his wife and second eldest daughter, shook his head and left the room.

Lizzie would have liked to follow him out but knew that would look like she was running away. What she had thought might happen was happening and she was not enjoying it one bit.

'You're wrong about Phyl,' she said to Lois as calmly as she could. 'She loves being on the stage. You know that. She doesn't want Alex!' There was a sudden desperate note in her voice.

'And if you believe that then I believe pigs'll fly,' said Lois. 'Why didn't she stick it out in London? It was what she went there for.'

'Because we had no money. And after Daddy ki— died she wanted to be with you. She missed you all.'

'Ha! That's a lie!' said Lois. 'Our Phyl always had an independent streak in her. No, this is all *your* fault. You've always liked Alex. Even when you were a kid you were always round at that yard.'

Lizzie knew that was true, so it was impossible to deny it. She glanced at Maisie, having expected her to put in her tuppeny ha'penny worth before now. She cared about what Maisie thought. 'I haven't done anything underhand, honestly.'

'Perhaps not intentionally,' said Maisie, sitting down as if she was really weary. 'If anyone's to blame it's Alex. He's older and should know better. You're a nice-looking girl, Lizzie, and I reckon he's using you to make our Phyl jealous.'

Using me! she thought. The idea had never occurred to her and suddenly she felt quite sick.

'I can see why you're attracted to him,' continued Maisie. 'He's a good-looking man and he's been kind to you. Probably taken the place of the father you lost.'

'The father I lost!' Lizzie could not prevent a bitter laugh. 'You're mistaken! Daddy didn't care about me in the least. If you'd known him you'd realise just how wrong you are.'

'So he wasn't like Alex,' said Maisie without hesitation. 'It makes even more sense then that you'd be looking for the things you'd have expected from a father.'

Lizzie could not believe what she was hearing. 'It's not a bit like that between us,' she said in a despairing voice. 'How can you say that?'

'Easy,' said Lois, rocking her son who had started to cry. 'Our Phyl encouraged you to look upon him as a father. She wanted the three of you to live together like a happy little family. More fool her! You're a Jezebel.'

'No!' cried Lizzie. 'Alex never wanted that. He told me ages ago it would be a mistake!'

'I thought he had his head screwed on right,' said Maisie. 'He saw the way you felt. Probably had some experience with that Black Widow. Now look at this sensibly, Lizzie. Alex ran out of patience with our Phyl so he determined to bring her to her senses. First by breaking off the engagement, then by using you. It was unkind of him but probably he was feeling desperate. Why else would he have kissed you in front of us? Alex isn't the kind of man to show his emotions to the world. I've known him since he was born, and he did it so it would get back to our Phyl.' She looked squarely at Lizzie. 'It'll have to stop, love. You're only nineteen and with our Phyl away I'm responsible for you. Men get frustrated and that's probably half the problem. You'll see – when our Phyl comes back they'll sort things out between them. In the meantime you're not to see him. I'll have a word with him about you and thank him for what he's going to do for our Billy.'

Lizzie stared at her, her head aching from the force of Maisie's argument. She felt as if she'd been hammered with words and now was horrified at the thought of Maisie speaking to Alex about her as if she was a child. 'No! You've no right! You're not my bloody mother!' The words burst from her. 'And all that you've said is cruel and untrue!'

Maisie's mouth set in a straight line. 'No, girl, I'm not your mother. More's the pity! Because if I had been none of this would have happened. Now why don't you go upstairs and get out of your working clothes and have a rest?'

'You're too soft with her, Mam,' cried Lois. 'If what she's just said isn't ingratitude, I don't know what is! The way you've cooked and washed for her, she ought to be ashamed of herself! And she swore at you! And what

about our Billy? That's another thing.' She turned on
Lizzie. 'You were going out with him not so long ago but
then he got crippled. Is that why you looked elsewhere?
I don't agree with Mam that you're such an innocent. I'm
going to write to our Phyl and tell her she's been nurtur-
ing a serpent in her bosom.'

'You're talking rot,' said Mary, taking them all by
surprise. 'You sound just like the other woman in a Mills
and Boon novel, Lois. Lizzie's no snake in the grass. She
cares about our Phyl and our Billy.'

Lois shot her a venomous look. 'And what do you
know about anything? You're only a kid! So shut up and
keep out of this.'

Mary looked at her scornfully. 'Why should I? You've
got enough to say. You don't even belong here any more,
so why don't you go home before Lizzie or I clock you
one like you deserve? Since when were you such great
buddies with our Phyl? Just tell me that.'

'She's my sister, *child,*' said Lois, her eyes glinting.
'And you only have to make one step towards me and it'll
be *you* getting clocked.'

'I think this has gone far enough,' said Maisie, slamming the flat of her hand down on the table. 'Not another
word. Lizzie knows how we feel and I hope she's got
enough sense to see what's the right thing to do. Don't!'
she added firmly as Lois opened her mouth. 'Haven't you
got a husband at home to go to?'

Lois pressed her lips together, stuck her nose in the
air and flounced out of the room, leaving a heavy silence
behind her. As if from a great distance Lizzie could hear

her muttering to the baby as she strapped him in his pram and moments later heard her saying, 'Goodbye!' in a sniffy voice to someone outside.

'Good riddance,' said Mary. 'She has too much to say, Mam.'

'Aye, and so have you, girl,' said Maisie. 'She is older than you and you should show her a bit of respect.'

Mary frowned. 'But she was saying all those awful things about Lizzie.'

'Aye, well, some of them were true,' said her mother, glancing at Lizzie. 'Remember what I said, girl. You aren't to see Alex tomorrow.'

She cleared her throat. 'You can't stop me. I'll see him when he comes in the morning to pick Billy up.'

'No, you will not.' Maisie's expression was stern. 'I'll lock you in your bedroom first. Now no more back answers or you'll be getting a smack.'

Suddenly Lizzie could not take any more. What was the point? Maisie wasn't going to listen or believe anything she said. And what about when Billy, Sam and Trev came in? And then Dot? When Maisie said her piece they'd all see things from her point of view. Steadying her voice, she said, 'I'm going to my room. I don't want any tea,' and walked out of the kitchen looking straight ahead.

She ran upstairs, half-expecting one of them to follow her. In the attic she dropped on to the bed, pressing her face into the cotton bedspread. Her heart felt like a pendulum too heavy to swing any more. She was gripped by a sense of horror. Her first instinct was to go to Alex. He would reassure her. Tell her that not one thing Maisie had said was true. She wished she could wipe the words out of her mind. They had sounded so feasible but they could not be true. Alex wouldn't use her! She tried to think sensibly but couldn't. 'He's used you, used you to make Phyl jealous!' No! It wasn't true, it wasn't! It wasn't! 'You're a snake! All what Phyl's done for you and you've betrayed her!' No! No! she cried inwardly, restlessly turning over and over on the bed. Unexpectedly that old memory of Alex lying on the bed with Phyl re-established itself. She could almost see them and felt pain and a grief so sharp that it made her gasp for air. Phyl had loved him and he must have made love to her. She thought of how Alex had not really answered her when she had asked him whether he still fancied Phyl, only parrying the question with one of his own about them making love. Even when she had questioned him about making love with Phyl he had not really denied it. Now that she had set herself to think, more memories came rushing in. She thought of how Phyl had taken control when her father had killed himself. How she had brought Lizzie to Liverpool and kept her out of her own pocket. There were so many things Phyl had done for her, but since her stepmother had gone away Lizzie had seldom thought of her except with a sense of guilt. She was torn by anguish and that same guilt. How many times had she said she owed Phyl?

Lizzie could not bear the way she felt. She wanted to stop thinking of Phyl. Phyl had gone. Phyl was acting. Phyl couldn't want Alex that much, not like she did. She wanted to hold on to the memories that she herself had shared with Alex. They were good memories and made it impossible for her to believe that he had used her. Yet was it possible that she had come between him and Phyl? And that if she had not been so willing to be loved by him, he might not have responded to that love in her reaching out to him? Perhaps if she was not there they could find each other again? The thought of walking out of their lives hurt deeply but she could not get rid of it. Perhaps they really did want each other? And maybe they didn't. She just didn't know what was the truth any more. She only knew that she owed it to Phyl to try and make her happy, whatever the cost to herself, but oh God, it was going to be painful!

She couldn't do it, Lizzie decided. It would hurt too much. There, she'd made her decision. She couldn't go. But she could not stop her thoughts. They continued to whirl around in her head and the one that lingered longest was the one that said Phyl had to have her chance with Alex. If Lizzie herself was to go somewhere, he would go and visit Phyl. For a moment Lizzie quailed once more at the thought of leaving Alex, of spending day after day without a glimpse of his smile or the chance of touching him. Would he be hurt at her going without a word or was Maisie right? After all, Lizzie had only been a part of his life for five years, while Phyl had always been there.

She thought of Alex coming in the morning for Billy, and Maisie's spoken intention of locking her in the bedroom and speaking to Alex about her. The thought of being treated like an inbetween, not a grown-up, not a child, made her furious. Why had she stayed with this family anyway? She didn't belong! She wasn't really one of them.

Lizzie decided she would not weaken and dragged her suitcase from under the bed. She packed as many of her clothes as she could, as well as the *Treasury of Poems* given to her by the twins and her Cinderella's slipper, taking the money she had saved in it out first. She hesitated over a photograph of Alex with Blackie, taken when she had borrowed Sam's Brownie camera a few summers ago, then packed it.

She gazed at the dolls' house under the window and knelt in front of it, regretting that she had to leave it behind. It was the best present she had ever been given. Alex had cared about her then. He did now, but did he really love her? She felt herself weakening and forced herself to think of Phyl lying on the bed with him in this very room. She squared her shoulders and hoped Mary would take care of the dolls' house. Perhaps she should leave a note bequeathing it to her? No! She couldn't give it away. Maybe one day she would come back for it.

Lizzie had no clear idea where she was going but as she snapped shut the locks on her suitcase she remembered that a Crosville coach left for London from St John's Lane, travelling overnight. The twins had used it when they'd gone down to see Matt and Lily and the new baby. It had cost them thirty bob each. The fare had gone up like everything else because of rising wages since then but she had enough money, having taken just over five pounds out of her Cinderella slipper. She also had a little money in her Post Office savings book. What about work? She'd have to send to Booth's for her cards. Perhaps she could phone them in the morning from London, making some excuse? A sick aunt maybe who lived in the south? The excuse sounded vaguely familiar but if she was to catch that coach she had no time to sit here wondering why.

She crept downstairs, feeling like a burglar, half hoping someone might hear her. She paused on the bottom stair and could hear the wireless and the murmur of voices from the kitchen. One of them was Billy's. Instantly tears threatened to overwhelm her. She would not be there when he started his job, nor would she see Dot marry her Ron. Unless . . . Carefully she opened the door, slipped out, and closed it gently behind her. Then she walked up the street, telling herself not to look back.

Chapter Fourteen

Lizzie's legs felt as if they didn't quite belong to her as she stumbled across the tarmac of Victoria coach station and out into Buckingham Palace Road. Everything felt strange. She had eventually fallen asleep on the coach to dream she was in Jerusalem standing on the pinnacle of the Dome of the Rock with Alex far below swimming in the sea. The only way to get to him had been to jump. She had woken instantly to find herself in London. She had experienced panic, wondering if she had gone quite mad to have run away from Alex when she loved him. Then she reminded herself why she had done it, and that mad or not she was in London and had to find herself a job and somewhere to live.

Although it was much too early in the morning to do either, she decided to leave her suitcase in the left luggage at Victoria and have a wander round. Her legs felt like they needed to be stretched, to run and jump after being crammed between seats for hours. The city was coming alive and the muted noise of traffic reminded her of the sleepy chirruping of birds just before they burst into the dawn chorus. She felt empty, having eaten nothing since lunch yesterday, although she had grabbed a quick cup of coffee in the Punch and Judy cafe in Lime Street before catching the coach.

She walked aimlessly, still feeling disorientated and trying not to think of Alex and the family. Eventually she did manage to concentrate on the scene about her, only to realise she was in unfamiliar territory, having wandered into a warren of streets where if there wasn't a pub on a corner or a small restaurant there was a grocery or a secondhand shop. None was open. A milk float passed her and stopped a few yards up the road. She realised how thirsty she was and broke into a run.

'Can I have a pinta, please?' she asked, fishing a coin out of her pocket.

'You anuffa one,' said the milkman, taking the money from her and handing her a bottle.

'Nuther what?'

'Bleedin' foreigner.' He grinned. 'Not that yer as foreign as he is in there.' He jerked a thumb in the direction of a dingy-looking door half open behind him. 'What I meant is, yer not from round 'ere, are yer, gerl? Yerra Scouser. I came across some of your lot in the war.'

She laughed, unable to believe what he was saying. 'I was born down here! My parents lived here for years, out Camden Town way. I'm looking for somewhere I can get something to eat and stay. D'you know of any rooms going?'

'Naw. The way housin' is they're snapped up quick. But if yer not fussy ol' Jan in 'ere might be able to help you with a bite to eat. This place is open all night and he's just tidying up before going 'ome.' He went over to the building behind him and poked his head through the doorway. 'Jan mate!' he yelled. 'Young damsel in distress out here.'

There was no response. The milkman shrugged and she was just about to thank him and walk on when a man appeared. 'What is it you want?' he asked in heavily accented tones.

'The gel's 'ungry and got no 'ome to go to,' said the milkman. 'Yer'll see 'er orlright, won't yer, mate?'

The man looked at Lizzie. 'You are hungry?'

'Yes.' She smiled but received no answering smile.

'You wait up road by pub on corner. I will come soon.' He went back inside the building.

'Do as he sez,' said the milkman. 'He's just being careful because he don't want any trouble.'

'What d'you mean trouble?' asked Lizzie.

'Ask no questions and yer get told no lies. Now get yerself on me float and I'll give yer a ride up the pub.'

She did as he said and thanked him before he continued his round. She glanced at the pub which was tiled in a bilious shade of green. There were signs of vomit on the pavement which she carefully avoided. Not the most salubrious of neighbourhoods. She thought of Scottie Road where there was a pub on every corner and wrenched the cardboard top off the milk bottle and drank.

A few moments later Jan made his appearance, stopping in front of her and taking from inside his frayed tweed jacket a brown paper bag which he handed to her. She thanked him. 'It is my pleasure,' he said, bowing slightly. 'Often I have been hungry.' He watched as she opened the bag and took out a doorstep sandwich. She thrust the half-empty milk bottle at him and bit into hardish bread and heavily spiced steak.

'When did last you eat?' he asked, picking up the paper bag she had dropped and folding it neatly.

'Yesterday lunchtime.' The words were indistinct as she spoke with her mouth full and unexpectedly her eyes filled with tears. Oh Lord, she was turning into a proper crybaby!

'Once I did not eat for two days and when I did it was raw sugar beet.' The words were spoken matter-of-factly.

She scrubbed her eyes and said unsteadily, 'Was it during the war?'

He nodded. 'I was in a labour camp in Germany but I escape and decide to return to my own country.'

'Where's that?' She was not really interested but he had helped her so she felt she had to make an effort.

'Poland.'

'You're a refugee?'

'When the Russians came we decided to leave. My family, they did not want to be communists.' He nodded solemnly several times and a lock of light brown hair fell on to his forehead. 'Ted, he say you have no home and you cry. So this, it is true?'

Lizzie thought of the Eccleses and Alex. It was corny but true that home was where the heart was, and hers was still back in Liverpool. That was why she felt so empty. 'I have nowhere I can go right now.' She finished the sandwich which she had enjoyed and licked her fingers before wiping them on a handkerchief. He handed her the milk bottle which she drained. 'That was lovely, thanks. I hope you won't get into trouble for feeding me? The milkman seemed to think you might.'

The smallest of smiles lit his eyes. 'There is no need for you to vorry. The boss he has left. The food it would only be thrown out but he would rather that to my taking it home.'

'That seems stupid,' she said politely.

'He is a mean man.' Jan took the empty milk bottle from her and placed it on the pub doorstep beside a couple of full bottles. 'This morning he go early because there was trouble last night. There was a man with a gun.'

Lizzie had been about to go but she hesitated. What he said sounded like something out of the flicks. 'He didn't shoot anyone, did he?'

'No. He wave the gun about and I worry because it remind me of the Nazis and I think that sooner or later men with guns are tempted to fire them. I decide then that perhaps I will find somewhere else to work. Maybe I go to the seaside. There is work there in the summer.' He fell silent.

Work! Refugee! They had so little. She took out her purse but he put a hand over hers. 'No. I did not pay for it. I explain to you.'

She hesitated again then held out her hand. 'It was kind of you. I really appreciated it and it was nice meeting you.'

'So polite.' He took her hand and a grave smile appeared in the eyes that appeared more silver than grey. 'It was nice meeting you too. I hope you will be OK.'

She was tempted to say dramatically, My life's ruined. I'll never be OK. Instead she freed her hand. 'I'd best go. Thanks again for the sandwich. Bye.' She turned and walked away and after a while found herself in the Tottenham Court Road. Where to stay? It was then she remembered Phyl had stayed in a Methodist hostel in the area once. She had told her that it was an improvement on a house she had stayed at near Clapham Common, infested by bugs. Lizzie tried to remember what the hostel was called but when she saw Emerson Bainbridge House, she knew it.

Her luck was out. There were no vacancies and the woman in reception told her she would have problems finding anywhere cheap at this time of year. Nevertheless she gave her the address of the nearest YWCA, but they were full too. Lizzie felt depressed and wished herself back in Liverpool. She decided to phone Booth's and went in search of a telephone box.

Wendy in Personnel was very sympathetic about Lizzie's sick aunt and offered to send wages and holiday money along to her address with her cards. The remark threw her completely and she could have kicked herself for not thinking things through. Then she recalled Booth's London office and suggested Wendy send everything there. She decided she might as well try for a job there as well. Wendy said she hoped her aunt would be better soon.

Lizzie felt a little happier when she left the telephone box. Now all she had to do was to apply for that job and find somewhere to stay. For a moment she considered Josie's relations but decided against it, realising she did not want anyone knowing where she was just yet. Her emotions were in such a mess she needed time to sort herself out.

At Booth's her luck was out once more. There was nothing suitable for her at the moment but if she would like to call in after the weekend she could pick up her cards and wages.

Lizzie left the building, feeling lost and lonely, and wondering what to do next. For a brief moment she recalled a younger version of herself standing outside Lime Street station feeling just the same. Her excuse for leaving then had been a sick aunt. She had intended asking for her address at the convent. It occurred to her then that maybe it was a good idea still. After all, what had she to lose?

Everything seems the same, marvelled Lizzie, as she walked up Queen's Road in Brentwood. There was the spire of St Helen's soaring above the roofs and trees. She remembered how during the war the lower windows had been blacked out and Benediction had been brought forward to three in the afternoon.

Unexpectedly she experienced a sense of fear and loneliness as she pictured a small girl with black pigtails saying goodbye to her mother. Sophie Knight had been a blonde but not particularly beautiful, her mouth being too big for her face, but she had possessed a strength of character which could be fearsome. Just like Phyl in a way, thought Lizzie, remembering her stepmother making her carry her suitcase all the way down the slippery road to the station way back in '47. Misery swamped her thinking of Phyl and Alex way up north.

She came to the school gates and hesitated. Perhaps Mother Clare was dead? She had been ancient when Lizzie had left. Then she decided she would never discover her aunt's whereabouts if she did not ask, and passed through the gates.

'So Elizabeth, you've come back,' said the old nun. The eyes in her wrinkled face framed by a starched wimple seemed just as penetrating as in the past.

She must be ninety if she's a day, thought Lizzie, thankful that nuns like clergy never seemed to retire. She cleared her throat, wishing she did not feel so in awe. 'I've come to ask if you can help me find my aunt,' she said clearly. 'I believe she was a pupil at the school just as my mother was?'

'May I ask why you wish to see her?' asked the nun after the barest hesitation.

'She's the only family I have and I'd like to get to know her. I don't even know if she's married and if I've any cousins or not.'

'Have you not been happy with your stepmother, child?' The old nun's voice softened. 'Was she unkind to you?'

The question took Lizzie by surprise. 'Oh, no,' she responded swiftly. 'It isn't anything like that! It's as I said. My parents are both dead and I would like to know my aunt.'

Mother Clare was silent a moment, then she seemed to come to a decision. 'Your aunt sometimes visits us. Our way of life interests her . . . but I'll say no more about that. I'll give you her address.' She took a pen from a holder on the desk and drew a sheet of paper towards her.

Lizzie came out on to Queen's Road and gazed in the direction of the Spread Eagle pub. She would have enjoyed a shandy but knew she'd be looked at askance if she went in the pub alone. Besides time was getting on and if she was to find the farm where Aunt Charlotte lived she was going to have to get a move on.

Broom Farm . . . Lizzie needed directions. She stood in Tindal Square at the top end of the High Street in Chelmsford, considering her next move. She thought of what Mother Superior had said about her aunt and found the nearest smithy.

'Sure I shoe Miss Broom's horses, miss. They're the love of her life. She has no time for us men.' He chuckled. 'You reckon on going out there?'

'Yes. Is there a bus I can get?'

'One goes to the village not far away but I reckon you've missed it.'

'Blast!' muttered Lizzie, her shoulders sagging with weariness. 'Is it within walking distance?'

He looked thoughtful as he took a swig of tea from a chipped white mug. 'Guess you could walk it but it's a few miles. If you hang on you'd maybe get a lift. Miss Broom's stable girl should be in any minute. She dropped a harness in this morning needin' mending.'

'Thanks!' Lizzie decided to wait outside where it would be cooler away from the forge.

She had not been there long when a girl drove up in a rattling truck. She jumped down, leaving the engine running. Her hair was long and blonde and she wore well-worn beige corduroy jodhpurs and a checked shirt. She and the girl looked much of an age, thought Lizzie.

She waited until the girl re-emerged from the smithy before approaching her. 'Are you from Broom Farm?'

'Yes. What can I do for you?' The girl had a harassed look about her.

'Could you give me a lift there?'

'Sure. Jump in.' She waved a hand in the direction of the truck. 'You'll have to make your own way back, though, and it's a good three miles.'

Lizzie smiled. 'Thanks for the information but I'm hoping to stay the night.'

'Miss Broom doesn't take paying guests,' said the girl hastily. 'She only hires mounts on a daily basis.'

'Miss Broom is my aunt,' informed Lizzie. 'I'm Elizabeth Knight. Her sister was my mother.'

The girl's expression changed and she surveyed Lizzie with lively curiosity. 'Is that so! You'd best get in quickly then and we'll see what she has to say.'

'Thanks a lot.' Lizzie climbed into the cab and within seconds they rattled off up the street. She clutched the seat as the vehicle clipped the kerb as it turned a corner.

'I'm Penny Smith,' said the girl. 'Your aunt has mentioned you a couple of times.'

'Has she?' That sounded promising. 'I wasn't sure if she knew I existed.'

'Oh, she knows all right. I heard your name only recently when they were talking.'

'Who's they?'

'Miss Broom and her solicitor. Not that we see much of him. She doesn't encourage men to call but recently she's been feeling her age. Her rheumatism gets to her in the winter.'

Lizzie could not resist a smile. She had been saying all along she had a sick aunt. Perhaps it was meant that she should arrive now? 'How old is she?'

'No idea. But she must be getting on. She remembers the Boer War.'

Lizzie did sums in her head. 'That could make her in her late-fifties. It's not exactly ancient.'

'No, but work's physically hard and most of it's outdoors.' Penny grimaced. 'She won't have a man working on the place, that's her trouble. The vet comes sometimes but more often than not she doses the horses with her own remedies.'

They were now outside Chelmsford and going pretty fast along a winding lane where trees grew on either side. A side window was open and Lizzie took in deep breaths of air laden with the scent of damp earth and growing things. She thought of her aunt and came to the not-so-welcome conclusion that Charlotte Broom might turn out to be as strong a character as her sister Sophie, but Lizzie was in no mood to be intimidated and was ready to stand up for herself.

What she was not prepared for was the family likeness.

Her aunt had Lizzie's black hair and brown eyes, as
well as her high cheekbones and dimpled chin, but there
the similarity ended. She had a stronger broader nose and
her facial skin was the colour of an oak leaf in autumn.
Her thick eyebrows were straight lines and bristled like
Robert Newton's Long John Silver in Walt Disney's
Treasure Island. She wore khaki twill cotton breeches over
bony hips, and despite the heat of summer had on a thick
Arran sweater over a man's shirt. Lizzie felt like a city girl
in a blue organdie dress bordered with broderie Anglaise.

'So you've come at last,' said her aunt briskly. 'About
time too.'

Lizzie held out a hand. 'I wasn't sure if you even knew
if I was born or not until today.'

'Of course I knew about you,' declared Charlotte.
'Sophie sent me a page from a newspaper – Births,
Marriages, Deaths. No letter with an address. Didn't want
me turning up on her doorstep. Stupid nonsense! And all
over a man!' She gave Lizzie a piercing look. 'I suppose
I should have enquired earlier about you from the nuns
but it's only lately I've started thinking about my own
departure from this fair earth. I had no idea your parents
were both dead until a couple of months ago. I was sorry
about that because I wanted to heal the breech. Too late
now but I thought maybe you and I could make it up. I
was told you'd gone up north so I had my solicitor set a
man to find you. Not so easy because we didn't know
your stepmother's maiden name, but Somerset House
helped us out there. I'm glad to see I haven't been wasting
my money and he found you.'

'Nobody found me.' Lizzie was puzzled. 'I'm here, Aunt Charlotte, because I wanted to meet you. As far as I know you're my only family.'

'You mean you haven't seen any detective or had a letter from my solicitor?'

'No. I'm here because . . .' She hesitated. 'I've just given you my reasons. I wish you'd started looking for me a few years back, you could have saved me a lot of heartache.' She glanced about her at several horses in a paddock, the red brick mock-Tudor farmhouse and stabling with more horses. She could not quite believe what she was seeing.

'This was my dream at fourteen. I was horse crazy.'

'You ride, girl?'

'Not for some time, but I'm sure it'll come back to me.'

'That's marvellous!' The bristling eyebrows twitched together over the powerful Roman nose. 'You can take over this place when I'm dead!' A twisted, nobbly hand encompassed the yard, house and stabling. 'I'll show you how to cope with it all, of course. We'll start work tomorrow.'

Suddenly Lizzie's head was spinning. One minute she had nothing. The next she was being offered a home, and something more than a home – the horses and the countryside she had once longed for more than anything. 'I didn't expect this,' she said shakily. 'You don't know me, Aunt. You mightn't like me. We mightn't get on.'

Charlotte smiled. 'I'm glad I've surpassed your expectations. You'll be staying then? It's the only way we will get to know each other.'

'I'd be daft to say no,' said Lizzie frankly, squaring her shoulders. 'I'll have to go to London on Monday, though. My suitcase is in the left luggage and I have to collect my cards from the firm I worked for.'

'As long as you come back,' said Charlotte, patting her shoulder. 'Now come inside, Elizabeth, and have some supper. Tell me how you managed to find me if it wasn't that damn' detective who gave you the information? I'll have to have him stopped.'

'I went to the convent and asked Mother Clare about you.' She followed her aunt, who walked with a limp, inside the house into a large untidy kitchen. There were red quarry tiles on the floor and a bare wooden table stood square in the centre of the room. A wooden dresser held cups on hooks, several mismatched plates and saucers, and sheaves of what looked like bills and leaflets. There were a couple of books and a set of leading reins on a shelf. On top of an Aga a large saucepan steamed and under the window was a white sink with a wooden draining board.

'You like stew?' said Charlotte, taking three plates from the dresser.

'I'd eat anything. I've had nothing since . . .' She remembered the Polish refugee. 'I had a butty this morning.'

'Butty?'

'Scouse for sandwich. I've lived in Liverpool since '47.'

'With your stepmother. I suppose you've had a difficult time with her? If only I'd known.'

'No. You're wrong,' said Lizzie swiftly. She would not have people believing Phyl had been cruel to her. 'We lived with her family. Four girls, two boys and a granny. Phyl's a lot younger than Daddy was, you know. She's twenty-nine, an actress, and very attractive.' Much more attractive than me, she thought helplessly, so how can Alex resist her if I'm out of the way?

'I like Greer Garson,' said Charlotte. 'Did you see her as Mrs Miniver? The film was set during the war. She was a strong woman. Women found their place during the war. The trouble came when the men returned. I'll tell you now, Elizabeth, I have no time for the so-called stronger sex.' She spooned stew awkwardly on to plates. 'If you've a girlfriend you're welcome to invite her. There's plenty of room. Christmas would be nice – make a party of it. Ask as many girlfriends as you like but no boyfriends. I don't want you to feel cut off out here.' She straightened. 'Now if you'll call Penny that would be a help to me. She'll be out in the yard somewhere. Strong girl and hard-working, but softhearted. Used to make the delivery men cups of tea.'

'I'd call that hospitable,' said Lizzie, heading for the door.

Her aunt shook her head. 'That's not all. She allowed the Driver boys to keep the apples they stole from my trees.'

Lizzie concealed a smile. 'Who are the Driver boys?'

'Two imps of Satan who live in the village. Now hurry, girl, or the stew'll get cold.'

Lizzie hurried, wondering what her aunt would have made of Billy in his youth and Trev as he was now. She felt instantly homesick and pushed them out of her mind.

As she crossed the yard to where Penny was shovelling soiled straw into a mound, she wondered what the male race had done to Aunt Charlotte and asked the groom.

'You don't know? She was in love with her cousin but he didn't want her.'

Lizzie was really interested. 'Tell me more?'

'He came to live here after your grandad died from TB when she was only a little girl, right? He was her only male cousin and your grandmother thought he'd settle here and eventually do all that your grandad did. But he didn't settle. He ran away to Wales and joined the HMS *Conway* training ship. Apparently he'd always wanted to go to sea but his parents wouldn't let him, but they gave in once he was there. He made captain eventually and sailed out of Liverpool. But it did mean that only the women were left in charge here.'

Lizzie understood now. 'What happened next?'

'Miss Broom kept this place going by inheriting money from a maiden aunt. The cousin died a couple of years back. I reckon she never forgave him for preferring the sea to her but regrets missing out on having a child.'

Penny paused and eyed Lizzie thoughtfully. 'And I reckon that's where you come in.'

Lizzie wrinkled her nose. 'I reckon you're right. She's as good as told me she's going to leave the farm to me.'

Penny nodded. 'You'll be staying then?'

She hesitated. 'I've nowhere else to go.'

'Right.' Penny eased her back. 'Did you come to tell me supper's ready?'

'Yes.' Lizzie smiled.

'I'll go in then.'

Lizzie nodded but did not follow for a moment. She stood looking about her. The sounds of the countryside had given way to an almost church-like silence as twilight fell. Even the horses were quiet. So much had happened since yesterday that it felt as if it could not possibly be only twenty-four hours since she had left Liverpool. The ache which had been within her all day intensified. What was Alex doing now? What was he feeling? Had she done the right thing? She was so unsure of herself. But she was here now and he was hundreds of miles away. She thought of what her aunt had said and still found it hard to take in. She did not know her well enough yet to understand if she was the kind of person who said a thing one day then changed it the next. Lizzie realised that possessing land and livestock was a terrific responsibility and she was not sure if she could cope with it.

She began to walk towards the building. The kitchen light was twinkling through the window as if beckoning her. She remembered how she and Phyl and Alex had joked about having a mansion in the country with a four-poster bed and curtains and footstools with tassels. Of course, the farmhouse was not a mansion and she'd bet a pound to a penny there were no four-poster beds upstairs. Even so it was bigger and better than she had expected, and perhaps one day might prove enough to compensate her for giving up Alex to Phyl and leaving Liverpool.

Chapter Fifteen

'Is she back?' said Mary, dropping her school satchel on the sofa and gazing at her mother. It was a whole day since Lizzie had disappeared.

Maisie shook her head and did not look up as she placed a handful of cutlery on the table.

'It's our Lois's fault,' burst out Mary. 'She shouldn't have said what she did. What if Lizzie never comes back? What's our Phyl going to say then?'

'Phyl'll accept it if she's got any sense,' said Maisie. 'The girl's gone back where she belongs.'

'What d'you mean?' Mary slipped off her blazer and hung it on the end of the sofa. 'Has she been in touch?'

'No, but I rang Booth's this afternoon. Apparently she's rung them. They say she's in London.'

'London!' Mary flopped on to the sofa. 'Are you going to tell Alex? You can't fob him off again with "She had to be in early for work". He was supposed to be going out with her tonight and he'll be here soon with our Billy.'

'I'm thinking about it,' said Maisie crossly. 'But the last thing I want is Alex haring off to London in search of her.'

'You're not going to tell him!' said Mary, staring at her wide-eyed. 'Why? Because of our Phyl? You're going to have to tell him something.'

'Then I'll think of something,' said Maisie and stomped out of the kitchen.

When Alex came home with Billy, Mary, who had been watching for them through the parlour window, rushed to the door. 'Mam wants to speak to you, Alex. Don't rush off after you've got our Billy in.'

'Is Lizzie home?' Alex smiled at her as he helped Billy ease himself down from the cab into the wheelchair.

Mary exchanged glances with her elder brother. 'Er – no.' She felt the colour rush into her cheeks. 'The back gate is open,' she added, and hurried indoors as Alex wheeled Billy up the entry, through the yard and into the house.

'What is it, Mrs Eccles?' he asked, entering the kitchen.

She cleared her throat, glanced at Mary then Billy. 'It's about Lizzie.'

'What about her?' His voice was instantly wary.

'She's not here. She's run away,' she said in a rush. 'Last night she was a bit upset because our Lois went and said things about the pair of you. I'm thinking that she might have run to our Phyl.'

For a moment Alex was stunned and then he pulled himself together. 'What did Lois say?' His voice was harsh.

'I can't remember everything. But she was upset about the pair of you seeing each other when you've only just broken off your engagement to our Phyl. And you must admit, Alex, it doesn't look right.'

'I suppose you told Lizzie that?' He was angry – no, more than angry, furious.

'Something of the sort.' Maisie was made uncomfortable by the expression on his face. 'I am responsible for her in Phyl's absence,' she said indignantly. 'She's only nineteen and you're nine years older. I'm telling you straight, lad. I didn't like it because you broke the engagement off so sudden after waiting for our Phyl for years. I thought you were using the girl to bring her to her senses.'

Disbelief flashed across Alex's face. 'How could you think that?'

Maisie bristled. 'All's fair in love and war. And that's what I thought.'

'You thought! I bet you didn't think about Lizzie, though, and how hurt she would be? I bet all you thought about was Phyl.'

'That's not true!' exclaimed Maisie, her face flushing as she realised he had her taped. 'I was thinking of the girl's good. I acted like I would for one of my own.'

'One of your own?' he echoed scornfully. 'What else did you say to hurt her? What other lies did you tell?'

Maisie was shocked into silence and for several seconds nobody spoke. Then Mary's voice broke the silence. 'Don't blame Mam. It really was our Lois who started on Lizzie. She said our Phyl had nurtured a serpent in her bosom. Going on about how you and her had been carrying on behind our Phyl's back and saying that it was her finding out which was the real reason behind the engagement being broken. But none of us really believed that.'

'None of you? Your mother did!' Alex's laugh had an ugly sound to it. 'Lizzie must have thought you all believed it! But you're wrong. I had plenty of other reasons for breaking off the engagement. You can't have forgotten the times Phyl put the stage before me? She wanted to have her cake and eat it, and nobody can do that.'

Billy, who had not taken his eyes off Alex, said roughly, 'Are you saying Lizzie really loves you?'

'Yes!' Alex insisted.

Mary looked at her brother and pitied him. 'Oh, our Lois threw you in her face as well, Billy. Accusing her of deserting you. But Lizzie said you didn't really care for her in that way. Is that true?'

'God! You females!' he said scornfully. 'I could strangle our Lois.'

'Me too,' said Alex, seething with fury. 'Lizzie and I were planning on getting married but we were keeping it quiet for a while. She wasn't sure if Phyl would give her permission. She was worried about hurting her. She cared about Phyl all right – and you, Billy.'

He grimaced. 'But not enough. I always thought she liked you rather too much.'

'Don't let it upset you, son,' said Maisie fiercely, placing an arm about his shoulders.

Billy shrugged it off. 'Don't treat me like a kid, Mam,' he snapped. 'I just thought Lizzie sort of fancied me because I could yell at her and she'd come back for more.'

'She cared for you like a sister,' said Alex quietly. 'Most of the time she felt part of this family, but it seems Lois and your mam never really accepted her.'

Billy nodded and Maisie half-opened her mouth to say that wasn't true then realised it was.

Mary went to Alex. 'What are you going to do? You have to help us find Lizzie.'

'And where am I supposed to start looking?' he said bitterly, thrusting his hands into his pockets. 'I take it she didn't leave a note?'

'No, but –'

'I think it's possible she's gone to see Phyl to sort this out,' interrupted Maisie, shooting a warning glance at her daughter.

'What!' Alex thought about it. Was it possible? She had wanted him to take her to see her stepmother, tell her the truth. 'I suppose it's worth a try,' he said, easing his shoulders.

'You know where Phyl is?' asked Maisie.

He nodded. 'She rang me the other day.'

Maisie exchanged glances with Mary as if to say, See! I was right! 'Did you tell Lizzie that?' she asked.

'Of course.' He stiffened and his eyes were as hard as marbles. 'I have no secrets from her.'

'Not like you had from our Phyl,' Maisie couldn't resist saying.

Alex opened his mouth, then shut it again. What was the point? She wasn't going to listen. He left before he said something he might regret and slammed the door behind him.

Mary looked at her mother. 'I don't know how you could lie,' she said incredulously. 'After the way you've brought us up to be honest.'

'It wasn't easy. But admit I was right?' said Maisie with a relieved smile. 'He and our Phyl are still in touch and that says something.'

'It says that our Phyl wants to have her cake and eat it, like he said,' muttered Billy, looking worn out. He glanced at Mary. 'Anyway, what is it Mam's lying about?'

'She knows Lizzie's in London.'

'You're joking!'

'No, I'm not. Mam phoned Booth's today and Lizzie'd rang them from London.'

'But what's she doing in London? She doesn't know anybody there.'

'How do you know?' said his mother. 'She used to live down there. She's bound to know someone.'

'No!' said Billy, scowling and tapping his fingers on the arm of his wheelchair. 'She spent most of her child-hood in that convent place in the country. I never remember her once mentioning having any friends in London.'

Mary, who had been thinking, said, 'She does know someone. The twins have relations down there. I remember Joe saying they lived not far from where Lizzie's parents used to live. If she was feeling desperate she could have gone to them. After all people do go to vicars when they're in trouble.'

Maisie clicked her tongue against her teeth in an exasperated manner. 'You're getting carried away, girl. Who said Lizzie's desperate? She's had a bit of an upset. Lots of people imagine themselves in love. Calf love, that's what it is with her! She'll get over it. Now I don't want to hear another word. Let's just wait and see what happens with Alex and our Phyl.' She stalked out the kitchen.

Mary and Billy looked at each other. 'I think Mam's whistling against the wind,' he murmured. 'She can't bear the thought of our Phyl not fitting into the little housewife and mother mould. She's not the least bit proud of her being on the stage.'

'What do you think we should do?'

'You get in touch with the twins tomorrow and we'll work something out.'

'Right!' said Mary, surprised but pleased at the thought of seeing the twins. She liked Joe a lot but in the past he had only seemed to want to spout poetry to Lizzie. As she left the room there was a spring in her step.

It was fortunate that Alex remembered the name of the play because he'd forgotten the name of the theatre, and Phyl's name wasn't even in the small print on the poster outside the theatre. There was a queue for the second performance which was being entertained by a man playing the accordion and singing about 'A Rambling Rose in the Wild Wood'. Alex strolled along the pavement, staring at faces, before it struck him that if Lizzie was here she was probably backstage or already in the auditorium. Surely Phyl would have given her a complimentary ticket? Unless they had argued so badly that Lizzie had already been and gone. He hoped not. He went round to the stage door and knocked loudly and when a man poked his head round the partially opened door, asked could he have a word with Mrs Knight.

'Dunno who you're talking about, Mister.'

'She plays the governess.'

'The Scouser?'

'That's right. Can I see her?'

The man rubbed his nose. 'Dunno about that. She'll be resting.'

Alex hesitated. 'We're engaged to be married. I just need five minutes.'

The man allowed him in and showed him to a changing room. 'Mrs Knight's fiancé,' he bellowed.

The three women in the room stared at him and Alex did not recognise Phyl until she sprang to her feet.

'Alex, how lovely! I never thought you'd come. Although I admit to having had hopes of Manchester.' She was wearing a long-sleeved dark green dress with white collar and cuffs. Its plainness suited her. She held out both hands and he could not help thinking, How theatrical, and in that moment felt sure that Lizzie had not been here. He took one of her hands. 'You haven't seen Lizzie, have you?' he said in a low voice.

'Tommy said fiancé,' she said softly, ignoring his words. 'Have you changed your mind about marrying me then?'

'No. That was a trick to get me in. Phyl, have you or haven't you seen Lizzie? She's gone missing.'

The warmth in her tawny eyes faded to be replaced by surprise. 'She's what?'

'She's left home. Nobody knows where she's gone. Your mother thought she might have run to you.'

Phyl stared at him. 'Why should she run away? I can't believe it. What's been happening at home? Is it Billy?' Her tone was anxious. 'Is he worse?'

'No!' he reassured her. 'In fact he's started work for me.' He paused, feeling at a loss for a moment about what to say or do next. 'I can't explain here, Phyl. Perhaps after the performance we can go for a meal?'

She stared at him and said slowly, 'You're so serious. You're really worried about her, aren't you?'

'Yes. But let it wait. I'll see you later.' He released her hand.

'I'll see you then,' she called as he walked away. 'Are you going to watch the performance?'

He had not thought about it but nodded and closed the door behind him.

Alex seated himself opposite Phyl and watched her take off her gloves. She placed them next to her handbag on the table and looked him straight in the eye. 'Well, tell me what's been going on while I've been away that I don't know about?' There was a sharpness to her tone which had not been there earlier and for a moment he was reminded of Lois.

'Let's order first. I haven't eaten since lunchtime.' He picked up the menu and held it out to her.

'I'll have the lamb chops,' she said, without looking.

'I'll have the same.' He caught the waiter's eye and feeling in need of a drink, ordered a pint of bitter and asked Phyl what she wanted.

'I'll have a sweet sherry.' Her eyes were thoughtful as she took a packet of Craven A and a lighter from her handbag.

Alex took the lighter from her and lit her cigarette. Their drinks were placed in front of them and it was a couple of minutes before he said, 'There's no easy way to say this, Phyl, so I'll go straight in. I want to marry Lizzie. I love her and she loves me. But your Lois and your mother have persuaded her that she's several different kinds of a skunk, saying she's the reason for our broken engagement. That's not true and you must know it.' He paused. 'I have to find her, Phyl. Have you any idea where she could be?'

She frowned and stubbed out her cigarette savagely in an ash tray. 'I've got two things to say to you, Alex Payne! First, don't you ever come in before a performance and say anything that might upset me. You almost spoilt my performance! And second, no way will I give you permission to marry Lizzie. How long has this been going on? I must have been blind not to see it!'

He scowled. 'Your performance? That's all you care about! Haven't you heard a word I said? Lizzie's missing!'

'Yes, I heard!' She rested her elbows on the table. 'Now answer my question. How long has it been going on?'

'I didn't touch her 'til I broke off our engagement,' he said forcefully, brows hooding his eyes.

She laughed sharply. 'And I'm supposed to take that for gospel? I should have listened to Dad all those years back when the Black Widow was there because I can only think it's you that's pushed it. I can't believe Lizzie would . . . but perhaps I've never really known her after all.'

'Perhaps you never spent enough time getting to know her,' he snapped. 'For the last few years all you've thought about is your acting career.'

Phyl half-opened her mouth and then closed it again. They stared at each other.

'Well?' said Alex in a hard voice. 'It's true, isn't it? She was at an age when a girl needed a mother but you were never really there for her.'

'You're speaking like I *was* her real mother,' she said impatiently. 'You expect too much, Alex. I took her on because I felt sorry for her and there was nobody else. I did my best by her.'

His expression eased. 'Sorry. I know you did. There's women who would have done far less. I'm angry because I'm worried. Although that snide remark about the Black Widow was below the belt.'

Phyl picked up the almost burnt down cigarette and drew on it. 'I'm sorry I said that. It's just that I find it hard to take it all in so suddenly, out of the blue. As soon as you get your ring back you discover it's Lizzie you fancy, not me.'

'I haven't had my ring back *and* I'd like it, please.' He smiled slightly. 'I can't have two women wearing rings of mine.'

Her mouth lifted at the corners and she covered his hand with hers. 'Why not? Think what people would say. Hell! It could make a good story with all kinds of complications! We could put it on in London.'

'Oh, behave Phyl!' His tone was vexed. 'This is serious. Have you any idea where Lizzie could have gone?

Your mother thought she'd come running to you but she was obviously wrong.'

She pulled a face. 'Perhaps Lizzie suddenly got scared? Maybe she realised that she was just infatuated with you? Girls her age get crushes. That's something for you to think about.'

He removed her hand. 'Thanks. You really make me feel good. But you're forgetting, she's nineteen not a kid of twelve.'

Phyl lit another cigarette and said moodily, 'If that's how you feel then there's nothing more I can say.'

He scowled at her. 'I'm disappointed in you. Don't you want her found? I thought you were fond of her.'

'Of course I'm fond of her. Although I didn't expect her to steal my man.'

'Oh, come off it, Phyl! I'm not your possession! Besides you really made your choice years ago.' He leaned back to allow the waiter to place a plate in front of him. 'Be honest with yourself and stop acting.'

Phyl said indignantly, 'How d'you know I'm acting?'

'I've known you too long, that's how,' he said grimly.

She picked up her knife and fork. 'It's sad when something ends.' There was a catch in her voice.

He nodded but remained silent, not wanting to say anything as hurtful as: it had ended years ago for him, and besides they had both already made a new start. He began to eat.

Neither of them spoke until they'd finished their food. 'Well?' said Alex. 'Have you thought about it? Where could she be?'

She frowned. 'I presume you've tried Josie's?'

He stilled. 'No.'

'Daftie! Try there. I'm sure you'll find she's been at the farm all the time.'

'Thanks, Phyl.'

'I still haven't given you permission to marry her,' she said, her smile honeyed. 'And I won't until I feel right about this.'

'We didn't expect you to give your permission right away.' He held out his hand. 'Ring, Phyl.'

'You are cruel.' She eased the ring from her finger and handed it to him.

'You've lost weight,' he murmured, pocketing it.

She smiled. 'It's all the hard work.' She began to talk about the play as they drank their coffee.

Alex was relieved that their encounter had not been any worse. He realised that it was going to be the early hours before he arrived back in Liverpool and he couldn't be turning up at the farm then, but he was impatient to find Lizzie. He was starting to feel angry with her, as well. How could she just up and leave without a word to him? It was hurtful. He thought, It's Saturday tomorrow, too, and I've a lot on. He would pick up Billy and take him to the shop, then he would call at the farm. He was presuming that Billy would still want to work for him. He had been keen enough talking about it on the way home yesterday. Hopefully his mam hadn't persuaded him against it by now.

Alex still felt angry with Lois and Maisie and hoped they would not be around when he arrived at the Eccleses' in the morning. But he doubted Maisie would keep out of his way. She would be too interested to know what had happened between himself and Phyl to do that.

Maisie bent to pick up the envelope which had just rattled through the letter box. She had been like a cat on hot bricks since last night and had stayed up late, hoping that Phyl might arrive home in Alex's company. She glanced down at the typewritten name and address and jumped when Trev spoke behind her.

'Who's that for, Mam?' He peered over her shoulder.

'It's not for you and that's all you need to know,' she said, placing the envelope in the pocket of her pinny.

'It's for Lizzie. It looks important.'

'It's got nothing to do with you,' she repeated, exasperated. 'Is our Billy ready?'

'Yeah!' Trev gave her an appraising look. 'That's if Alex turns up for him. He mightn't want him working for him after all what you said to him.'

Maisie had the same worry but one of her mottoes was: When in doubt carry on as normal.

'You shouldn't have lied to him, Mam,' said Trev, as if he could read her mind. 'He's going to be really annoyed you've wasted his time. But maybe if you give him that letter he can take it to London and deliver it to Lizzie. Then he won't sack our Billy.'

'Your nose is too big for your face,' she said severely. 'This letter is going in a drawer until our Phyl comes home. She can decide what to do with it. Anyhow we don't know where in London Lizzie is.'

'Our Billy and Mary think they know.'

'Guesswork. At the moment they've no proof,' she muttered. 'And don't you dare mention this letter to anyone. It's our Phyl who'll make the decision about what to do with it.'

At that moment there was the sound of a vehicle drawing up outside and Maisie hurried to open the door. It was another nice day with blue sky and fluffy clouds, although the heatwave was over and it was slightly chilly for the time of year.

Alex climbed down from the cab and nodded coolly in Maisie's direction. 'Billy ready?'

'Yes. Did you see our Phyl? How was she? Trev!' She turned to her younger son. 'See if our Billy wants any help.'

'He's coming,' said Trev, not moving, glad to hear the rubbery kiss of wheels on the lino as Billy propelled himself towards them. Besides he was not going to be got rid of. He'd always thought Alex was OK, had not forgotten the time he'd rushed him to hospital, and was really grateful to him for giving Billy a job. 'Tell Alex, Mam.' His tone was insistent.

'Hold your horses.' Maisie sounded vexed because she would have liked to know the outcome of Alex's visit to Phyl before mentioning London. 'Give him a chance to speak.'

Alex's smile did not reach his eyes. 'The show goes on, Mrs Eccles. And no, Lizzie wasn't there. Phyl thinks she could be at Josie's. So I'm going to the farm after taking Billy in.'

'She's not at the farm.' It was Billy who spoke. 'She's in London.'

Alex stared at him in frozen silence.

'I was just going to tell you,' said Maisie hurriedly. 'I phoned Booth's.'

'Where in London?' he demanded. 'Have you an address?'

'No. They're sending her cards to Booth's London office, but –'

Billy interrupted her. 'We think she could be staying with Josie's relations. They live not far from where Lizzie used to live. Our Mary was going to get the twins around so we could ask them to get in touch.'

Alex smiled and asked Trev to help him with the wheelchair. Within minutes the lorry was roaring down the street.

'Can we go to the farm first?' asked Billy hesitantly. 'I know I've got a cheek asking but I'd like to know if Lizzie has gone to the relations. And besides, I've been thinking about what I could say to the twins all night. I've been bloody horrible to them.'

'I've already decided to go to the farm first,' murmured Alex. 'You sit back and relax.'

Billy sat back but could not relax and Alex was aware of it. He felt all keyed up himself. London! He could barely take it in that Lizzie should have run so far. She must have been in a right state. He could hardly credit that she might have believed what Maisie had said about him using her to make Phyl jealous. Surely she knew him better than that?

They arrived at the farm just as Josie emerged from the dairy carrying a gleaming pail. Alex jumped down from the lorry and seized hold of her arm. 'Have you heard anything from Lizzie?'

'What d'you mean?' Her eyes shifted from him to where Billy sat in the cab.

'Lizzie's left. We know she's in London but we don't know where,' he said rapidly. 'Billy thinks she might be staying with your relations.'

'Billy does? He must be worried about her if he's made the effort to come here with you,' she muttered, not looking in Billy's direction again.

'He's not as worried as I am,' said Alex emphatically.

She stared at him and her expression lightened. 'Lizzie always liked you,' she said shyly. 'Even when I was younger I remember her defending you.'

He lowered his voice. 'Billy says he's treated you horribly. Meet him halfway. Then if you don't mind phoning your relations in London for me?'

'Joe'll do it for you.' She placed the pail on the ground. 'You go straight in. I must just have a word with Billy.' She ran in the direction of the lorry while he headed for the house.

'They're not answering,' said Joe, putting down the receiver.

'They could be on holiday,' said his sister Vera, placing her baby daughter against her shoulder and rubbing her back.

'Or they could just be out,' said Joe, looking at Alex. 'What are you going to do? Try again in an hour or . . .'

His eyes lit up. 'I'll go with you if you like. I don't start work 'til Tuesday. I wouldn't mind taking a look at Fleet Street.'

'Don't be cheeky,' said his sister, gazing at him reprovingly. 'Mr Payne won't want you along.'

Alex said, 'I'll try again in an hour, but if you could give me the number I can phone from the office. I'll have to get some work done.'

Vera gave him the number and Joe followed him out. They found Josie sitting close to Billy in the cab. Joe nodded in their direction. 'You OK, Billy?'

'Not bad. Did Alex tell you I'm working for him now?'

'No.' He hesitated. 'You won't be coming inside then?'

'Not now. Maybe you and Josie could call round tonight, though?' He faced Alex. 'Any luck?'

'No answer.' He helped Josie down from the cab and took her place, thanked the twins and drove off.

It was several minutes before he spoke again. 'I'll probably be taking a few days off, Billy, and going down to London. If I can find out where Lizzie is I'll need to talk to her. I'll get Harry to pick you up. Now Trev's finished for the school holidays he can give a hand with your wheelchair.'

If Alex had said such a thing a few weeks ago Billy would have got touchy but now he just thanked him.

Eventually Alex received an answer to his call to the vicarage in London, only to be told that they had not seen Lizzie and would make no promises to inform him if she did seek their help which angered him until he remembered it was probably part of a vicar's calling to keep confidences.

He was at a loss what to do next, then remembered Booth's shipping line and after dealing with a customer who wanted a secondhand engine for an Austin Seven, phoned a friend of his in the Liverpool office.

The information he received caused him to pack a suitcase the next morning and to head south, planning on being in London by the evening. It being a weekend the roads were busy but he had not reckoned on several tail-backs and just outside Stratford-on-Avon his car overheated and the cylinder head gasket blew. He could go no further, and after a walk into the town soon discovered that Sunday was the worst time possible to break down. It was not until Monday afternoon that he arrived at Booth's in London, to be informed that Lizzie had been and gone, leaving no address.

Chapter Sixteen

Lizzie watched the car bounce along the unmade track and through the farm gates. Her smile faded. Another satisfied customer but Holy Mary, Mother of God, she felt tired and it was only ten in the morning! She had been at the farm almost a month now and although there was a lot she liked about her new life, such as early-morning rides through the woods, she often felt restless. Sometimes the quietness got to her and she missed the sound of children playing in the streets and the noise of the ships' hooters on the Mersey. She would have given anything for a view of the river from King's dock and the smell of the sea. Most of all, though, she missed Alex. When the long day was over and she lay in bed, she wanted him so much it was a physical pain. She had hoped that as the days went by the pain would have lessened but that had been a forlorn hope. Sometimes she imagined him and Phyl happy together, but not often because it hurt thinking of them in such a way. Yet it was the reason why she had left so she knew she should be praying for them to come together if it had not already happened.

As Lizzie hung a bridle on a hook in the shed that housed the tackle and put away a saddle, she was conscious of a weariness which went beyond that of previous weeks. She remembered during the first week of her arrival, when she had taken to horseback again, feeling so saddle sore due to her attempts to please her aunt that she could have cried. Charlotte Broom was something of a perfectionist.

She went outside and rested her back against the wooden wall of the shed, looking across the yard towards the stabling.

There were a dozen stalls and each was inhabited. The horses required a fair amount of looking after and she helped Penny with the bulk of the work. Her aunt had decided she would concentrate on schooling now that Lizzie was on the scene. As well as the horses to take care of, there were the gardens and hens and the house. She had not had a day off in ages, her aunt and the horses not recognising Sunday as a day of rest.

Lizzie felt rebellious and suddenly came to a decision. Work could go hang for the rest of the day! She needed a break from the place. She had to see the sea. She would get a train to Shenfield where she could change for Southend and have a few hours at the seaside.

She hurried across the yard but as she reached the kitchen door her aunt came out. 'Elizabeth, just the person I want.'

Lizzie groaned inwardly. Being called Elizabeth made her feel as if she was at school again and also a different person to the real her. 'What is it?'

'Will you deal with the Dawson girl for me? She has Diamond. I thought I'd go and get my hair cut and set. It's getting much too long.'

Lizzie hesitated, then made up her mind. 'No, Aunt Charlotte,' she said cheerfully. 'I have to have a day off or I'll collapse or go mad. Do you realise I haven't had a whole day off since I've been here?'

Her aunt looked affronted. 'I'm sorry, dear. I thought you were happy working away? But if you need a day off then take it tomorrow.'

'No, Aunt. I need it today while the sun's shining. Tomorrow it could be raining and it wouldn't be the same at all. So if you don't mind, please can I have it today?' Lizzie smiled, determined to get her own way but to be pleasant about it. She could sense her aunt struggling with what she had said, heavy brows twitching ready to form a frowning line. 'Please?' Lizzie repeated.

Charlotte's eyebrows gave up the struggle. 'I suppose I can get it done tomorrow,' she said at last. 'But if it rains, Elizabeth, I shall blame you! I presume you'll want Penny to give you a lift into Chelmsford?'

'If you could spare her for half an hour?'

'Very well then,' said her aunt in a long-suffering voice and went back inside the house.

Lizzie followed her. She had a quick bath and donned a primrose cotton frock, took the allowance her aunt gave her out of the flower bedecked pottery jug where it was housed, and wished there was more of it. Her aunt seemed unaware that since the war a Labour government had allowed the wages of the working classes to rise. Not that Lizzie was going to complain. She was thankful to have a roof over her head and food in her stomach. She also had the security of knowing that one day the farm would

be hers to do what she liked with. So after putting on a
dab of lipstick, she hurried outside in search of Penny.

Lizzie took deep breaths of salty air and tried not to think
of Alex and New Brighton as she gazed at Southend pier,
but her thoughts kept returning to how that evening out
had ended. She bit her lip and hoped that it was the change
in her way of life that was messing up her monthly cycle.
She turned her back on the pier and began to walk. The
tide was in so there was not much shingly beach to sit on
but that did not bother her. The August sun was still shining and she was content to watch people. One woman had
her skirts tucked into a huge pair of khaki knickers and
was paddling at the edge of the water. Lizzie admired her
courage.

She eased her way between people and went along the
promenade, past stalls selling cockles, sticks of rock, KISS
ME QUICK hats and comic postcards. She paused to buy
an ice cream. Later she planned on having fish and chips
and a pot of tea before catching the train back to the farm.

She had been walking for perhaps ten minutes, and
had paused to watch some children jumping in the waves,
when a man stopped beside her.

'Excuse me, please. Have we not met before?'

Lizzie looked into the features which were pleasant
enough and was about to say, 'Sorry, mate!' when she
recognised the silver grey eyes and felt a moment's pleasure. 'You're the refugee!'

He smiled. 'And you are the young woman Ted told
me to feed. You will tell me your name?'

'Lizzie Knight.' She returned his smile. 'What a coincidence. Although if I remember rightly you did tell me you were thinking of finding work at the seaside. It just seems odd that we should meet on the first day I've been here in years.'

'If you had come yesterday or tomorrow or last week or next week we could have met. Every day I walk along here at this time when I have an hour off. But in a few weeks I will have to return to London. The summer season it will end and,' he shrugged in a very foreign way, 'there will be no work.'

'Surely you won't go back to the same place? Wasn't there a man with a gun?'

'You have a good memory. I find somewhere else. I am useful in kitchen and my English it is good, do you not think?' His tone was earnest.

'Very good,' she said, hiding a smile as she walked on because he seemed so much to want to be reassured when really he must know his English was good.

He fell into step beside her and for several minutes neither of them spoke but gazed over the beach. Then suddenly he said, 'Why is it you British have this liking for cold water?' His eyes twinkled at her.

'I think it's expected of us,' she said with mock gravity. 'We're an island race surrounded by the sea. Perhaps, too, we're so unused to sun that we have to cool off quickly if we get too much of it. I presume it's not like that in Poland?'

'In Poland in summer it is dry and warm. In winter it is very cold, much snow. So that some of my friends come to school on sledges from outlying farms.'

'Your family weren't farmers?'

'No. When I leave school I work in office. Then Germany makes threats to my country and I have to go to armaments factory elsewhere. It was bombed and afterwards I am taken to German labour camp.'

'But you escaped.'

'Yes. I am sixteen and I try to get to Switzerland but it is difficult and my family are still in Rozwadow. So I go back to Poland but not to Rozwadow because it is occupied by the Germans and they would take me back to labour camp. Instead I hide in Carpathian Mountains where my mother's cousin lives. Then we hear the Germans are retreating and I go home. But Germans only leave Poland because the Russians are coming so we pack as much as we can carry and leave. We go to refugee camp and there I meet Yanks and British Tommies and I join the army.' He paused, took a deep breath and looked about him, appearing surprised at what he saw.

Lizzie knew how he felt, remembering the sense of disorientation she had experienced when she had first arrived in Liverpool. She touched his arm. 'You were back there for a while, weren't you? You must miss it terribly.'

'I miss Poland, yes.' He sighed heavily and delved into his pocket, bringing out a handful of change. 'I will buy now an icecream. You would like one?'

'Thank you.' She was not going to say no to another. 'Then you can tell me more about your life during the war. You must have had adventures.'

'No, Lizzie!' His tone was firm. 'I talk enough. Now it is your turn.' He left her and walked towards a kiosk.

She went and stood beside him. As he handed the first icecream to her, he said, 'You are down here from London for the day?'

She shook her head. 'I'm living with an aunt in the country here in Essex. She keeps horses and hires them out. It's hard work but peaceful.'

'You are young to have that need for peace that older people desire.' There was a question in his eyes. 'You are running away from something or someone? Or is it life itself you seek to escape from? Life as only the young can live it.'

His words took her breath away and she thought of telling him to mind his own business. Then she remembered that he was almost a stranger so what did it matter what she said to him. 'You're not so old yourself,' she murmured, and took a lick of icecream.

'I am twenty-nine but I have lived through much. You would only be a small child during the war here in England and you would know nothing of the fear of having the Nazis knock on your door.'

'No. But my father killed himself.' The confession was out before she could recall it and she did not remember even thinking about it. Her heart was suddenly beating fast and she turned her back on him, scowling up at the lift which led to the hotels and houses higher up in the town.

He came and stood in front of her and bowed slightly. 'Jan Swietlik is sorry. It was a great shock so you run. I understand. I am glad that you live with your aunt and find peace.'

She stared at him and then realised what he must be thinking. 'No! You don't understand. My father killed himself years ago and my stepmother took me to live with her up north.'

'So it is your stepmother you run away from? She was cruel to you?'

'No!' She felt exasperated. 'Not all stepmothers are tarred with the same brush. I've run away because – because –' Her voice trailed off. She could not tell him. Instead she said, 'It's only a month since I found my aunt. She and my mother quarrelled, you see. Mother died in the war and I never knew where Aunt Charlotte lived.'

'But now you have found her and that is good. It explains why you run away. You wish to be part of her family.'

Lizzie found that funny. 'Aunt Charlotte's a spinster and has no time for men.' She smiled wryly. 'She regards them as the weaker sex. She'd have a blue fit if she knew I was talking to you. I'm to follow in her footsteps if I'm to inherit all that she has.'

'But you are young and attractive and not like her,' he said forcibly. 'Can you do this thing she asks of you?' He took a mouthful of icecream and stared at her gravely with a moustache of the creamy confectionery above his lip.

Lizzie thought of her missed period. 'Probably. I've been in love. I don't think it'll happen again.'

He continued to stare at her with that grave expression. 'I, too, have been in love. Perhaps we can just be good friends?'

Uttered so seriously the words made Lizzie laugh because they reminded her of what film stars were reported to say when they were much more than that. 'Haven't you listened to a word I've said? We can't be good friends. I still love Alex so I'll stay single.'

'Good friends,' he repeated. 'When you visit Southend again, Lizzie, we will meet.'

She was silent, having no intention of seeing him again.

Yet when he left her a short while later she did not throw away the piece of paper he gave her with the name of the restaurant where he worked, and she had given her address to him, even as she warned him with a smile that her aunt would take a shotgun to him if he came near.

She had the fish and chips she had promised herself, eating them out of the paper and washing them down with a small bottle of cream soda. She considered how much she had enjoyed a man's company, thought of her aunt and the farm, of Alex and Phyl, and her missed period. Then she went and caught her train.

Two days later no sooner had Lizzie put her feet out of bed than she was overcome by nausea and had to rush to the bathroom. Her aunt was unaware of her sickness as she was always up with the birds despite her rheumatism.

After a week of sickness Lizzie had little doubt about her pregnancy. It seemed unfair that such a thing should happen when she and Alex had only made love once but there it was and she had to decide what to do about it. Only momentarily did she worry about mortal sin, being more concerned about what her aunt would say.

She thought of writing to Alex, remembering how he had been with Syd and picturing his delight. The two of them could set-up home with the baby in that house on the outskirts of Liverpool he had spoken about . . . The happy daydream did not last, replaced by what she thought more realistic imaginings. He and Phyl had found each other and her news would ruin everything. There would also be Maisie's shocked disapproval and Lois's horrified delight at Lizzie's fall to contend with. There were several choice epithets Lois would find pleasure in getting her tongue around to describe Lizzie's predicament. She might even say that Lizzie had planned getting pregnant deliberately to catch Alex. Lizzie felt sick thinking about it. And what about the rest of the family, her friends and the neighbours? If she had been certain that Alex still wanted her then she felt sure she could have coped with any tribulation imaginable. The trouble was she could not. He hadn't even tried to find her and a man of his commonsense would have enquired of Booth's, knowing she would need her cards if she was to support herself. But there had been no mention of his ringing when she had returned there a month ago. That fact did not stop her loving him because she guessed that she had hurt him a lot leaving the way she had but it did prevent her from writing a letter informing him of prospective fatherhood.

She decided there was nothing for it but to tell Aunt Charlotte. It was possible that she might be pleased once she had recovered from the shock. Having lived with her aunt for over a month Lizzie had a fair idea how her mind might work. After all, when Lizzie herself died who would inherit her property?

She waited until the day's work was done and her aunt was relaxing over a glass of dry sherry in the sitting room. 'I have something to tell you,' she burst out, after building herself up to the announcement. 'This is going to come as a shock to you and I'm sorry about that, but –' She drew in a deep breath. 'I'm having a baby.'

Charlotte did not drop the glass as Lizzie thought she might but placed it carefully on the stone hearth. 'Are you sure?'

'Pretty sure.' Her aunt's expression was hard to read.

'Do you know who the father is?'

'Of course I do!' Lizzie was shocked by the question. 'What do you take me for, Aunt Charlotte? Once, only once it happened, and I loved him.'

'And I suppose he took advantage of that, the dirty dog!'

'Alex is not a dirty dog,' she said, flushing. 'He asked me to marry him.'

'Then why didn't you?' There was something of Lizzie's mother in Charlotte's direct stare.

Lizzie opened her mouth, then changed her mind about what she was going to say. 'I'm not explaining. All I want to know is – are you going to throw me out?'

The muscles in Charlotte's face relaxed. 'I suppose that's what a girl in your condition would expect. I remember in my young day a girl in the village was whipped within an inch of her life and sent to a Home. In my opinion they should have castrated the father! Who, of course, got away scot-free because she was too ignorant to have known what was going on and had done it with several of the lads.'

'That's barbaric,' said Lizzie. 'I bet her mother never told her the facts of life so how was she to know what was right and wrong?'

Her aunt cleared her throat. 'But you did know the facts of life, Elizabeth?'

'Yes.' Her cheeks burned. 'I'm making no excuses for my behaviour. Do you know, though, Daddy and Mummy never hugged or kissed me? They only did that to each other. I was an intrusion. A child needs love to be shown to it.' She rested a hand against her belly. 'This child is going to be loved if I'm allowed to keep it. I know that depends a lot on you, Aunt Charlotte. Are you going to throw me out?'

Charlotte's bushy eyebrows drew together over her large nose. 'I'm not going to throw you out. If the child's a girl then you may keep her.'

Lizzie had not thought about the sex of the child and said carefully, 'And if it's a boy?'

'Then we'll have it adopted. And don't look at me like that, Elizabeth. I will not have a boy inheriting my property! Now fill my sherry glass and stoke the fire. We'll have to decide who's going to look after you when you give birth. I believe there's a couple of midwives round about who know their job.'

'I'm perfectly healthy,' said Lizzie, her voice brittle.

'All right, don't see the midwife. We'll wait until nearer the time,' said her aunt, looking at her keenly. 'Now that sherry, Elizabeth.'

Lizzie fetched the sherry bottle but was not about to accept her aunt's ruling on what was to be done with her baby if it was a boy. By her reckoning it would arrive towards the end of April if nothing went wrong, so there was no hurry to decide things yet.

Penny was amazingly philosophical about Lizzie's being pregnant. 'Well, if you have to be a mother without a man, you've come to the right place,' she said, brushing the chestnut's flank with firm strokes. 'I bet your aunt blamed the fellow?'

'You'd win your bet.' Lizzie paused in the act of spreading clean straw in Diamond's stall and said quietly, 'Thanks for not acting like I've committed all the seven deadly sins.'

The girl smiled. 'We all make mistakes. I suppose he's the reason you're here?'

'I would have probably come sooner or later with Aunt Charlotte hiring someone to find me.'

'But you wouldn't have stayed?'

Lizzie glanced about her. 'There's a lot I like about living here. I still like horses. They give affection and don't say hurtful things. I like the countryside. But if I could have Alex and the semi-detached he offered me, then I'd probably take it. This is a heck of a hard life and I'm not sure if I can cope with it for ever. I might have some of my aunt's looks but I take after my parents more than I realised. I need love and I'd like nothing more than to have a man around the place.'

'Me too,' said Penny, and they both smiled.

After Penny had gone home after supper, Lizzie thought about the baby and hoped it would fill that emptiness in

her life. If it was a boy she prayed that she could make
Aunt Charlotte see sense and keep him. A boy could be
so useful in a place like this as he grew. She remembered
Trev as a ten year old being capable of helping Sam with
jobs. She also thought of Syd and the pleasure she had
found in watching him develop. Thinking of such things,
she was reminded of Lily in London and wondered about
helping her with her children and housework. She dismissed the idea almost immediately. How could she
believe that Father Matthew, that High Anglican vicar, and
his wife Lily would welcome her now she was carrying
an illegitimate child? They would probably thoroughly
disapprove of her. She was spoilt goods. No, it was no
use looking to them for help if the child was a boy.

Worry over the sex of her baby continued to plague
Lizzie as autumn tinted the woods brown, yellow and red.
She had Penny teach her to drive, not wanting to be
stranded in the winter if the weather got bad.

One morning she received a letter which surprised her,
and was aware of her aunt's curious stare. When she slit
it open, she saw it was from Jan Swietlik and felt less
lonely. She read the short note swiftly. He had returned
to London and was giving her his address in case she
would like to visit her 'good friend'. He told her about
his new job working in a restaurant in Soho and of his
ambition to own his own restaurant one day. He was
working and saving hard. He asked after her aunt and the
horses and that made her smile. She put the note away in
her underwear drawer and felt comforted thinking about
it as she went about her work.

One day Lizzie woke to mist and bare-branched trees and felt the baby moving inside her. It seemed a miracle to her. She was still conscious of the wonder of life when she saw her first red-breasted robin. Strangely it was then she realised that September had come and gone and so had Dot's wedding and she had been too wrapped up in herself to have thought about it.

It was one of the most lonely moments in her life since she had been at the farm and tears clogged her throat as she imagined those she loved up north enjoying themselves. Dot had always been friendly towards her and Lizzie would have liked to have been there to see her marry her Ron. She remembered telling Alex the news, and her hope that the event would be a means to bring Billy and the twins back together again. She longed to know if it had happened but most of all she wanted to know if Phyl and Alex were a couple. It was then that she made up her mind to find out.

Charlotte was not pleased when Lizzie told her she needed to go to London. 'What on earth for? There's work to be done.'

Lizzie said irritably, 'I've done my work. I can't do anything in the garden now – and I am entitled to a day off. I can't understand, if people have money, why they can't spend it making life easier for themselves. We're going to need an extra pair of hands, Aunt Charlotte. I know some of the girls who ride help out voluntarily but it's not going to be enough. Now, I want to do some Christmas shopping and I want to do it in London.' She almost stamped her foot.

'You can do that in Chelmsford. Did you know that
Trollope once stayed there? He was something in the Post
Office and used to stay at The Saracen's Head, working
on the proofs of his books. He's not a bad writer.'

The remark surprised Lizzie. A compliment for a man!
Things must be looking up. Her aunt was reading more
and Lizzie had recently picked up *Barchester Towers* in
the library in Chelmsford for her because it was good and
thick. The onset of cold weather had triggered off
Charlotte's rheumatism and she was spending more time
indoors in front of the log fire in the sitting room.

'I'd like to visit Westminster Abbey,' said Lizzie.

'Why?'

She was exasperated. She hated being questioned in
such a way but remembered that her aunt found great
satisfaction in there being a woman on the throne of
Britain. 'The Queen's Coronation's going to be there and
I can't see me getting to London once the baby's born.
I'd just like to go inside and imagine it all happening.'

Her aunt gave her a look. 'I suppose it's your condition
that makes you say such peculiar things and be so bad-
tempered. Go then if you must, but tell Penny she'll have to
come in and see to the fire for me. And run upstairs and
fetch me another blanket.'

Having got her way, Lizzie was happy to acquiesce
with both requests. Then she left the house as quickly as
she could before her aunt changed her mind.

Lizzie realised as she reached the top of Primrose Hill
that despite her pregnancy she was in better physical

condition than she had been a year ago. Although the hill was not steep when she compared it to that street in Everton she had climbed with Alex and Nan Eccles. That seemed such a long time ago but she could almost feel the magic she had shared with Alex that evening. She stood gazing over London, letting the chill wind blow through her hair and wondered why she had given in to the impulse to stand here. Perhaps it was to gather courage? Yes, that was the reason. Standing high up looking down made her feel elevated, like a long ago lord on the battlements of his castle gazing down on his vanquished enemies. She told herself fiercely that she was not going to feel guilt and shame. She had loved and been loved, and yes, she would have no regrets if the baby was a girl. But what if it was a boy? She did not want to think about it but the thought would not go away.

Lizzie turned away from the view and went down the hill, past rows of shops and tall terraced houses with basement areas behind wrought iron railings. There were also big houses with garden walls adorned with the odd late rambling rose.

At last a church came into view, part of which was covered in scaffolding, and she remembered how Josie had mentioned the church being damaged during the blitz. It was now Lizzie hesitated. What would Father Matthew and his wife think if she went knocking on their front door? Did her condition show despite the loose-fitting swagger coat? She changed her mind about going into the vicarage but noticing the church was open she slipped inside there.

She sat listening to the silence and looking about her.
There was a small circular stained glass window close by,
depicting what appeared to be a curly-haired Saint George.
He wore gold armour and a crimson cloak and was slay-
ing a green dragon with a lance. Strange how she had
thought of vanquished enemies and gaining courage up
there on the hill. A blast of sound from an organ startled
her into movement and she stood up but the organist was
invisible to her so she sat again and allowed the Bach
Fugue to sweep over her. For a while she did not consider
her worries as hymns followed the Bach.

When the music stopped, and after she heard a door open
and close somewhere, she rose. Turning, she saw a man
dressed in black with a clerical collar. He seemed to have
made his appearance as miraculously as a genie from a lamp
but she recognised him. She hoped he did not recognise her.

'Marvellous music,' he said.

She swallowed, attempting to get rid of the tightness
in her throat brought on by an attack of nerves. 'Yes,' she
managed to get out.

'You're in trouble.' His concerned grey eyes met hers.
'Can I help?'

If she had not recognised his face she would have
known his voice anywhere. He was a good, understanding
man she told herself. Josie had said so many times. Yet
again she was aware of her ringless left hand and the baby
growing in her womb, and had a terrifying urge to confess
to what the nuns would have called her mortal sin. 'Father,'
she gasped. 'I've done something terribly wrong.'

*

It was only later when Lizzie was standing outside a restaurant in Soho that she questioned why she had behaved the way she had. She'd confessed to having lain with a man whilst unmarried, then refused to accept any help from Father Matthew when he offered it. She'd asked him no questions about the family up north, not wanting him to recognise her. The outshot was she knew no more about Phyl and Alex than when she had set out that morning. She guessed now it was her pride that had got in the way of making herself known to the priest. She really did not want any of them up north knowing about her condition. As long as the baby was a girl her future lay in the south.

Lizzie stood on tiptoe to gaze over the red gingham curtain which covered the bottom half of the restaurant window and decided to go inside. She planned on thanking Jan Swietlik for his letter and telling him it was a waste of time his writing again. She knew she could have ignored his letter and just let him think she was uninterested but she liked him and did not want him to think the English were ignorant. She pushed open the door and went inside.

There was a table near the door which was empty but before she could reach it, a man in black trousers, white shirt, waistcoat and bow tie came over to her. He wore a grave smile and she recognised him even before he took one of her hands between his own and bowed over it, saying, 'It is Miss Lizzie Knight, is it not?'

'Hello,' she said, trying to stem a rising blush. 'I hope you don't mind my coming here? But I went to the address you gave me and they told me you were here.'

'It is OK. The lunchtime rush it is over and I was about to go off duty. We can go elsewhere and talk. Unless you are hungry?'

'No, I'm not hungry,' she lied, relieved that he was gazing into her eyes and not at her waistline. 'Perhaps we could go to Westminster Abbey?'

'Westminster Abbey?' he echoed faintly.

'I told my aunt I was going there and I don't like telling lies.'

'Then we shall go,' he said immediately. 'As long as I am allowed to sit down when we get there?'

Lizzie smiled and agreed. Jan left her a moment to put on an overcoat and then rejoined her where she was waiting outside in the not so salubrious street, and offered her his arm.

After a moment's hesitation she took it, murmuring, 'I hadn't planned on this.'

'What did you plan on, Lizzie?' His expression was serious.

'Saying thank you for your letter, don't bother again, and leaving.'

'Ah, but why? That would not be the act of a good friend and that is all I am asking of you. Is it that since we last met you have seen your lover and he would not approve of your friendship with me?' He glanced at her sidelong.

'I haven't seen Alex, and I don't plan on seeing him,' she said as cheerfully as she could.

'Why not?'

She was silent, not sure if she wanted to answer his question.

'I am sorry,' he said after several minutes had passed. 'I intrude. You do not need to answer.'

She sighed. 'Alex was my stepmother's fiancé and that's the reason I left Liverpool. I can't go back.'

'Do you still love him?' Jan asked stiffly.

'What has that to do with anything?'

'Everything. If we are to mean anything to each other.'

Lizzie reddened and pulled her hand from his arm. 'You hardly know anything about me, Jan. We can't mean anything to each other. It was a mistake my allowing you to change my mind.' She held out a hand. 'Goodbye.'

He stared at her. 'You intrigue me and I think I am in love with you.' He took her hand and, pulling her towards him, kissed her passionately amidst the milling crowd.

Instinctively she struggled and then suddenly her mind took over and she thought of how much she needed a husband, telling herself that she might not be able to pass the baby off as his but if Jan felt this passionately about her, then in time, if the baby was a boy, he might just accept him and marry her. So she returned his kiss. And when they parted she promised to write.

Chapter Seventeen

Billy clamped the joint together and carefully wiped away the excess glue that oozed out. Christmas had come and gone but there were people who had asked if they did outside repairs to furniture and so the business had expanded.

Harry ambled into the back room of the shop. 'Someone to see yer, lad. She's a bit of a smasher – tall, blonde, beautiful, and in a nurse's uniform.'

'Josie.' Billy's expression clouded. 'I suppose you'd better tell her to come through.'

Harry shook his bald head. 'What's up with yer, lad? A beautiful girl comes to see yer and yer've got a face like a wet Whit weekend.'

'What good am I to any woman?' There was a bitter note in Billy's voice as he wiped his fingers on a rag before manipulating his wheelchair so he faced the door.

'Now stop that!' Harry squeezed his shoulder. 'There's always someone else a damn' sight worse off. Put the smile back on your face and look like yer pleased to see her.'

'I am pleased to see her. It's just that . . .' Billy closed his lips on the rest of the words and gave a ghost of a smile. 'Send her in.'

'That's the spirit, lad.' Harry grinned and went out.

A few seconds later Josie entered and immediately Billy sensed a suppressed excitement about her. 'What's up?'

'You'll never guess.' She strolled across the room with the relaxed confidence of a Siamese cat and sat on a chair so their faces were on a level.

'Tell me then.'

'You remember Matt who assisted at Dot's and Ron's wedding?'

'Of course. Your *holy* relation. What about him?'

'He's been on the phone asking what my friend who went missing looks like.'

'What!' Billy's hands reached out and gripped hers. 'You think he's seen Lizzie?'

'He didn't say. I said I'd send a photo. He thanked me and put the phone down.'

'Mysterious.'

'Very. Do you think you should tell Alex?'

There was a pause and their eyes held, hesitantly seeking from the other their hidden feelings about that question. 'You think I should,' said Billy at last.

'He hasn't got back with your Phyl, has he? And he refused Dot's and Ron's invitation to the wedding,' said Josie eagerly. 'And you told me and Joe that he bites your and Harry's head off at the least little thing. I think he's really missing Lizzie and we should help him find her.'

'I'm not so sure,' said Billy slowly. 'If Lizzie wanted to be found she could have made it happen. She could even write to us. In fact I think it's blinkin' wicked of her not to have written,' he declared hotly.

'Pride and fear,' said Josie promptly. 'It's what's wrong with you. It's why you won't ask me out on my own.'

Billy scowled. 'How can I ask you out? We can't even go to the pictures without there being steps to cope with. I need Joe then.'

'Joe won't always be around. You know he's got his eye on Fleet Street,' she said softly. 'And I'm no eight-stone weakling. Nurses have to be strong.'

Billy's expression relaxed. 'Don't be trying to kid me you lift blokes my size all the day long. You work in St Paul's eye hospital, not men's surgical at the Royal.'

'I'm still strong.' She raised one of his hands and kissed the back of it. 'Pride,' she said.

'You're getting off the subject.'

Josie smiled. 'If you don't think we should give this information to Alex, what about Phyl? She's still supposed to be responsible for Lizzie. Perhaps Matt would say more to her?'

'Maybe. She's doing a week in Southport at some awful theatre on the promenade by the pier.'

'You'll write to her then?' she said persuasively.

He was silent. She pinched him and he winced. 'OK!' he said crossly. 'I suppose you won't give me any peace 'til I do.'

'That's a good boy.' Josie kissed him lightly on the mouth before standing up. 'I'll see you tomorrow and you'd better have written that letter by then.' She fluttered her fingers and walked out.

*

Phyl took a last bow with the rest of the cast, and as soon as the curtain came down hurried off-stage. She had been offered a small part in the company pantomime and had said yes. Her star was not rising as she wished so she could ill afford to turn down work despite the theatre's drawbacks. The wintry wind that blew across Liverpool Bay seemed able to find every gap in the tongue and groove boards of the little wooden theatre. There were also rats which climbed the piles of the pier and headed straight for backstage, seemingly to relish sticks of grease-paint for snacks.

But she was not going to think of the rats now. She had a splitting headache due to a letter she had received from Billy saying she had to come home, that it was urgent and about Lizzie. No further information, damn him! She felt guilty about her stepdaughter. Five months since Lizzie went missing and she'd done nothing about it. Phyl headed for the women's dressing room on the first floor and changed as swiftly as she could before leaving the theatre with other members of the cast, having a terrific battle with the wind because the stage door faced the sea.

It was not until she was seated on the last bus to Liverpool that she allowed herself to think some more about Lizzie. Why did she want to cry just because Billy had mentioned her? She knew where Lizzie was but she had not told a soul, not even her mam. Perhaps it was time she did? Her heart felt heavy as she gazed at her reflection in the darkened window. Damn! She looked a hundred and five. She needed a rest.

She set her green velour hat at a more flattering angle and almost wished she was a child again. That's what she needed, to be cosseted, not to have to make any decisions, to get enough food and sleep. She needed home, but home meant family who believed they knew the real Phyl Knight. The one they knew would not have kept Lizzie's whereabouts a secret.

She remembered being home for Dot's wedding and her mother handing her an envelope addressed to Miss Elizabeth Knight. It had been from a solicitor informing her stepdaughter that her aunt, Miss Charlotte Broom of Broom Farm, nr Chelmsford, Essex, wished to make contact with her. It had thrown Phyl completely off balance. It had come on top of being told that Alex had declined an invitation to her sister's wedding, just when she had hopes of taking advantage of such a special occasion to persuade him to take up with her again. She hated not having a man to go around with. The play's tour had finished and she had not yet been offered another part. It had been exciting, fun but exhausting, so she was glad to be *resting* but in no mood to think kindly of Lizzie. After all she had done for the girl, for her to scoot off the way she had was inexcusable. The information that she had gone to London had only confirmed what she'd believed when she recalled the times Lizzie had spoken of going south to find her aunt, of seeking her whereabouts at the convent school in Brentwood, and she'd felt certain that was what her stepdaughter had done and now was safe in Essex. So what could all this urgency Billy had mentioned be about? Surely Lizzie hadn't come home or he'd have said so. Wearily she rested her head against the window of the bus and tried to stop feeling guilty.

'You feeling better now?' Mary placed a tray on the bed and sat alongside her sister.

'Heaps!' said Phyl, watching her sister pour milk in cups and then fill them from a tea-cosied brown pot. There was a Sunday feel about the place enforced by the sound of church bells and the smell of salt fish and butter on the plate on the tray. 'Where's Billy?'

'Waiting for you downstairs.' Mary took off her slippers and stretched out beside Phyl. 'Alex giving him that job has done wonders for him, you know. Although the man himself seems to have gone hard. He never stops and talks to any of us when he picks Billy up and drops him off.'

Phyl drank her tea and had a couple of forkfuls of the fish and a slice of bread and butter before saying, 'At least he's not taking his grievance with Mam and our Lo out on our Billy. How are things with him and the twins now? And are you still carrying a torch for Joe?'

Mary stared at her, wide-eyed. 'How did you know? Was it always so obvious?'

Phyl leaned back against her pillows and was silent a moment. 'At least with Lizzie off the scene you've a better chance of grabbing his attention. I think he had a pash on her at one time despite her being a bit older than him.'

'He might still have because I think he doesn't really see me.' She pulled a face. 'The only thing he thinks about is seeing his name in print more often.'

'He'll notice you soon enough if you stick around. You're not a bad-looking kid.' Phyl filled her teacup again and lit a cigarette. She had cut down on them because they played havoc with her singing voice but there were times when she needed one. 'D'you know what it is that Billy says is so urgent about Lizzie?'

Mary placed her teacup on its saucer. 'No. He hasn't said a word. Is that why you've come home? I wonder what it's about?'

Phyl shrugged and blew out a stream of smoke. 'The sooner I find out the better. I have to go back to Southport tonight. I have a script to learn. Tell Billy, love, I'll be down in ten minutes.'

Mary nodded and swung her legs off the bed but she did not leave the room immediately. She stood looking down at her eldest sister. 'Do you really love the life, Phyl? Is it living up to your expectations?'

Phyl took time to answer. 'Most of the time I enjoy what I'm doing but whether I could answer honestly that it's everything I want, I don't think I can. I'm not sure if I wouldn't give it all up tomorrow if I met the right man.'

'You're over Alex, though?' Mary's voice was anxious.

Phyl's expressive tawny eyes dropped and she stared intently at a small milky bubble on the surface of her tea. 'I'll know when I meet him.'

'You're planning on doing that?'

'I think I need to. Now go away, little sister, and let me get dressed.'

Mary went.

*

Billy looked up as Phyl entered the parlour. He'd been in bed when she had arrived last night and now, looking at her, he thought some of the glitter had left her. She looked tired without make-up. He worked out how old she was and realised she must be round thirty. No spring chicken to be trying to make it on the stage. Then she smiled and he changed his mind.

'You OK?' she said.

'I'll never be completely OK, but I'm coping. Sit down, Phyl. I hate having to look up at people.'

She sat on Nan Eccles's old rocking chair, feeling chastened and took a deep breath. 'Right. What's this about Lizzie? Do you know where she is?'

'We think she's still in London. Josie's vicar relation phoned her and asked for a description of her friend who'd gone missing. We don't know any more than that but we think he's seen her and wants to make sure it's her before raising our hopes.' He paused, expecting her to speak, but she remained silent so he cleared his throat and continued: 'We think she's in trouble. Why should she suddenly turn up there if everything's hunky dory?'

Phyl's smile did not quite reach her eyes. 'Now there's a question.' She stood. 'I'm going to see Alex. I'll talk to you later.' Before he could speak she walked out of the room.

The small door in the gates was open much to Phyl's relief. She did not immediately enter but stared up at the newly painted sign. Gone were the words WOOLLENS, COTTON RAGS AND BAGGINGS and instead were SECONDHAND CAR

PARTS. At least Alex was progressing, and she was glad of it. As she went through the small door she found herself reaching for a cigarette before remembering she had not bought another packet. She swore inwardly. She was nervous and knew why.

Phyl began to make her way across the cemented yard, only to stop when she saw Alex talking to a couple of men just outside the office door. He glanced at her but did not reveal by the flicker of a smile that he recognised her. So she had to stand there waiting until the men had gone, carrying a car engine between them, before approaching him. 'Hello, Alex.'

He nodded in her direction. 'What can I do for you, Phyl? Bought yourself a little car, have you, and it's gone wrong?' He spoke in that abrasive tone she remembered him using in the past when he didn't want anyone to know what he was feeling.

'Don't be daft. Where would I find money for even a secondhand car?'

'Haven't hit the big time then?'

'You'd have heard if I had.' She paused, huddling inside her coat. 'Can we go inside? It's freezing out here.'

He pushed the door, holding it open for her.

She went inside and he waved her to a chair. She hesitated then sat down, watching him seat himself the other side of the desk. She had rehearsed this moment but now it was here she was tongue-tied like she had never been on stage.

'Lost for words, Phyl? It must be something serious.'

'It is,' she murmured. 'It's about Lizzie.' From her handbag she took an envelope and placed it on the desk. Then she rose and walked out.

Alex caught up with her outside the Mission Hall on the corner of Dawber Street. He waved the letter in front of her face and demanded, 'Did you hate her that much, Phyl?'

'Hate is too strong a word,' she said wearily. 'I was hurt, tired, and I didn't want to think about her.'

'What about me? I suppose I was being punished too?'

'I suppose you were.' She looked him straight in the eye. 'Sorry, but I'm only human. What are you going to do? Go and see her?'

He nodded. 'What about you? Don't you want to see her?'

A smile lit Phyl's eyes. 'Don't be daft, man. It would be the worst thing going if we arrived there together. I'll get to see her sometime. In the meantime you go, and the best of luck.'

'Thanks, Phyl.' He squeezed her shoulder before walking away.

As she made her way home she felt an enormous sense of relief, although she felt like crying as well. Lizzie was off her conscience but Alex was still in her heart. She supposed he had been part of her life too long ever to be completely ousted. She wished there was another man she could turn to but who could possibly fill his place? In the meantime she would tell Billy to stop worrying about Lizzie and then it would be back to work learning the next script.

*

Alex drove slowly along Chelmsford's busy High Street and then stopped outside an impressive building. Just beyond it he could see what was too big to be a church and was most probably a cathedral. It was no use. He was going to have to find the solicitor's office or ask a passer-by to direct him to Broom Farm. When he had set out he had not realised Chelmsford was so large but pictured it the size of a village.

He got out of the car and stopped the first man he saw, who happened to be elderly and red-faced. 'Excuse me, sir, can you tell me the way to Broom Farm?'

'Certainly, my boy,' he said, placing a hand on Alex's arm and leaning on it. 'But take my advice and don't go. You won't be made welcome.'

Alex smiled, wondering why the old boy should say that, but he was not going to turn back now. 'I'll take that chance.'

The man's blue eyes looked up into his face. 'You're not from round here, are you, my boy?'

'No. I'm from up north. So if you could tell me the way, sir?'

The man gazed at Alex's car and patted the bonnet. 'I'll get in and show you. Turn its nose, my boy, and we'll be off.'

Alex did as ordered and zoomed off up the road. Once outside the town he drove carefully along the icy road, thinking about how Lizzie had once declared her liking for the countryside. 'How far is it?'

'Two, nearer three miles. I presume it's horses you've come about? My neighbours say Miss Broom is potty about them. I wouldn't know myself. I've only lived in the village a few years but the Broom family are known in the area. Strong women!' He nodded jerkily. 'You can drop me off in the village if you don't mind? The farm is about another half mile and a turning further on. I once took a walk up there but wasn't made welcome.' He fell silent, a brooding expression on his face.

Alex did not enquire as to why he had not been made welcome. His attention was all for the narrow winding slippery road. They came to the village and he stopped to let the man out. They thanked each other and Alex carried on past cottage gardens which contained the odd straggly rose or cluster of flowering winter jasmine. His heart was starting to pound in a peculiar way. Would Lizzie be pleased to see him or would she tell him to go back home the way he'd come? After all, she'd known where he was all this time. She could have been in touch if she had wanted to. He felt on edge, unsure what to expect and how to behave.

He came to a sign post which said 'Broom Farm' and turned right and rattled up a lane past a field containing several blanket-covered horses until he saw another sign and some open gates. He drove the car in past a barn which looked in danger of falling down and a frozen pond on the other side. He drew up in front of a Tudor-style house and got out and looked about.

Nobody came running so he walked up to the house and knocked on the only door he could see. Nothing. He knocked again and thought he heard a faltering step inside. He tried the door and it opened so he stepped inside.

'Who's that?' called a querulous voice.

'Miss Broom?' said Alex, walking across the kitchen.

'Good God!' said the voice, which appeared to be coming from the other side of a door.

He opened it and saw a middle-aged woman leaning on a stick. 'Miss Broom?' he repeated.

'Out!' she said, and resting a hand against the wall she waved the stick at him. 'Out, out! I'll have no men in my house! Get out immediately. How dare you come in without being asked!'

Alex was so startled that he backed away. 'I'm sorry but nobody answered. Are you Miss Broom?'

'It's nothing to do with you who I am! Out, I said, young man.' Balancing herself against the wall she advanced on him, brandishing the walking stick.

'There's nothing for you to be frightened of.' He held up his hands in a pacifying manner. 'I've come to see Miss Elizabeth Knight. I'm Alexander Payne, a friend of hers from up north. There's nothing for you to be frightened of.' He knew he had shocked her rigid.

Then she said in a croaky voice, 'My niece isn't here. I've made approaches but not one answer did I get from her. You're wasting your time, Mr Payne, so get out of my house.'

It was Alex's turn to go stiff with shock. 'But she has to be here!' His tone was desperate. 'Her stepmother gave me this.' He took the solicitor's letter from his wallet and held it out to her. Reluctantly Charlotte relinquished her stick. Placing it on the table, she took the paper. She read it swiftly. 'You say her stepmother gave you this? But it's dated July. Why has she waited so long before doing anything about it?'

He hesitated. 'She's been on tour with a play and doesn't get home often. She was sure Lizzie would be here.'

'Well, she's wrong.' Miss Broom's mouth set firm as she handed the letter back to him. 'You can tell her from me the girl isn't here. Now outside, Mr Payne. I will not have you on my property.' She picked up her stick again and waved it at him.

Alex did not budge. 'Have you any idea where she could be?'

Charlotte made an exasperated noise. 'How can I if she hasn't been here? Now will you go before I call the police?'

Alex thought that remark quite ridiculous but was in no mood to laugh about it. He'd rather smash something. But there was no point in staying if Lizzie was not here. He turned and then hesitated in the doorway. 'If she turns up here, will you tell her I was looking for her and that my feelings haven't changed?'

'If!' She sniffed. 'Can you see it after all this time? Now outside, young man, or I'll have the law on you for trespassing.'

Alex left the house, closing the door quietly behind him. For a moment he stood looking about him, feeling the silence and aware of the smell of horse manure. Then he got into the car and drove away.

He was angry. Had Phyl deliberately sent him on a wild goose chase? Yet as the car ate up the miles he remembered what the old woman had said and realised Phyl could not have known Lizzie wasn't going to be at the farm. She must be in London still, but where? Billy had mentioned before Alex had left that Josie had received a phone call from her clergyman relation. He had been a bit vague, saying that Lizzie might have been seen but he was not sure. Was it any use trying the vicarage? Alex decided as he was in the vicinity he might as well have one last try at finding Lizzie and headed for London.

'So you're the Alex Payne who didn't come to the wedding?' The grey eyes of the clergyman were searching as he shook Alex's hand. 'Do come in, I'm Matt Gibson.'

'Thanks, padre.' Alex had not had anything to do with the clergy since he'd been in the army. Feeling ill at ease, he wiped his feet on the coconut mat with WELCOME on it and followed the older man into a large high-ceilinged room at the back of the house overlooking a garden. He was waved to a comfortable-looking sofa covered in chintz which was pulled up close to the fire.

'You're fortunate my wife and the boys are out or we wouldn't have a moment's peace,' said Matt, seating himself on a chair. 'Lily'd be bombarding you with questions about the family. As it is I presume you've come about the missing girl?'

'Lizzie, yes!' Alex leaned forward eagerly. 'Have you seen her?'

Matt nodded. 'I feel pretty sure it was her. I remember we had a conversation with her and her stepmother at a party. In some ways she hasn't changed that much.'

'So you can tell me where she is?' Alex's hands trembled where they rested on his thighs.

'I wish I could but she refused to give me her address. I did wonder if she thought I'd recognised her so she was not taking any chances at being found.'

'Then why come to you?' Alex could not conceal his disappointment. 'I mean – it's tantalising of her, isn't it?'

'She came to see me in my role of clergyman,' said Matt.

'I don't understand! Why should she . . .?' He paused. Matt was silent.

Alex gripped his hands tightly between his knees as he gazed back, remembering the thunderstorm and how he and Lizzie had made love on the rug in front of the fire. A mortal sin, she had called it, despite being C of E. That convent education had been strong within her. 'She is OK, isn't she?' he said passionately. 'I mean –'

'I think I know what you mean, and I give you my word if she turns up again I'll tell her you've been here. I think it's imperative that the two of you get together as soon as possible.'

Alex felt a strange thrill as well as a sense of shock. 'Did she say why she ran away?' He jumped to his feet and paced the floor, suddenly unable to sit still. 'Dear God, why hasn't she written? She must know I've been worried about her.'

'I haven't an answer for you,' said Matt firmly. 'I've said more than enough.'

'She must know I'd marry her!' Alex just could not understand the way Lizzie's mind must be working.

Matt was silent and Alex realised that he was not going to get any more information from him. He held out a hand. 'Thanks for everything. Josie can find me if you want me.'

They shook hands firmly before he was seen out.

As soon as Alex managed to escape London's chaotic traffic, which had needed all his concentration, he tried to think clearly. Was he right in believing Lizzie was pregnant? It was the only answer he could come up with to that 'it's imperative the two of you get together as soon as possible'. Hell! What was Lizzie thinking about not coming home to him? He could not make sense of it at all. She must know he'd be pleased. Why go to a padre? Another man knew about her having his child before he did. The thought hurt. He had believed he understood women but was starting to think he didn't know how their minds worked at all. To him it made perfect sense if a woman got pregnant to get in touch with the father to let him know. Especially if she was not married and had little money! The thoughts went round and round in his brain until his head ached with thinking. The road seemed to dance before his eyes and he realised how tired he was and pulled off.

He climbed into the back seat and lay down, trying to relax. But a new thought was now chasing the old one. Perhaps he wasn't the father and that was why Lizzie had run away in the first place? Maybe it was even Billy's? The accident hadn't taken the possibility of being a father away from him. Lizzie had been so thrilled when he had given Billy the job. He could see her face now. She had kissed him. He imagined the feel of her lips. He dozed off and was soon having a nightmare. Lizzie was being attacked by a man in an entry and he could not get to her to prevent him from raping her.

He woke with a jerk, stiff and cold. His teeth began to chatter. Maybe that time in the entry with that nasty bit of work had affected Lizzie? Perhaps it had twisted her somehow and she wasn't the woman he thought he knew? He was unable to bear his own thoughts so got out of the car and walked up and down in the dark until he felt wide awake. Then he drove off but he still had no peace of mind.

When Alex eventually arrived in Liverpool he felt drained and knew he had to stop thinking about Lizzie if he was to remain sane and rebuild his life.

Chapter Eighteen

'Push now, push!' urged the midwife. 'I can see its head. Come on, girl, you can do it.'

Lizzie did not need any coaxing, her whole body was demanding that she give birth to the child. She pushed and panted and did as she was told. There was now no room in her mind to worry about the baby's sex. There was a fierce stinging pain and she cried out but knew the head was through.

'Carefully now,' said the midwife from somewhere between her legs. 'No need to rush it. When you feel the next push coming, gently does it and we'll have the shoulders out . . . that's a good girl!'

Lizzie found some comfort in the praise. Her pains had started yesterday evening and had continued right through the night, gaining in intensity until she thought she would not be able to bear them any longer.

'Now one more push. Ahhh! That's it. You have a lovely daughter, dear. She's tiny, mind.' The midwife sounded taken aback.

Lizzie was surprised herself. She had been so large. But, oh, the relief! The blessed relief! Thank you, God. Thank you!

She attempted to lift herself higher so she could catch a glimpse of her baby, but flopped back, exhausted. Alexandra Rose, that was what she had decided to call her. She heard a slap and then a baby's cry and tears filled her eyes. 'Tell my aunt it's a girl,' she croaked.

'There's time soon enough for that, dear. You and baby need my attention at the moment.' The midwife was feeling Lizzie's belly and frowning. 'I wish I'd been called in earlier. You really should have seen the doctor. Do you feel another push coming?'

Lizzie felt something, expected something because she had read up about the birth process and knew about the afterbirth needing expelling. What she hadn't expected was the strength of the pain that now followed. She swore beneath her breath and felt as if she was being torn apart.

When the midwife said, 'Twins! A boy this time and he's all there. He must have been lying behind his sister,' Lizzie could scarcely believe it but nothing could take away the joy of her ordeal being over. Never again, she thought, as she turned her head and looked at the babies lying on a towel on the bed beside her.

Five minutes later there was a vigorous tapping on the door. 'Mrs Slater, is everything all right?'

'Everything's fine, Miss Broom, but it might not have been,' shouted the midwife. 'Your niece should have seen me or the doctor long before now. Get Penny to put another kettle on.'

'What about the baby?' The door opened cautiously and Charlotte's face appeared.

'The babies are all there.' The midwife looked at her severely, scooped up an armful of soiled linen, and brushing past her, left the room.

'Babies?' Charlotte's wrinkled face wore an astonished expression as she tapped her way across the linoleum towards the bed.

'Twins,' said Lizzie in a croaky voice. She gazed down at the babies wrapped tightly in a length of sheeting apiece as they lay in her arms, and knew she wouldn't be able to bear parting with either of them. Their tiny features were scarlet and screwed up with the effort of having entered the outside world and for a second she marvelled that half an hour of passion on a tiger skin could have resulted in these tiny but perfect human beings.

'What are they?' said Charlotte, leaning on her stick and staring at Lizzie.

'Can't you tell?'

'Of course not, girl! They both look alike to me.'

Lizzie sought to put off the moment of telling her aunt the truth. She rocked gently the baby cradled in the crook of her right arm. 'Aren't they tiny? I think this one is Alexandra. She was born first.'

'You're not naming her after him!' sniffed her aunt. 'You'll call her Charlotte after me and change your surname and hers to Broom so there'll be three generations of Brooms at Broom Farm.'

Lizzie lifted her eyes from her baby. 'I want to call her Alexandra after her father.'

Charlotte's jaw dropped. 'You want to name my greatniece after a man who disgraced you?' she rattled out.

'Where's your dignity, girl? You'll name her Charlotte and have done with it.'

Lizzie was annoyed. She had just been through hours of extreme pain and had made up her mind that if she had a daughter she was going to be Alexandra Rose. She was in no mood to be told by her aunt what to do. 'She's my daughter.' Her arms tightened about the baby. 'I shall name the other baby after you. Probably get called Charlie but there you are.'

Charlotte's expression changed and her tone was milder when she spoke. 'I've never heard such impudence in all my born days, Elizabeth, and I do wonder where your gratitude is, but I expect you've had a rough time.'

'Yes,' said Lizzie shortly, rocking her son who seemed to be pleading with her from unfocused eyes.

'I'll forgive you then.' Her aunt smiled down at the babies. 'Some of the girls used to call me Charlie at school – and Alexandra is one of the Queen's names. I suppose if it's good enough for royalty it'll have to be good enough for me.'

Lizzie looked at Charlotte and realised what her aunt must be thinking. She could not resist a smile even as she wondered just how long she could get away with Charlotte believing both babies were girls.

Her aunt tapped her stick on the floor. 'You must forget that man, though! You've got a good life ahead of you here now and a secure future for your girls.' She gazed down at the baby in Lizzie's left arm. 'I think Charlie here is the best-looking.' She touched his cheek with a hand that quivered.

At that moment the door opened and the midwife reappeared with a cup of tea in her hand. 'If you could leave mother now, Miss Broom,' she said firmly, 'she must have some rest. I want your permission to send Penny down to the village to get a couple of tins of Ostermilk and some feeding bottles. Mother might need some help to feed these two and it's best to have it in.'

Charlotte inclined her head and smiled at the woman. 'Alexandra Rose and Charlie after me. What do you think of that, Mrs Slater?'

The midwife glanced at Lizzie as she placed the tea cup and saucer on the bedside table. 'Very nice, Miss Broom. I think it's very noble of you to take them on. But I'm sure you'll get an extra jewel in your crown when you get to heaven.'

Charlotte smiled graciously and, leaning heavily on her stick, walked out of the bedroom.

'Charlie!' exclaimed the midwife, taking Lizzie's son from her. 'I'm wondering why you didn't name the girl after your aunt instead of the boy? As if you and your aunt haven't already set the tongues wagging enough. There's going to be more talk in the village now. First lad to live on Broom Farm for more than forty years, I reckon.'

'My aunt seldom gets to the village,' said Lizzie, gazing at her steadily. 'And besides, she doesn't listen to gossip.'

'What is it you're saying, my girl?' She placed Charlie in the old fashioned wooden cradle that had come down from the attic.

Lizzie smiled wearily. 'My aunt said if the baby was a boy he had to be adopted.'

The midwife was silent as she handed the cup of tea to Lizzie. 'She's going to find out sooner or later.'

'Better later than sooner.' Lizzie sat up against the pillows and sipped the tea. 'I'm hoping she'll get so fond of him that she won't be able to bear parting from him.'

The midwife smiled mirthlessly. 'You don't know your aunt! But it's nothing to do with me.'

'So you'll say nothing?'

'As I said, it's none of my business. But you'd best keep it from Penny. She's a nice girl but her mother likes to talk.'

Lizzie thanked her and wondered why she was prepared to keep quiet about things, and came to the conclusion that maybe it was as she had said and it was none of her business. She watched the nurse wash the babies and put nappies and vests and nighties on them both. Lizzie thought she would have to buy more clothes. Then the midwife had her put the babies to the breast.

'Give then turn and turn about, Miss. Bottle, breast, bottle, breast, and you'll just about manage that way. I'll be back later and see how you're doing. And I'll be around for the next couple of weeks.' A small smile lifted her mouth. 'Seeing as how you're a special case.'

After the midwife had gone Lizzie lay back, feeling worn out and wanting nothing more than to go to sleep, but her thoughts would not let her. How long could she get away with deceiving her aunt? Not for ever so she had to think of a contingency plan. She'd had one already if the baby had been a boy, and it had involved Jan. It was no good now, though. He might have accepted one baby but not two. Not for the first time in the last twenty-four hours she thought of Alex and Phyl. Could they forgive her and help her? Then she considered how she would feel if it was Phyl who had borne Alex's children and forced herself not to hope for any help from them. There was something else that had been fluttering on the edge of her consciousness for some time and perhaps the next few weeks was the time to do something about it . . .

Penny came to see her, bringing a bar of chocolate and a bunch of tulips, as well as the tins of Ostermilk and feeding bottles. 'They're little beauties.' Her voice was full of admiration. 'You aren't half lucky! I mean, some girls in your position would be at their wits' end, but you've got your babies and all this.' She gazed about the large bedroom with its leaded bay window, carpet and walnut furniture. 'But golly, you're going to have your work cut out looking after them.'

'I know that,' said Lizzie, her eyes narrowed in thought. 'I'm going to get up as soon as I can.'

'Ten days,' said Penny sagely. 'Miss Broom's asked me to sleep in for that time to help you out.'

'Thanks.' Lizzie bit into a piece of chocolate. She was starving but offered Penny a couple of squares. 'I can't stay in bed that long. The sooner I'm up and about, the sooner I can start getting things sorted out.'

Penny sighed. 'We could do with some more help.'

'Exactly. And I'm going to see we get it.'

'You'll have trouble persuading your aunt,' warned Penny.

Didn't she know it! thought Lizzie, but said no more, only giving Penny instructions on how to make up a bottle.

Lizzie found the following few days frustrating, but she fed and changed her babies herself from her bed, before defying the midwife and getting up after five days. Despite soreness and occasional bouts of dizziness, she managed to keep on her feet. She knew that going to London was beyond her just yet but wrote to Jan telling him about the twins and that she would not be writing again. She thought how useful interchangeable names were, because her aunt caught her writing out the envelope and presumed Jan was a girlfriend of Lizzie's. Charlotte suggested she have her visit, saying perhaps she could help the regular girl riders whom she had coerced into helping with the horses while Lizzie was so tied up with the babies. The idea amused Lizzie but she put her aunt off by telling her that Jan owned a restaurant and was much too busy to come and see her.

Towards the end of May Lizzie decided she was fit enough to go to London and considered it safe to leave Alexandra for Penny to bottle feed but was too anxious about the girl and her aunt discovering Charlie was a boy to leave him behind.

She told her aunt she was going into Chelmsford to register the babies' birth but instead caught an early train to London and went to Somerset House, using a shawl as a sling to carry Charlie against her as she had seen African women carrying their babies in a film. She needed both hands free.

Lizzie was at Somerset House some time but when she emerged there was a curve to her lips which signalled her satisfaction with what she had discovered. She fed Charlie in the ladies' toilets at Liverpool Street station and caught the next train to Chelmsford. There she registered the twins' births before hurrying to the farm, prepared for the day when she might have to do battle with her aunt.

The day arrived quicker than Lizzie had planned.

'I think you should get Charlie and Alexandra christened,' said Charlotte over breakfast on the last day of May. In a couple of days it would be Coronation Day.

'We can't,' said Lizzie instantly.

Her aunt's eyebrows bristled. 'Why not? The priest in Chelmsford's a reasonable man. He won't blame the girls for your sin.'

'I can't,' insisted Lizzie. 'I'm not Catholic, unlike you and mother.'

'You can have instruction.'

'No, Aunt.' Lizzie thought she might be able to deceive her aunt but she could not deceive God. She took a deep breath. 'Charlie isn't a girl. He's a boy.'

Charlotte's eyes almost popped out of her head and her jaw dropped. She said stiffly, 'I do not find that remark the least bit amusing, Elizabeth.'

'It wasn't meant to be.' Lizzie couldn't finish her egg and pushed it away, resting her elbows on the table. She was trembling inside and prayed she had not been mistaken at Somerset House, but she had taken a copy of what she had read so she couldn't be wrong. 'Before you threaten to throw us off the farm, may I say that I've been to Somerset House.'

'You've what!' Charlotte almost choked on the words and her eyebrows bristled as she thumped her stick on the floor.

'I've seen Grandmother's will and I know half the house and the land was left to my mother,' said Lizzie. Her aunt blanched and Lizzie felt mean but reminded herself that her aunt had been dishonest with her, as well as telling her that she had to have her son adopted.

'The horses are mine and you've no money, Elizabeth.' Charlotte's voice was harsh. 'Your mother had her share of that.'

'I know. She spent a fair amount of it on my education.' She paused and added as calmly as she could, 'Let's be sensible about this, Aunt Charlotte. Without meaning to sound cruel, your rheumatism isn't going to get any better so you're going to have to hire extra help with the horses or accept me and the babies as they are. You have a nephew and he has as much right to a quarter of the house and land as Alexandra does.'

Her aunt was silent for what seemed ages before she said slowly, 'There's a lot to be said for animals and I must say that I prefer them to most people. I love my horses and you can't imagine what it means to me not to be able to ride any more.'

'I do understand loss,' said Lizzie gently. 'I was twelve when mother died and fourteen when Daddy went. If it had not been for Phyl, I don't know what I'd have done.

Animals can be good companions but they can't help in the way other human beings can. Phyl showed me what caring meant when I needed it most.'

There was another silence broken by Charlotte's noisily clearing her throat and saying in the manner of a grande dame. 'Your mother should have told you about the farm.'

'But she didn't and she mustn't have told Daddy either. I don't know why.'

Her aunt continued imperviously, 'I will not accept an ultimatum from you, Elizabeth. Do not think that I have not considered your leaving because once you mentioned Alexander Payne, I knew it might happen one day. I will sell the farm and you can have your share.' She paused and added dramatically, 'I will take the veil! The nuns will look after me and you will not get a penny of my money. I will give it to the church.'

Her words were so unexpected that Lizzie felt laughter rising inside her. Her aunt dedicating herself to a Christ who had been man and God! She took a deep breath. 'Right. We'll sell this place. It's probably the wisest thing. You'll get in touch with your solicitor?'

Her aunt nodded. 'Now go away and leave me in peace.'

Lizzie left her and went outside to where the babies lay top and tail in their pram. She had a lot to thank her aunt for but perhaps it was best that things had ended this way. Maybe she could still have a father for her children. She would have some money now and perhaps Jan would be prepared to accept the three of them, if she brought enough cash with her to help him buy that restaurant he had his mind set upon. As soon as things were settled she would go and see him.

She thought of Alex with a painful longing but she had accepted that reality had long ago taken over from the magic she'd experienced with him that night of the firework display. But thinking of that night reminded her that soon the whole country would be celebrating the Coronation. Just for a moment she wished fervently that she could be up north with Alex, could see Josie and Joe, Phyl, Billy and Mary, even if it was just for one day, before this time saying a proper goodbye to them all.

Chapter Nineteen

Mary carefully fastened the base of the blue crepe paper rose with a twist of wire before placing it down on the table next to a white one. 'D'you think that's enough, Mam?'

'Do another half a dozen. I want to be sure,' said Maisie from across the table where she was making red roses. 'That trestle your dad's put up over the front door and down the sides is a fair size, yer know.'

'I know! But we must have done hundreds of flowers,' said Mary, but obediently took up the scissors, despite her thumb getting a weal across it, and cut another strip of crepe paper. 'I wouldn't mind but I'm not even going to be here for the street party.'

'Mmmph! I don't know why you can't be like the rest of the family and be satisfied to watch the Coronation on the telly. Why do you think your dad bought it?'

'I didn't ask him to buy it,' said Mary. 'I'm not turning down an offer to go to London with the twins. Joe might just notice me once in a while if we're on holiday. I only wish our Billy would come but he's that positive he'll be a nuisance, he's digging in his heels.'

'He'll enjoy himself just as much here,' said Maisie, her eyes narrowing with concentration as she peered through the spectacles she'd had to start wearing. 'I know Josie means well but did she tell you if he went he'd have to travel in the luggage van?'

'We'd stay with him,' said Mary, resting on her elbows. 'We'd be happy to do it.' Her expression was earnest. 'Try and persuade him, Mam. Josie's getting real desperate. You must know how she feels about him.'

'Mmmph!' said Maisie again. 'I know she thinks love can conquer all but life with our Billy ain't going to be that easy, girl. And she's only young and her feelings might change in a year or so.'

'I don't think so. But what d'you want out of life for him, Mam? That he stays with you for ever?'

'For ever is a long time,' said Maisie, not looking up. 'And I'll remind you that it's not me that's stopping him going. He made the decision himself. Now, not another word about it.'

Mary fell silent. She wished Phyl was there. She was back in Southport at the Scala theatre after being here, there and everywhere, and hadn't been home for what seemed ages. Not since Alex had returned from the south just after New Year without Lizzie in tow. She remembered Billy saying he'd been real difficult to deal with ever since. Which seemed to indicate that he still cared about Lizzie, and it must be all of – Mary counted on her fingers – ten and a bit months since she had left Liverpool. Wouldn't it be lovely if when they were down in London they could find her? She told herself not to be so daft. As her mam had said, life was not that simple. Even so she decided to write to Phyl and hope she would come home before waltzing off somewhere else in yet another play. If anyone could persuade her brother to go to London it would be Phyl.

Mary spoke her thoughts about finding Lizzie to Billy.

'You're a dreamer,' he muttered, glancing up from the book which had not managed to hold his full attention because he had other things on his mind. One of them due to something Harry had said about a Mrs Bradshaw who had once worked at the scrapyard, having been asking after Alex. He could only remember three women who had worked at the yard in the past, and only one who was young.

'What's wrong with that?' insisted Mary, sitting sideways on a chair and dragging it close to him. 'Fairy tales can come true. It says so in some song. You've just got to be young at heart instead of behaving like you're ninety-two. Unless you dream, Billy, you can't possibly have one come true. Why don't you come to London with us?' she pleaded. 'We might go wild without serious old you there to keep us in check.'

A reluctant smile tugged the corners of Billy's mouth. 'I'd like to see it. The three of you are far more serious than I was at your age. When I think . . .' His voice tailed off.

Mary waited for him to speak again but he didn't so she said, 'Come on, Billy! Make Josie happy. Making people happy is within your scope. You've just got to think of what they really want instead of what you think they want.'

'Easy said,' he muttered.

'Easy done,' she replied.

He was silent and she realised that she had gone as far as she could for now and left him.

Phyl came out of the railway station, carrying a suitcase, and walked across Lime Street to the bus stop near the lions in front of St George's Hall. A Sunday calm lay about the place at such an early hour in the morning and she was glad of that. Pigeons fluttered about St George's plateau and she watched one land on the head of the statue of Prince Albert, consort of Victoria, and considered how useful it would be to be able to fly. Once again she was returning home because of a letter from a member of her family. Fleetingly she thought, Why can't they visit me at the theatre? Then it occurred to her that it might be their way of getting her to come home where she would give them more of her attention.

She remembered the last time she had been in Liverpool. She had been convinced Alex would find Lizzie but she had been wrong and guilt had returned in some small measure. Most of the time it remained submerged because most hours of the day were filled with her doing a play a week with different repertory companies, mainly in the north and the odd time in the Midlands. She had been asked to stay on at Southport for another week but had refused. It was times like now that her guilt resurfaced.

A bus drew up and she climbed aboard, having decided that her guilt was foolish, that Lizzie was a big girl now. Twenty years old if she was correct, and knew where they

lived so it was up to her to make a move if she wanted
to see them. But Billy was to tell Phyl something that was
to cause her to have second thoughts.

'The Black Widow! Are you sure?' she said, leaning
back in the chair and staring at her brother.

'Would I say it if I wasn't? I've seen her with my own
two eyes. She's been to the shop twice. It appears she's
having difficulty in catching up with Alex. He's a busy
man these days. Hardly ever in one place for long. It's as
if he can't keep still.'

'In case it gives him time to think,' said Phyl dryly. 'I
know the feeling.' She smoothed the dress over her knees.
'You say her second husband's dead?'

'I told you. And I told you what I think.'

She looked amused. 'That Alex could be caught on the
rebound? I can hardly believe she's out to catch him when
she actively hated him in the past.'

'People's feelings change. You've got to do something,
Phyl.'

'Such as?'

'Anything. You don't want him marrying her, do you?'

'I'm not in love with him any more,' said Phyl, but as
she looked at Billy she was thinking of Lizzie and the
way Alex had spoken of his feelings about her, and knew
she had to do something.

The gates to the yard were locked though when Phyl
arrived there so she decided it would have to wait until
Monday. So the next morning she went round to the yard
again, only to find not Alex but the Black Widow talking
to a man who was a stranger to Phyl.

Doreen looked up as she entered the room and said, 'Blinkin' hell! I never expected to see you here.'

'I could say the same,' said Phyl in hard tones. 'But I don't see why you shouldn't have expected me.'

'I saw your picture in the *Echo*. You were acting your heart out on the stage in Southport. Congratulations! Who knows? One day you might be a star.'

Phyl shrugged. 'Have you seen Alex?'

'Not yet. This gentleman here,' she waved a beringed hand, 'says he's at the shop. I was thinking of going along there. I presume Alex's the reason you're here?'

'Well, I didn't come to buy scrap,' drawled Phyl, remembering the trouble Doreen had caused in the past.

Doreen smiled. 'Only scrap parts. Have you got a car? I have. My husband left me it and I've learnt to drive. I've been lonely so I thought I'd come and look up old friends.'

Old friends! Phyl felt like laughing at that but wasn't prepared to antagonise Doreen yet. 'Where's your little boy?'

'At school. I believe Lizzie's gone back to London? Pity. She was the best of the bunch round here.' Doreen smiled sweetly. 'I'd best be going if I want to catch up with that man.' She walked past Phyl and outside.

Phyl followed immediately. 'I wonder if you could be nice and kind and give me a lift to the shop? My brother's working there and he forgot his sarnies this morning.'

Doreen looked at her speculatively before waving her to the other side of the car. It was not until they were driving along Sheil Road that she said, 'You still don't like me, do you? But you're wrong about me, you know. I've come back to try and make amends. I treated Alex rotten in the past and I want to say I'm sorry.' Phyl remained silent and after a couple of seconds Doreen continued: 'I was surprised to find him still at the yard, actually. He could really make something of himself instead of being stuck in that dump back there. I wonder now how I survived living there so long? I've a lovely house on the Wirral now.'

'You had no choice if I remember,' said Phyl, controlling her anger. 'You were hard up and far from home.'

'True.' Doreen's hands moved confidently on the steering wheel to take a corner. 'That's why I feel I owe Alex and I thought it would be nice to make up to him for my past behaviour. Besides I've sort of missed him and I think Syd has. He was so accommodating, and even when I was hating him I was still aware he was an attractive bloke.' She glanced at Phyl. 'You don't mind, do you? After all, you gave him up to go on the stage, didn't you?'

'I mind,' said Phyl, 'but I don't think that's going to stop you doing whatever you've got in mind. You might find, though, that Alex isn't as accommodating as he once was. He's hardened.'

For a moment Doreen looked disconcerted and then several different expressions flitted across her face. Phyl could see the moment when she decided she was still going to make a play for Alex.

No more was said between them and when they reached the shop they got out of the car without speaking and went inside, setting the bell jangling.

Alex, who had been talking to the girl behind the counter, glanced at them. Then he turned and stared at them. 'What's this? Get Alex Anonymous?'

'Funny, Alex,' said Doreen, moving forward. 'I'm glad to see you haven't forgotten me.'

'How could I?' His tone was sarcastic. He glanced at Phyl who had stayed by the door. 'What are you doing here?'

'I was hoping you hadn't forgotten Lizzie either, Alex. Or is it out of sight, out of mind with her?' said Phyl.

Pain showed in his face and she felt ashamed, which made it harder to walk past Doreen and reach up to kiss his cheek. 'Sorry,' she whispered, 'but I needed to know.'

'My turn next,' said Doreen, dragging on Phyl's arm.

'Wait your hurry,' she murmured. 'I haven't finished, and I think I have priority over you as Alex and I are old friends.'

'Old being the right word to use,' said Doreen. 'You must be thirty if you're a day.'

'Correct. But looking good, don't you think?' Phyl linked her arm through Alex's and gazed up at him. 'What do you think?'

'You look great,' he drawled, his expression not giving anything away.

'Thanks. You must have a ticket for my next performance whenever that is. I'm thinking of taking time off to go to London and see Lizzie. Why don't you come with me, Alex?'

His eyes caught hers. 'You've heard from her?'

'No, but I thought I'd have a go at finding her.'

His expression hardened once more. 'Not again, Phyl. I've tried. It's a waste of time. She doesn't want finding.'

'That's because she thinks you're not looking.'

'No. I'm sure it's not that. Anyway, why is it you want to look for her now? Why the sudden concern?'

'Mrs Tarantula here,' she said, being honest. 'I hate the thought of her getting her hooks into you, love.'

Suddenly his eyes blazed. 'You're bloody jealous, as well as cruel! How could you act like you knew where Lizzie was, knowing how I feel? But then everything's bloody acting to you.'

'That's not true,' she protested. 'I'm over you, Alex.'

He did not answer but seized hold of Doreen's arm and stormed out of the shop.

Phyl kicked the nearest thing which happened to be the base of the counter. The shop assistant giggled. 'Someone's in a temper.'

'Oh, shut up,' said Phyl, and turning the doorknob of the back room she walked in and closed the door behind her.

Billy was painting a wooden figure and was on his own.

'What are you doing here? What was all the noise about outside?'

'Me making a mess of things.' She leaned against the workbench. 'I'm an idiot. He's gone off with the Black Widow and might do something stupid. I've got to find Lizzie.'

His face brightened. 'You're going to London?'

'Where else?' she said.

'I think I'll come with you then.' He smiled. 'Go via luggage van. The only way to see the world.'

Phyl stared at him and hugged him round the neck before going out of the shop, singing.

Mary was not as pleased as Billy when Phyl came into the backyard where she was sitting with the twins, and told them she was going to London with them, but she could hardly give her reasons and say she didn't want her eldest sister watching everything she did to get off with Joe. Sisters had a bad habit of saying things that embarrassed a girl.

'Your relatives will put me up, won't they?' she asked the twins.

'Not put up rising star Phyllis Knight?' said Joe. 'You must be joking.'

Phyl smiled at him and stroked his cheek. 'You are a love. You really do make me feel better. I'm going inside to pack.'

'What's wrong with her?' said Josie, pulling a face. 'Why does she want to come with us?'

'She wants to find Lizzie,' explained Mary. 'But the great news is that Billy's agreed to go with us.'

A smile split Josie's face but Joe only touched his cheek absently, a frown in his blue eyes. 'How does she think she's gonna find Lizzie? She never turned up again at Matt's church.'

'That's a question,' said Mary in a subdued voice, hoping Joe would not start fancying Lizzie all over again. She was much too mature for him.

There was a brief silence before he said, 'We could put a piece in London's *Evening Standard*. "Wanted, Lizzie

Knight! Come home all is forgiven. Your family in Liverpool is missing you".'

Mary pulled a face. 'That's the newspaper man coming out in you but I suppose it might work.'

'Our man Joe was on the scene to see Lizzie Knight reunited with her stepmother, up and coming actress Phyllis Knight. Lizzie ran away after being accused of having had an affair with the man who was to have been her future stepfather.'

'You can't say that!' Mary hit him in the chest and sent him toppling off a chair. 'If you use my family to advance your career,' she said angrily, 'I'll never speak to you again, you – you toad!'

'Keep your hair on.' Joe straightened his tie and sat up. 'As if I'd do a thing like that!'

'You better hadn't,' said Mary firmly. 'Or I'll break your legs.'

'Holy hell,' said Joe, smiling. 'Little Mary, meek and mild, is changing. I certainly hadn't better do it then. Now what say me and you go for a walk before Josie and I go home and pack?'

Mary agreed with alacrity while Josie went in search of Billy. She found him in the parlour lying on his bed, reading. Without hesitation she went and lay on her side beside him so they could be on a level.

'I'm glad you've changed your mind. It'll be fine, honestly.'

He placed his book on the bedspread. 'You can read the future, can you? It'll probably be bloody awful but who the hell cares?' He pulled her against him and kissed her.

*

Lord, I feel like a gooseberry, thought Phyl, as she followed in the footsteps of an arm-in-arm Mary and Joe. Josie trailed a little behind pushing Billy in his wheelchair along Regent's Park Road. Phyl hoped she had not made a mistake in not having been in touch with Alex before leaving and prayed he'd have some common sense where the Black Widow was concerned.

She looked about her, reflecting on how it had been last time she was in London. What had made Lizzie stay in the Smoke when she'd loved the country? Another of life's little mysteries, she thought wryly, and hoped the vicarage was not much further. She should have had more sense and worn something other than her best high heels.

'Here it is,' said Joe at last, stopping in front of a pair of wrought iron gates and pushing one open.

'Looks a big place,' said Phyl, as they walked through a shrubbery towards the house that could just be glimpsed between the leafy branches of a couple of enormous sycamores.

'It's a Victorian monstrosity built in the days when vicars were either as rich as Croesus and the wife had loads of servants, or poor as the proverbial church mouse. Lil has a daily, two kids and five cats.' He glanced at Phyl. 'They get the odd mouse and three of the cats are strays she took in. Much the way she took us in during the war so that gives you an idea of the kind of person she is.'

'We have met,' said Phyl, smiling.

Joe said, 'I'd forgotten. It seems so long ago.'

They came out between the sycamores on to a gravel path, which ran along the front of the red brick vicarage with its double bay windows, and vanished out of sight round the side.

Before they could knock the front door opened and Lily stood there, a smile in her eyes. 'I was watching and hoping you'd be here this early.'

'Why?' asked Josie, kissing her.

'Because there's a sale of work on at the church hall and Matt and I want to get out of it. It's too nice a day to be stuck indoors. I promised the kids that as soon as you've unloaded your stuff we'll go fly their kites up Primrose Hill and have a picnic.'

Matt appeared at her shoulder and his smile embraced them all. 'Is it settled?'

'Not half,' said Josie happily, flinging herself on him.

'How about you?' Lily addressed Phyl. 'Do famous actresses fly kites and eat butties?'

'I haven't made it to the top yet,' said Phyl, shaking hands. 'I sometimes wonder if I will.'

'Of course you will,' said Matt, 'and when you do we'll come and see you.'

'That's nice of you,' said Phyl, giving him one of her most charming smiles.

Lily put a proprietary arm through her husband's and said jocularly, 'We always support Liverpudlians – Arthur Askey, John Gregson. More recently, Lita Roza of 'How Much is That Doggy in the Window?' fame. And besides, vicars and their wives have to be nice to everyone. I did what Joe asked, by the way.'

Phyl looked at her uncomprehending. 'I beg your pardon?'

'The advertisement concerning your stepdaughter. Joe phoned me up so I put it in the *Evening Standard* and told them to tell her to get in touch with you here.'

Phyl stared at Joe, who glanced at Mary, who said, 'Ooops! I forgot to tell her. Sorry, Phyl. But you did say you wanted to find Lizzie and we thought it would save time this way. We've only got a few days.'

Phyl could not be annoyed because she had only thought of going knocking on old neighbours' doors. 'It was a brilliant idea. Thanks.'

The twins and Mary and Billy looked jubilant, almost as if Lizzie had been found already.

'Everything's OK then,' said Matt, looking satisfied.

'We've got a bed fitted in a downstairs room, Billy, and there's a lavatory just up the hall for anyone who's desperate. Lily will make a quick cuppa while I show you to your rooms and then we'll go fly kites.'

Phyl stared at her face in the mirror as she creamed it with Pond's last thing that night. She had felt almost carefree up there on Primrose Hill, watching the Gibson boys flying their kites. Billy had taken a turn and even now she could see the rapt expression on his face as he controlled the kite. It had seemed for the moment he had been flying free himself, having forgotten he could not walk. Thinking about him, she suddenly stopped worrying about where her career was going and whether she would become famous. She pulled a face at her reflection and thought of Lizzie. She hoped something would come from the newspaper advertisement. It would be terrible if she never got to see her again, and Alex ended up trapped forever in the Black Widow's house on the Wirral, and Lizzie never saw him again either.

The morning before Coronation Day a still sleepy Phyl happened to be coming downstairs when the doorbell rang and she went to open it. A man stood on the doorstep. He was of medium height, thirtyish with light brown hair and eyes that were an unusual silver grey. She yawned. 'D'you want the vicar?'

'I am looking for Mrs Phyllis Knight.' His voice was deep and serious and he bowed slightly as he spoke.

For a moment Phyl, still caught up in a dream, could only think that some agent had discovered her whereabouts and wanted her to appear on the London stage. She swallowed a yawn and fixed on a smile. 'I'm Phyllis Knight. What can I do for you?'

'You do not look like I imagined!' He sounded dazed. 'You are younger and prettier. I did not expect this in Lizzie's stepmother.'

Phyl realised she'd made a mistake. This was no agent. Besides, agents generally got you to go to them. 'You know Lizzie?' she demanded.

'Yes. I am Jan Swietlik and I have come in response to this.' He held out a newspaper and indicated a place with his thumb.

Phyl seized hold of his arm and pulled him inside the vestibule. 'Where is she?'

'In the country. But –' Jan removed her hand from his sleeve and held it firmly. His eyes smiled into hers. 'I am pleased to meet you, Lizzie's stepmother. You can perhaps answer a question for me?'

'About Lizzie?' She was wondering how he came to know her stepdaughter. He had nice eyes and his accent was fascinating. Was he a new boyfriend of Lizzie's? Phyl's heart sank.

'No, about you. Your name, it is still Knight in the newspaper. Am I right in understanding that you have not married the Alex Lizzie gave up for you?'

'So that was it!' she muttered, staring at him. 'Damn! Where exactly is Lizzie? I have to see her. Although –' She cleared her throat. 'I hope you don't mind me asking this, Mr . . .' she hesitated.

'Call me Jan,' he said, his hand tightening about hers.

She returned the pressure of those strong fingers and smiled. 'Jan. Are you a close friend of Lizzie's?'

'I ask you first. Are you married to the Alex?'

'No.' Phyl could not stop smiling. 'What about Lizzie?'

'She has babies. Two of them,' he said solemnly. 'They are Alex's and he should know about them, do you not think?'

Phyl's mouth fell open. She could not believe it. 'Are you sure about this?'

He released her hand and from his pocket took a letter and handed it to her. She read it swiftly and then looked up at him. 'It says Broom Farm. That's where her aunt lives.' She frowned. 'I don't understand. Alex went there and the aunt said Lizzie had never been there.'

'When was this?'

'This year.'

'Then the aunt lied. She does not like men, you see.' Jan looked thoughtful. 'You read the letter where Lizzie says about the boy baby? I think that maybe you have come at the right time to help her.'

Phyl raised her eyebrows and gazed at him. He gazed back at her in a way that made her heart suddenly feel light. 'Are you a refugee, Jan?'

'I have been in England for six years. I feel I belong. I am Polish. You do not mind?' He sounded almost anxious.

'Mind?' said Phyl, and flashed him a dazzling smile. 'I like it. Will you come with me to find Lizzie?' It was her turn to sound anxious.

'Of course. You want to go now?'

'Yes. I'm worried in case she disappears again.'

He nodded. 'I have a motorbike. It will get us there fast.'

'It sounds thrilling.'

'You like speed?'

Phyl nodded and went and fetched her coat and handbag. Without a thought for anyone else, she left the vicarage with Jan.

Chapter Twenty

Lizzie tied Diamond loosely to the wooden pole fencing and began to unbuckle the girth strap. She could do most things for the horses without thinking now and her fingers worked automatically as she heard the roar of a motorbike in the lane. Her eyes scanned the yard and the paddock, past the barn and the pond, to the entrance as the motorbike came through it and into the yard where it stopped by the house. A woman dismounted from the pillion, dragging off a headscarf and running a hand through her copper-coloured hair. There was something familiar about the gesture and Lizzie's breath caught in her throat as she heaved off the saddle.

Voices sliced through the unseasonably cool air and the weight of the saddle dragged on her arm muscles but she was barely aware of it as she peered beneath the horse's head. For a moment her mind could not accept that it was Phyl. It must be someone just like her, that was all, and the man couldn't be Jan surely? Because how could he and Phyl have got together?

Lizzie balanced the saddle on the fence and began to walk towards the couple. Then she saw the woman catch sight of her and touch the man's arm. It was then Lizzie knew for sure it was Phyl and shock and pleasure rippled through her. For a moment she did not know what to do but Phyl took the initiative and started to run towards her.

They met by a heap of manure, stopping a few feet short of each other, and for a moment neither of them spoke. Lizzie thought, She's just as attractive as ever while I must look like something the cat brought in. She took a deep steadying breath. 'Hello, Phyl. What are you doing here – and with Jan?'

'We advertised in a London newspaper and he came in answer to it.' Phyl's tone was exuberant. 'And here we are, and here you are, too! I hope you don't really fancy him because truthfully the pair of us have been getting on like a house on fire!' Her tawny eyes were quizzical as they met Lizzie's stare.

'You've what?' Lizzie could barely comprehend what Phyl was saying. She ran a trembling hand over her pony-tail. 'What about Alex?'

'He's not so good.' Phyl's expression changed and she frowned as she looked about her. 'He came here, you know – just after New Year. Your aunt said she'd never set eyes on you.'

'What!' Lizzie could scarcely believe it. She thought of all the anxiety she had suffered in the last few months and fury erupted inside her. 'She never told me,' she said angrily. 'But – but why?' Then she knew why. Alex was a man and he would have taken Lizzie away.

'He came for you, of course. He came and your aunt lied.'

Something fluttered free inside Lizzie. 'He came!' she whispered. 'Alex came looking for me!'

'Yes.' Phyl smiled.

'I've been here from the very first day,' babbled Lizzie. 'I went to Brentwood and they told me my aunt lived here.'

'The thought did cross my mind you might do something like that but I was so bloody cross with you I didn't do anything about it. It was a letter from your aunt's solicitor that brought Alex here. But he was in London even before then. He went to Booth's and just missed you.'

Lizzie could scarcely believe it. She released a long breath and a smile lit her face. 'I thought he would have married you. You loved him! That's why I ran away. I thought I owed you.'

Phyl linked her hand through Lizzie's arm. 'I did love him and I still do in a friendly kind of way. He doesn't love me, though, you idiot! It's you he loves. But if you don't get your skates on and get back up north the Black Widow just might snaffle him in one of his weak moments. We all have them.'

Lizzie blinked. 'What on earth are you talking about? The Black Widow left years ago.'

'She's back, and blacker than ever! She's lonely, says she wants to make it up to Alex for the way she treated him.'

'I don't believe it!'

'It's true! You ask our Billy.'

'Billy?'

'He's in London. Josie's done wonders for his spirits, just as you said she would. She's in London too, and so are Mary and Joe. They were coming down for the

Coronation so I thought it was time I found you before Alex ruins his life altogether by marrying you-know-who.'

'He couldn't possibly marry her! What am I going to do? I can't believe this about the Black Widow!' Lizzie knew she was babbling.

Phyl licked her finger and made the sign of the cross over her heart. 'Cross my heart and hope to die if I'm not telling you the truth about the Black Widow.'

'OK! I believe you,' said Lizzie, sighing deeply as she gazed in Jan's direction. 'Did he tell you?'

'About the babies?' Phyl squeezed her arm. 'You don't do things by halves, do you, love?'

Lizzie flushed and stopped in her tracks. 'It was only the once we did it, Phyl,' she said earnestly. 'We wanted to get married but thought we'd best wait. Then there was a thunderstorm and we got carried away. Then everything went wrong. Your Lois –'

'I believe you,' she said mildly.

Lizzie hoped she was telling the truth. There was a silence and then Phyl nudged her arm. 'Well, are you going north? I've rushed to get here so you can do something. What are you going to do?'

'Give me a chance to take it all in,' said Lizzie. She scowled in the direction of the house. 'Of course I want to go but I've hardly any money, and what about the twins? I'm still feeding them. I'd have to take them with me.'

'Of course you'll have to take them,' said Phyl firmly. 'They're your ace in the hole.' She laughed. 'I'd love to see the Black Widow's face when you turn up with them.

I'll give you the money to buy a train ticket, although God only knows what Mam'll say. She never got over you going on about mortal sin.'

Lizzie's mouth lifted at the corners. She'd forgotten how infectious Phyl's laugh was. 'Don't remind me. Even so, Phyl, it's not that easy. I could cope on the train with one baby but I'm pretty sure I can't with two.' She began to walk towards the house.

'I suppose not.' Phyl's smile faded and she was silent as she fell into step alongside Lizzie.

Lizzie felt ashamed as she looked at Jan but it seemed he read her mind because he smiled and said, 'It is OK. I understand why you not tell me. But I could hear you talking with Phyl about the babies and the train just now. Did you not tell me you could drive?'

'Yes, but I haven't a car. There's just the old truck that belongs to my aunt.'

'You could borrow it?'

Lizzie stared at him and a sharp laugh escaped her. 'You haven't seen it! And besides, I've never driven further than Chelmsford.'

'What if Phyl and I came with you? A British soldier taught me to drive when I was acting as translator with the British Army. We can take turns with the driving.'

Lizzie thought how the back of the truck only had a canvas cover and how its floor needed a good scrubbing. It wouldn't be very comfortable but she supposed Jan's idea was feasible.

Phyl said, 'You do want Alex, don't you, Lizzie? You don't want the Black Widow getting her talons into him.'

That decided her, although with part of her she didn't really believe Alex could be so stupid. 'I was prepared to give him up to you but not her!' she said, lifting her chin. 'She'd make him bloody miserable. Let's go.' She glanced at Jan. 'What about your motorbike?'

'I shall leave it here. Phyl and I will bring the truck back. She'll want to be in London for the Coronation.'

'Damn! I'd forgotten about the Coronation,' groaned Lizzie. 'You couldn't get back in time, Phyl.'

'Shut up,' she said, adding in a whisper, 'I owe you one for finding Jan. I think we really might suit. He has an old fashioned charm that appeals to me. Anyway, I'm not bothered about the Coronation. I can watch it on telly with Mam. You get your twins packed and let's be on our way.'

'I'll have to have a word with my aunt first,' said Lizzie. She grinned suddenly. 'I can't wait for her to see you, Jan. She thinks you're a girl!'

A clock on the brick mantelpiece chimed two o'clock as the three of them entered the sitting room where Charlotte was seated in front of the fire. She looked up from her book in annoyance. 'Who are these persons?' Her voice trembled slightly.

'Jan Swietlik,' he said, bowing slightly.

The book slid from her knee. 'But you're –'

'A good friend of Lizzie's,' he said, and lifting Charlotte's hand, kissed it as to the manner born.

She blushed and withdrew it hastily. 'What are you doing here?' she said stiffly.

Before Jan could answer, Phyl moved in front of him and said in a charming voice: 'I'm Phyllis Knight, Miss Broom. I'm Lizzie's stepmother. I believe you've met the twins' father, so I don't think you'll mind if we borrow your truck and take Lizzie and her babies north to see him?'

Charlotte looked like a cushion which had had all the stuffing knocked out of it. She did not look at Lizzie.

'You should have told me about Alex,' said her niece, the anger in her voice barely controlled. 'It's going to take me a while to forgive you that! But I'll be back to see you in the not too distant future and we'll get everything sorted out about the farm then.'

Her aunt nodded stiffly. 'Just as you wish, Elizabeth. But it's going to be very inconvenient for Penny not having the truck.'

Lizzie made no answer but walked out of the room. Now the decision had been made to see Alex she wanted to be on her way. Her only fear was that he might have changed his mind since last travelling south and not want her or the twins after all when he saw the three of them.

It was the early hours of Coronation Day when they caught their first glimpse of the Mersey gleaming like pewter before them. Lizzie started to feel that she was nearing home. The journey had been uncomfortable and taken longer than they had planned because they had lost their way a couple of times.

She was reminded of that first journey more than six years ago when she and Phyl had been delayed by ice and snow. Then she had been running away; now she was running to. Then she had been unsure of her welcome; now, despite her earlier fears, she was pinning her hopes on Alex being as dependable as she had believed him to be, almost from that first moment they had met. She remembered how she had always felt able to be herself in his company and how they had laughed at the same things, and prayed it could still be like that between them.

As they drove along the quiet, lamplit streets decorated with pictures of the Queen hanging amongst garlands of flags and artificial flowers, she was reminded of the Festival of Britain and the evening that had ended so sadly with Nan Eccles's death. She hoped that Alex still remembered how it had been between the two of them then, too.

Where to go first? she wondered. Jan and Phyl were in the back of the truck with the babies so the decision was hers. She thought of how people showed their true feeling when taken by surprise. She needed desperately to know how Alex really felt.

Lizzie could scarcely believe it when she stopped outside the yard and saw the TO LET notice on the wall. A grey, drizzly dawn was lighting the sky as she descended from the cab. Unable to take her eyes from the sign, she despaired. Did this mean that the Black Widow had grabbed Alex already? What was she to do? For a moment she could not think. Then she tried the small door in the gate and rattled it, but it was locked. She eyed the gates and then turned as Phyl climbed awkwardly out of the truck, accepting the babies from Jan's arms before he also stepped down on to the ground. 'Where are we?' he asked.

'Alex's yard,' said Lizzie, turning to Phyl. 'Have you seen the sign?'

Phyl stared. 'What the hell!'

'You didn't know about this?'

She raised her eyebrows. 'Of course not! It's a right turn up for the book. I hope he hasn't left already.'

Lizzie eased back her shoulders. 'There's only one way to find out.'

'You're going to knock him up?' said Phyl, handing one of the babies to Jan.

Jan patted the baby's back as it started to cry and stared at Lizzie, a slightly worried expression on his face. 'How will you do this?'

Lizzie smiled grimly. 'I'm going to take a leaf out of Phyl's book – but keep your fingers crossed that I don't break my neck!' She took several paces back, glad of her flatties and slacks. Jan said something but she ignored it. She ran and leapt, got a grip and clawed her way upwards. Without a pause she swung her legs over and dropped. She lost her balance on landing and toppled over. Getting to her feet, she made her way towards the office.

Before she could reach it a light went on and the door opened. Alex stood in the doorway, a cricket bat in his hand. Lizzie's knees gave way unexpectedly and she collapsed on the ground in front of him. He seized the shoulder of her jacket and dragged her up. 'What the hell do you think you're playing at, you little –' He stopped abruptly.

'Alex! It's me, Lizzie,' she whispered, her heart suddenly pounding like a military drum.

He dropped the bat and said hoarsely, 'I know who you are. I'm not blind as well as stupid.'

'Of course you're not. I'm sorry, Alex.' She put her arms round his waist and pressed her head against his chest. He only had vest and pants on and she could feel his skin against her cheek. 'I'm sorry, I'm sorry!' She felt weak with relief that he had not gone away.

'Sorry for what?'

'Sorry for running away! Sorry for what I put you through! Sorry for not following my instincts when they told me to go to you!' She clung to him, loving the solid feel of him against her body. 'Phyl seems to think you knew why I ran away. Do you Alex? Do you understand my stupidity?'

'So you admit you were stupid?' He seized hold of her hair and pulled her head back. She winced but was forced to look up at him.

'Haven't I just done so? But Lois and Maisie said such horrible things about us. Especially Lois.'

He nodded, his blue eyes dark. 'Where've you been all this time?'

'At my aunt's farm. I only discovered yesterday that you'd been there, too. My aunt lied to you. Phyl told me everything.'

He drew in breath sharply so it hissed between his teeth. 'So it was Phyl who found you?'

'Yes. With Jan's help.'

'Who's Jan?'

'A good friend of mine. He's Polish.'

'He?' He twisted her hair around his hand, trapping a single strand.

She yelped. 'That hurt!'

'He's not the father of your baby, is he?'

'Don't be stupid!' Lizzie stared at him and said weakly, 'How did you know I was having a baby? There's two of them, by the way.'

'You're joking!' He loosened his hold on her hair and she almost fell. He saved her before she hit the ground.

She hung on to him, determined to have him listen to her. 'I've registered them as Alexandra Rose and Charles James. They're outside with Phyl and Jan. I really needed you there when they were born. I was in deep trouble but I thought you and Phyl had got together and I would spoil everything.'

He gazed down at her and she could not read his expression. 'Let go of me,' he murmured.

Her heart seemed to drown in the pit of her stomach. 'You don't believe they're yours?' she cried in an anguished whisper.

'I didn't say that.' He took hold of her hands and prised them apart. He went indoors and reappeared minutes later fully dressed with a bunch of keys, making for the gate.

She went after him but even before she reached the gate he had the door open and was outside, talking. As she climbed through she saw Phyl and Jan handing the babies to him.

'You get their paraphernalia,' said Alex, still sounding very in control of himself. He manoeuvred himself and the twins through the door without another word.

Lizzie looked at Phyl and Jan, who both smiled. 'He told us to go home,' said Phyl, handing over her suitcase and a holdall. 'I'm taking Jan to our house to knock up the parents. Jan tells me he's Catholic but Mam doesn't have to know that yet. What I need is to speak to Dad and get him on my side. I'll see you later.'

Lizzie nodded. 'OK. Although I'm surprised at your leaving me here. The tongues'll soon be wagging. What do you think your mam'll say?'

Phyl raised her eyebrows. 'Probably something about mortal sin. Tell Alex he has my permission to marry you – that he's to buy a special licence because the sooner those babies are legal the better.'

'OK!' Lizzie put down her suitcase and bag and hugged Phyl and Jan before going back inside the yard.

Alex was in the kitchen, kneeling on the floor. Both babies were on the tiger rug in front of a newly lit fire. Charlie was crying but Alexandra was stretching, blinking up at her father.

Lizzie cleared her throat. 'He's probably hungry.'

'How d'you know he's the he?' said Alex gazing at her with an expression of wonder.

'He's got longer eyelashes and is the prettiest.' Her smile teased him and suddenly he reached across the babies and kissed her. Their lips clung for what felt an eternity but Charlie's cry turned to a scream. His parents drew apart.

Lizzie felt a little shy as she shrugged off her jacket and picked up her son. She began to undo her blouse.

'Lizzie,' said Alex, his eyes dark with emotion, 'I don't know what to say about what you must have been through when you knew you were having these two.'

'I didn't know – not until they were born. So say you'll marry me and make them legal?'

'I'll marry you,' he said obediently. 'Doesn't that go without saying?'

'I was scared it mightn't,' she said in a low voice as she settled Charlie to the breast. 'Phyl said Doreen was back. Then I saw the yard was to let.'

'Did Phyl really think I'd be taken in by Doreen? I sent her packing. But I decided I needed to get away from this area. It had too many memories of you. I was thinking of going to Canada and joining the mounties.'

She smiled. 'You're joking.'

He grinned. 'There's a larger yard than this for sale in Bootle up near the railway. It's a good site. It might mean I can't buy that house on the outskirts of Liverpool for a year or so, though. Would you mind, Liz?'

'It doesn't matter to me where I live,' she said promptly knowing that they would probably be able to buy that house he had set his heart on but that news could come later. She felt a glow inside her, considering how happy they were going to be. She said quietly, 'North or south, east or west, it's corny but true that home is where the heart is. Now could you get a bottle out of the holdall, as well as the tin of Ostermilk, and feed Alexandra?'

Alex laughed and kissed her in passing as he did her bidding. She wanted to cling to him, knowing for certain that she would always be able to depend on him.

When eventually Alexandra was suckling contentedly in the crook of his arm, Alex said, 'I can't believe this is all happening. It's like all my dreams have come true. Although I didn't picture twins.'

'They are the reality and they're hard work, Alex.'

'I'm not complaining. I always wanted several children. But later I'm looking forward to having you to myself.'

She felt a thrill run through her. 'Later,' she echoed, her eyes like stars.

Later was to be much later because no sooner were the babies asleep in a couple of drawers taken from the sideboard than Phyl and Jan arrived in the truck. They were accompanied by Maisie, wearing her best frock. They had with them Lizzie's dolls' house.

'We thought,' said Maisie, her cheeks pink, 'that you might want this for Alexandra to play with.'

Lizzie exchanged glances with Alex who grinned. They knew that the dolls' house was an excuse to make peace. 'Thanks,' they said.

'I also thought,' said Maisie in a low voice, drawing Lizzie aside, 'that you might like to wear this.' She took a wedding ring from a pocket. 'It was Nan Eccles's.'

Lizzie took it from her and turned it round the tip of her third finger left hand, remembering that day Nan Eccles had played at brides. 'You mean wear it now when I'm not married?'

Maisie nodded.

Lizzie shook her head. 'I know you mean well but it would be hypocritical. Besides Alex'll give me a ring soon enough.' She handed it back. 'I appreciate your coming when I know how you feel about people living in sin and all that.'

Maisie swallowed and said in an even lower voice, 'Don't tell my girls but Sam and I had to get married. I've never forgotten the feeling of shame. Maybe that's why I am the way I am? Forgive me, Lizzie. I'm sure you and Alex'll be happy. You've courage and you've suffered for each other. You'd be surprised how that can bind a couple together.'

Lizzie was touched by her confidences. 'Thank you.'

Maisie touched her arm and said in a voice more like her own, 'It's a pleasure, luv. Now are you going to come and watch the Coronation on our telly and bring the twins to the street party later? They won't remember it, of course, but you can tell them about it and I'll see they get a Coronation mug each.'

'I'm not sure,' said Lizzie gently. 'I'm really tired.'

'Come later and have a dance in the street,' said Phyl, coming over and hugging her.

'Perhaps,' said Alex, slipping his arm around Lizzie. 'Later.'

It was to be much later because Lizzie and Alex watched the Coronation on Alex's television. Her eyes drooped because she was so tired but she kept telling herself to stay awake because she was seeing history in its making, and besides she wanted to see if she could spot Billy, Mary and the twins in the crowds lining the streets. But she didn't. It did make her realise, though, how important those four people were to her and that she wanted them at her wedding.

So later, after they had fed and changed the babies and shared a meal of bacon, eggs and chips, and having spoken to Alex, she phoned the vicarage in London where it sounded as if a party was going on and spoke to Billy and Josie. After all the explanations were finished she asked them how quickly they could be home because they were wanted for best man and chief bridesmaid at her wedding.

'We'll be home the day after tomorrow,' shouted Billy down the telephone. 'And tell Ma that there's another party on the cards. Josie and me are getting engaged!'

'I couldn't be more happy,' said Lizzie, tears prickling the back of her eyes. 'See you soon.'

She put down the receiver and told Alex.

'It's great news,' he said, looking thoughtful. 'I'd like to do something for Billy and Josie. He mentioned the other week that the shop next-door was moving its premises. It might be worth taking over the lease and extending ours. There'd be space in the back he and Josie could turn into living quarters.'

'You'd need to take on more staff.'

'Trev might be interested. I'll talk it over with Billy when he gets home.'

So it was decided, and after washing the dishes they went walkabout from street to street, admiring the decorations and simply enjoying being together and watching people letting their hair down. They talked a lot about the time they had spent apart. As darkness fell they reached the street where the Eccleses lived, just in time to watch a bonfire being lit and fireworks set off.

'Sheer magic, isn't it?' said Phyl, coming to stand next to Lizzie.

'Yes,' she answered, her eyes dreamy.

'Jan's charming Mam,' whispered Phyl. 'She's never had her hand kissed before, but mostly she thinks he needs mothering because of what he went through in the war.'

'So there's hope for you and him making a match of it?' said Lizzie, smiling.

Phyl's eyes twinkled. 'It's early days but I think it's a possibility. One thing's for sure, though – we'll live in London. Jan's got loads of drive and ambition so he's bound to get that top class restaurant he wants one day – which will be useful for throwing parties when my name's up in lights in the West End.'

'Alex and I'll come down for the occasion.'

'Naturally,' said Phyl and laughed. 'Who'd have believed it, kid, that our meeting in the convent would result in this one day?'

'I wouldn't have – never in a million years,' said Lizzie. For an instant she thought about her parents and felt sadness that their lives had ended so tragically. Perhaps when she went south to see Aunt Charlotte she would place some flowers on their grave.

She kissed Phyl fondly. 'Thanks for everything. For bringing me to Liverpool. Everything!'

'Ah, away with you girl!' Phyl hugged her in return before pushing her away. 'Go and dance with Alex now, while me and Mam look after the babes.'

So Lizzie went and danced with Alex, feeling the better for being back in the family circle.

It was past midnight when she and Alex went back to the scrapyard and let themselves in. They talked about the evening and Maisie's offer to look after the twins while they had a honeymoon. It was an unlooked for treat. They saw to their children's needs before, without hesitation, Lizzie put her hand into Alex's and climbed into bed with him. They turned to each other and Alex's mouth came down over hers in a kiss that Shakespeare could have written a sonnet about.

Pure homespun magic, thought Lizzie, glad that at last she was home.

Also by June Francis:

LILY'S WAR

Torn between duty to her family and a last chance at love...

Busy bringing up her motherless brothers and sisters, romance is the last thing on Lily Thorpe's mind. But when the handsome preacher Matt Gibson asks Lily to return with him to Australia as his wife, she finds it very hard to say no.

But with rumours of war on the horizon, will she have to choose between her head and her heart?

EBURY
PRESS

Also by June Francis:

A MOTHER'S DUTY

A family at war...

Raising three boys and running the Arcadia Hotel almost single-handed are enough to keep widow Kitty Ryan busy. She has no time for romance – unless it's in the form of a rare evening out at the local picture house.

Then along comes John Mcleod, bringing with him a second chance at happiness. However, Kitty finds her sons unwilling to accept another man into their household.

Unless she can reunite her menfolk, the future looks set to be that of a family in conflict, in a world on the eve of war...

EBURY
PRESS

Also by June Francis:

A DAUGHTER'S CHOICE

**Seventeen-year-old Katie is about to discover a
devastating family secret...**

Katie is the apple of her mother's eye and is being groomed
to take over the family business. But when Celia, her
natural mother, re-enters her life, her world is turned
completely upside down.

Tormented by her divided loyalties, Katie is plagued by
a question Celia refuses to answer – just who is her real
father?

EBURY
PRESS

Also by June Francis:

A SISTER'S DUTY

She will do what it takes, for the sake of the children…

Rosie Kilshaw is only fifteen when her mother Violet is killed in a tragic accident, but as the oldest of her siblings, she vows to keep her family together, no matter what the sacrifice.

But as distant family members begin to resurface into their lives, Rosie quickly realizes that there is a lot more to parenting than she first thought. And when her estranged aunt Amelia decides to take them in, she will have a difficult choice to make…

EBURY
PRESS

Also available from Ebury Press:

WORKHOUSE ORPHANS

by Holly Green

All they have left is each other...

Life has always been tough for May and Gus Stirzaker. Their father went away to sea never to return, and then their mother falls victim to the typhus sweeping through Liverpool. Regarded as orphans by the authorities, May and Gus are sent to the Brownlow Hill Workhouse.

Like all workhouses, Brownlow is the last resort for the poor and the destitute. May and Gus will have to rely on each other more than ever if they are to survive the hardships to come...

EBURY
PRESS